MAGRATH

A novel by

Justin Tuts

For Ashlynn,
Hopefully something
within these pages
resonates with you.

Justin
Tuts

This book is dedicated to my brother Mathew

Mathew, though you don't like to read books, you've always supported my passion and have always been there for me; supporting me and being the best brother I could have ever asked for.

Prologue

IN THE STILL, RECYCLED AIR OF HIS APARTMENT, Jack Lewis slept soundly. It was a deep and dreamless sleep, one in which he did not toss or turn, one where the fragments from the recesses of his mind couldn't reach him. This sleep was not due to a perfect mental state, or some miracle drug administered by his general practitioner. No, this sleep was brought on by his nightly tradition, one that originated in the depths of addiction and necessity.

Behind the empty bottle of black label that sat precariously upon the edge of the oak nightstand, his phone began to ring. It was a shrill tone, downloaded specifically to pierce through the depths of his dreamless slumber. The noise penetrated the air and the device buzzed once more; the display flickering to life as it tried to show what little information could be provided. UNKNOWN NUMBER flashed across the top of the screen.

Jack slipped out of unconsciousness, unsure if he'd heard something or not. As the remnants of sleep slowly drifted out of his memory, he heard the phone ring once more. But, as he turned over in bed, the wet tightness of his clothing stopped him. *Did I piss myself?* He gripped his shirt between his thumb and forefinger, pondering the possibility of urine reaching this high up his front. *No, thank God it's just sweat.*

Jack groaned as he reached out from his bed and fumbled in a drunken stupor as he groped around in the darkness. Though only in his late twenties, his body was sore and stiff, as though rigor mortis was threatening to encroach on him then, not waiting until he'd shuffled off this mortal coil. His fingers slipped across the screen several times, yet he failed to grab it in time as another shrill ring hit his ear drums and rattled his brain.

Finally, he picked it up and squinted against the foreign presence of the bright light flowing off his display, unable to read the caller ID. He sighed and thumbed the small green phone icon, bringing the phone up to the side of his head in one swift effort.

He listened first to the other end of the line, if someone on the other end of the line needed his services desperately enough, they would be speaking as soon as the dialing tone ended. He was right.

The voice came through in a rough and authoritative tone. The hair on the back of Jack's neck rose. *Cop.* "Jack Lewis?"

He tried to hide the sigh building up inside of him but ultimately it came out on the first word responded. "Speaking. Who is this, and why are you calling at this hour?" *What hour was it?*

Jack was about to put his phone back when the officer responded, "I'm officer-" static cut into the conversation, "with Magrath police department. There's uhh, there's been something happening in town and we figured some fresh eyes on the case might do us a world of good. Dominic Thompson vouched for you; said you'd be reliable. I can't stress how badly we need your help here, please, come down and at least see if there's anything you can do. We'll pay whatever price you desire, regardless of how ludicrous." he paused, "again, Jack. We need your help."

Dominic Thompson? Magrath? The two names probed Jack's aching head, threatening to disturb the hangover building up inside. He swung his legs out from under the covers and sat on the edge of his bed, looking over to the alarm clock he'd kept there for reasons unknown. These days all his alarms were on his phone. Despite this, the alarm clock came in hand at this moment; the display illuminating 5:15am. He recalled his first swig from the bottle came around eleven, and he stumbled to bed around two in the morning. Were three hours of sleep enough to sober up? He didn't know and reflecting inwardly, he shrugged. He didn't care either.

Jack thought a mere moment longer before uttering his reply to the man on the other end of the phone, "Sure, I can be there, but I charge significantly more for police work. It'll be double my usual hourly rate." He paused, "When do you need me there?"

Jack began to marvel at the lengths he'd go to for cash, even though he wasn't strapped for it when the voice came through once more, firm and assertive, "as soon as possible, come to the Glendale apartment complex, it's located at -"

Jack cut him off, the man's voice was starting to irritate him, getting under the thin layer of consciousness to the alcohol fueled headache growing underneath, "I know where it is, I'm about 11 hours away. Give me enough time to get ready and head over; I'll be there around 5:00pm." Jack thought for a moment then added, "*preserve* the crime scene. Take pictures, keep locals away, do whatever you need to, but leave whatever you found where it is until I get there."

There was a brief pause, no more than ten seconds before he responded, "sure, whatever you need. And Jack?"

"Yes Officer?"

He let out a long, relieved sigh, "Thank you for taking the call."

The call disconnected then, leaving Jack in a world of resounding silence that settled over the entirety of his apartment. Not for the first time, he reflected on how quiet it had gotten since Emma left. Since the world he'd built up had been torn down around him and he was rendered alone. Sometimes, the silence was deafening.

He rose onto unsteady feet and shambled around in the dark, groping along the wall for the light switch. When the light flicked on above, the light swathed the room in its yellow glow; shining warmly from the incandescent bulb above.

He sighed heavily through his nostrils as he reached under his bed and pulled out his small suitcase. Over the next several minutes, he gathered several pairs of underwear, socks, dress pants and shirts, and a few pullovers to help combat the cold October air.

Within a matter of minutes, Jack was packed and ready for what he presumed to be a regular case, regardless of the town. He grabbed his keys off the credenza that stood next to the door and walked out of his apartment complex, mind set on returning to a city he swore he'd never return to. After a decade of running from Magrath; it was time to return, to run headfirst into a town steeped with history of his past and of his family. As the apartment complex faded to little more than a blur in his rear-view mirror, he hardly realized he was shaking.

Part 1
Welcome Back

October 3, 2015 - October 4, 2015

Chapter 1: Old friends

~ 1 ~

THE SMOKE CURLED ABOVE HIM; the scent ingrained itself in his clothes as the tar embedded itself within his lungs. He recalled the events of the prior night as he took another drag of the cigarette, relaxing slightly as the nicotine flowed through his body; alleviating his stress. He exhaled, casting smoke from the depths of his lungs like the billows of a chimney. The smoke clung to the air above, illuminated brightly by the streetlamp, casting dancing shadows of tendrils along the side of the Glendale apartment building. He shifted his eyes from the light, moving them over the scene in front of him, he wished he could obscure it in the very smoke he held within him.

She was in her late thirties by the looks of it. He'd grabbed her wallet from her pocket but had yet to look at the contents for an ID or other clues as to who she was. Her dyed brown hair swept across the ground beneath her, as if melting into the blood that pooled around her broken skull. Jack watched as a fly landed on her face, rubbing its front legs together in a hungry manner before launching into flight once more, joining the small swarm above her corpse.

He returned his eyes to the woman. By the fullness of her cheeks and contour of her lips, he could tell she had once been beautiful. Though it was hard to tell now, considering the top of her head had been dented inwards; as if the top of her head was reaching for her lower jaw from the inside. He flipped open her wallet and examined the picture ID within, looking at what her face had once been. It described her eyes as blue, yet, looking at her decimated corpse, he couldn't tell where her eyes even were. He shook his head slowly.

Looking around the scene, he took inventory of the skull fragments that littered the ground; small flecks of white against the blood spattered ashen black of the asphalt. He took another long, deep drag from his cigarette; the smoke curled its way down his throat and into his lungs as if trying to kill him. *Not this time.* He held the smoke in momentarily, as though doing so would allow him to absorb more of the precious nicotine within.

When he couldn't hold it in anymore, he exhaled, expunging the white smoke out of his lungs in a large white cloud that hung in the air momentarily before dissipating. When the cloud was all but a smell stinging the back of his nostrils, he tossed the cigarette butt onto the ground, stomping it out with the bottom of his dress shoe while he studiously stared at the corpse in front of him.

Her legs were broken at both joints and several locations along the shin and thigh. Causing an effect akin to her attempting to run in four directions at the same time. Her spandex jeans stretched and pulled; twisting to match the position of her legs, bulging against the swelling onset before rigor mortis kicked in. Her arms were tucked underneath her back, making her back arch into a partial bridge position. The only parts that maintained contact with the ground were her shoulders and her rear. Jack looked to her baby blue shirt that was now stained in several places; showing evidence of the struggle that had taken place.

He slowly approached the body and crouched next to it, looking at the way the head caved inwards; trying desperately to match it to a weapon of some sort. There seemed to be a single indent in the center that dragged the remainder of the skull downwards with it, pulling until it broke free and the weapon was halted. He shook his head, unable to come to a conclusive decision. Footsteps came from somewhere off to his right and he turned to see who was approaching.

The man was around his age, and was dressed in a familiar blue police uniform, "Fuck me, Jack, what do you think happened to her?"

The man was none other than Dominic Thompson. Someone Jack had once considered his best friend. He was the one who encouraged Jack to become a private investigator; knowing full well that he would operate better without all the red tape. Of course, there was still the red tape of the law in general, but being a private contractor, Jack was able to take some liberties unavailable to the police; so long as he wasn't caught.

Unfortunately for their friendship, Jack had left shortly after twelfth grade ended, leaving everything and everyone behind. Leaving his old friends to fade into to nothing more than distant memories. Though sometimes he wondered if it was Dom's influence that had spurred him to get his license. He was, after all, one of Jack's happiest memories of growing up in Magrath, and their steadfast friendship helped him deal with the horrors he experienced in those years.

It had been just under ten years since the night Jack left the town behind. He recalled watching as the orange haze in his rear-view mirror faded to little more than a light on the horizon behind him. Jack wondered to himself, though not for the first time since the call, if Dom would hold his sudden disappearance against him.

He looked into Dom's eyes, "Honestly Dom, I'm still wondering that myself. Surely you've looked at the wound on her head?" Dom nodded, "The shape of the indent suggests something with a blunt point, like a bat or sledgehammer, yet there's no mark from where the handle would have connected on the outside of the crater. It's curious… How many does this make?"

Dom shifted nervously on his feet, "Uh, eight disappearances and three homicides, including this one. So far, we have no suspects but aren't ruling out any group effort. Though, this could have been one person."

Jack looked back to the remains in front of him, wondering if the others were like this, and what fate had befallen the missing, "What's the time frame?"

Dom shuffled closer, as if embarrassed, "Two weeks, nearly three."

Jack looked at him, shocked. *'Fuck me, Jack' was right.* He looked at the body of the woman in front of him and thought about the brief run down he'd been given concerning her discovery and the poor kid that found her the previous morning while running his paper route. He'd been so scared that he peddled all the way home before calling the police; by which point several others had come across her body as well and called it in.

Jack trundled over to one of the cruisers, nodding grimly to one of the uniformed officers who reached into the trunk and produced a white linen sheet from within. It emitted a small rasping sound as it unfolded, and caught the eye of a couple of the other officers that were gathered around.

Jack watched the officer place the sheet over the dead woman's body, as if hiding the atrocities of man from the eyes of God. A shudder went through his body. He turned to the other officers, who'd returned to their previous activities as the detective walked over, head held low. Jack studied him, noting the defeated look in the detective's eye. Perhaps it was the result of sympathy for the departed, though Jack suspected it was due to his diminished pride.

The man had been introduced as Detective Hanson of the Magrath police department, he had a firm voice that hinted at the authority he'd grown accustomed to, "What are you thinking Lewis, suicide?"

Jack looked at him, then at the body, then back at him once more, dumbfounded that he'd considered it a possibility. "No, detective. By looking at her, there would have to have been a struggle. That much is simply evident by the blood splatter on her clothing. Her legs look dislocated and severely broken, as are her arms. Both would have to be done with a weapon of significant weight or someone with significant strength. Perhaps both. The damage to her head was most likely done last, I assume that whoever did this was intent on inflicting as much pain as possible. The likeliest weapon used would be a hammer of some fashion. Large, like a sledge. Though the shapes of her wounds suggest otherwise. An autopsy would be needed, though I'm not sure the coroner would be able to determine anything from the wounds; though, if we're lucky, residue may be left behind. Hopefully a metal alloy from the weapon, skin particulates from the perp.

"So, to answer your question detective, there's no way that this was a suicide. Sure, she could have jumped and either broke both legs, or collapsed her skull, but not both in that position. But assuming this isn't a cartoon, I don't suppose an anvil followed her down either. No, there was foul play involved. I'd bet my business on that."

Jack paused, trying to gauge the detective's reaction, but when he appeared to be indifferent, Jack continued, "In the morning, I'll set about speaking to the locals, perhaps they witnessed something. Maybe I'll be able to build up a profile."

Detective Hanson didn't respond immediately, instead he walked over to the white sheet covering the body. He lifted the corner and recoiled at the sight within, covering his mouth with the edge of his sleeve as if to contain the bile rising up within his throat.

Finally, he spoke, "Do we have a name at least? I don't suppose she had her wallet on her. It would be pretty hard to get an ID on her in this state."

Jack looked down to his hand, which still held her ID, and read it aloud, "Elizabeth Wildbrooke, thirty-seven years old, one hundred and five pounds, five feet, four inches tall. At least, that's what her license says. Though, I'm sure the last two things matter little at this point, you'd have to reassemble her entirely to get those measurements again."

Jack shivered at the thought of someone meticulously piecing her back together as Detective Hanson resumed his walk around the crime scene, inspecting the blood splatters and most likely thinking dull thoughts. Jack snickered to himself, then looked away innocently when Hanson looked up at him. Jack reached into the depths of his pocket and slipped his hand around the familiar box of Marlboros he'd always kept within. He wrestled free a cigarette from the tight grip of the foil and stuck the filter in between his lips. He cupped the end of the smoke, though unsure whether it was out of necessity or habit at this point. The sweet release of nicotine flowed through his lungs, taking off the edge of the stress he'd acquired while looking at Elizabeth's corpse. He bit down on the filter as he let the smoke billow out the sides of his mouth, forming a large white cloud that obscured his vision.

He pondered how to address the case and determined that the best course of action would be to study the past occurrences in chronological order. As he stood there, he poured his mind over possible causes and motives; his mind always returning to manslaughter. He realized he'd need to see the other files, determine if there was a connection of some sort between the other homicides and this one. He chuckled, *perhaps this is all one big fucking joke and I'm the punchline*. Jack knew he'd need to convince Dominic to let him see the other files before things went further south.

Jack exhaled a large cloud of smoke and waved Dom over. He slid his eyes upwards to where the cloud clung, illuminated a dull yellow in the incandescent light of the streetlamp above. He sucked in another lungful, filling his chest with the toxic gas that threatened to contaminate his very cells. He didn't care, and as he watched the smoke twirl and mingle with the dark clouds that had gathered above, he reflected on his life, wondering how in the world he'd let himself come back to this small town. He watched Dom saunter over and realized that it was going to be a very long night.

~ 2 ~

Hours later, long after the sun had fully descended into the indifferent horizon and the crickets began to chirp their forgotten songs, Dom and Jack found themselves at a bar a couple blocks south of the apartment complex. They'd bid the crime scene farewell once the blood was cleaned off the asphalt and the body had been removed from the premises. The barflies chattered noisily amongst each other, filling the bar with an air of nostalgia that reminded Jack of his younger days.

The bar was one of the few left in the town where one could freely smoke, but Jack opted not to, considering the half pack he'd already burned through that night. Instead he'd pined for a pint of Guinness, and by now, the froth nestled halfway down the tall curved glass. He shifted in his seat, getting more comfortable and looked across to Dom, who'd appeared to have aged significantly over the course of several hours.

With blood alcohol levels slowly rising, Jack finally got up the nerve to ask Dom the question he'd been dreading, "So - uh, Dom. You said she was the third murdered. What happened to the others?"

His eyes flicked up from the table and met Jack's eyes, "honestly Jack, I'm surprised it took you this long to ask." He smiled weakly, "The missing people, that's something no one understands, as for the murders… this one was by far the worst, though I'm not saying the others were better by any stretch of imagination. It's a fucked-up case, some were kids. Some were fuckin' kids."

Jack lowered his voice, "what did they -"

Dom cut him off, "look, Jack. I'm not so inclined as to talk about work right now. I really appreciate you lending a hand in this investigation and all, but I don't like talking about work outside of work. You know? It's the one thing that's really kept me sane all these years. Tomorrow we can go to the precinct. I'll get you the files and you can look at them to your heart's content. You can see for yourself what happened to the others."

Dom shifted his eyes down to the table once more and Jack remained staring at him, unsure of how to proceed. It appeared to him that he was on thin ice as it was.

Dom chuckled dryly and met his gaze, "I guess some things never change Jack. You get your mind set on something and you can't drop it until you know everything there is to know about it. Hell, you did that back in grade school too, remember? The damn thing with the aquariums?"

Jack laughed at the memory, "Oh yeah, I nearly drove you mad with facts about breeding habits of cichlids. It's a damn shame my parents never let me have an aquarium, maybe I'd be a marine biologist now."

Dom let out a hearty laugh, "you? A scientist? Jack, you were made to investigate, made to work cases and find clues, discover secrets and unearth things no one else could. It'd be wasted talent in any other field."

Jack chuckled, "You were always so adamant about that. Lo and behold I became a PI. I should have listened to you sooner."

This elicited a gentle smile from him, "Jack, if everyone listened to me, the world would be much better off."

He burst out laughing and Jack joined shortly after. With each bellow stress was flung from their bodies and into the stagnant air of the bar, mixing in with the aroma of beer and cigarette smoke. As a tear of joy trickled down Jack's stubbly cheek, he wondered how long it had been since he'd last laughed so hard.

After some time, Jack shifted the conversation, "So Dom, you have a girlfriend, any small Thompson's running around that I should know about? What's been going on for the past ten years?"

Dom brightened up, "Yeah I got married a few years ago, we currently live together, though there are no plans on having a little one just yet." He paused, "Perhaps in the future though. What about you, are you still with Emma?"

In that moment, Dom took a quick, sharp breath inward, as if wishing he could retract the question. His sorrowful gaze returned as if he knew exactly what the next story Jack told would reveal. Though he'd had the general idea right, he'd strayed in one key aspect.

Jack met his eyes with a crestfallen gaze, his voice betraying the emotions inside, "Well, we - uh - we split up. Though, saying 'split' doesn't do it justice. That would imply that there was a conversation held, that would assume there was some sort of mutual agreement to be held. The typical 'you deserve better, it's not you it's me' sort of conversation held when one party feels like the other is no longer adequate. No, it definitely wasn't a traditional split."

Dom's eyes softened, "Tell me about it?"

Jack choked back the wet anger that was rising in his throat, threatening to bust the seams of his emotional control and turn him into a blubbering imbecile. He blinked rapidly, keeping the tears from spilling forth, finding it difficult to control his emotions while the alcohol made his facial muscles feel numb and slow.

As his remaining strength began to fade, he began, "I was working a case. It was a pretty normal one; man suspects wife of cheating. He was rich, like marble pillars in his house rich, anyway, he brought me in to investigate. He was right of course, though he had been under exaggerating. His wife was one adulterous act away from being a full-fledged pornographic actress by the time I'd been involved. She'd slept with the pool boy, gardener, mail man, pizza delivery boy, hell, if there were still milkmen around, I'm sure she'd have gotten more than just one type of white fluid, if you catch my meaning. After I reported it to my employer and took my check, I returned home, but something was very different. All her stuff was gone; her clothes, jewelry, anything that was hers had just vanished, along with her. Poof, up in the air like she'd packed up and shipped off. The whole place was spotless Dom. The whole place was fucking spotless."

Jack lifted his pint and knocked back the remaining Guinness inside, then settled his face into his hands. The feeling of the beer worked its way across his cheeks and nose, bubbling with warmth though he nearly wept the closing words, "All my successes as an investigator and I still couldn't find her Dom. I couldn't find her, and I don't even know how she was able to move everything out in one day."

Dom reached across the table, planting a firm yet gentle hand on Jack's arm. The gesture softened Jack, and calmed him, building a dam out of a friendship that he'd once thought extinguished. As the wet anger receded and the urge to break down dwindled, Jack came to the realization that Dom was still a very good friend. Someone to rely on, not only when times were good, but when times were tough.

He felt a mixture of grief and guilt - not for the first time that day - over the friendship he'd lost over the years. Though, as they sat in that dingy bar just a couple hundred yards away from where a murder had taken place hours prior, he felt happiness for the first time in years. And although, it could have been a side effect of the alcohol that coursed through his veins, he smiled and a tear of happiness rolled down his cheek, dripping delicately against the stained oak table. Where friendships had been formed and lost; brawls had been started and finished; and tears were shed for lost lovers and family, though Jack didn't know about any of that. For in that moment; sitting at that very table, he was happy, he had his friend back. His brother. The one he'd met all those years ago in kindergarten, in the small, yet bustling town of Magrath.

The fires of their friendship were rekindled that night under the loving gesture of lifetime friends, though those initial fires quickly turned into a roaring inferno in the fumes of alcohol. They spent the remainder of the night recounting tales of their younger days; the drunken misadventures and close calls of their youth. When last call was roared across the bar, and the moans escaped the few remaining patrons, they stumbled out of the bar; their breath a sure giveaway of their inebriated state. Their laughs trailed high into the autumn air above, echoing off the tall buildings and homes that lined either side.

With no inkling as to the degree their lives would change, they carried themselves drunkenly down the street towards Dominic's house, their laughs fading to little more than mere whispers in the night.

~ 3 ~

High on a hill over Magrath, he watched. he watched as the last of the barflies flitted out onto the streets below like ants mindlessly carrying out their duties. Waiting to be squashed underfoot.

He sneered as he witnessed the stumbling duo stagger down the street, arms over each other's shoulders, laughing incessantly. By God, he hated that festering weakling, Jack Lewis. He sneered as he watched him, wishing he could run down there and tear him apart right now, but he couldn't. Killing that girl had taken more out of him than anticipated. He recalled the feelings that coursed through his body as he bashed her head in and folded her like a pretzel. He recalled the feeling of her brain matter running over his fist, how the blood spurted out and covered him. Oh, the screams she made when she'd first seen him. So… delicious. He couldn't wait until he was strong enough to act again, he sure missed being out in the air. It had been a long, long time.

He was watching, waiting, hoping that Jack would face him once more. He looked down the haggard path he had taken to the top of this hill and the sneer spread out further across his face, displaying sharp teeth that poked out from his grey gums. He was hungry.

He didn't shiver, despite his nakedness, those sorts of feelings were reserved for the weak. For the cattle. He thought back to a time when he was significantly younger; when he last walked among the others below. He thought of the rolling hills and the blue sky, undisturbed, untouched by mankind. In current times, he fed well, though he had little taste for the world in which man had created, its monolithic structures and automobiles. No, the world was different from when he had last walked the earth, significantly different, and that angered him. As the anger boiled and curled inside of his abdomen, he readied himself to let out an unearthly scream. One that would wrap the town in terror and drive them mad.

Yet, as he tried to bellow, all that came out was a light wisp of a noise. One that barely allowed him to extend his power further than a couple feet in front of him. He still needed time, time to regain his strength from the years he'd spent asleep, from the years he lay dormant. He sneered once more at the town of Magrath, then turned and ran back down the path that led him up to the promontory overlooking the town.

As he ran, a rage overcame him, he would get his revenge on Magrath. Soon.

Chapter 2: Murders in Magrath

~ 1 ~

Jack awoke to a loud banshee-like wail that pierced his ears and punctured his hungover brain, sending shooting pains up the sides of his head to right behind his eyes. He groaned and felt his dry tongue stick to the equally dry roof of his mouth, then turned and tried to find the source of the incessant noise. He slowly opened his eyes, struggling to fight the dryness that held them closed. He saw his phone flashing sporadically on the coffee table mere feet away and winced each time it pulsed as the flash sent resounding pain surging from his eyeballs deep into his brain.

He reached out and snatched it off the table, hitting 'dismiss' on the display. Rising on wobbly legs, he stood and took in his surroundings, his mind clouded with profound confusion. He looked down to the olive green couch which until recently, he had laid, a large flatscreen TV was mounted to the wall directly adjacent to the couch, and between the two stood the oak coffee table where his phone had sat throughout the night. He plopped back down on the couch and rubbed the sleep out of his eyes as he tried to sober up. He had almost succeeded in granting himself some semblance of cognitive sobriety when he heard a light, melodic feminine voice ring out with a surprised gasp from somewhere behind him. He winced before turning, as the noise brought forth the knowledge of the hangover that had since ridden in the periphery.

As he turned and saw her a wave of nostalgia washed over him. Grasping him gently as his mind recalled all it knew of the woman before him. Her smell, her laugh, the times they'd spent together over their youthful years. Her name was Shannon, though he knew to just think her name elicited so much more than just a word. A string of seven letters, two vowels and five consonants. She'd been a tight member of their little group of misfits and her beauty only increased in Jack's years of absence.

Her bright red hair hung loosely over her shoulder, ruffled slightly from a good night's rest. Although disheveled, her hair glimmered in the morning sunlight that poured in through the den's window. Jack couldn't help but think that it looked soft. He looked at her soft white porcelain skin and the way it traced from her face down her neck and delicately into the large plaid shirt she was wearing; re-emerging at the hem once more, and down her sculpted legs. He felt the wave of nostalgia get replaced by a burst of lust, which was quickly replaced by guilt as his mind pieced everything together. *She's probably Dom's wife.*

Jack smiled sheepishly, his hoarse voice came out embarrassed, "Hey Shannon. It's - uh - it's been a while." He raised a hand and rubbed the back of his neck with his palm.

She gently returned his smile and small crinkles appeared at the outer corners of her eyes, "Hiya Jack. It sure has."

They stood there a few moments, unable to find the words needed to communicate the passage of time between them, to close the rift that forms when two people who separated on inexplicable terms part. Jack looked into her dazzling green eyes, marveling at the way the light reflected jade, emerald and peridot sparkles into the containment of the iris. His heart lurched, longing for something he'd once had. He smiled once more, about to speak, when he realized how awful he must look. It'd been a long time since he'd seen her, and he felt embarrassed about his appearance. Regardless of this, she caught him off guard.

A whimsical expression crossed the edges of her mouth and eyes, "You look good Jack."

"It's uh - been a long time." God, you already said that, you awkward idiot. "Er - I mean - you too."

The gentle smile returned, though in a much more somber tone and she flicked her eyes downwards, "Yeah Jack, yeah it has."

They once again fell into the boughs of silence, only this time they were spared from any additional awkwardness by the footfalls on the steps leading down to them. Shannon gave him one more lingering smile before turning her head towards Dom's feet as they carried him down the stairs and onto the first floor.

Jack was glad to know that he wasn't the only one to feel rough. Dom looked about as good as Jack felt, which was awful. His eyes were red and puffy, and his hair stood up in clumps at odd angles, giving him a look of having several horns protruding from his head. He smiled painfully and raised a hand in greeting. He breezed past them without so much as a word and continued across the wooden expanse between them, dragging the hems of his pajama pants across the hardwood. They watched as he reached the coffee machine and turned it on, closing his eyes in pain as it loudly ground fresh beans. Allured by the promise of coffee and knowing they were unable to hold a proper conversation, Jack and Shannon walked over to the counter and joined Dom as the coffee began to brew.

Jack and Shannon watched as Dom walked over to the four slotted toaster and popped four slices of toast in, pushing down the lever to begin cooking them. Walking over to the fridge to grab the margarine, he wiped at his eyes with the back of his hand. He turned and faced them in silence - groggily blinking as the coffee machine brewed the dark elixir they were all craving - and smiled as he realized he had an audience.

Jack welcomed the silence, he felt comfort in it as he always had. He'd never found it awkward or tense, regardless of the situation, instead he always saw it as a liberating moment from which he could think in respite. As he stood there that morning, he mulled over the details of the case, wondering what the files could tell him that Dom had avoided. Were there children involved? He wasn't sure. Though as he watched his friend pour coffee from the pot into three white ceramic mugs, he figured there were. For Dom was a gentle man, and if children were involved, Jack knew it would scar him.

Dom slid one of the thick ceramic mugs across the granite surface of the island to Jack along with two Tums and an Advil. He graciously scooped them up and slid them into his mouth, chasing them with the scalding liquid. He looked to Dom and Shannon, who'd since moved to watching him as he stood there. Dom with worrying eyes and Shannon with something else.

He set his mug down and quietly excused himself before meandering to the couch on which he'd spent the night prior. He plucked his coat off the arm rest and shrugged it on; sliding his hand into the pocket to feel the familiar comfort of the box of Marlboros within. He maneuvered the box from the folds of his coat and flicked it open, hungrily eyeing the fixation of his addiction within. He pulled one free from the aluminum foil and slid the filter into his mouth as he stepped through the threshold and onto the front porch.

The autumn air was cool on his skin. He loved the way it ruffled his hair like a loving parent, enjoyed the way it rushed up his nostrils as if its sole desire was to aid in his respiration. He marveled at the way it carried the scent of the leaves and the grass through the air, as though bestowing the gifts of the season's change upon any and all who were so fortunate to have not caught the common cold.

His smiling lips clamped onto the filter, holding it firmly in place as he lit the end and inhaled deeply. He closed his eyes as a wave of relief overcame him. He was unsure of whether it was a placebo or not, but the feeling of the smoke filling his body had always helped to take the edge off his stress, clear his mind, and allowed him to focus. Jack released his breath, blowing a large cloud of smoke; an homage to the sky he'd spent many days of his youth staring into, wishing he could fly away.

His smile faded as he looked towards the hill that stood over Magrath and the disheveled building that lay on top of it; remembering a time when the house stood tall and proud, overlooking the town like an idol, giving an air of prosperity and wealth. He felt queasy looking at it, and decided he was done with his cigarette for the time being. He walked down the porch stairs and hunkered over, stubbing the burning end on the concrete below. Leaving smoldering ashes behind as he turned back to Dom's house and ventured inside.

As he walked down the hallway that connected the entryway to the dining area, he heard them speaking in low hushed tones. Growing suspicious, he slowed, and crept along the wall, straining to hear their quieted words and eavesdrop on their conversation.

Dom's voice flitted through the air, "... when he got home."

Shannon's voice came out strained and concerned, "That's horrible! She just up and left him?"

"Yeah, he told me last night, she took all of her things, and vanished poof into thin air…"

Shannon cut into the conversation, "Shit, I never expected her to do such a low-grade bitch thing like that. To make matters worse for him, he must come back to a town he left behind and find us together, hitched."

Dom's voice came out serious, "What do you mean?"

So, Dom didn't know? Jack felt his heartbeat quicken, his breath shorten and his palms begin to sweat as he wondered what Shannon would say. He wanted to barge in and stop the conversation, but he was afraid it would become too obvious. He wondered if Shannon would force him to unintentionally relive the night they'd broken off what they'd had all those years ago. He gulped.

Shannon surprised him, however, "I mean, his girlfriend of what, 10 years ups and leaves him high and dry. He comes back to a town he probably doesn't want to be in and finds his two best childhood friends enjoying a very healthy marriage, with a house of their own, and are both successful. Dom, you must realize how hard this must be on him. He's lost everything we have; I can't imagine the emotions he must be feeling right now."

Dom's voice lost it's serious edge, "I know hun, it must be terribly hard on him. I wish I was able to take his pain away. Do you think…"

His voice trailed off as Jack entered the room; eyes downcast and movements slow. That sadness etched into his features gave them the realization that he'd heard their conversation and upon this epiphany Shannon walked over and wrapped him in a tight hug. Her soft hair poured between them and her scent flowed welcome up Jack's nose. He breathed her in, not hearing the quivery apologies spewing from her. He held her tightly, reveling in the feeling of her body pressed against his; from the placement of her hands on the crux of his lower back to the feeling of her head nestled just under his jaw.

He blinked back a series of tears that threatened to break free. They were tears of loss, though not just for the loss of Emma, but for the profound loss he felt in that moment for letting Shannon slip from his grasp years prior, for the loss of the life he'd never experiences, and for the guilt bubbling inside of him as he coveted his friend's wife. But for the moment, he savored the feeling of her body on his, the scent of her unkempt hair and the wet spot growing on the nape of his neck from the tears she shed for him. He felt another tinge of loss when Shannon finally broke off the hug.

--

After accepting their heartfelt apologies, Jack spoke up, “You guys have nothing to worry about, it’s kind of a relief that you both know now.”

He smiled uneasily at them as they sat around the kitchen table eating the breakfast that Dom had prepared for them and they dug in without further question, plunging the room into silence. Jack happily ate, enjoying the silence, using it to further delve back into thoughts of what his day would hold.

Jack and Dom left shortly after breakfast and getting ready, abdomens unsettled. Though, neither of them could begin to guess if it was the result of the prior night’s drinking or the trepidation building up inside of them. For they had no inkling as to the depth this investigation would go, what fruit it would bear, or what secrets it would dig up. As they stepped out into the autumn air and made their way towards where Jack had parked the day prior, Jack cast his eyes up to the charred skeleton of the mansion on the hill, where the fate of Magrath had been decided nearly ten years before.

On a night he’d quite like to forget.

~ 2 ~

They stopped on their way to the precinct, outside of an old and familiar storefront. ‘Ferguson’s General Store’ was plastered above the door, and Jack smiled sadly as he took it in. It was different than Jack remembered it, though he was unsure of whether it had been from the lens of childhood being stripped from his vision only to be replaced by a cynical and pessimistic worldview. The windows, once crystal clear, stood streaked, catching the faint grey light that flitted through the clouds above at an odd angle. Giving them an appearance as though an indifferent hand had wiped them some time ago, leaving trails of soap and dirt to intermingle on the surface for the world to see. The once vibrant red bricks had faded significantly from the sunlight, giving Jack a surreal feeling as he realized how inconsiderate the passage of time could be; noticing how it stripped his idyllic memories of the building of their color unapologetically. He frowned as he stepped through the now rusted metal-framed door.

As Jack stepped through the threshold of the store, he was hit with a wave of nostalgia upon seeing Mr. Ferguson working the cash register. Jack smiled at him and could see Mr. Ferguson's brain working behind his eyes, trying to assign a name to the face he seemingly recognized, but couldn't place. He hesitated a moment, as if decided the best way to address him, then a whimsical smile splayed across his liver-spotted face.

His eyes lit up with grand-fatherly affection, as they had all those years ago when they'd visit the store to get candy, "Well helllloooo Jackie."

The old man's mouth remained smiling as he looked affectionately at Jack, seemingly pleased with how he'd grown up. His smile willed Jack with the pleasant feeling of nostalgia once more, whisking his mind away momentarily to the days when he was younger.

He recalled the way that he and his friends; Dominic, Shannon, Emma, and a few others would spend their days biking through the town's streets, stopping to acquire more of the kids that they'd grown up with since kindergarten. They'd have short races up the street, as if trying to decide who was the fastest by who could reach the end of the block first. He recalled the way their chests would burn with the desire for air; the exertion of vigorous exercise sending sweat trickling down their spines and foreheads, threatening to soak through their thin t-shirts at any moment.

When a victor was crowned for the evening, they'd make their way over to Ferguson's - high on the rush of adrenaline - for candy. They'd grab frozen desserts and sodas, then bike to the park, where they'd talk about plans of being firefighters and superheroes. Jack smiled at the memory, remembering fondly how Mr. Ferguson would always give the night's victor a free piece of candy, and if he was in a good mood - which was most days - he'd give a few to everyone else as well. Jack blinked slowly, as if to savor in the memory of a childhood he'd long since forgotten. The present came crashing back and the traces of his smile faded from his eyes, as he struggled to keep it on his face.

Jack's voice came out even and without inflection, "Hi Mr. Ferguson, how've you been?"

Mr. Ferguson's smile faded slightly, evidently wounded by Jack's monotonous tone and the fake smile that he'd put on his face. Jack's heart broke slightly for the old man who'd been such a positive impact on his childhood but given the pain he'd been experiencing he'd figured monotony was better than tears. Mr. Ferguson gave a slight shrug as if to say, 'same as always,' and looked into Jack's eyes, giving an almost pitying look.

Jack held his gaze for a few seconds longer, then turned right as Mr. Ferguson was about to start talking once again, not wanting to linger on the tradition of conversation, afraid his colloquialisms would give his current state away. He walked deeper into the store as the tears began to slowly fall, collecting on his lower lashes in the process. He wiped them away as he found his way to the products he was looking for; Tums and Ibuprofen.

He heard hushed conversation between Dom and Mr. Ferguson, and shook his head, knowing Dom was explaining the situation as a way of apologizing. His kind heart will get him killed one day. Jack smiled sadly and walked back out with his items, ready to pay.

Their conversation cut off as he approached; their eyes slid curiously over his face, as though to glean any indication of whether he'd heard what they'd been talking about. Jack placed his items on the counter and fumbled in his jacket pocket for his wallet, he met the eyes of Mr. Ferguson as he produced his debit card.

Mr. Ferguson smiled sadly, hinting that he understood what Jack had been going through and began manually entering his items into the machine, "What have you been up to Jack? Dom tells me you're a big shot Private Eye now."

Jack chuckled dryly as his mind drifted off to thoughts about the earlier days of his work. The simpler days. The days with rich old men who'd wondered if their stay-at-home-20-year-younger supermodel wives were remaining faithful. He thought about the years of working such cases, and how it was a stroke of luck that a client hosted a police charity event at his manor and invited Jack out of kindness; effectively kick-starting his career into cases alongside police.

Jack's mind lingered on the crime scenes and long nights, the travelling and staying up late in motels working the case with little more than his laptop and notepad. The days spent away from home, wondering if this was what his life had become. He enjoyed the work, sure, but it put an unanticipated strain on his relationship with Emma, and he had little doubt that it was a contributing factor in her untimely departure from his life. He thought of the times when he'd come home after a big case and how he'd work one of those tame scandalous cases once more, as though anxious to return to the life he'd unknowingly left behind.

He smiled weakly at Mr. Ferguson and told him none of that, however, he shrugged, "Yeah, I guess I get around from time to time."

Mr. Ferguson laughed a deep and hearty laugh. One of a man who'd spent his life with joy and friends, who'd known hardships but had always come out on the other side unscathed. He bellowed the laugh of a man who'd known the measure to which laughter heals and Jack couldn't help but laugh along with him.

He smiled wide and winked at Jack, "good to see you're humble in your old age Jackie."

Jack smiled back and took a twenty out of his pocket to cover his bill, sliding it over the counter to Mr. Ferguson, who'd punched it into his cash register, then tilted his head to peer at the display through his glasses.

Jack nodded to the old man, then turned for the door, "keep the change Mr. Ferguson"

Jack and Dom left the small store smiling. Dom, for seeing a smile on Jack's face, and Jack for the nostalgia. He knew it wasn't much; the tip he'd given the old man, but when he'd given him the change, he'd done it as a repayment to a sweet, kind hearted man who'd sweetened the eves of his childhood and shined a beam of light into the darkness that clouded Magrath.

He looked back once more before opening his car door and sliding behind the steering wheel. It was a 2006 Pontiac Sunfire, and though he could have afforded a much nicer vehicle, he liked the familiarity of the car. From the way the engine rumbled when he turned the key to the way he sank deep into the seat when he drove.

He looked over as Dom got into the passenger side and settled on the seat, before looking at him. Jack met Dom's gaze and found himself feeling glad that he was there for him, which came a surprise, he'd found that over the past several years, he'd never been so grateful for someone else to be with him.

Jack's voice came out a little shaky, "Hey, I just wanted to say thank you. You've been a great friend, even though I haven't seen or spoke to you for the past ten years. It means a lot to me Dom. I mean it."

Dom turned in his seat so he could place a hand on Jack's shoulder, "no problem, I just hope you know that you don't have to face these things alone. I'm not entirely sure why you left, but now that you're back, I want to do everything I can to make sure you don't feel like an alien in your own hometown. Welcome home Jack."

Jack felt the tears well up once more, but he suppressed them and steeled himself for the day. He turned back to the road and began to drive, heading down the asphalt that, like Ferguson's store, had dulled with age; now an ashen grey that contrasted heavily with the black road that remained in his childhood memories.

~ 3 ~

Within five minutes of leaving Ferguson's, they pulled up to the lonely Magrath police department. Jack's car sputtered to a halt and he smiled as Dom shot him a curious glance; clearly put off by the noise his engine had produced. Jack simply shrugged as he met Dom's gaze, and slid the transmission into park, giving the old car a rest as they left to go about their business within the old brick building.

They walked through the double glass doors into the precinct, and Jack was hit with a lingering scent of coffee, paper, and the musty smell that accompanied the old building; it was the smell of bureaucracy. He smiled to himself, happy - though not for the first time - that he'd passed up a life with the police for one with less constraints on his actions.

They approached the large wooden front desk and the female officer that sat behind it. Jack's eyes fell upon the name tag and saw that her name was "Smithson." His brain went cloudy as he tried to grab the edge of the memory from the periphery in some vain attempt to understand why the name sounded so familiar. Yet, as he stood there, struggling to place her face and name, his mind was filled with an image of a petite girl with long, wavy blonde hair.

He frowned, then finally matched her face to the picture in his head. She'd grown considerably; having packed on a significant amount of muscle. Her hair was cut into a short bob, though her sparkling blue eyes still showed the high level of intelligence he came to know her for in their youth. He chuckled to himself, thinking of how much someone can change in a decade. Her once narrow shoulders were now broad and powerful. Even though he could now place her face, it still took several seconds for her name to fall into place and finally find its way onto his tongue.

His voice came out astounded, “Darla?”

He recalled how growing up, she’d been timid; in fact, she’d never spoken much in class, though she’d always scored superbly on exams. She wasn’t known for being super social and had no close friends to speak of. Jack felt guilty as he studied her, waiting for her to recognize who he was; ashamed that after the night he’d left, he’d never thought of her again. The guilt intensified as he recalled how she’d sit next to him almost every class, how she’d bashfully look away when their eyes met or when he’d ask her questions. Those mannerisms had followed them from kindergarten all the way into twelfth grade and he’d never once seen them as anything more than her being socially awkward.

Her eyes finally widened as the realization set in, “Holy shi- I heard you were coming back, is it really you Jack? I haven’t seen you since - hell - since you left, what nine years ago?” She stood, “is this your first time back? How the heck are you?”

Her cheeks flushed red as she stood there staring at him, waiting apprehensively for an answer, embarrassed but unwavering. Her words caused him to think about the night he left, and he choked on his reply as his mind flitted through the nightmare that caused him to leave.

“Almost ten years, and yeah… it’s my first time back. You look really good Darla.” his lips formed a smile as he said the latter part.

She let out a small squeak, and her cheeks became even redder as she managed a strained, “welcome back!” Smiling all the while.

Jack smiled back at her before turning to Dom, “Well, we should probably go and check out that filing room, then I can get to work.”

Dom rolled his eyes and shook his head slowly, receiving a confused look from Jack. He signaled for him to follow as he began down the linoleum corridor.

The filing room was little more than a broom closet with metal shelves running up the wall on either side and a lonely desk jammed in between them. Though the shelves were packed full of old filing boxes - each covered with a thick layer of dusk - the desk stood empty. An old leather office chair with several tears and a very worn out seat was positioned next to the desk. Jack looked at it and smiled. Perfect. He slowly shrugged off his jacket and hung it on the high back of the chair, ensuring that it wouldn't fall off the moment he turned away.

Dominic walked over and grabbed one of the boxes before bringing it over to Jack who looked at him bewildered as he took it from Dom's hands, "Really? A bit archaic don't you think?"

Dom smiled, "it's a bit outdated, but a lot of us prefer pen and paper over keeping the files on the computers. We feel safer that way."

Jack, who didn't think his eyes could open any wider, discovered that they could, "What next? You're going to tell me about the microfiche that's stored at your desk? Are you gonna grab some slate for me to take notes on? Oh! Maybe, if I want to make copies of anything, I can bring it over to the printing press and duplicate it."

Dom shook his head and put his palm against his forehead, trying to prevent himself from laughing. Meanwhile, Jack placed the book on the desk and stared at the front of it. "2015 MURDERS" was written across the front and sides in thick black marker. Jack rolled his eyes as he pulled the top off it, barely noticing as Dom turned and walked out of the filing room, still chuckling lightly to himself.

Jack reached into the box and pulled out the three files from within. He set them down and looked at the size of them, pondering how much investigative work had happened since the murders. The files were thin; containing only preliminary questioning and pictures of the crime scenes. There simply wasn't enough inside of them. He read off the names printed neatly on each.

His voice was flat and even; inquisitive, "Noah Brackman, Veronica Stillwell, and Elizabeth Wildbrooke, let's find out what we can about you."

He placed down the files on the table, praying silently that this wouldn't lead to an inquisition, though if it did, at least he'd be paid well. He looked at the fronts of each of the files, trying to decide where to start, eventually settling on chronological order. He picked up the one labelled "Noah Brackman" and opened the file, anxious to read the report inside.

Jack spread the contents of the file over the desk and picked up the first report; the one that listed Noah's age. *Sixteen years old. Fuck, just a kid.* He shook his head sadly as he continued to read. From the report, he was a prodigy football player, to the point where his parents had decided to move to a larger city that had a better scouting rate. They were set to move in the spring once the school year had finished. They'd been hysterical when they found out about his death and often cut their answers off with sobs when they answered the detective's questions.

Jack could picture them in his head vaguely. Imagining the way that they would have clung to each other as they stared into the distance, unable to fully comprehend the depth of the loss they'd experienced. They'd spend the next few weeks distancing themselves as they tried to figure out how to cope with their grief, blaming themselves for the loss. Saying things to themselves like, "If only we'd kept a closer eye on him" or "I should have loved him more." Jack had seen it often enough over the years, grief raged across families. He figured in some time, they'd go to grief counselling and their grief would eventually solidify their dying marriage, they'd figure out how to live again and they'd return to a life that was a husk of what it once was.

Jack shook his head sadly and returned to the files. Noah's parents had found him in his bedroom on the afternoon of September 20, 2015, and Jack imagined how their hearts must have shattered upon viewing their son in such a state. They were advised to speak to a psychologist by the detective and given the card of a grief counsellor the police department kept on retainer. They'd accepted and bid the detective farewell.

Jack placed down the report and began to sift through the crime scene photos. He found himself quite disturbed by them. There were several pictures of various angles of Noah's body spread out over his light grey comforter, though, there was a red halo of blood staining under his head. His body appeared to be in remarkable state and Jack only felt queasy as his eyes panned over the deceased boy's face; where there was absolutely no skin to speak of. It was as though the skin had been filleted off with expert precision, keeping all the muscles and tendons intact. The flesh had only been removed around his facial features, leaving a macabre remnant in its wake.

Jack looked in a sort of morbid fascination at the muscular structure of the boy's face, amazed at how uncanny the resemblance was to the anatomy books he would frequently look at as a child. He looked at the seamless cut that ran around the exposed muscle, noting how there was no presence of jagged flesh that would have suggested the use of a serrated instrument. It was as if whoever had performed the action, had done so with surgical precision.

He looked back to the initial report to see what was recorded pertaining to the location of the boy's face. He scoured the page and finally found what he'd been looking for. "It remains unclear what became of the victim's face, as of right now we are assuming that whoever has committed such atrocities has taken it as a trophy of sorts." He shivered and exchanged the initial report for the coroner's report.

The initial inspection proved to further solidify his own observations, revealing there were no external injuries to Noah's body, save for the removal of his face. Though, it was upon the preliminary internal inspection, that Jack felt bile rise in his throat. As the coroner propped open Noah's throat, he was met with a fold of what appeared to be flesh.

He reached with forceps and attempted to remove it, and after some time, had managed to remove from the boy's throat and screamed in abject horror as he realized what it was. It was the flesh that had originally constituted the face of Noah Brackman. After a thorough investigation of the corpse, the coroner determined that the cause of death was suffocation. He deduced that Noah Brackman had died from asphyxiation from his own face.

Also included was a small note by the coroner; "This has not only mortified me, who deals with death on a daily basis, but also the several officers stationed here in Magrath as well. It concerns me to think of what sort of man, no, monster has the capacity to commit someone to this kind of death." Jack read the full report several times, absorbing the information even though it made his stomach churn.

He pulled back from the desk and put his elbows on his knees as he drew in a deep breath, trying not to vomit. His mind struggled to think of a time when he'd felt this way over a crime committed but turned up nothing. Elizabeth's death the night before, yes, but what bothered Jack wasn't the gore of the crime, it was the thought of this kid being forced to choke on his own severed face. Jack sucked in another deep breath and held it for a few seconds before slowly releasing. He maneuvered the chair back to the desk and picked up the forensics report.

There was no discernible DNA left at the crime scene, in fact, there was no foreign organic matter on the scene to speak of. As Jack combed through the report, he reckoned that whoever had killed Noah, would have been not only highly skilled with a knife, but would have known to some degree the minute amount of genetic material required to figure out who the perpetrator was. He read the file again and pulled out the small notepad he'd kept with him at all times. Attached to it with a thin chain was a pen, so that should the pen slip from the small elastic holster on the side of the pad; he wouldn't lose the pen altogether.

Jack scribbled across the first blank page he opened to; 'NOAH BRACKMAN: No traces of spittle or flecks of skin left on the scene. They covered their tracks well. Professional?'

He paddled through the remaining files in the span of several minutes, covering Noah's basic details, parents' names and income, their acquaintances, neighbors, friends, where his parents worked, where he went to school, and what city they had planned on moving to. After flipping through some of Noah's information Jack concluded that he'd been a well-liked individual. He'd had good grades, great athleticism, and from his parents' account, it seemed like he'd had ample friends. The police took his parents' word for it and had not pushed the investigation further. This caused some frustration to bubble in the depths of Jack's chest, and he felt the anxiety that accompanied it clench tighter on his heart. He picked up the pen once more and jotted down 'talk with Noah's parents, classmates, friends, and coaches.'

Jack placed the file down on the desk and slowly rose to his feet, retrieving his jacket from the back of the chair. He needed a cigarette. He felt his mouth begin to water as he exited the filing room; the hankering only growing larger as he walked down the old hallway. He walked past a bulletin board filled with missing persons signs that had been brought in by the grieving families and carried on, trying to focus solely on the murders, though he knew he wouldn't be able to stop himself from worrying about them too.

He walked slowly and deliberately through the lobby towards the doors he'd entered through no more than an hour prior. He caught Darla's eyes and she reddened visibly and waved at him. He raised his hand in response, though didn't stop, afraid that stopping to talk would bring forth the tidal wave of emotions welling up inside of him. *Just get outside and smoke, there's nothing more you can do.*

He smiled sadly, passing Darla by entirely on the way out.

~ 4 ~

Jack stepped outside and closed his eyes momentarily as the crisp autumn air bit into his face. He quite enjoyed the little moments like this; when he was still warm enough from the indoors, and he could just enjoy the change in the environment. He liked the feel of the soft breeze as it sent shivers down his spine in such a way that it brought back the memories of his youth; walking to Dom's house in the early winter with a new game his parents bought him to play on Dom's Nintendo 64. He smiled as he reached into his pocket, feeling the outer edges of the box of smokes.

His anxiety eased as he felt the familiar shape of the package of Marlboros that he'd always kept there, and as he finally removed the tightly wrapped stick of tobacco from the confines of its space, he felt that ease kicking in even more. He knew he was an addict, there was never any question in his mind. Yet, he'd always justified it with the mindset that he could and most likely would die working one of these cases and the cigarettes wouldn't have time to affect his body.

Jack propped the filter in his mouth and withdrew the small lighter from his pocket and sparked it against the end. When the lighter refused to hold a flame, he cupped his other hand against it, digging his teeth slightly into the filter to hold the smoke in place. When the wind proved relentless, he knew he'd have to move to an area where it would be unable to reach him. He sighed and plucked the cigarette from his mouth, then trudged off, around the corner of faded brick and stepped into the back alley.

As he finally set the smoke ablaze, he noted the reduced level of noise in the back alley. He reveled in it, allowing himself to close his eyes once more and attempt to clear his mind. He felt the muscles in his forehead relax and frowned, he hadn't even realized they were flexed.

He sucked in a lungful of smoke and exhaled through his nose as he opened his eyes and stared at the grey sky above. *How long has it been since the light shined on Magrath?* He felt a gentle tug on the hem of his Jacket, and turned, surprised to see a little girl standing there.

She was no older than five, though, her eyes pierced through him with an incomprehensible depth of wisdom. He looked her over, noticing the dirt surrounding her eyes and covering her cheeks. Her light pink bed dress was similarly soiled, and stains of dirt, blood and tears lined the front of it. Her feet were bare and in a sorry state. Having been exposed to the elements, they'd begun to grow fungus inside of the numerous lacerations that covered them. Jack reckoned that her small and tender feet had been cut by rocks, as the thin skin would have been torn like paper.

What caught Jack off the most were her eyes, which shone with a hyperawareness, he'd seen in no one else. They didn't match the rest of her, nor were they the eyes of a child. They were the eyes of someone who'd experienced hardships and overcome adversity, and as Jack thought back to the first time he'd met her, he remembered why.

--

Jack had been working one of his first 'big' cases, he had only been contacted because it had caught the local media's attention and the police wanted the family to be out of the public eye as soon as possible. Jack hadn't worked for the police before, though he knew police departments had been known to hire PI's when they were unable to pursue the case any further. He'd accepted the job with little to no inkling as to the profound effect it would have on his career. As Jack soon found out, when you have the backing of one police department, soon you'll find yourself getting calls from others.

Jack reviewed all the clues the police department had collected until that point, and he concluded that all the evidence was suggesting a kidnapping. There were a few things that simply didn't sit well with him.

Her second story bedroom had been broken into via the window positioned next to her bed; and the glass was strewn across the floor. This proved that the perpetrator had in fact broken that window from the outside. However, there was no awning below the window, nor were there any signs that a ladder had been placed below. This confused Jack, but not as much as the single tuft of hair that appeared to have been ripped from her head, which lay perfectly strewn across the pillow in a fine blonde heap, as though it were deliberately placed there.

Jack still had no doubts that she'd been taken from the house, though he began to suspect that some parts were staged, as if to make whoever was investigating think someone had broken in through the window to grab her. This in and of itself didn't cause Jack concern, sometimes criminals would send investigators on a false trail. So, Jack treated it as he would any other case, and eventually he ended up in a back alley in a rather impoverished area.

It was there that Jack first saw the little girl. He'd been looking at a rather curious stain on one of the building's walls when he caught sight of a flash of pink disappearing further down the back alley, around the side of one of the buildings. On a hunch, Jack stood and ran after the girl, finally catching up to her outside of a large white metal door that was dented and rusted in several spots, as though someone had tried to break into it.

He quickly realized that she was the missing girl that he'd been looking for though her eyes looked significantly different than they had in the photographs. They pierced through him, rendering him frozen on the spot. He gazed into them for what felt like an eternity, every second passing feeling like hundreds if not thousands. He tried to speak yet nothing came out, and the silence that encroached on the back alley was becoming unbearable for him.

Finally, she spoke, and though her voice was that of a little girl, she spoke with the ease of someone that'd walked the earth for decades, "I'm afraid your investigation will reveal little of the results you desired. I've perished, and for little more than a week I've been rotting away, slowly, as the insects writhe and churn inside my cadaver I've decided to help. Jack Lewis, you will find me behind that door. Though fleeing is always an option, I must warn you, that doing so will not yield the answers, you'll never know the truth and he'll only do it again. So, go on, but there is one more thing. Ask my father about my birthday."

As her body began to dissipate into the surrounding air, Jack finally found he could move again. He looked to the large metal door and began to walk up the couple steps leading up to it, wondering what the hell he'd just witnessed, reasoning to himself that he must be going insane. You're stressing yourself out too much Jack, maybe it's time to take a break, disappear for a while, you know it's long overdue.

He almost walked away from the door then, unsure of whether he'd want to see what was or wasn't on the other side, afraid for what either answer would imply. If he found her body, then that would mean he was just speaking to her spirit, though he wasn't entirely sure he could deal with that. Alternatively, if he opened the door and found nothing, that would mean he had been hallucinating the apparition and would mean it was time for him to be sent to the looney bin. Jack weighed the two outcomes with the third. Walking away. If he walked, he'd be turning his back on the investigation, he had no reason not to explore what lay beyond the door, though as he stood there, he began once more to reason with himself, to ponder the outcomes again and again.

Finally, he set about one decision, I'll try the door, if it's locked, I walk if not I'll enter. And thus, leaving his actions up to the hands of the fates, he reached for the handle and pulled, his heart both sinking and rising as the door swung open. He felt excited, sure, it was an advancement in the investigation surely, though if that were true, then that would imply several things that he wouldn't allow himself to think about at that moment. For now, he had to do a thorough investigation of the room in which he'd entered.

It wasn't as large as he'd originally thought, and it seemed to be abandoned perhaps an old storage room long since forgotten by the tenants of the building. He pulled a flashlight from his pocket and panned it around the edges of the room, illuminating the walls on the four sides, realizing that there was no door leading into it. A design flaw perhaps. It was only when he panned the light over the floor that the smell hit him, as if waiting for him to determine the source before it made its presence known.

Laying on the ground before him was the body of the little girl. Maggots clambered over her face, crawling across her cheeks and into her now empty eye sockets as they consumed her flesh. Jack vomited then, spilling the contents of his stomach onto the concrete ground. It splattered and his body racked as it purged him from any and all food. It was the first time he'd seen a corpse up close in such a state, and it was not something he ever wanted to see again.

Her dress was stained with a mixture of blood, dirt, and something else, though he struggled to determine what it was in the darkness of the room. Just as the apparition had said, it was clear that she had been dead for a week. He felt sick and threw up several more times before he was finally able to stop the dry heaving. His stomach was empty, devoid of any and all substance within.

Once he stopped shaking and his body stopped racking with the aftereffects, he pulled out his phone and called the police department, giving them a very brief message, followed by the address.

"Hello"

"Yeah, it's Jack... Uh, Jack Lewis"

"Oh, how are you?"

"Not good, I found her, send… well, send some officers, some EMTs and some forensics guys. Bring a body bag."

Silence.

"I'm at 10020, Baker Street. Go around back, you'll find a white steel door. I'm in there."

He clicked the phone off and waited for the mechanism of the law to come and remove the child's remains. Jack moved to the stairs outside of the room and sat on them, placing his head in his hands. He was in shock, and the tears didn't come then. They would come later though; he was sure of it.

Sometime later, when the sun began to dip into the horizon, the EMTs carried out the body on a stretcher in a large black bag. Jack watched with morbid fascination as the sun cast its indifferent orange rays over the scene, casting all of them in an amber haze as the body was loaded onto the waiting ambulance. Jack closed his eyes and cursed God above for the actions of one of his creations. He cursed him for snuffing out the life the little girl lived and the future she could have had. He cursed him for turning his back on humanity. On that day, Jack Lewis lost his faith in not only God, but humanity itself.

As the sun finally crossed the threshold, Jack walked back to his car and off towards one final destination; the house of the girl's father. When he arrived, he knocked on the large white French style doors and waited for him to answer the door. He had his hand in his pocket and was grateful for the way it muffled the light click that sounded inside of it.

The crocodile tears were streaming down his face, and though Jack saw through them, he played along.

"I'm sorry for your loss, sir. My name's Jack Lewis, I just wanted to let you know that I was the one who found her."

A small glint of anger flickered across the man's face, a micro expression of the hate he was harboring, "Thank you Jack, I uh, I don't know how to move forward here." The tears streamed down his face and dribbled onto the carpet.

Jack kept his poker face on full display, "That's an understandable feeling, sir. From what I know of grief, it's birthdays that are the hardest."

He quickly flicked his eyes to Jack's, "Yeah, those will probably be filled with a lot of drinking, I reckon."

Jack held his stare, acutely aware of the tension building in the space between them, "Oh definitely, I've heard it helps to tell happy memories. Why don't you tell me about her last birthday?"

The man's expression went tight, and the fake tears came to a halt. His eyes narrowed and his mouth went taught. His voice came out through clenched teeth, "Well we had a cake. Of course."

Jack was done playing games and he put as much authority into his voice as possible, shattering the man's demeanor, "What happened on her birthday?"

The man drew back for a second, intimidated by the increased volume of Jack's voice. He began to tremble, then started sobbing as he came to terms with what he'd done. "Her... Her birthday was last week. I just missed my wife so bad…"

Jack's heart fell and he felt bile rise in his throat as he began to put all the pieces together. The shattered window, ripped hair, the other stain on her nighty he that he couldn't make out in the dim light. The fucker raped and murdered his daughter.

Before he was able to control himself, he saw his fist flying into the man's jaw with all his strength. He collapsed in a heap on the floor, blood streaming from his mouth. Jack reached into his pocket and removed the tape recorder that he'd started before the interaction, clicking the stop button on it. He slid it back into his pocket and for the second time that day; called the police department, telling them of his findings.

--

In the days following the police concluded their investigation into the missing girl, ruling that the corpse Jack had found, was in fact hers. The semen found on her dress matched the father's and she had in fact been raped and killed the week prior, on her fifth birthday. He was sentenced to life in prison on charges of infanticide, murder, child endangerment, pedophilia, among several others.

The guards at the maximum-security prison didn't go easy on him either, and ensured that everyone in his cell block had known exactly why he was there. They did not go easy on him. After repeatedly raping him, they strung him up to the highest railing and hanged him for all to see. Crudely carved into his torso was the word "DIDDLER." He'd lasted no more than 48 hours before he was pronounced dead. No one shed a tear for him, and no one showed up at his funeral.

Jack, on the other hand, had begun to deal with nightmares. The terrors of the investigation haunted him, and most nights, he'd see her body, the crawling maggots, and the stains that covered her entire body. He cursed at himself for his own feebleness, his inability to halt the situation. Despite being called in after the crime had already happened and the girl had already been dead; he still blamed himself, and eventually found himself turning to the bottle for comfort. It offered him dreamless sleep where he wouldn't have to face his demons, he could simply stumble from one town to the next, assisting with investigations. Though no matter how many people he saved, or crimes he prevented, he couldn't forget the girl.

She helped him on several occasions to solve cases where he'd hit a wall, following him around from case to case like a paranormal partner. Even though he'd always appreciated the help, seeing her always jarred up the memories of his failure, the failure by which he'd defined his career. The failure that turned him to drinking, night after night, so he'd fall asleep in a drunken stupor and awake on the other side with a hangover.

She never stayed longer than it took to get her cryptic message across, leaving him with the questions that would help him solve his case. She'd never deliver good news, and he'd come to recognize her as an omen of sorts. A prophecy of bad things to come, of hurdles to face and obstacles to avoid. Thus, as she stood in front of him once more, dirty and haggard, he knew what this would bring. His skin broke out in goose bumps that festered all the way up his arms and down his back. Jack Lewis was scared.

Jack looked at her, grateful that he was no longer paralyzed by her presence. He tried to lighten the pitch of his voice, but it came out shaky, "hey, it's you, are you -"

She cut him off with an intense stare that cut through him and caused him to lose his train of thought. Her voice was soft however, and had a somber tone, "There's a malicious presence here Jack. Head home, leave, forget Magrath, forget the life you had here all those years ago. Go home and forget about this case, forget everything about it and never return. There's nothing that you find here that won't cause you pain, that won't threaten to break your already paper-thin mental state. Jack, the road you are travelling will bring you nothing but misery."

Jack smiled half-heartedly, not sure he understood the implications of her cryptic message, he puffed his cigarette thoughtfully, "I don't suppose you're going to tell me exactly what I'm up against this time, huh?"

She shook her as she met Jack's gaze, a sad look splaying across her dirt stained face. The gentle light of the afternoon refracted off the single tear that trickled down her cheek as she slowly began to dissipate; becoming one with the cold air that surrounded Jack in that cold back alleyway behind the precinct. The goose bumps remained as he stood there, the smoke in his hand slowly burning away as he stood there, staring off into the distance as if trying to look into the future. After some time, he turned, hearing the sound of approaching footsteps coming from the front of the building.

~ 5 ~

While Jack was buried in Noah Brackman's file, Dom was sitting at his desk staring at the monitor in front of him; unable to form the coherent thoughts required to finish the report he'd been working on.

To say Dominic was worried about Jack was paramount to saying that Noah Brackman had died of an unfortunate accident. It was technically true, though it barely scratched the surface of the complexity of Dom's emotions. He was concerned. Yes. Concerned for not only Jack's mental health but for his friend's overall state.

Jack had said that Emma had left him. Had said she left him high and dry, taking all her worldly possessions with her in the process; moving out within the timeline of a single day. This worried Dom. Worried him deeply, for Jack hadn't mentioned taking on any work, hadn't mentioned leaving his apartment for anything else since she'd left. Hell, he could have, but Dom suspected different.

Although Dom never really knew why Jack and Emma left all those years ago, he was certain that it had been highly correlated to the damage left to the town in the months following. Regardless, he wouldn't try to pry open any old wounds as of now. He couldn't. He knew Jack and Emma had their reasons for leaving, and though Jack had never sent letters or anything of the sort over the past decade, Dom suspected that he had thought about him at least a couple times over the years Hell, they were best friends since birth basically. They had playdate while they were still in diapers, their parents had been somewhat close. Then again, Jack's parents were close with every family in Magrath.

He shook his head, trying to shake away the thoughts of his friend and focus on the report he'd been slowly typing up for the majority of the day. It was to be his initial inspection of the crime scene the day prior. Yet, he was unable to think clearly and recall the events in perfect order. He just couldn't think straight with all the information swarming in his mind about Jack.

Surely he had to be self-destructive, right? Why else would he return to the town he'd left behind so many years ago, knowing he'd find little else but pain and guilt. Dom had seen him holding back tears at breakfast and had seen the way his crestfallen gaze had befallen him when he'd heard his and Shannon's conversation that morning.

He rubbed his face with his rough hands, feeling the start of stubble forming on the edge of his chin. He closed his eyes and rubbed them with his thumb and forefinger. He figured the best way to ease his ever-growing concern would be to just speak to Jack, though, he found himself growing anxious at the mere premise. He hadn't had a heart-to-heart with Jack in years, and he was uncertain if Jack's receptiveness would be what it once was. Simply put, he was afraid.

He slid out from his desk and walked around the precinct, nodding to other officers and detective Hanson. He often thought about how undermanned the Magrath PD was for cases like these. At any given time, there were at least two officers on duty and one deputy. The Sheriff was on duty during daytime hours and at night he was on call, though it was rare for there to ever be trouble in Magrath after dark.

Magrath had been a relatively quiet town during his time as an officer, though, he'd only really been an officer for a few months. He'd been a deputy officer much longer. He chuckled at the memory of the massive reorganization that had taken place shortly after his graduation from the small training camp that the police department held every couple years. It was six months of grueling physical training on a standardized level. He'd aced the written test and the physical, having lost at least ten pounds of fat and gained at least fifteen of muscle in that time. Finished top of his class.

It wasn't long after however, that shit hit the fan and the whole organization had been brought down for corruption, the whole powers shifted as the Sheriff, two deputy's and one of the detectives were brought into federal custody. The department had been bigger in those times, as there was more money floating around in it. Now, after reorganizing the entire force, there was little talent and strong ideals. Dom, having only been on the force for a couple of months, was moved up a rung within the force. However, more senior officers were moved up higher, and Hanson was one of those. He'd been an incompetent officer, and he was an ever less competent detective. Dom was not his biggest fan.

He'd just nodded to Hanson when he caught sight of Jack stepping out of the filing room. We could sure use someone with your deductive thinking around here Jack. He watched Jack disappear down the hallway and around the corner. He saw the grim look on Jack's face and reckoned that he'd seen Noah's file, had been disturbed by it and was going outside to smoke to help relieve the inevitable stress that was building up with him. He was just about to follow Jack through the front doors when he heard a voice from behind him.

Darla spoke, "Hey Deputy Thompson, is everything alright with Ja- I mean Lewis?"

Dom nodded slowly, thinking up his answer, deliberately picking his words, "I think so Darla, he's just been going over the Brackman case."

Her face paled considerably, "Oh god. Yeah, that poor boy. I hope Jack doesn't take it too hard. Though, I would have thought he'd seen worse in the big city."

Dom understood where she was coming from, though, "I think it's always hard when there are kids involved. You can't quite scrub that thought from your mind, nor can you get the visual out of your head."

She nodded knowingly, her grey eyes meeting Dom's, "well, I guess you better go and check on him then deputy."

Dom nodded once more, and met her eyes, offering a weak smile, "That's the plan."

He turned towards the front door and noticed that Jack wasn't out front anymore. Confused, Dom walked to the door and opened it, eliciting a spasm to course across his body as the cold air swept across the back of his neck. He stepped out and turned in a 360, looking for Jack, seeing if he'd wandered off anywhere. When he found he was unable to see him from where he stood, he decided to take a gander around the building, perhaps Jack had stepped off to the side to get a break from the wind.

Dom rounded the corner and saw Jack standing there, staring intently at a pocket of space with an almost unsettling intensity. His cigarette sat smoldering between his fingers, setting a thin stream of smoke trailing into the sky above.

He was about to speak up and call out to him, when Jack spoke to the space before him, "I don't suppose you're going to tell me exactly what I'm up against this time, huh?"

Dom frowned, wondering if Jack was speaking to him or to something else. Curious, he stood there watching Jack for a time, saw him indifferently stand still for moments before looking around and meeting his gaze.

Dom's voice came out with more concern than he'd been intending, "did you find anything Jack?"

Jack took another puff of his smoke, and exhaled it as he spoke, "Not yet, but there are a few things I'll need to dig a little deeper into. That first death… that was something." he paused, "Uh, is everything okay Dom?"

He flicked his eyes to just beyond Jack and then back to him, "Yeah Jack, let's just get inside. I just want this case to be done and wrapped up as soon as possible. Freaks me out knowing there's a killer on the loose."

They walked back through the lobby and Darla gave Dom a cursory glance. An expression crossed her face as if to say 'well?' He just shrugged and continued following Jack back into the filing room. He felt apprehensive after seeing Jack talking to the air, and now he'd grown more concerned than ever. Afraid of what could be going on inside his mind.

It wasn't long before they found themselves within the filing room once more, the shine of the incandescent bulb above casting a dull yellow over the entire space. Jack walked up to the desk and removed his jacket once more, hanging it on the back of the office chair. Dom watched as he turned to look at him, curiosity in his eyes.

Dom shifted on his feet, "is everything okay Jack?"

Jack gave a weak smile, "yeah, everything is fine, why?"

Dom thought for a moment, choosing his words carefully, afraid that Jack may have an undesired reaction to his next sentence if it didn't come across as intended. "I'm just worried about you man; you've had a lot going on and I'm wondering if you just needed someone to talk to about this stuff. I know it can be heavy, hell, I was one of the officers that reported to the scene when Noah was found. It was difficult, man. Real difficult."

Jack held his gaze and for a moment Dom was afraid that he'd blown it, that Jack would blow up at him for what he said, for implying that he needed help. Though, to his surprise, Jack looked down sadly, "Yeah, it's been a rough one. That's for sure. I've just been looking at this damn file and it makes no sense. Why would someone do this to a kid? What bastard in their right mind would hurt a child like that? What sick fucker would do that to anyone?"

Dom struggled to come up with an answer, but Jack continued, "I know you don't have the answer, that's why I'm here, I have to find this sick son of a bitch and make sure he's locked up for good. You know though Dom, this isn't the first case I've worked where a kid died and there was nothing I could do about it. Here," Jack pulled out one of the stacks of boxes from the shelf and brushed off the layer of dust that had formed on top of it. "Sit, I'm going to tell you a story."

So, Dom sat down on that stack of filing boxes as Jack told him the story of his first case with a police department. He told him the story of how he'd found the body of a little girl in some backwater town, of the stains that contrasted with her bright pink nightie and the truth she'd led him to seek. As he revealed the atrocious acts committed by her own father Dom wept for the child, but he also wept for Jack. For in hearing of the case, he'd begun to understand Jack's pain, his demeanor and his afflictions.

He'd been living with this pain inside of him for years, bottling it deep down where he thought it couldn't reach him. Where the images of the girl's destroyed body would no longer be able to come forth and haunt him in his dreams. Jack just wanted to be free of his memories of his guilt.

That's why he'd come to Magrath, in an attempt to mend the bridges that had long since burned down and crumbled away to little more than piles of soot and ash. He'd come back to Magrath in an act of penance for his perceived sins, to cure himself of the demons that dwelled just beyond the periphery, threatening to take over at any moment and render him useless. Finally, Dom understood that the best way to help his friend was to be there when he needed a shoulder to cry on or somebody to lean on.

And Dom was just fine with that. He'd be the person Jack needed him to be.

~ 6 ~

Jack found himself alone inside the filing room once more. Dom had left minutes prior, needing to use the facilities to 'get his mind straight'. Jack could only hope he hadn't made a mistake by telling him that story. He'd hoped Dom didn't think he was crazy or was seeing things. A dense feeling of unease came over him, working its way over his body as he sat in the office chair with his head tilted back and his eyes closed.

The unease faded the longer he sat there. Eventually he raised his head and looked back to the pile of files splayed out over the table. He narrowed his eyes and picked up the second case file; the manilla folder felt heavier than the last, though he thought that may just be a figment of his imagination.

He opened it up and read the name written across the top, "Veronica Stillwell," Still-well, yeah, right. She most definitely is not well.

He produced the first report from inside and sat back in the chair as his eyes devoured the page, transporting him to a world far beyond that of the page. Jack began to picture the scene described within, from the small apartment to the dirty dishes that were toppled over on the table. In his mind he was experiencing walking onto the crime scene firsthand, witnessing everything through the eyes of Veronica's friend, Serena Williams.

In his mind's eye, he found himself in Serena's body. He imagined himself looking down as he checked his phone, anxious to see if Veronica had texted him back yet. It had been a few days and he was growing increasingly concerned. She'd been acting strange before, yet he was unsure of whether it was boy trouble or if she'd gotten pregnant or something else of the life changing variety. Regardless of the circumstances, he figured he would ease his concerns by simply walking over there and checking on her. He got into his Toyota Camry and drove several blocks to her house, rushing, though not frantically. He still assumed she was alive, just playing some dumb game.

After the few minutes behind the wheel, he pulled up outside the apartment, and parked his car. As he stepped out of it, he noticed someone entering the building ahead. He ran the distance, using his long runner's legs to carry him over. He smiled as the man held the door open for him and looked at him appreciatively. He winked in return and continued through the familiar hallways, headed towards Veronica's flat.

When he was standing directly outside, the smell hit him. At first he frowned, assuming it was nothing other than someone's garbage, though, when he knocked on the door, he became aware of just how much more pungent the aroma was.

He knocked again, growing increasingly panicked as he did so, now fearing what sort of setting he was going to walk into, fearing for the life of his friend that was just on the other side. Finally, he tried the knob, his heart jumping momentarily as it turned, allowing him to swing the door open.

The celebration was short lived, his victory was cut short by a wall of death. The smell caused him to gag, though he covered his nose and walked through the threshold into the apartment, calling out Veronica's name as he entered.

When he got into the living room, he realized that he need not call out for her anymore. Though he did let loose a scream that was produced from the depth of his abdomen, coursing through his lungs and out through his mouth. An ear shattering, blood curdling scream that summoned a few of the other tenants. When they walked into the room to see what the fuss was about, they understood why.

Veronica was splayed out over the couch; her head was pulled back over one of the armrests and her eyes showed nothing but pure white. Her jaw hung open in a permanent scream. Her neck was red and there were already holes beginning to form where the maggots were beginning to eat through her skin. She was covered in bruises from head to toe, as if someone had slowly and deliberately inflicted enough slow and arduous pain to fill the entire subcutaneous layer with blood, causing her to turn purple. He doubled over and threw up as he took in the sight, from somewhere on his left, someone called the police.

--

Jack closed his eyes as he imagined the scene splayed out before him, the pained look on Veronica's face as she lay dead. It's as if the poor girl died of fear. He looked at the pictures he had spread over the desk in front of him, all various shots of the horrific scene. He sighed heavily as he read her background.

According to her parents, she'd been recently accepted to an Ivy League university on a full academic scholarship. She was ecstatic, she'd posted the news to her multiple social media accounts and was telling anyone who'd listen in person. Her future had been laid out for her, it was waiting for her, all she had to do was reach out and grab it. Her dreams had come true, they'd never seen her that happy before. They had begun to break down as they told the officer how upset they were that it had been Serena Williams to find her. They'd known her since the girls were children, and couldn't bear the thought of the trauma that would cause the young woman.

Jack reached for his notebook to jot something else down but stopped when he caught another glimpse of one of the pictures. In the top left corner of one of this particular photograph, he saw a strange thick substance on the floor. Though he hadn't read anything about it in any of the reports. Confused, he made a mental note of it as he resumed writing his thoughts down on the notebook.

'Speak with Serena Williams, ask old school mates about her? Also, jealousy?' He sighed once more and leaned back in the chair, uncertain of how to proceed. Should he speak to this Serena Williams first - he had her contact information and place of employment right there, he assumed she'd be working on a Monday as it was. She worked at "Debbies Diner", and Jack knew he should probably eat something soon. He nodded to no one as he resigned himself to the idea. He'd go to the diner and if she was there, he'd ask her some questions.

He stood and once again grabbed his jacket, slipping it on as he walked through the precinct hallway and out through the lobby. He strode past Darla and waved. He knew that something wasn't right, and he was intent on getting some answers to the questions tumbling around in his head.

As he walked up to his car's door, he heard a remnant of the little girl's voice echoing through his mind, "The road you are travelling will lead to nothing but misery."

Jack climbed into his car and slid it into gear, I know kid. It always does.

Chapter 3: Asking Questions

~ 1 ~

Jack pulled up outside of "Debbies Diner" less than ten minutes later. He had many fond memories of getting lunch here with his mother on weekends while his father recovered from yet another bender. It had become their place. He reckoned he should probably check in some time soon.

The diner's name was a clever play on the names of the founders. It was founded by two friends named Debby who'd met where anyone in Magrath met. School. They'd grown up together, though they'd only bonded when they discovered their shared passion for cooking in their home economics course. Over the years they'd grown close and began cooking together, creating new dishes and enjoying themselves all the while. Eventually, they set out to create a fifties themed diner in the small town of Magrath. It was a huge success, garnishing attendees from all over who wanted to experience what they'd only seen in movies and tv shows.

As Jack walked up the sidewalk towards the diner's entrance, a feeling of nostalgia began to wash over him and he found himself hoping that they still served the same special that he'd always eaten when he was a child; the Debby Double burger. Or simply the Double D.

He stepped through the front door and rising tide of nostalgia crashed over him. His eyes scanned the red cushioned booths and the polished white bar. The swinging doors on either end of the bar led to the kitchen where Jack didn't doubt they were still using the same vintage ranges they had used when he was a child. His eyes lit up as he saw the chef place an order on the small window ledge that stood between the kitchen and dining area. He smiled so wide he was afraid his face would split.

He'd momentarily forgotten all his troubles as he stood, soaking in the memories of a youth he'd long since repressed. He walked over to one of the booths and sat down. When he picked up the menu and saw that the special had remained the same, he couldn't help but beam. For a moment, it was as if he was in heaven.

The illusion was sent crashing to the ground as his waitress came up to take his order. She introduced herself as Serena and he immediately recalled why he had come to the Diner in the first place.

Serena, who didn't seem to notice his smile slipping off his face, took his order, in a false, but still somewhat decent southern drawl, "And what're you havin' sugar?"

Jack tried a fake smile, but gave up almost instantly, "Uh, hi, I'll get the Double D please."

"Anythin' to drink with that?"

"No thank you. Actually, a water please."

She smiled, "So a Double D and a water? Sure thang. Comin' right up sugar."

She winked at him and swung her hips over to the counter to pass on his order. She returned momentarily with his water.

"Say, you're not from around these parts, are you mister?"

Jack sighed, and looked at her with a straight face, "No, though I was once. A long time ago, went to the school and everything. Hell, I used to eat here as a kid with my mother. Anyway, I was wondering if I could ask you a couple questions, er, I guess I should introduce myself. I'm Jack Lewis, I'm a private investigator. I'm currently working with the…"

He trailed off as he saw her face go pale. She slunk into the booth with him and put her head in her hands, any energy she had been displaying prior dissipating into the air around them. Fuck, I'm a piece of shit.

Jack raised a hand hesitantly, "Is everything alright? I'm sorry I just-"

She cut him off, her playful southern drawl fading, "No, don't. It's fine. I just wasn't expecting to talk about her so soon. The officers came and went, and I guess I assumed that it was over, that I could finally grieve. Though, I guess, seeing as your here, that means they haven't found the bastard yet." She let out a quiet chuckle, "Fire away Mr. Investigator."

He met her large, tear filled brown eyes and was faced with the soul crushing sadness that embodied them. Jack found himself unable to speak as he saw himself reflected in them. He loosed a shaky sigh, and stared into her eyes, trying to figure out the best way to go about asking the first question that was bouncing around inside his brain. The words were there, though he needed to find a way in which to pose it without causing her to deepen into her sadness.

A cold feeling spread through his abdomen as he realized he needed an answer regardless, and it wasn't his job to worry about how she felt, "So, Serena... could you tell me how Veronica was acting in the days prior to you... finding her?"

She cast her eyes downward and he couldn't figure out if she was going to cry or not, but eventually she spoke, "We hadn't seen each other for weeks, to be honest. Life got kind of hectic. She was busy preparing for school and I was busy trying to find a new place. I guess we were just too busy. We stayed in contact though. We'd text daily, though even those had been growing less frequent over the weeks prior as well. I guess that's why it took me so long to figure out something was wrong."

She sighed deeply and dabbed at the corners of her eyes with one of the napkins that had been placed on the table. Good job idiot, you've gotten rusty with your people skills. Why would you start with the hardest hitting question first?

Serena continued, "Maybe if I'd been a better friend I could hav-"

Jack interrupted, tired of feeling sorry for himself, "hey. Serena, you did nothing wrong. Hell, you saw her body, do you think you honestly could have stopped someone that could do something like that? You did what any good friend would do, thank you for finding her. And thank you for answering my question, I won't ask any more for now. I should probably let you return to work; I think I smell a fresh Double D."

She looked at him and burst out laughing. She tried to contain it within her hand, though she found she couldn't and ended up doubling over in the booth as she tried to contain herself. Jack was unsure of whether she was laughing from stress or laughing from the oddity of his statement, though he figured it was a culmination of the two.

Several moments later, she was finally able to stop, though by that point the tears of sadness that had streaked her pale face were replaced with tears of joy. She smiled warmly at him and slipped back into character, leaving him with a wink and a "comin' right up mister."

She returned shortly after, carrying a plate with a steaming mound of fries and a large juicy burger on it, she leaned over to Jack and whispered, "Thank you for making me laugh, it's been a while since I've done that. Though, you also made me cry, so I guess it balances out."

She stood and winked, before uttering a "let me know if you need anythang." She blew him a kiss as she walked away.

Jack sat there a moment, confused by the emotional switches he'd experienced within the past few minutes. He assumed that she had been affected worse than she'd let on. Poor girl. Probably needs a therapist. He leaned forward over his plate and picked up his burger, marveling at the way the juices dribbled off it and hit the plate with a steady drip. He dug in and his stomach grumbled in appreciation, nostalgia once again overcoming him. He was surprised how in ten years; the flavor of the burger hadn't changed in the slightest.

~ 2 ~

Sometime later, Jack found himself at the second stop of the afternoon. The house of Noah Brackman. He stood on the sidewalk, looking up the thin concrete path up towards the front door, which was a simple metal screen in front of a metal core door. He smiled at the thought of how quick the journey from the diner to this destination had been. Though, he reckoned that was the biggest benefit of a small town. You could travel every single road within the city limits over the course of a few hours. The only drawback was that there wasn't much to see in these small backwater towns.

Jack began the short walk from the curb to the front door, looking closely at the grass and the path he walked on. They looked well maintained, but the grass looked like it hadn't been cut in a while. About two weeks? He shook his head and resumed his journey towards the door. He walked confidently up the stairs, though inside, he felt anything but. He thought about potential motivators, though his mind kept coming down to Jealousy. Noah had been a prodigy with a promising future, and Veronica had been accepted into an Ivy League university. For people in a small town, those achievements were nothing short of miraculous; surely that would spur someone on to feel jealous. After all, they were leaving the town. Certainly, if the other factors didn't make them jealous, then that fact alone would have done it.

Jack thought about how ugly of an emotion jealousy was. It was a useless emotion, and very rarely did it ever result in anything good, in fact, Jack would have bet any amount of money that at least half of assault charges were the result of jealousy. But although it was an ugly emotion, it very rarely resulted in a murder, sure, at times there would be someone so overcome with jealousy and rage that they kill their spouse's mistress, but even then, that was far and few between. As Jack reached the door, he concluded, jealousy may have been a factor, but he didn't think it was the only reason.

Jack knocked on the front door of the Brackman house. It was a series of three solid knocks, loud and announcing, but not poundingly tumultuous to cause any intimidation. When there was no answer after a period of several minutes, Jack knocked again, louder this time. The result was almost immediately apparent as he heard shuffling coming from the other side. A moment later, the door swung open slowly, revealing a defeated looking Edward Brackman with downcast eyes full of shame and sadness.

Jack studied him for a moment, trying to discern anything from him, ultimately, he figured he was merely a husk. A shell of the man he would have been before his son was killed. His bathrobe hung open, revealing plaid pajama pants and a thin white t-shirt, though both were terribly stained with various liquids and food particulates. His face was unshaven and his eyes sunken in. This man hasn't slept in days. Jack's heart ached for him, but he steeled himself, this would not be easy.

Edward didn't look up from the ground as he said in a small voice, "h-hi, can I help you?"

Jack gave a sympathetic smile, "Hi, my name's Jack Lewis, I'm a private investigator employed by the Magrath Police Department. Would you mind if I asked you some questions? About Noah? I won't take a lot of your time; I just need to know a few things."

He looked up, a slight amount of surprise displayed behind his weak smile, “sure, come on in, I have some tea on, though I suppose I could make coffee if you’d like.”

Jack was caught off guard by the invitation, “Oh no, I couldn’t, you don’t-”

He held up a hand, silencing Jack immediately, “I don’t have to, but I want to. It’s been very quiet around here; I could use the company. If the fee for conversation is answering a few questions, I suppose that’s a price I’m willing to pay.”

A puzzled look crossed Jack’s face as he wondered where Edward’s wife was. Though as Edward met his eyes, he saw nothing but unfathomable pools of sorrow and despair. Jack wanted to ask what happened, but he couldn’t find his words. He’d never witnessed such profound sadness in the eyes of another. He was baffled by the sheer depth of the sadness Edward possessed so as he turned and trundled deeper into the house, Jack could do nothing but follow.

The house reflected his appearance, Jack cringed away from several concerning globs of mold that had begun to grow on discarded food containers that lined the hallway. Pizza boxes were piled up on top of dishes that were piled up on top of any and every surface. Jack saw a fork embedded into the cushion of the couch and several more green globs of mold littered the floor. He felt queasy and was afraid that he would lose his lunch.

A squealing sound resonated from somewhere in the house and Jack assumed it was the tea kettle. This was confirmed as Mr. Brackman excused himself and walked off towards the kitchen. Jack didn’t follow as he was afraid of what may lay inside.

Instead, Jack took note of his surroundings, taking in the two ‘his & hers’ chairs that sat side by side, both were green lay-z-boy recliners facing the small tube tv that sat in the corner of the room. Though one of the chairs still looked in good condition, the other was covered in stains and flattened tissues that looked like they had been sat on and one point or another. The table next to that chair was also covered in used tissues that had begun to spill over onto the floor below.

Between the chairs and the television was a small coffee table that looked to be worn with age and neglect. It was covered with pizza boxes that, like the tissues, had started to topple over onto the floor. Jack studied the floor and noticed that spilling out from Mr. Brackman's chair was a congealed glob of green fuzz that looked like it may reach out and snatch Jack's hand. He cringed away from it and continued to study the room.

The air was thick with a musty smell that Jack assumed was a result of the mold that had encrusted a vast majority of the surfaces in the room. The scent held in his nose and lungs as he breathed, and he noticed undertones of decay and rot with every breath. The aroma was so pungent that Jack bet even a hog would turn away from it. Jack realized that after the loss of his son, the light of his world had dwindled and diminished, resulting in him becoming little more than a husk of what he once was. He was drained of any remnant energy he could have had, and Jack felt sorry for him.

A grave realization overcame Jack then, an epiphany that shook him to the core. He realized that over the many years he'd been working as a PI, he could have been met with the same fate, he'd come near when he'd received the call that brought him to Magrath. He realized just how easy it was to drop off and stop caring once the focal point of your life flitted away. The dishes pile up and the time spent cleaning lessens, you sit down and know you're rotting away in a mound of filth, yet you can't muster up the motivation to clean. You simply don't care; you don't feel worth it. Jack shivered at the thought and cleaned off a spot on the couch for himself to sit. This was a messed-up world, and he only hoped that eventually Noah's father would be able to come out into it one day and realize that there's sometimes a light at the end of the tunnel. The sun can't be obscured behind the clouds every day and eventually there will be good days again. He hoped more than anything that he would have one of those days soon.

For now, though, he sat back and set his mind to working the case. They say laughter is the best medicine, though for Jack, getting lost in his work was better. Distraction is the best medicine. For what is laughter but a distraction? He sat back and waited anxiously for Edward to come back into the room.

Mr. Brackman came back into the room moments later carrying two mugs; one surprisingly clean, and one visibly dirty one. Jack watched with growing horror as Edward approached him, fearing that he would be handed the dirty one. He shuffled over and handed Jack the clean one, much to Jack's relief. Jack took a hesitant sip of the earl grey tea and watched as Edward Brackman sat down in his chair. Jack slipped his hand into his Jacket pocket and brought out the small recording device he carried with him for when he would ask people long strings of questions.

Jack never liked taking notes as people talked, he found the experience useless and unnecessary. Years prior when he'd needed to visit a therapist after a rather gruesome case; they'd refused to stop jotting down everything he said and really listen to him. Sometimes they'd get him to slow down or stop so they could catch up. Jack found that experience extremely patronizing. Thus, he began carrying a recording device with him almost everywhere, it had a 64gb SD card, so he could record for hours on end without needing to stop - and once he'd returned to his laptop, he was able to transcribe everything. It not only allowed him to have proof of what they'd said but allowed him to go over their wording and verbiage to see if they were lying or hiding something.

He placed it on top of one of the pizza boxes that had toppled off the coffee table after pressing the 'record' button, "Mr. Brackman -"

Mr. Brackman held up a finger, halting Jack, "Please call me Ed. You need a family to consider yourself a mister." Tears began to well up in his eyes.

Jack continued, "Okay, Ed, just so you're aware I'm going to be recording this conversation, just so I can reference it later if needed. Is that okay."

Ed looked from Jack down to the little device, "Yeah, I don't see why not, I don't have anything to hide."

Jack smiled kindly and continued, "So Ed, what can you tell me about your son Noah?"

Ed's voice came out shaky, "What, like school things? Friends?"

"Anything you want to talk about is just fine."

Ed nodded, "Alright, I can do that." He cleared his throat, "Ah, Noah is - was a good kid. Hell, I remember when he was born, he came out with these striking grey eyes - you know how all babies have the same eyes - but there was such intelligence behind them. I guess all parents say this, but there wasn't a doubt in my mind that he was destined for great things. And he was. Growing up, he was always surrounded by friends and playing sports. God, he loves - sorry - loved sports. I think he just loved being outdoors most of all. When I got him his first football, it wasn't long before he'd learned just about everything I could teach him, I knew he'd go places. He gave his mom and I such hope for the future. That's something they don't tell you about raising a child Mr. Lewis. You could be the poorest sombitch out there, but as soon as you see your child enjoying what they do, I'll be damned if it doesn't make you feel like a million bucks." he paused as if getting lost in the memory of Noah.

"Any who, my wife and I - well - we weren't the best parents. We just couldn't provide the type of life we felt he deserved. You know? He always wanted to grab life by the balls, but we, we couldn't afford to let him do that. He wanted a higher education, but we simply couldn't afford the hundreds of thousands of dollars to give him that. So, you could imagine how happy we were when we found out he could play football that well. It opened the door for him. He was only sixteen and he was playing better than everyone else in the division. He was set to make it big Mr. Lewis, we just needed to find a way to get him that scholarship. For a while there, the future there was looking up, though, now… well. Shit's gone sideways."

The tears began to stream down his face, dribbling off his stubbled chin, and dripping onto the moldy floor below. Jack realized just how broke this man was, he was one who centered his life around his son, and when his son died, so did his world. Yet, despite all he had done for his son, he still blamed himself for not giving him a better life. Jack's heart reached out for him.

Jack placed a tender hand on his shoulder, and he tried to emulate Dominic, "Look, Ed, you did everything you could for Noah. By the sounds of it, you were an amazing father. You did the most with what you had available and you gave him a promising, happy, and full life. You were a great dad."

Ed broke down further, "Tha-thank you, it's so nice to hea-hear that."

Jack brought his tea up to his lips and took a slow sip as he watched Ed slowly compose himself. He wanted to ask about his wife, where she'd disappeared to, but that wasn't the priority. The priority was finding out who killed his son. Jack lowered his mug as

Ed composed himself and wiped the last of the tears away from his face and fetched one of the used tissues from the table next to him, crinkling it open before blowing his nose with it.

Jack waited until Ed finished to ask the next question, "Noah was killed a couple weeks ago, as you are undoubtedly aware." Ed nodded, "Sorry Ed, would you be able to say yes for the recording."

His eyes widened as he looked down to the recorder, as if he'd forgotten entirely about it, "Sorry, yes, Noah was murdered a couple weeks ago."

Jack nodded, then continued, "As far as you know, would anyone want to do something like this to Noah? Was he acting strange at all in the days leading up to his death?"

Ed's eyes widened, "No, no, goodness, he was loved by everyone. He hung out with people from all walks of life and treated everyone equally. Everyone went to games to watch him play and a win for him was like a win for the town. He was the hope of Magrath.

Though I'm not certain if he was acting strange, I didn't see much of him in the days leading up to his murder, though when I talked to him, I always felt like he was looking up into the distance, as if he was waiting for something to happen."

Jack nodded, "what about close friends? Anyone he'd hang out with quite frequently? People he's been friends with since childhood?"

Ed smiled, "Yeah of course, they were a group of five, they'd always hang out either here or at one of their houses after school. They were super tight knit. There were three other boys and a girl, though, she was more of a tomboy herself."

Jack nodded, hope growing inside of him, "Would you be able to tell me about them? What are their names, what they're like?"

Ed nodded, "Yeah, sure thing. There was a small rat like boy named Robert Fielding, though he's anything but a rat, he's just short and has mousey features. You know the type I'm sure. Anyway, he was always good with computer things, I would always overhear him talking about new websites and such with Noah. Noah didn't have much time for computer games or anything like that, but it mattered to Robert, so it mattered to Noah.

"Then there was this boy named Larkin - uh - Larkin Grace, he's on the other end of the size scale. I'd put him at six foot four? Yeah, that sounds about right. He's a gentle boy. The football coach wanted him on the team as well, but Larkin refused, he doesn't like physical confrontation and all that. He enjoys reading though if you walked into him on the street, you wouldn't guess that. He's probably a good two hundred and forty pounds. Big boy, but a great friend.

"Next there's Zachariah - er - Hastings, though I'm sure everyone just calls him Zach. I don't know a lot about that one, if I recall correctly, he only became part of their group a few years ago. Though, he seems like a nice boy. He played on the football team with Noah, though he was average build, so he was a pretty average player.

"Lastly is Trix, I was seeing a lot more of her lately, though I'm not sure why. She'd come over to hang out with Noah and they'd talk for hours. Oh, that's not her real name by the way, I think it's Patricia though everyone calls her Trix. With an 'x' like the cereal. She's a sweet girl, though her parents aren't around much, I think due to work, though I can't be certain. I think that about covers it."

Jack thought for a second before reaching into his pocket and pulling out his notepad and pen, "Do you know where any of them live? I should probably ask them some questions too."

Ed nodded and reached out, taking the notepad from Jack then writing down the addresses of the bunch, before passing it back, "Just one thing, please take it easy on them. I've had it bad, but I think they had it worse. He was the center of their group of friends. I don't even know how they're doing."

Jack nodded as he looked down at the page of the notebook and the several addresses written down on the sheet. I'll have to get Dom involved on this one. It's a lot harder to speak to kids all willy-nilly. He smiled at Ed who was once again reaching into the pile of tissues that sat next to his chair. Jack wanted to get out of the house now that he had his answer. But there was still something that wasn't sitting right with him.

He spoke cautiously, "So Ed, where's your wife? You never mentioned why she left."

Ed looked up from the tissue he'd been wiping his eyes with; his expression had paled significantly, "Well, we were both put on leave from work to deal with our grief, though in hindsight, I don't think that was the best idea." he gestured to his living room and I understood immediately, "I had been trying to hold it together for her, you know, so she could let the emotions out. Anyway, she asked me to run to the store one day to get a few things, milk, cereal, eggs, you know, benign things like that. When I came home, she was gone. That's all there is, everything that was solely hers was gone too, all her clothes, toothbrush, razor, everything. I figured she'd been planning it for a while to have completed it that quick. I guess Noah's death was just the tipping point for her. It still caught me off guard though. I mean, it's like she hired professional movers and had them show up immediately after I left. There was no trace of her anywhere in the house."

Jack felt his heart thud deep in his chest, growing tight as it struggled to keep some semblance of normalcy in its rhythm. It couldn't though, and it beat one solid beat followed by a flurry of others Ed's wife had vanished. Gone. As if she'd planned it, as if whoever helped had taken everything that was solely hers. Jack stumbled a bit, then excused himself, apologizing for the abrupt departure as he gathered up his belongings. With rushed "goodbye" he turned and practically ran back to his car, sliding behind the wheel.

He drove a little over a block away and pulled over, unable to stop himself from hyperventilating. Everything was gone. No trace of her. As he sat there in his car, the thought overcame him and thundered within his skull, crashing about between the bone. Just like Emma.

Jack needed a smoke. Bad.

He sat in his '06 Sunfire chain smoking Marlboro's repeatedly. He'd finished one pack and was long into the next when he finally pulled away from the curb. He needed to find out more answers, needed to know if there was somehow a connection between the two. He couldn't focus, so he lit up another cigarette and began puffing on it with fervor. This trip sure was stirring up a lot of old memories.

Jack knew that memories often attracted the demons he'd long since thought he'd killed under torrents of alcohol he tried to drown them with. But, alcohol doesn't kill demons, as Jack was quickly realizing. No, it quiets them, it subdues them and keeps them at bay long enough for you to think that everything is fine. It pushes them deep, deep enough that no light can reach them, that no amount of poking and prodding can bring them to the surface. But they're still there. They're biding their time, waiting for a time when you no longer think you need the drink and then they come. They scorch your mind in a hellfire until you relapse and pound back more alcohol than before. You know it'll kill you, but you don't care, you'd rather that then face them. When another drink keeps them at bay, then you may find peace at the bottom of another bottle. They'll leave you alone as you stumble mindlessly from one bar to the next in a blurry haze.

Jack had more than his share of alcohol over the years, it wasn't a matter that could be debated. But then again, he had more than his share of demons too.

~ 3 ~

Jack found himself back in the filing room no less than thirty minutes later, typing away on his computer as he transcribed his conversation with Edward Brackman. It had been an enlightening conversation though, as he performed the mundane task of typing, he found his mind wandering.

His mind drifted to Emma, and he thought of when they began dating those years prior in Magrath. Though he'd been a small, tired and naïve boy; she was already a woman. She'd matured long before the rest of the group; and slowly took over a nurturing role among them. Though he couldn't be sure, Jack assumed it had something to do with the love he'd often lacked so much in those years. Thus, he found himself complete enamored by her, wrapped up in the way her hips swayed as she walked, the curve of her breasts as they poked through her shirt. It didn't take long for the throes of his lust to blossom into something more, something akin to the love he'd longed for, needed, and desired.

--

They were in junior high when they first met. Her family had moved to Magrath from a nearby city and they were still settling in. There was always such a buzz of conversation whenever a class found out they were getting a new student. It didn't happen frequently, and when you've grown up in class next to the same people year after year the promise of new blood can be exhilarating.

She'd walked in behind the teacher, hiding her face shyly and had been made to sit next to their little group of friends. She integrated flawlessly and soon she was teasing Dom just as much as Jack and Shannon did. Though Jack had never seen her as anything more than a friend in Junior high. However, after he and Shannon split abruptly due to rather malignant circumstances, he started spending more time with her. It wasn't long before he found himself looking forward to seeing her smile both in school and outside of it.

One evening, as they sat in his backyard gazing up at the stars, he rolled over and kissed her. He breathed in her scent, ran his fingers through her hair and pulled her into him. With that simple action, they plunged headfirst into a relationship that changed Jack's life.

They were together for nearly twelve years before Jack got home on the day she'd left. His mind flitted through those memories, dwelling on the nights they stayed up watching movies, slipping under the covers next to each other; bodies intertwined as they wrapped themselves in each other's loving arms. His mind drifted to the late-night conversations spent talking of the future, and the nights spent dreaming of things to come. Lastly his mind drifted to the night they fled Magrath and the orange sky they left far behind as they sped down the road towards the city. They had nothing but each other, though, they didn't need much else. They were in love and that's all they needed.

The years had flown by with reckless abandon; his nights spent working cases gave birth to a space between them. The rift expanded exponentially until finally Jack found himself alone. His mind came back to the present as he finished typing up the last of the conversation between himself and Edward Brackman, he found himself wondering why she'd really left.

He frowned, and closed his laptop, rationalizing that it was pure coincidence that Ed's wife left by the same means as Emma. He shook his head as he stood, now is not the time to linger on coincidence, we need to focus on what we know. He stretched his weary muscles as he began to walk towards the door of the filing room, he needed to find Dom.

Walking out into the bullpen, he eyed the clear skies through the skylight, noting that there was no trace of any clouds above. The blazing ball of heat had moved to its last quarter in the sky and had begun to cast a friendly orange light over Magrath. Jack smiled, for he knew that no matter the outcome of this case, and regardless of what the little girl had told him, he knew that the sun would carry on shining and the world would go on turning. There was no future where those environmental constants ceased. Once more, he found the motivation to go forward and headed towards Dominic's desk, he needed to ask a favor.

To Jack, it felt like days had passed since he'd last spoken to him, though it was only a few hours prior. It seemed even longer since they'd shared coffee in his house that morning, and Jack recalled the sincerity in Dom's voice on both occasions. The way he seemingly exuded sympathy to every single one of Jack's struggles. He couldn't fathom any measure of repayment for such kindness. Yet, he figured Dom wouldn't expect it, such was not his way.

Dom looked up from his computer and smiled at Jack as he approached, "Hey Jack, any headway?"

Jack answered truthfully, "To be honest, a little, not a whole lot though. I may have a lead with some kids from Fairmont secondary though. They're in school this time of year, yeah?"

Dom's eyes studied Jack's face, as if looking for something, "Yeah, that's right. Jack, how did you come across this lead?'

Jack shuffled uncomfortably, "I went to Edward Brackman's house. He seemed grateful for the company."

Dom's smile picked up a bit, "Yeah we heard that, though I wasn't expecting you to be making any house calls today." He noticed the strange look on Jack's face, "Word travels fast in small towns as you might have forgotten. Magrath is full of oldies Jack, any 'outsider' goes poking around, they think they're robbing the place."

Jack chuckled, “Well, I guess that makes sense. In any case, I’m going to need to question a few of the students. Although I don’t need a warrant because I’m not acting in any official capacity of the law, I figured the administrative offices could easily call you guys and have you remove me from the premises.”

Dom beamed, “So then, you need my help is what you’re saying?”

Jack exhaled heartedly through his nose, “Yeah, I guess. I figured that if one of you beautiful boys in blue were to say, call them, maybe give them a heads up to my arrival. It would go a lot smoother. Perhaps, you could even tag along. That way they’ll figure I’m acting in an official capacity.”

Dom’s smile grew even wider and Jack feared his face would break, “So we’d work the case together then? I’m game. I can make the call in a little bit, just need to finish up this report on Elizabeth Wildbrooke. What were their names?”

“From what Ed told me, three boys, one girl. The boys go by Larkin, Robert and Zach. Girl goes by a nickname, though Ed didn’t know what her actual name was. It’s Trix, like the cereal.”

Dom looked at him startled, “Trix? Are you sure Jack?”

Jack raised an eyebrow, “Yeah, why? Do you know her?”

Dom’s voice came out a little guarded, “That’s my niece, we can go see her if you’d like. May I ask what sort of questions you plan to ask.”

Jack thought for a second, “I was hoping for them to come by organically, though they’d be the typical sorts of questions of non-suspects. I was planning on asking if Noah had been acting strange, if there were any notable events before his death, how well she knew him, etc.”

Dom visibly relaxed, “Okay, yeah that sounds good. We can go see her as soon as I’m off if you’d like.”

Jack nodded, “That sounds good, but after that, I have a bit more running around I’d like to do, there’s some other leads I would like to touch up on.”

Dom nodded, then pulled up his wrist to check his watch, "That's fine. It's three o'clock right now, meet me here at four and we'll leave."

Jack nodded, "Alright, I'm back to the filing room now, there's something that's been bothering me. If it leads to anything, then I'll let you know."

Dom smiled, "Sounds good, glad to see you're progressing through this case Jack."

Jack smiled back then turned and walked the short distance back through the bullpen, towards his dark and dusty workspace once more. He paused as he walked back under the skylight and took the time to look out into the blue sky above. He wondered where Emma was and what she was doing. He hoped she was okay, wherever she was. Though, as he resumed his walk towards the filing room, he had a nagging suspicion that she wasn't alright and that she was somehow tangled in the mess of a case happening in Magrath.

~ 4 ~

The cardboard filing box for the year was pristine, the corners came to sharp points and the edges were crisp and unblemished. Jack reckoned that this box would look this good for as long as the precinct stood. And he realized, not for the first time that this was just a small town, they were unequipped for serial killers and serial kidnappers; he couldn't fault them for requiring his help.

Jack reached up and plucked the box from the shelf, stirring up a voluminous cloud of dust that cascaded over his arms and chest. He chuckled as he shook his head and walked over to the desk, noting how much lighter the box felt in relation to the murder box. He set it down on the desk and could help but be surprised as he read the words printed on the front of it fully through for the first time.

When he'd first seen the box, he'd only focused on the "MISSING PERSONS" portion. As it was the only box on the shelf, he'd assumed it was the most recent. Though, as he read the date printed underneath, there was a date that he'd not expected to see. "1990 - ____." Jack couldn't help but laugh as he realized it was a sort of "all cases box" as the blank end date suggested they'd add it once the box was full.

He slowly plucked the lid off the box, uncertain of how few files would be inside, even less certain as to the quality of the reports inside. A smirk edged onto his face as he took note of the miniscule number of files inside of the box. Eyeballing it, he supposed there were around ten. He frowned, there should be a lot more from before I left. He shook his head as if trying to rid himself of the thought and turned back to the present matters. He plucked out the full stack of Manila files and flicked through them, returning the ones that didn't happen in 2015 and setting down the relevant files on the surface of the desk.

He looked down to the neat pile of eight files that were related to the case, at least he hoped they were related to the case by some stretch, if only by coincidence. He didn't like how thin the files were, and supposed they only had the reports from the citizens and the initial report from the investigation officer.

He hesitantly reached down and picked up the top file, dating back to a mere three weeks prior. The name printed on the Manilla folder was "Brathford, Gina." He tried to place the name in his mind, yet came up empty, she must have moved to Magrath or had been from a younger generation than him. He'd known most of the family names of the area, yet he couldn't place Brathford. He flipped open the folder and took out the citizen's report.

The report was submitted by her common law partner who'd she'd met in university several states over. Though they'd only recently graduated, they wanted to settle down somewhere quiet where they could build a family. They'd settled on the small town of Magrath to lay roots for their family tree and began actively trying to conceive.

Her degree was in education, and she'd found a job at Magrath's Primary school teaching young children in the second grade. According to her partner, Susan Locksar, she'd taken to it better than either of them could have dreamed. The kids loved her, and she'd hoped to teach them acceptance and kindness from a young age. Susan explained that they'd been afraid of moving to Magrath due to the stigma about same-sex couples in small towns, yet they were happy to find that everyone was too excited about having new blood in the county lines to care about such trivial things.

Jack scanned the document with fervor scrutinizing every detail described by Detective Hanson on the second page. According to Susan, Gina had disappeared within the span of ten minutes. This caught Hanson off guard, as when they'd arrived, the house only appeared, "half furnished." He elaborated further that it was as if someone had broken in, kidnapped Gina, taken only her things, then had disappeared without a trace. In the brief amount of time it had taken Susan to go to the store to cash in their lottery ticket that had won a free play, she'd vanished.

Jack's breath caught in his throat. There, on the page lay the one piece of evidence he'd been looking for, yet not wanting to find. He was hoping it was mere coincidence that Ed's wife and Emma had disappeared in the same manner; up and vanishing as if by some whim, taking everything that could have been theirs along with them. Sure, Jack and Ed assumed they'd been abandoned, but they were broken people. People who at one point or another had been in a rather emotionally volatile state. Jack wondered how many people had gone missing that people had just assumed to be kidnapped. Not liking where his thoughts were headed, he re-read the last part of the report several times.

"The disappearance is interesting as all of Gina's personal effects have disappeared with her. It is only with my due diligence that I am typing this out, as my investigation has led to little conclusive evidence. If I were to write this report on the evidence alone, I would speculate that Gina had simply left Susan. Perhaps this was a result of a lover's quarrel, some scandalous affair or even a slight tinge of imposter's syndrome that led her to flee Magrath. Though my heart truly aches for Susan, I do not believe that this is a missing person's case in the slightest."

Jack's mind couldn't comprehend the implications of the line. He'd had his suspicions, though his mind kept tracing around and around the thought that he had been wrong. Emma had not left him. Couldn't have. Though he had more than enough evidence to prove this thought, he wanted more. No, he needed more.

With a trembling hand, he placed Gina Brathford's file back onto the old oak desk and hesitantly picked up the second file. This one was marked with a name that appeared semi familiar to him. And though he didn't recognize the first name, he did recognize the family name of "Peterson, Shawn." They'd been a moderately prominent family in his youth, he recalled his mother owning the flower shop next to their home furnishings store. He smiled weakly at the vague familiarity as his thoughts lingered on his mother. His smile faltered. He returned to the folder and opened it, turning to the report first.

He barely noticed the familiar scent that seemed to come off the manila folder, it was the subtle smell of cologne intermingled with a desiring perfume. Before his mind and olfactory system could communicate the data they were pouring over, Jack read the reporting officer's name, Dominic Thompson. So, Dominic wrote this report. Jack frowned, though for reasons that remained unbeknownst to him at that moment. He thought of proper procedure, it wasn't abnormal for officers to fill out forms on investigations, Hanson had only done the last one because he was most likely bored of sitting around in the empty station. Jack's face tightened, though he didn't know why, it was just a report.

Then, as if on cue, his mind finally placed the smells that lingered on the folder and Jack could picture Dom wrapped in Shannon's arms before going to work that day. He thought of their freshly applied scents intermingling as they embraced. Dom would have spent the day smelling like both cologne and perfume, just like this folder. Jack finally understood the frown and the tightness of his face, he was jealous.

He scoffed inwardly; I have nothing to be jealous of Dom for. I have a successful business in a large city, with rich clients. He rationalized that he was enough in all aspects of life, except for love. You're all alone. Dominic has Shannon, you have… no one. Jack's mind lingered, rationalizing further that Emma still could have left him, that she was out there enjoying another man's company. The evidence of it being something else lay in his hand, all he had to do was look. So, look he did.

Shawn was no older than Noah had been, sixteen years of age and went to the same secondary school as the others. Jack devoured the file with fervor, skimming over details he deemed unimportant, though he went back to read them not long after.

According to the file, his parents had returned home after a night out; they'd recently sold their store to an anonymous source and had more money than they knew what to do with. They'd gone out to one of the fancier restaurants in town; a local two star that served steaks in addition to burgers. Though, when they'd returned home, they were surprised to find their son no longer on the premises.

At first they assumed that he'd simply slipped out to go and party with some friends which wasn't an abnormal scenario for a Saturday night. Though, as time progressed and the night floated by, they fo9und themselves worrying that he was out a bit too late. They tried texting him, though he didn't reply, so they tried calling him, though he didn't answer. They began to get worried, though they figured maybe he had crashed at whichever friend's house he'd snuck out to. So, they went to bed.

When they woke up the next morning, they poked their heads into his room to see if he'd returned throughout the night. They were shocked to see that there was nothing left inside. As Jack flipped the page, his heart clenched. This was the information he was after.

Dominic was studious of the kid's bedroom, he had to give him that much. "Shawn was last seen by his parents the day prior, before they left for their weekly date night. They'd figured he'd slipped out during the night, though in the morning when they went to see if he'd returned, they noticed that there was nothing within. They immediately called it in, to which I arrived, and began to inspect the room. I am appalled at what I must report, though, there was absolutely nothing in his room, not even the faintest speck of dust could be found. It's as if all traces of anything other than the room itself had completely disappeared."

Jack's mouth hung agape as the heart palpitations began and his breath shortened. His brow broke out with sweat, as did his hands and armpits. It began to trickle down his back and pool on the hem of shirt. He wiped at his brow as his mouth started to feel cottony. The culmination of guilt and fear overtook him as he began to introspect.

Jack ran his mind over the facts; Emma had disappeared in almost the exact same way as the others had. For the child it would seem as though the only items taken were those in his room. But Jack reasoned that as a child, there isn't much we own save for the items we identify in the space we call our own. For the adults, however, it appeared as though it was anything that they'd personally paid for and legally owned. Their personal effects were seemingly wiped out of existence alongside them. As the realization overcame Jack that Emma hadn't left him, he began to curse himself more. If he'd tried harder, he might have found her, might have been able to save her from whatever fate had befallen her.

As Jack placed the manilla folder back on the desk, he realized that Emma would have been ground zero; for her disappearance had happened a week before the first disappearance in Magrath. But why? We were hundreds of miles away. Jack shook his head before he could fall down the rabbit hole of madness, though he found himself unable to pull out.

Fortunately, as he sat there spiraling, a final thread of hope appeared in the doorway, saving him from the thoughts that lay ransacking his mind. Dominic Thompson stood in the doorway with a bemused smile on his face, though Jack realized he wasn't looking directly at him, but at the clock on the wall above.

"You know Jack, you're not super punctual. Here I was thinking I'd be seeing you at four, right at my desk. But no, imagine my surprise when you're still in this room, fifteen minutes after four, pouring through files like a junkie." His eyes finally met Jack's, and concern creeped up his face, "hey, is everything okay?"

Jack looked up at him and smiled weakly, "yeah man, I - uh - just figured something out. We can discuss it on the way, I'm ready to go."

Dom smiled, "alright, let's go."

Jack stood up, "good, I think if I spent another minute here, I would go insane."

Dom winked at him, "you already look insane."

He turned and walked out the door, leaving Jack to follow behind. Jack turned back as they reached the threshold and looked back to the desk that still had the eight files for the eight-missing people on it and felt a shiver course through his body. He'd figure out the rest tomorrow, but first, he needed to interrogate a sixteen-year-old girl over the death of her friend. He sighed and resumed following Dom through the hallway towards the front of the precinct. Darla was no longer at reception, now there was a burly man sitting behind the desk. He eyed Jack curiously as he passed, though he remained silent.

Jack stepped out of the oppressive building and into the warm rays of sunshine that washed over Magrath. The molten gold poured over him, warming him in contrast to the cold that still clung to the air. Jack stood and faced it as the sun began its last descent into the horizon, crossing into the final eighth of its trek across the evening sky. Jack stood still in the radiant warmth, closing his eyes as if to soak up all of it that he could.

Jack looked up towards the dilapidated ruins that stood over Magrath and noticed how little to no light reached the burnt pillars and overgrown plants. He figured it might be due to the blackness of the coal, but the chill that simply looking at it sent down his spine suggested otherwise.

He exhaled and turned towards Dom, who'd already made his way to the Sunfire that sat idly by in the parking lot. Jack smiled and walked over, his mind compartmentalizing the information he'd learned from the files and his interview with Edward Brackman.

~ 5 ~

Dom and Jack sat in the comfort of Jack's car. It's worn fabric seats were significantly comfier than the old leather office chair he'd spent most of his day sitting in. The Sunfire sputtered to life as Jack turned the key in the ignition, whining hesitantly before finally turning over. Jack sighed, then reached over to the glovebox, smiling as he popped it open, revealing the several boxes of Marlboros within. He plucked one out and took the thin plastic wrap off it. Dom shot him a curious glance with his eyebrow raised, as if to say, 'is that normal?' Jack chuckled self-consciously as he removed a smoke from the package and stuck it between his lips, cracked the window open and lit the cigarette.

He inhaled deeply as he shifted the car into first, then exhaled as he eased off the clutch and accelerated down the road. The nicotine eased the stress from his body as his mind began to wander once more, pouring over the details and mystery surrounding Emma's disappearance. He took in another breath and held it, perhaps hoping that his body would absorb more of the addictive substances and not allow his lungs more time to take in the tar. When he released; the smoke was sucked out the window, being carried out like a forgotten memory, illuminated by the golden sun above.

Jack had been driving for all of three minutes when he finally realized something. In his haste and strange mental state, he'd completely forgotten that he had no idea where he was going. He felt his face flush with embarrassment as he pulled the car over and parked alongside the curb.

Avoiding the curious glance Dom sent his way, he muttered, “Uh, I don’t know where we’re going.”

Dom stifled a laugh, but managed to get out from between tight lips, “I was wondering when you’d say that. Thankfully, we’ve been going the right way all along. The house is just a few more turns. Take your next left, then hang a right and we’ll be there.”

Jack slugged him gently on the arm, then his smile fell, “so about those files …”

Dom slowly turned his head towards Jack, and Jack was surprised to see how wide his eyes were. “Jack. I really don’t want to talk about them. I lose enough sleep at night without thinking about them.” He let loose a deep and breathy sigh, “but I guess I owe you that much.” he looked to the clock then back to Jack, “alright. Stay here for another fifteen minutes, we can talk, then we’ll go to Trix’s”

Jack took a moment to work his thoughts into a coherent string of words as opposed to the malformed jumble of information he’d been tumbling around in his head for the past several hours. He struggled to form a sentence as the words kept getting stuck in his throat or he realized the sentence wouldn’t sound wholly accurate.

Jack hesitated, then finally began to spout the words that he’d been holding in all day, “Something fucked is happening in Magrath Dom. I think you know that. I think that’s why you don’t want to talk about it. It’s fucking terrifying. The implications of what’s going on lead to nothing but wall after inconceivable wall. There’s no rhyme or reason for the murders, or the disappearances. No one person can vanish that quickly or to that level of detail. Which brings me to another point. I think Emma is wrapped up in this somehow. I think she was the very first victim.”

Dom’s eyes widened, and Jack found that by some miracle, he’d put it out in the open. Dom smiled hesitantly, as he visibly worked his head around what Jack had said, formulating his own response to the statements made.

Finally, through a clenched Jaw, he got out, “Jack. I’m terrified. Terrified beyond belief. Magrath is - er - was a quiet town. I was happy to just take on the regular small call or the occasional missing goat, but this, this is way beyond my paygrade. As far as the missing people, I don't even know what to think about all of that. I went to Shawn Peterson's house as I'm sure you're aware by now. There was nothing. Not a speck of dust nor a single hair on the ground. No one should be able to do that. Let alone a sixteen-year-old kid. Would you be able to elaborate on the whole Emma thing? How is she tied up in this?"

Jack thought for a moment, "Dom; when I went to see Edward Brackman, he mentioned that he had been so lonely. Initially I figured it was solely caused by the death of his son. However, he said his wife had left him too. Though it was understandable, when I'd heard the reason he thought so. I couldn't help but leave there as quickly as possible."

Dom cut him off, "What happened to her?"

Jack shot him a look and continued, "he said he'd left to get some supplies for the house and when he'd come back, she was gone. All her stuff had disappeared along with her and he found himself in their home all alone by himself. She vanished Dom, in no longer than the time it took him to get some basic groceries."

Dom paled, "Just like the others… Just like you said Emma had disappeared. Holy shit Jack, I'm so sorry."

Jack continued, "Dom, things in Magrath are going sideways. People are dying - kids are dying. There's a handful of people missing and even more that I'm sure people just assumed had walked off. I don't know what's going on, but I plan on finding out. I initially thought I could solve this on my own, but it's far worse than I thought. I'll need help Dom; I need you by my side on this. Please."

Dom splayed a pitiful smile over his otherwise grim face. The lingering rays of sunlight showed the early signs of wrinkles beginning to form along the creases of his face. Dom swallowed, but didn't say anything at first, his mind was running a million miles a minute, just as it always had when they were just kids. For a moment, Jack saw the scared boy he'd met in kindergarten. The one who'd been too afraid to leave his parents side, the one who'd only calmed down when Jack promised to be friends with him. The one who'd run out of the forest they'd played in after hearing the hoot of an owl. Dom steeled himself and all traces of fear vanished off his face, he'd finally gotten his emotions back under control.

He met Jack's eyes, "Jack. I'm terrified, you know this, though, I don't sleep most nights, you can ask Shannon that. I typically lay awake long after the sun has gone down. That is, unless I drink myself to sleep, but then, I'll wake up the next morning with one hell of a hangover. What I'm getting at is that yes, I'll help you. Not because we stand a better chance together. No, I'll help you because I believe in you. I don't know why you came back to Magrath, or who tipped you off to the events transpiring here, but I'm glad you did. You may be the only person who can solve this case and return peace to Magrath. So yes, Jack. I'm in."

Jack smiled, though it didn't last long before it was replaced by a look of puzzlement, "Dom, what do you mean you don't know who tipped me off to the events in Magrath? I was called the other night by someone that works with you, though…" His face went pale, "I never did get their name."

Dom raised an eyebrow in confusion, "Jack, you emailed us a few days ago, saying you were going to come down to visit and not to disturb any new crime scenes that may pop up within the next few days so you can personally inspect them."

Jack was baffled, "Dom, that makes no sense whatsoever, a few days ago, I was drunk out of my mind, I wouldn't have been thinking of Magrath in that state."

They both reached into their pockets to take out their phones, each anxious to prove the other wrong and themselves right. Yet as Jack combed through his call logs and Dom combed through his emails, they both came to the same realization.

Jack spoke first, "The call… it isn't here. But I was called, I remember it perfectly."

Dom concluded, "The email isn't here either, this makes absolutely no sense."

Both stared in borderline insanity at their respective devices, unsure of whether or not they should be screaming or crying for the sudden revelation that there was someone else - something else - at work here. They began to not only question themselves, but to also question each other, swearing up and down in their minds that they knew what they had seen or heard. They both assumed the other was wrong, but a small voice at the back of their heads was telling them otherwise. Panic coursed through Jack's body as he stared into the blank call history on his phone; seeing no incoming calls over the past few weeks. Jack's body began to shake.

Dom slowly glanced over, "Something fucked up is going on here, I think - I hope - that working this case may provide the answer."

With that, Jack slid that car back into first and trundled the car down the road once more, taking the first left and then the first right, maneuvering down the road that would lead them to Trix's house. Jack hoped that asking her questions may lead them towards an answer, or even another clue as to what has been happening in this town. He hoped answers would be gleaned and minds would be mended. Though as they pulled off the faded asphalt onto a less travelled road, Jack's mind wandered to the words he'd heard earlier that day and he found himself wishing he'd been more prepared for the horrors he'd found in Magrath.

"The road you are travelling will lead to nothing but misery"

~ 6 ~

They arrived at Trix's house shortly after five o'clock. Though, as Jack realized, it was more of an acreage that bordered the town of Magrath. The sun cast its rays across the lands as it descended into the far horizon. Illuminating the world in its final pink brilliance before plunging the world into darkness. Jack slid out from behind the wheel and stretched.

He breathed in the sweet autumn air and reveled in the moment. He enjoyed the fresh air and thought about how much easier life would be if he'd pursued a life as a search and rescue officer. Though, he supposed any job would have its downsides. He took in another deep breath and extended his hands towards the sky, stretching his back in the process.

He focused on loosening his tight muscles, trying to remain as limber as possible. He stretched his arms, his legs and his shoulders. He enjoyed the crisp autumn air as it flowed through his lungs. He looked over to Dom, who stood silently facing the lone acreage as if deep in thought. Jack was anxious to focus on anything other than the subject discussed on the ride over and based on Dom's demeanor; he was too. He figured that acknowledging it now, would be paramount to accepting insanity. So instead of acknowledging it, he simply watched Dom, waiting for a signal.

As if sensing Jack's eyes on him, Dom turned to him, "Before we go inside, there are some things I want to share with you. Basically, Trixie is almost always home alone. It's nothing to be concerned about, however, my brother Liam teaches law at the university a couple cities over, he's only home on weekends. His wife works as a doctor at the hospital here in town, every couple weeks she works night shifts. I stop by to visit at least three times a week to spend time with her and make sure she's all caught up on her homework. She's a very good kid. But, a word of warning; she gets very emotional whenever Noah gets mentioned. She's had a very tough time with his passing." He paused, "they were kind of dating when he was killed. It absolutely destroyed her. Although she's been getting better, I don't think the mention of his name will be doing her any favors."

Jack nodded slowly as he looked knowingly into Dom's eyes, "alright, noted. I guess this is going to be difficult for all of us, then."

Dom nodded then turned back towards the house and began walking. He pressed the small white button on the wall and listened to the resounding chime as it echoed throughout the house. A smile played upon Dom's unsure lips as they heard shuffling coming from the other side of the door. The shuffling subsided momentarily before the door swung open, revealing a young girl with the tell-tale Thompson's brown hair and Hazel eyes, she was no younger than sixteen.

Jack smiled as she threw herself at Dom, "Uncle Dom!" She exclaimed with a wide grin.

All of Dom's unease and stress vanished in that moment and Jack saw the wide smile spanning his face as tightly hugged Trix and twirled around with her in his arms. Jack realized that this wasn't the Dom he'd grown up with, nor was this the Dom he'd grown to know over the past twenty-four hours. No, this was the man who had all that Jack desired. A large heart that was filled to the brim with love; an overflowing vestibule of compassion that would undoubtedly earn his place in the heart of anyone he interacted with. Jack was overcome with a brief, though intense feeling of jealousy that coursed through his body and twisted his heart inside his chest. The feeling was almost instantaneously replaced by an equal measure of guilt that cascaded over his body and caused his face to feel immensely hot. He kept his eyes on Dom as his mind lingered dangerously into the realms of ‘what ifs'. What if I’d never left, if things had been different? Could this have been my life?

Jack shook his head slightly, as if to shake out the thoughts that were coagulating inside. He watched in awe as Dom kissed Trix on the head and they exchanged greetings. Jack thought for a moment that Dom looked like he was her father.

Dom turned to Jack, “Jack, this is Trix. Trix, this is a very old friend of mine, we grew up here in Magrath together.” he paused, “his name is Jack… Lewis.”

Her eyes widened as Jack outstretched his hand, “hi Trix, it’s nice to meet you. I suppose you know why I’m here.”

Trix smiled mischievously, “well, if Uncle Dom’s numerous stories about your young escapades are true, then you’d be quite the detective. My guess, which is most likely right; is that you’re here to fix all the messed-up crap in this town. The stuff that everyone would just turn a blind eye to and forget altogether.”

Jack looked to Dom, whose face had turned a light shade of scarlet, “oh Dom, I like this one.”

They walked through the doorway onto the finely tiled entryway that served as a sort of shoe area from the looks of it. Jack couldn’t help but compare the clean-living space to the dirty home of Edward Brackman. Jack hadn’t known what to expect, though he realized that Dom’s brother and his wife had done quite well for themselves. They’d gotten prestigious jobs and earned quite a lucrative combined income. Though from the outside, the house matched the others for the most part, the heavy interior renovations were evidence enough that they’d invested a large sum of money into the home.

The lacquered hardwood stretched out across the floor. The entryway was slightly lower than the other floors, and Jack had little doubt that it was there to keep away any water brought in from outside to protect the expensive hardwood inside.

A masterpiece of masonry and bricklaying stood against the wall in the form of a fireplace, inlaid with a cast iron stand on which one could place the logs. Running above the hearth, fixed into the rockwork was a rustic wooden plank of long aged dark oak. Strewn across its surface were several portraits and family photos depicting perfect moments held still, as though giving Jack a window into the family life he hadn't experienced in almost twenty years.

Jack cast his eyes around the room, taking in every detail from the fine Italian leather couches that stood parallel to one another - to the ornate coffee table fashioned from a large piece of lacquered driftwood, smoothed and machined to allow the glass top to be placed on top of it; giving it a look as though it was jutting out of water.. It was evident to him in abundance that Dom's brother and wife had ample resources to draw on. He smiled to himself, happy to see the fruit of their efforts.

As Jack stood there, smiling dumbly at the interior design - momentarily forgetting the purpose of their visit - Dom wasted little time. He slid his feet out of his shoes and followed Trix around the small railing that stood as a barrier between the entryway and the rest of the open concept house. Jack shook his head from its stupor and refocused on the task at hand, chiding himself for getting distracted by the interior design of the space. He slid his own feet out of his own shoes and followed Dom and Trix; anxious to get this informal interrogation over with.

They sat on the two couches regarding each other over the large coffee table, Trix on one side, Jack and Dom on the other. She smiled as Dom launched into a story about a prank that she'd pulled on him a few years prior. Jack didn't pay much attention. His mind was running through the various questions he wanted to ask; molding them from the incoherent jumble of words into a much more palatable format. Jack hoped she'd be able to reconcile the events as described by Ed, though, if not, he hoped she'd be able to at least point him in a new direction.

Jack joined in as the other two reached the crux of their retelling of the prank and burst into laughter. His mind already set on what came next. The questions. Let her finish laughing before you stir up the painful memories you apathetic asshole.

He watched as the laughter slowly died down; feeling guilty he was about to take away the smile that had spread across Trix's face.

The corners of her eyes scrunched up slightly and light tears had begun to form. She dabbed at them with the back of her hand and flashed the whites of her teeth as she met Jack's eyes. I guess it's time.

With the air of laughter still clinging in the space surrounding them, Jack began, "so Trix, by now I'm sure you know why I'm here, though you may not know exactly the subject matter. I know you were close with Noah, and those are where my questions lay. Is it alright if I ask you a few questions? Perhaps glean some information regarding the weeks leading up to his untimely death?" He paused as her smile began to fade, she nodded. He continued, "Good. What can you tell me about Noah?"

Though tears had begun to well up, her eyes displayed an immense amount of emotion, brightening up as she recalled their time together. "We met in kindergarten, like the rest of our group. I guess maybe I had a crush on him then. Though, when we'd met, we simply became the best of friends, y'know? He really solidified our group. See, he was everything. A leader, an athlete, smart, he had charisma; you name it, he had it. He would lead us on our adventures; take us into the woods, teach us about the local flora and bring us on all his favorite trails. Hell. one time the group was walking at a brisk pace when we heard a loud bird call. Without skipping a beat, he looks back at me, places a small piece of trail mix in his hand and stuck it up as though offering it to the sky. You could imagine my surprise when all of a sudden, this small grey bird - a whiskey jack - he'd called it, had flown down right into his hand and took the damn thing right out. It was amazing.

"Anyway, our lives were all full with him in it simply because he was in it. It's no wonder I fell for him. Though, I didn't even realize I was falling for him until high school started up. See, I'd been such a tomboy that I didn't even consider the fact that I could have those feelings, let alone for Noah - who until that point, I'd seen simply as a friend." She loosed a chuckle, "I guess those things kind of sneak up on you huh? Well, one day, we were sitting on the lawn in his backyard gazing at the clouds as they moved across the sky when he interrupts the silence with a simple 'you know Trix? I think I love you.' That was that. He wasn't looking for reaffirmation or even my response, that was just the kind of boy he was. He said what he meant regardless of the outcome. I was ecstatic. Though, in hindsight, I looked too much into the future. I was thinking about becoming his wife and -"

She cut off and looked at Dom, who'd grown slightly red hearing about his niece's love life, "Anyway, about a month ago, we were in his room and he told me that his parents were thinking of moving. My heart dropped. He said they were doing it for him, and that because he was a prodigy in football they wanted him to get accepted into a big fancy university with a full ride, 'blah, blah, blah' they hadn't even consulted him though. I instantly told him I'd follow him anywhere, I'd convince my mom and dad, and I'd move with him. Deep down though, I was heartbroken, there's no better way to put it. It felt like my whole world was uprooted. And I guess that now it really doesn't matter. Because h-he's - he's dead."

Her voice gave way and she sat there with her head in her hands sobbing loudly into them. It had begun to fester slowly in her story, her voice had shaken at regular intervals that ebbed up and down in her throat as it contracted from grief. Jack was surprised she'd made it to the end, and as he sat there dumbly staring forward, trying to think about what she'd told him, he felt Dom stand and walk over to her. Jack didn't push further, he couldn't, he knew that she'd only backed up what Ed had said about Noah being an upstanding child, being great in all facets of life. As Jack sat there, he knew he couldn't push it, he wouldn't, not with Dom there, not now. For now, he would sit and watch quietly as Dom comforted his niece, pulling her face into his chest. He closed his eyes as he rested his head on top of hers, as though protecting her from any external threat.

So, Jack waited. He simply stared into the wall beyond and mulled over her words, attempting to latch onto anything that could have proven useful to the investigation. He still would need to speak to the boys, though he hoped he could get some pointers from her answers to his questions. If he could find out more information, then he would be able to push the boys in the right direction. It would take some time, though, for now he'd remain silent. He'd just sit there and observe. At least until she was done crying.

As the spaces between her outcries began to space more and more, Jack realized that she was still just a child. A child whose world revolved around the life she'd built in her classes, with her classmates, and the conversations they'd have in between them. She had yet to experience the sleepless nights lying awake as she contemplated the weight her actions had on her entire life, she still needed to spend time questioning the feebleness of her actions in the grand scheme of things. She'd yet to experience the existential crises that would shape a lot of her adult life. Thus, her world was narrow and confined to a space even smaller than the town she resided in. As Jack looked at her, his heart softened. He couldn't push her, couldn't force her further, for he knew that forcing her to relive the trauma could cause damage and would do her more harm than good. She still needed to heal, so he'd leave it up to her. Not only out of respect for Dom, but out of respect for Trix, respect for the person she was and the person she would become. He watched as Dom rubbed her back slowly and kissed the top of her head as her sobs finally ceased, feeling like an asshole.

When her eyes were wiped clear of the final tears and her sobs had all but disappeared, Dom pulled away and smiled sympathetically at her. She leaned in and whispered something into Dom's ear. Dom's eyes softened and he looked over to Jack with a sad yet stern expression.

"Hey Jack, no more questions about him tonight, okay? She's just not quite ready, the wound is still very fresh for her. She needs time to heal."

Jack nodded and looked down to his hands. His fingers were interlocked tightly, though he was unsure of whether it was due to anger, stress or guilt. Perhaps, it was all three; Trix was a child, yes, but in relativity, he wasn't much older. Sure, he had twelve years on her, though he still had self-doubts, still contemplated his position in the world and whether there was a meaning to anything he did. He turned to the bottle to take his mind off things, perhaps this was something else he'd need to add to the list. He closed his eyes and tried to focus, simply being in Magrath was stirring up a lot of old memories for him, painful memories he'd rather not dwell on. So, he pushed them down, deeper and deeper, figuring he'd deal with them later, once he'd figured life out. What a joke.

With his mind lingering in the past, he drew on happier memories from the times he and Dom were children and how they raised hell in Magrath. He told Trix stories of how he and Dom grew up together causing trouble for both their teachers and parents alike. He told her how though they'd caught out late, playing 'ding-dong-ditch' well past curfew, they could walk up to any house and be greeted with open arms and smiling faces. Dom joined in and mentioned the late-night town-wide games of tag they'd play and the unparalleled hospitality of the residents in

Magrath. That, even though they ran around with flashlights as they chased each other, they could go into any house if they needed a break or wanted to opt out for the night.

Jack conveyed memories of their explorations of the forests and the wooden structures they'd built that likely still stood. As he told her of their adventures in their youth, Trix's eyes lit up with a level of wonder and excitement at the prospect of a safer, more peaceful Magrath. She hung on Jack's every word; drawn into the tales of a Magrath she'd never known. Jack felt sorry for her, for in this changing world the children were the ones to suffer. The string of murders and disappearances had weighed heavily on the town, and yet it was still on the children that it hurt the most. They were missing the prime days of their lives when they should be out being foolish, being reckless and building memories.

So, Jack did what he could, he told her more stories of all of their shenanigans, and by the end, she was smiling. If only she knew that Magrath's sullen decline was due to that fateful night, nearly ten years prior.

Chapter 4: In the Dark of Night

~ 1 ~

Jack trundled the Sunfire along the curb outside of Dom's house, resigning to the idea of staying in the cheap motel down the road that probably hadn't changed its sheets since he'd lived here. He looked to the small digital display and noticed that the time read 8:15pm. They'd been at Trix's for over three hours and he realized that he'd grown rather hungry. The last time he'd eaten was at Debbies Diner over eight hours prior. Jack sighed and figured he could stop and grab something on the way to the motel.

Dom stopped as he was easing out of the passenger seat, "hey, do you need a place to stay, Jack?"

Jack shrugged, "I'm planning on just checking into the motel just up the street, why?"

Dom waved his hand as if wiping the words away, "No sir. There will be none of that, can't have you catching some fiendish motel sickness. That place probably hasn't been cleaned since we were kids, and no friend of mine is staying in that motel."

Jack's eyes widened, "are you sure man, I don't want to impose or anything-"

Dom let out a hearty laugh, "Impose? Never, besides, I'm sure there's enough leftovers for you to be able to have some food as well. Shannon's most likely in bed by now – I swear sometimes I'm married to an old woman with her sleep schedule. She usually wakes up early and goes to bed early too. Anyway, she'll usually leave dinner out if she knows I'm working late. Funny thing is this month has been the only month I've ever had to work late."

Jack let out a light chuckle, "okay man, but only if you're sure."

As he slipped out from behind the wheel, his mind lingered on a thought, one that stirred up repressed memories that he knew he'd eventually have to share with Dom. To do anything else would be tantamount to betrayal. He watched as Dom walked into the house, leaving the door slightly open so Jack could enter shortly after. *Fuck, I need a smoke.*

--

Jack watched the clouds move slowly across the horizon as the cold air bit into his flesh. With cold fingers he fumbled the Marlboro from the depths of the package. He placed the familiar filter into his mouth as he fished his lighter from his pocket to light the end of the cigarette. He inhaled and let the smoke trickle out of his mouth, allowing the wind to carry it off as the nicotine began to work its much-anticipated magic on his mind. He finally allowed himself to exhale as the stress began to fade into the recesses of his mind. He watched the smoke coil through the air and out under the streetlamp, coalescing against the slowly darkening sky, visibly only where the light happened to touch it. Jack slowly took another drag and closed his eyes, trying to focus solely on the feeling of the smoke flowing through his lungs. When he finally opened them, he wasn't surprised to see the familiar face peering out at him from under the streetlamp.

She smiled solemnly, although her eyes remained as intense as they had been hours prior in the back alley behind the precinct. Jack looked sadly at her, once again seeing her as a grim reminder of his failures. Her torn pink dress still lined with dirt, and grime hung limply off her shoulders. Beneath, her bare feet were barely visible in the glow of the streetlamp. Jack's heart felt like it was sinking lower in his chest, for the girl never brought anything other than bad news.

Jack eyed her as she regarded him studiously, he'd never seen her twice in one day, though by now, he knew he'd never worked a case quite like this one.

Breaking the silence, Jack posed the first question, "It's you again, can you at least tell me if I'm on the right track?"

The little girl looked down towards the ground, but for a moment Jack thought she had smiled, "This may be the last time I'll be able to appear before you Jack, this path, this journey that you are on, though it will fill you with grief, suffering, and agony, you will gain some piece of mind. You will find answers. Answers to questions you did not ask, and answers to one you have. You may find yourself lost in the sea of grief, though know that tomorrow will be a different day. Tomorrow you will need to face your demons and overcome the hurdle that has kept you from Magrath. After all these years, Jack, you must face it, your past, your present.

Only when you face it, will you be able to remove the dark cloud that hangs over this town."

Jack stood there, attempting in vain to comprehend the implications of her words. He had the vague notion that it was a warning, if only due to the typical nature of the little girl's visits. As his mind worked to decrypt her message, one question lingered in the back of his head and though he knew she would not provide a direct answer, he knew he still needed to ask it.

He pleaded, "Where does it all lead? Is it a single person or a group of people? What is going on here? Can you at least tell me that? Help me, please."

She cast her sad eyes at him, some of the intensity had faded, replaced only with sorrow, "The road will lead to where it began Jack. You know the place, even if you do not realize, for it is the place where the fires of guilt were kindled and where the gates to the night of tears burst open. You must return to the horrors of your past, for they contain the answer."

As she finished her sentence she closed her eyes; began to slowly fade into the blackness of the surrounding night and when the last of her face began to dissipate, Jack could have sworn he saw a faint tear trickle down her small and delicate cheek. He stood there for several moments after, realizing that for the first time after seeing her he was sweating from the implications of her words. He realized that in order to solve this case and discover the root of the problems in Magrath he'd have to unearth old skeletons he'd long considered buried for good. Though, he subconsciously understood that there was no permanent resting place for the secrets he'd long since pushed deep down inside, only temporary fixes.

He looked out into the overwhelming darkness realizing he'd been standing outside longer than he'd anticipated. His eyes lingered in the direction of the burnt down mansion that overlooked Magrath and he wondered how on earth he'd be able to explain his past to Dom without breaking down, without withdrawing from the world entirely and getting himself stuck in another state of introspection. Jack sighed and turned towards the house, I guess that's an issue for tomorrow.

Jack shrugged out of his jacket as he entered the house; his nostrils heavily appreciating the delectable smell that wafted towards him from the kitchen. His stomach grumbled and he realized just how hungry he was. He hung his coat and strained his ears to hear if anyone was talking in the next room but was relieved when the only sound he'd heard was silverware clinking against itself.

Jack walked into the kitchen moments later, being greeted by the sight of Dom serving food onto two ceramic plates. Jack's stomach growled in anticipation as he eyed the two large chicken breasts next to mounds of mashed potatoes that Dom was spooning onto each plate. His mind went blank as his primal instinct for sustenance kicked in and he found himself unable to take his eyes off it. Without even thinking about it he began walking towards Dom, who had just scooped another spoonful of potatoes out of the steel pot.

Dom's eyes flicked up to Jack and he smiled before handing him one of the plates, "Shan made enough food for both of us. That woman, I swear, she's something special. She knows me well enough to know that I would have invited you here to stay."

Jack met his gaze and saw the sheer amount of affection in Dom's eyes as he spoke of his wife. Jealousy coursed through him momentarily, though it was quickly replaced by another surge of guilt that he struggled to force down; not wanting his emotional swings to register on his face. By some grace, Dom didn't appear to notice, instead, his smile held as he turned and trundled over to the kitchen table then sat down in one of the chairs.

Jack took the seat across from him and began making quick work of the meal. As his stomach began to fill, his mind slowly eased off the thoughts of eating and back onto the case.

Okay, so we have three dead. Eight missing - potentially more. Somehow Emma leaving could be mixed up in all of this, yet I don't understand how. We lived several hundred miles away; would the killer seriously make that long of a trek just to grab her? Why would he grab her? I don't understand this case, I sure hope that the boys are able to shine some light, if any, on this case. There's no telling just how deep this all runs, for all I know, it could very well be tied up in my past.

Jack scolded himself and tried desperately to tear his mind free of the case, not wanting to fall back down that rabbit hole. Instead, he decided to focus on the food in front of him. Although it was a typical meal, the food was absolutely delicious. The crispy thin skin was seasoned to perfection and had contained all the juices within the breast. The meat itself was succulent and tender, not like how it had always come out whenever he'd try to cook it. He smiled as he forked another slice of chicken into his mouth, then turned his attention to the soft potatoes. They appeared to be whipped to perfection, as if they had been infused with the care of a master chef. There were no chunks that had escaped the mashing process and the potatoes themselves were light and fluffy.

Jack smiled once more at the food, and Dom piped up, "You gonna eat it or just sit there smiling at it? Maybe you'd like to take it out on a date first?"

Jack looked up as Dom winked and laughed, "nothing of the sort, I was just thinking of how good it is. I was just thinking of how nice it is that some things never change."

A look of confusion crossed Dom's face, "what do you mean?"

"Shannon's cooking. She was always such a good cook. Remember how she'd always demand to be the one to do the cooking whenever we'd hang out? Hell, her cooking was always so much better than any of the restaurants in town. Does she still make those quesadillas?"

Dom beamed, "Of course she does! Why else do you think I asked her to marry me?"

Jack laughed, "Very true. So, when did you and Shannon get hitched?"

Dom smiled fondly, as though remembering their wedding day, "Well, after you left, we were both pretty messed up. She was in a very emotional state and so was I, so we ended up being each other's shoulder to cry on. We confided in each other and as the months turned into years, we began dating. Shortly after we both turned twenty-two, I finally manned up and proposed. Best decision of my life, I've never regretted it for one second. Shannon's a great woman Jack."

Jack nodded sadly, "Yeah, you're both great people, I'm happy you both had each other. I know it's a little late, but for what it's worth… I'm sorry I left, you deserved better, you both did."

Dom went quiet as his smile faded, his eyes softened and after some time, he finally said, "Jack, I don't accept your apology. Not right now. I know life's been hard for you, I understand that. But until the time comes when you're able to forgive yourself, I won't forgive you. There are things you need to face. I don't know what happened the night you left, and you don't have to tell me, but I think you need to come to terms with the skeletons in your closet."

Jack nodded sadly, remembering the words the little girl had told him not too long before. "Yeah, I've been thinking about that a lot lately."

Dom reached out and put his hand on Jack's forearm, "You know I'm good if you need to talk. You can tell me anything Jack, Shannon too."

Jack simply smiled as tears began to form in his eyes. *I need to get my damn emotions under control.* He quietly turned back to his food and resumed eating, though, he found his appetite had significantly lessened.

They sat in silence for a while, staring at their food and filling their stomachs. They were tired, and weary of the day's work and though Jack wanted to talk about the case, perhaps just to soundboard off Dom, he didn't. He knew that Dom didn't like talking about cases, though, Jack found that quite peculiar as he'd always rationalized that the most important part of thinking was vocalizing, through written or spoken word. It's the reason he carried his notebook with him everywhere, as he'd jot down thoughts to come back to, to meditate on later when his emotional state had changed. He'd solved a great deal of cases this way, as in the different state of awareness he'd be able to see the case from another perspective.

He looked up as Dom finished off the last of his potatoes and stood; his plate now clean. He walked over to the sink and Jack found himself wishing, and not for the first time, that things had been different. He figured that if only his father hadn't been the man he was, or hadn't committed the atrocities he did, that things very well could have.

Dom's voice cut through his thoughts, "I'm off to bed though man, I'm beat." he turned, then stopped, "oh yeah, you can sleep in the guest bedroom, I forgot about it last night, but if you go down the hallway towards the front door, it's the second room on the right."

Jack looked up and nodded, "thank you Dom, have a good sleep, I'll see you tomorrow morning, big day ahead of us."

Dom turned and lifted a hand, "night Jack."

Jack smiled sadly to himself, "night Dom."

Jack found the room with ease and brought his small suitcase in from his car shortly after, knowing he didn't care to wear the same clothes three days straight. He stripped down to his underwear and left his clothes in a pile by the foot of the bed, flicked on the bedside lamp, then let himself fall back onto the top sheet.

He laid there a while, staring blankly at the ceiling above. Though his thoughts drifted to benign regions, he found himself unable to fall asleep. This wasn't a surprise to him however, though he did feel guilty as he lifted himself off the bed and walked over to his suitcase to retrieve his 'medicine.'

He reached in between the folded clothing and his heart lifted as his hand found purchase on the familiar cold glass inside. He sighed and pulled out the bottle of whiskey he'd brought just for this occasion. He uncorked the bottle as he sat down on the edge of the bed, letting the sweet fragrance burn his nose. He hesitated as he raised the bottle to his lips, hating himself for needing to resort to such methods to sleep, though not for the first time.

He closed his eyes and knocked his head back, allowing the contents of the bottle to splash as they poured into his mouth. He barely noticed the burn, he'd grown too accustomed to drinking like this, no longer drinking for the enjoyment of it, but drinking simply to quell the demons that threatened to rise when he was most vulnerable. He took another swig before recorking the bottle and setting it down on the floor next to his suitcase.

Once more, he lay back on the bed, wiggling himself under the blankets this time as the heat worked its way from his chest and into his face. His breaths grew long, and he felt his pulse in his face, though, he soon ceased to notice at all and simply rode the wave of the alcohol, smiling. Moments later that wave brought him gently through the doors into a deep and dreamless sleep.

Though he didn't remember the dreams that came that night, he did have them. As his self-prescribed medicine worked its magic, he found himself whisked into a realm where the dreams couldn't find his waking mind. Where the dreams of a past encapsulated by demons and monsters in a world his father destroyed didn't appear. This was the benefit of the medicine he took with an almost religious fervor. The side effects went unnoticed mostly by Jack, though over the past few days, they began to present themselves as withdrawals took over him. If the alcohol was a catalyst for the apathy that had initially washed over his existence; then the withdrawals that plagued him were the inhibitor.

He'd consumed significantly less alcohol than normal in the last forty-eight hours, and thus, he'd become emotionally unstable and his demons began to worm their way to the surface. Wriggling and writhing amongst the mass of memories they'd stirred up as he entered the town he fled.

As he laid there unconscious, in a dark and seemingly dreamless sleep, a thought presented itself, as though brought forth from the recesses of his mind; undulating, pulsing and mingling with the once dormant demons of his past. Poking and prodding its way to the forefront, surfacing briefly before returning to the depths, letting Jack know it would always be there. It'll be there when he goes about his daily tasks, remembering he was part of an event that shook the town of Magrath. I'll be there when he shoots awake in the depth of night as the obscured dream continues to fade into the ignorance of his drunken stupor and he'll know that it will never go away until he's able to face his actions and own them, though that thought terrified, made him break out in a cold sweat. His heart thundered heavily in his chest as the thought presented itself once more.

By God, how on earth could I face them if they knew the truth?

~ 2 ~

As Dom and Jack were talking over dinner, Shannon lay on the bed of the master bedroom, listening to the faint murmur of conversation that flowed up the stairs and into her ears. She thought of Jack, thought of how different he looked, how mature he seemed.

She recalled the brief time they dated back in high school. He was her first for many things; first kiss, first love, first time. She supposed there was always a special place in one's heart for their first, some sort of strange nostalgia that holds in one's mind for all time. Though, she figured it was as much for the person as it was as much for yourself. To her, the fondness that remained in her heart when she thought of Jack Lewis was something to do with herself opening to him, and the way he'd opened up to her.

Sure, some may have seen them dating as a way for her to gain prominence in the community, but it was never anything like that; they'd simply been friends for the longest time, though they only started dating when they'd realized just how much they cared for the other. Dom knew, of course, that they'd been an item for a time, though, he didn't know the pains that forced them to break up.

She'd blamed Jack for so long, blamed him for the loss sustained at the hand of his father. It wasn't until years had passed that she was finally able to forgive him. She recalled the day, quite vividly, though wouldn't allow herself to dwell on such things; there was a price of pain that came with thinking of those times, her younger days.

Instead she thought of the times they spent as children, the three of them at first, then the four of them when Emma came into town. She recalled the late nights talking on the edge of town, watching the star speckled sky pass above, they'd point out the constellations and talk at length about the possibility of life on other planets. She smiled lightly to herself, and closed her eyes, trying to use the happy memories to carry her off to sleep.

The sound of utensils clinking on the level below prevented her from doing that however and instead she turned over in bed and face the window, seeing the small LCD display on the nightstand next to her. It read 8:45pm. If I fell asleep right now, I'd have seven hours and fifteen minutes of sleep. That should be enough, right?

Instead, she kept her eyes on the picturesque window and watched as the town quieted before her very eyes. She sighed, though didn't close her eyes again, she simply watched the world float outside, worrying about the influx of emotions brought on by seeing Jack again. She subconsciously moved her hand to her lower abdomen and lay there for a while, wondering what sort of world it would have been for her if Jack was the son of somebody else.

Sometime later, when Shannon had finally closed her eyes once more; the door clicked open and Dom walked in. For reasons unbeknownst to Shannon; she kept her eyes closed and feigned unconsciousness as Dom walked throughout the room, going about his nightly rituals. He walked over to the corner of their room where the laundry hamper was, then walked to the closet where he removed his socks, he then slipped out of his uniform and hung it up next to the other sets. Finally, he sighed loudly then slipped into the bed next to her.

He lay still for a few moments, then turned as though to prop himself up on one elbow, and whispered, “Hey Shan, you awake?”

She didn’t reply, instead she kept her eyes closed, her body still and her breaths deep, feigning unconsciousness. Dom reached out and place a hand on her shoulder and soon he placed his head back on the pillow. She lay there, wondering how long it would take for him to fall asleep.

Instead, he surprised her, “I know you’re asleep, but there are some things I need to get off my chest, so I’ll talk to you. Even if you can’t hear me.”

When the silence encroached, he resumed, “I worried about Jack, Shan. We never expected him to come back and for a long time that was alright, I figured it was better for him, I mean, there was no house for him to really return to, right? Anyway, several times today I caught him looking up towards the manor; which I guess is normal enough, but the look on his face… well it’s hard to describe. It’s almost like he’s afraid of it, yet there’s a longing there. It’s taking all my will power not to ask him about it, I don’t want to add to that bottomless sadness he appears to be harboring. I guess I’m just worried about him.”

Dom yawned and for a moment, Shannon thought about turning to him and replying to him, but then he continued, “In a way I’m happy that he’s home, though I wish - for his sake - that is was under different circumstances…”

Dom trailed off then, and for a while Shannon believed he’d speak again. Though, as the minutes passed, she began to hear the deep sounds of sleep coming from Dom's mouth as he slept, and she smiled. She turned onto her back and stared at the ceiling, worried that she may be up all night with worry, though, in time she drifted off into the realm of sleep as well.

~ 3 ~

Trix sat in the quiet of her room, reading from a P.F. McGrail anthology she'd 'borrowed' from her father's collection. The writing was eloquent, she found, and though the premise was something she'd never considered, it was the tragedy of the short she was reading that drew her in. She wiped a stray tear that formed in the corner of her eye free and set the book down. She sighed as she rose onto her unsure feet; another night spent home alone.

She meandered through the darkened hallway between her bedroom and the kitchen passing her parents' empty room on the way. She'd never been fond of their absences, but she did enjoy the visits from her uncle. She figured that was the silver lining that came from the job-oriented nature of her parents. She just hoped they didn't try to push their ideals onto her. She'd been getting good grades, so they knew that she'd be well on her way to a good university and they'd had a significant amount saved up for her to do such a thing. Should she choose.

She didn't think too much about that though, she was only sixteen, how was she to know what sort of job she'd wanted to do for the rest of her life. She wanted to explore the world, see monuments and temples undisturbed for centuries. She wanted to spend nights in tropical paradises and days in foreign markets; she wanted to explore the world - leave the confines of Magrath's city limits and see what else was out there. She sighed and meandered the rest of the way into the kitchen.

She thought of the Parthenon in Athens and the ruins of Knossos, wondering if she'd ever get to see them. She'd been getting very anxious lately, as far as she was concerned, Magrath wasn't safe anymore. Though, she was unsure as to why the general mood of the people here was so damn calm. Perhaps they knew something she didn't?

She walked over to the fridge and looked at the half-eaten pizza that lay within and the note her mother had left on top of it.

Dr. Watters called in sick. I'll be working until tomorrow evening. I love you, MOM.

She looked to the small display on the oven. The time read 10:30pm, and though she was hungry, she knew that if she wanted any chance to sleep tonight, she'd need to hold off. Sighing she closed the fridge, figuring she'd settle for a single slice of bread.

As she went about the task of pulling out a slice she thought about her uncle Dom and that man he'd brought with him. Jack Lewis. The name sounded familiar, though she wasn't sure why. He seemed nice enough, though, she figured he was a bit more messed up than he'd let on. There was a deep sadness behind those dark eyes of his, especially when compared to the loving and compassionate eyes of her uncle.

She didn't dwell on it too much, instead focusing her attention on the single slice of bread that she was now slipping into the small toaster oven they kept on the counter. She turned it on and waited, thinking about school. It had been a while since she'd been there; her parents let her take as much time as she wanted, even told her it would be of little consequence if she needed to take additional classes during the summer to build back up her GPA. Even if they need to enroll her in a school to upgrade courses after, it would be fine, so long as she focused on getting better.

"The brain can't retain additional knowledge if the heart is hurting," her father had explained to her shortly after Noah's death, "we'll support you in any way we can, and when the time comes, we'll get your grades to where they should be."

She smiled to herself as she listened to the incessant timer tick away on the toaster. Her father had always been like that; his heart was kind, much like Uncle Dom's, yet, his kind words were always followed by academic platitudes. Those were always the forefront of his mind. He'd probably sooner see me dead than see me working at Debbies Diner or one of the other two-bit restaurants in this town.

Finally, the toaster dinged, and she took the now lightly toasted bread out from under the hot element. The aroma was a welcome smell, filling her nose with a smell reminiscent of the Sunday mornings she'd fondly remembered from the times before grade school; when her parents were home to enjoy meals with her. The nostalgia faded, leaving her with an empty feeling in the pit of her stomach, she took her first bite of the steaming toast and let the warmth flow through her mouth and into her body.

She nibbled absentmindedly on the toast as she turned to walk back to her bedroom. She moved slowly down the darkened hall, relying on her mental map of the corridor to bring her there. She smiled as she reached the door and pushed it open, hoping to get a little more reading done before she resigned to bed, though she wasn't going to school the following day, she figured it would still be best to maintain the routine of going to bed around the same time she normally did and waking up early the following day.

As she crossed the space between the door and her bed, thoughts turning organically to the interaction between Uncle Dom and that man, Jack Lewis. She couldn't place why his name sounded so familiar so her mind kept turning back to the nagging feeling that she was forgetting something important, as though that simple thing could change everything.

A shiver went down her spine then, and without provocation she found herself terrified. Is someone watching me? She turned slowly towards the window on the far wall of her bedroom, her breath growing quick as the terror spread throughout her body, causing her muscles to twitch in a fight or flight response. Her eyes widened in horror as she saw what had caused her to feel so scared. It clicked open the window and stepped in with ease. A moment of clarity overcame her and as the thing laid eyes on her she suddenly remembered why Jack Lewis' name had sounded so familiar.

She screamed, though even as the sound reverberated throughout the house, bouncing off walls and filling the space; there was no one around to hear her. The horror of being alone settled in, causing her to scream louder, hoping with her very being that someone, anyone, could hear her. Her vocal cords strained and eventually her screams were reduced to a mere whimper. She shuffled back, tripping on a discarded article of clothing as it approached. Its smile stretched across its slick wet face, it reached towards her, its small dark eyes never leaving her face. Suddenly, she felt very lightheaded.

The world spun as blackness encroached on her vision. It wrapped one hand tightly around her throat as unconsciousness swept in and Trix fainted.

Part 2
Headway

October 5, 2015

Chapter 5: Fairmont Secondary

~ 1 ~

THE SMELL OF COFFEE graced the morning air while somewhere on Jack's nightstand, an alarm was going off. The shrill sound pierced the veil of sleep, tearing Jack away from the safe darkness of his dreams. He opened his eyes slowly as he tried to remember where he was. Bed. He frowned, where? He panned his eyes around in the darkness, confused momentarily before the events of yesterday finally came back to him. Dom's house. Right.

He slowly untangled his legs from the mess of blankets then swung them out over the edge. Using his left hand, he rubbed the sleep out of his eyes as his right groped around in the darkness, seeking out the source of the high-pitched siren that was emanating from the nightstand. His hand found purchase and he quickly dismissed the alarm, condemning the room to a welcome silence. Jack sighed appreciatively.

Still partially drunk from last night's 'medicine', he raised himself onto unsteady legs and rubbed the last of the sleep from his eyes. Fumbling in the dark, he worked his way along the wall to the light switch; wincing as the light filled the room and assaulted his dry eyes.

Regaining his bearings, he sauntered slowly over to his small suitcase and moved aside the bottle that he'd place before it the night before. He reached in and pulled-out a t-shirt and sweatpants then slipped into them before turning for the door.

His socks absorbed his light footfalls as he made his way down the hallway towards the kitchen and he found himself really pining for the coffee whose aroma filled the air. As he neared the kitchen, he began to hear the faint echoes of conversation drifting around the corner. Jack knew it would be rude to eavesdrop, though he quelled the guilt and decided to remain hidden.

Jack could hear Dom's faint voice, "... but Shan, you must know something about the night he left; why won't you tell me? I know something happened, his house didn't burn down for no reason, he didn't leave for no reason, and Emma didn't disappear for no reason. Something fucked is going on here; far longer than these past few weeks. I've looked through the old files, there's no reports on anything happening in the town before the police department was scrapped and fixed. No records on anything from before Jack left, though I feel like you may know. It may coincide with Jack and his family. You were close to them at one point, surely you must know something?"

A stifled gasp came from Shannon's mouth as if the words had physically struck her, "where is this coming from Dominic? Why on earth do you think I know what happened? Why not just ask Jack?"

Dom's voice came out frustrated, "Shan, I've asked subtly what happened that night, and every damn time, his eyes space out - like you see in war vets when they hear about the war. Do you know what it could do to him to force him to relive that? He's already got one foot in the grave as it is, I don't think he's gone to bed without the sauce's aid in years and he smokes more than a pack a day. He's self-destructive and he has a lot of problems, I don't want to add to them."

A small fire was kindled inside of Jack's chest as he ran his mind over Dom's words. *Does he think I'm inept?* He creased his brow and balled up his fists as his heart rate grew quicker. The anger built, *I don't need his opinion on how I live my life, what my habits are or any of that.* Jack got ready and steeled himself to face him. He would walk around that corner and let out the bubbling rage on him; give him his two cents. He took his first step when a sound from the other room became audible, stopping him dead in his tracks.

It started as a series of strange and repetitive foreign exhales, and it took Jack a moment to realize what they were. Dom was crying. Empathy washed over Jack and he felt the anger that had so rapidly built up inside of him dissipate. He realized that Dom wasn't judging him, wasn't criticizing him or anything of the sort. No, what Dom had said came from a place of warmth and kindness, said with the utmost compassion for his friend. He'd said it not with spite in his heart but worry. Jack realized just how much he'd worried Dom, even though he'd only been back for a couple days. His shoulders sagged as the realization overcame him. *I'm sorry I ever doubted you Dom. You deserve a far better friend than me.*

Jack finally stepped out of the hallway he'd been listening in from, Shannon stood behind Dom; her arms wrapped tightly around him with her eyes closed as he sat there weeping with his head in his hands. He walked slowly over to them, marveling at just how vulnerable they looked in that moment. Jack felt a pang of jealousy but quickly dismissed it as he closed the remaining distance between them.

Shannon's eyes shot open as he neared as she met his eyes with a bewildered expression. Quickly, she glanced between him and Dom as if to say, "how much did you hear?"

Jack said nothing; instead he smiled gently at her and gestured for her to move away from Dom. She frowned, though obliged, watching curiously as Jack approached his crying friend. Dom slowly looked up and met Jack's eyes, giving away a clear visage of sadness at the state of his friend. Jack simply met his eyes in silence.

He thought it over, the absurdity of seeing someone he respected crying. He reckoned it's much like the first time a child realizes that their parents are people too and not this immovable force that carries no common emotions. As Dom stared deep into his eyes with tears running down his cheeks and dripping off his chin, Jack felt something in his heart click. Jack realized that respect builds up something false in the mind, dehumanizes people to a certain degree in the eyes of those that respect them. It builds up a false image of the person, constantly in the state in which they are respected. It's a strange contradiction, Jack thought, for as the respect for the person grows, you begin to stop associating human traits to them. In his mind he'd built Dom up as someone strong, resolute and infallible, yet, as he laid his eyes upon Dom, the facade melted away.

Jack saw someone who, underneath their firm and tough exterior, was just as human as he was; was just as prone to heartache and loss as anyone else. He realized that Dom wasn't this person who was a hardened cop with a firm respect for the community, whose life was wholly perfect, and had nothing but positivity in his life. No, he began to see him as a man facing a dilemma. Someone who had empathized with his own pain and put his emotions first, Dom had placed himself in Jack's shoes and Jack realized that it had only made him respect him more.

Jack placed his hand gently on Dom's shoulder, much like Dom had done in the bar a few nights prior and held his gaze. He smiled and Dom smiled in turn, an understanding passing between the two men.

Jack's voice came out steadier than he was expecting, "Dom, I'll tell you about my past. Not right now, but later. After today, let's go to the bar, have a few drinks and I'll spill everything. I'll tell you the tale of my father, the things he took from this town, from us, and everyone living here. I'll tell you about the night I left, the night that the culmination of events reached the boiling point and I set fire to my house. I'll tell you about the night I fled Magrath with Emma, leaving everything behind."

Dom looked at Jack with a surprised expression, eyes wide and mouth agape. Quickly, he re-composed himself, "sounds good Jack, whatever you need."

In an attempt to lighten the mood and shake his mind from slipping into his past, Jack let out a shaky chuckle, "what I need is a damn shower, I smell like ass."

Dom and Shannon let out hearty laughs in kind with Jack, though he was unsure if it was the sound of stress leaving their bodies or if they had genuinely found it funny. He seriously doubted they found it funny, more so, he thought they were the laughs of two people desperately trying to cling to something that would hold them afloat; spare them from the dark places of the mind.

When the roars of laughter subsided and they wiped tears from their eyes, Dom sent Jack on his way to the shower, telling him to take a fresh towel from the cabinet on his way. Jack nodded graciously and trundled his way up the stairs, feeling their weary eyes on the back of his head. He wondered what they'd talk about while he cleaned himself.

--

Under the torrent of hot water, Jack felt the stress leave his body and the anxiety melt away. He ran his hands through his hair as he thought about recounting the night, he left Magrath. He'd never recounted the events of that night to anyone before, never in full anyway. Emma had known most of what happened, but they never really talked about it.

Looking down, he realized his hands were shaking. I'm going to need a lot of alcohol to get through this.

~ 2 ~

Sometime later, Jack and Dom were sitting in Dom's Honda Civic outside of Fairmont Secondary school. The wind blew idly by, sweeping the remaining leaves from the naked branches of the trees that lined the sidewalk running adjacent to the school grounds. It was a colder day, one that made Jack grateful that he'd brought a warm enough coat to face the chill that rode the wind down from the neighboring mountains. He reached forward and warmed his cold hands on Dom's heating vent while he shuffled in his seat. He was getting antsy.

They sat in silence watching the casual flow of students; neither one wanting to break the anxiety that clung to the air between them. They were waiting for the day of classes to start, but neither of them had realized that simply because they were early, didn't mean that class would be in session any time sooner.

Jack shifted again in his seat, moving his hands from the vents and back. He was growing restless. He wanted answers, wanted to move this case forward, and most importantly, he wanted to figure out who killed Noah Brackman and the others, who had been the one to snuff lives out like nothing and leave the families in mourning. He shook his head and moved his hands once more. He was beginning to feel the walls of the car closing in on him, he figured it would be better to be out there turning over rocks, looking for clues in the most obscure cases; anything would be better than waiting in the car impatiently for an indifferent bell to sound the start of classes.

Dom realized the level of anticipation coursing through Jack's body, "Jack, buddy, just a few more minutes then we can go inside and wait in the office for the kids. Why don't you have a smoke or something? Take your mind off whatever is causing you to act like this."

Jack frowned, his mind latching onto something that hadn't happened in years. He couldn't remember the last time he'd gone so long without a cigarette. He'd always have one before bed, one or two throughout the night when he'd wake up with the shakes, and then he'd have one first thing in the morning with the sunrise. Yet, he'd done none of that in the past several hours. He reflected on this, pondering how his obsession with this case had been able to outweigh his addiction. Though, now that the thought of lighting one up had entered his mind, he couldn't help but desire the safe and familiar feeling of the cotton wrapped paper between his lips.

He nodded to Dom and slipped out of the car, shoving his hand into his coat pocket to fish out his cigarettes. The autumn air bit into his face as he stood outside, and he pressed the filter to his lips; feeling calmed by the gesture alone. He smirked to himself, reckoning that Pavlov knew a significant amount about human conditioning.

After a few tries, the end was alight, and he began to inhale the familiar smoke with an unanticipated fervor. The nicotine flowed through his body and he could feel his muscles relaxing with every drag, as though the act of smoking was paramount to mediation. He focused solely on the act of inhaling and exhaling the smoke. He closed his eyes and surrendered himself to the action, experiencing the feeling of the smoke as it rolled over its tongue, tinging it in the sour taste of the cigarette.

He took another deep drag and was surprised to see that it had been reduced to nothing more than the smoldering butt. Why not another? Unable to argue with his own logic, he fished out another from the box and lit it. This time he savored each deep inhale and the feeling of the smoke filling his lungs. As he exhaled the smoke, he watched it flow up into the air, dissipating in the cool breeze that had rolled over Magrath. He found himself envying the freeness of the smoke as it flowed up and over the town; free of the confines of the city limits.

A loud bell resonated over the field and interrupted Jack's thoughts of freedom and smoke. He hunkered down to peer at Dom through the car's window, smiling despite himself at the prospect of officially starting their day's work. As Dominic Maneuvered himself from the car Jack flicked the remaining cigarette onto the ground and stepped on it, then followed Dominic towards the oppressive brick building that lay before them.

--

They strode through the front doors of the school and headed straight towards the office, relying on their memories of the school's layout to find their way to it. They were hit by a wave of anxiety as they saw the familiar linoleum lined corridor spanned out before them; as though the years of angst and teenage hormones had remained there. Waiting for the perfect moment to latch back onto them and remind them of the children they once had been.

Jack shook his head as though to rid himself of the feeling and noticed that Dom was doing the same. He smiled at him and they resumed their march towards the office, anxious to meet the boys and hopeful to glean any information that may be of use for the case.

They walked into the office shortly after, met by the perplexed stare of the geriatric secretary working the front desk, "Good morning officer Thompson, who's this with you? What brings you here today?"

Dom smiled, "Good morning Martha, this is Jack, he's a PI that the police department hired to assist with the - uh - on goings here in Magrath. I was wondering if we'd be able to speak to a few of the sophomores today."

Martha looked to Jack, "Pleasure to meet you Jack…"

Jack's face reddened slightly, "Lewis."

Her eyes widened, but as she was about to open her mouth to ask the question Jack knew was coming, Dom coughed, "about those students."

Martha shifted her eyes back to Dom, "Yes, am I right in assuming this is about Noah Brackman?"

Dom nodded sadly, "I'm not at liberty to say, would you be able to pull them from class for me?"

She nodded, "of course, what were their names?"

Jack spoke up, producing the page from his notebook, "Uh, let me see here; Robert Fielding, Larkin Grace, and Zachariah Hastings."

Martha nodded, and although she maintained a look of professionalism, she could hardly contain the cursory look that edged its way onto her face as she looked at Jack, "Sounds good… Mr. Lewis." She clicked something on her computer, then paused, "Ah, here we go, it looks like they are all here today. I'll page them."

She turned to the microphone that rested upon the cream colored desk and picked it up, sliding the switch to "on" in the same motion, "Would Robert Fielding, Larkin Grace, and Zachariah

Hastings come to the office please, that's Robert Fielding, Larkin Grace, and Zachariah Hastings. To the office. Thank you." The turned back to Jack and Dom, "Just another moment."

Jack looked to Dom, who raised an eyebrow at him before turning towards the line of chairs running along the office's wall. He walked to them and plopped down on one, Jack followed suit.

--

No more than two minutes later, the three boys entered the office looking confused. Dom and Jack rose to their feet and approached the boys, "Martha," Jack spoke, "Is there a conference room or office we could use to speak to them in private?"

Martha nodded and showed them to the conference room that Jack figured would have been for staff meetings. The room was large enough to house a long dark oak table with eight chairs on either side, as well as a television at the end. Seems like the school isn't struggling financially. Interesting.

The three boys sat across from them, their eyes wide and postures nervous, evidently still confused. Jack felt sorry for them, but had to quell his empathy, he needed answers and these boys were his best shot. Looking at them left to right, he assigned the names to the faces based on Ed's descriptions. He chuckled to himself as he realized they'd arranged themselves from smallest to largest subconsciously.

Sitting on the far left was a small boy who was no larger than 5'4 and most likely 95lbs soaking wet. He had small features that erased any confusion as to why Ed had referred to him as "Rat-like." Despite his clearly nervous composure, his face still held a latent expression of mischief; one that would surely result in his associated guilt and punishment in things he hadn't even participated in. His eyes flicked around the room as though he was trying to avoid eye contact with everyone and everything in the room at the same time. Jack smiled to himself; This must be Robert.

Seated in the middle was a boy of a medium athletic build, Zachariah, or Zach; as Ed had said. Though he was of average height, a solid 5'10, he appeared to be covered in a thin sheet of lean muscle that poked through the thin fabric of his shirt. He remained almost calm, despite the few beads of sweat that bordered his hairline. Based on his appearance and demeanor, Jack figured he was an athlete of sorts. Most likely dominant on the field, yet not so much as to inspire arrogance, but enough to instill confidence. His eyes were focused on the table and his jaw was set in concentration.

Jack slid his eyes over to the mountain of a boy next to him. Though he easily stood over 6'5, Larkin had a kind and gentle face. His forehead was slick with sweat and his blue eyes flickered back and forth between Jack and Dom. Jack studied him, noting how his body - that was a healthy mixture of muscle and fat - was trembling. Out of the three boys, he appeared to be the most afraid. Jack reckoned that if any of the three knew anything, it would be him; and based on his demeanor, he would be the most willing to spill everything.

Jack reached into his pocket and produced the small recorder he'd used the day prior at Ed's. He placed the device on the conference table between himself and the boys, then met each of their eyes as he hit the large red 'record' button. He took a step back as they all looked at him, nervous to see what he had to say.

He gestured to the recorder, "do you all know what this is?"

The three boys nodded slowly.

He nodded in kind, "Good, I'm going to be recording our conversation for my own reference; with your consent of course. Do you all consent."

The boys nodded again.

He let out a light chuckle, he'd said this spiel hundreds of times over the year; "Sorry, I'll need you to verbalize it. You understand, legal reasons and all that."

The three of them let out pitiful, shaky responses, subtle "yesses" that barely disturbed the thick air of anxiety that had settled over the room.. Jack thought about the best approach to get information out of the group. He wanted to ask Larkin but didn't want to single him out in front of his friends, thus, he knew that in order to get an answer, if any, he would need to ask the group as a whole first.

Jack met each of the boys eyes individually and smiled, "Now, you all seem like fairly bright kids, so I assume it's no wonder why we brought you here; it's because you are - were - friends of Noah's. But, before we get into this, I'd like to mention that you all are not in any sort of trouble whatsoever."

The opposite of what Jack was expecting happened. Instead of the anxiety that clung to the air dissipating, it seemed to thicken. Robert and Larkin both looked to Zach who was still staring at the table. Slowly his eyes shifted up to Jack's, causing him to suck in a breath. He'd only ever seen that kind of silent ferocity when speaking to old war vets who were reliving their wildest nightmares. Why does he look like that?

Dom spoke up from next to Jack, "Again, you boys aren't in any trouble, we just want to get to the bottom of this and solve your friend's murder."

Jack nodded, "Exactly, we don't want you to feel like you're in any sort of predicament with the law, we just want to ask you some questions." Jack reached into his pocket and brought out the notebook, turning it to a blank page, "Ah, here we are. Firstly, did Noah have any enemies? It could be anyone who wanted to hurt him; from an outraged teacher to a fellow student, does anyone come to mind?"

Robert and Larkin exchanged glances, yet it was Zach who spoke up, through clenched teeth, "No sir, no person we can think of."

Strange. Jack noted the way he answered the question. It was to the point, concise, yet it didn't give away any information that didn't directly pertain to the question. Jack nodded thoughtfully as he ran through other questions, he might be able to ask that wouldn't give away too much information.

Still pretending to read off the sheet, "Did anything of concern happen in the weeks leading up to the night of Noah's untimely demise? Any parties or anything?"

Though Robert and Larkin went white, Zach remained stiff and guarded as he answered, "No sir, the weeks were fairly average."

Jack smiled as he realized he would get nowhere with all three of them together. For whatever reason, Zach had deemed it necessary to protect the other boys from whatever event had caused them to act so nervously. He reckoned separating them would be the best course of action. One on one; remove the cop and everything would be fine.

Jack turned to Dom, "Would you be able to take Robert and Larkin to the waiting room, I'd like to ask them the questions one at a time if that's alright." He looked back to the boys, specifically Robert and Larkin who now looked like deer in headlights. "Would you two follow officer Thompson back outside? I just think it will be easier to have a little one on one. If that's okay."

Dom flashed a cursory glance to Jack, who stood deep in thought as he continued to mull about the various ideas that were beginning to pool in his mind. He needed Zach to open, regardless of the other two's statements. Each one of them knew something, though it remained to be seen as to whether they each knew the same amount.

Dom stood and the two boys followed suit, nervously rising from their seats and following him out of the conference room. Jack marveled at just how large Larkin was. As he and Robert followed Dom out of the room Jack couldn't help but think of how comical it was to see such a short boy next to such a behemoth. It's like if David and Goliath were friends.

As they cleared out the room, Jack shuffled so he was seated directly across from Zach.

He coughed lightly into his hand, then began, "So Zach, why so clenched up? Is everything okay?"

Zach met his gaze, "Yeah. Everything's fine."

Jack nodded, "That's good. Good. You know, whatever you're not telling me, the others will most likely spill. Not that it's any fault on them, they're scared, as I'm sure you are as well. You don't have to protect them; they'll do fine on their own."

A moment of realization crossed Zach's brow, breaking the stern face he'd been displaying up until then, "I'm fine."

Jack pressed, "you can tell me Zach, no matter how far-fetched it sounds. I won't even tell your parents if you don't want me to. Please, just give me a bone here."

Jack could see Zach's internal struggle as a slew of emotions crossed his face; resistance, panic, and finally resignation. His lip began to quiver, and he quickly ran his hands through his shaggy blonde hair. Jack could see the hidden frenzy stirring behind his eyes as Zach's demeanor broke.

He loosed a deep sigh as he resigned to the question, "We went to a party about a week before Noah died, I believe it was September 11th. Yeah, that sounds about right. Anyway, it was Me, Noah, Robby, Trix, and Larkin. The party was at one of the senior's homes, asshole by the name of Corey Speilding."

Jack frowned, "what makes you say that?"

Zach sighed again, "Well, you see he's always kind of had it out for me, I don't know why exactly but he's always gone the extra mile to piss me off. Whether it was pushing me into lockers, kicking the backs of my shoes or even stealing some food from my plate occasionally. Basically, he's a typical Jock, like the type you'd see in movies, though I think he's jealous of me."

"Why's that?"

"Well, he's always had football, and always wanted to be Noah's friend. Though He's two years older than us, so naturally I got closer to Noah and became one of his best friends. I just don't think Corey liked that too much and decided that all his problems were my fault. At least it sure felt like that.

"Anyway, he was throwing a party and really wanted Noah to go. Y'know, invite the prodigy and suddenly your party becomes a rager? Well, he invited Noah and Noah flat out told him if he wanted him, he'd need to invite the rest of us." He paused a as large childish smile crossed his face. "According to Noah, the bastard squirmed. But he eventually agreed."

"Alright, so what happened after the invite?"

"Noah told us of course, and regardless of who's party it was, we were all stoked. It was our first invite to a party, let alone a senior student's party. You can imagine how hyped we were. We talked about it all week; I mean, during lunches, breaks, between classes, hell, even in classes. If we had a chance to talk, we talked about it. We formulated a sleepover plan as well."

"Care to elaborate?"

He shyly looked down, “Yeah, this is the part you can’t tell my parents though, although, I’d rather they didn’t know any of it.”

Jack smiled, “Zach, I’m not a cop, I’m not required to tell your parents anything about your whereabouts, I’m only responsible to report to my employer.”

Zach visibly relaxed, “Okay, well, we decided that the best course of action would be to stay at Trix’s. Her parents are almost never home, so we figured her house would be empty. She confirmed that it would be and so the plan was set. The guys decided we were ‘staying’ at Robby’s house, but then Robby told his mom that he was staying at my house, that way all of them thought we were somewhere we weren’t. They had no Idea we were going to a party and I assume they still don’t know.

“We met at Trix’s around seven and began to hype ourselves up, Noah and Trix wandered off at one point and Larkin, Robby and I just kind of sat in the living room wondering what we could do after the party to spruce up the evening while Noah and Trix… Well…”

Jack chuckled as Zach’s face went red, “Yeah I get it, no need to explain further.”

Zach nodded, “Yeah… so anyway, we left shortly after seven forty and arrived just after eight. The walk from Trix’s house took around twenty minutes, but it was quicker on the way there because none of us were drunk at that point, hell we hadn’t ever had anything to drink at that point.”

Jack nodded as his mind wandered to the first party he’d ever gone to. He recalled the music, the brilliant green hues that slayed out across the dark night sky above. The first taste of alcohol that trickled past his lip and down his eager throat; numbing the pain he’d been trying to bury for years. Looking back, he reckoned that should have been his first red flag to stay away from the stuff that he’d later cling to as medicine. He thought of the way Shannon bounded happily around the room, dancing with her fingers entwined with his, singing along to their favorite songs as the night drifted by with reckless abandon. He smiled as he recalled the blurry night of dancing and loving, the kiss he planted on Shannon’s supple red lips that sealed their relationship all those years ago.

He shook his head as the memories threatened to take him back down the rabbit hole and refocused on Zach's face as he told his story undisturbed.

"... the music was loud. Noah and Trix wandered off and mingled while the other three of us kind of clustered along the wall, sipping absentmindedly from the red solo cups that we'd filled with the punch Corey had made for the party. It was a good night and after some time I even began mingling as well, a few of the senior girls seemed interested in me too. Man, it was a great night."

Jack nodded as the kid reddened up, "what happened after the party."

Zach's relaxed expression disappeared, and he clammed up, "Uhh, nothing. The party began to dull down around one or two in the morning, and we initially were going to do some urban exploring, you know, check out some of the abandoned homes on the way back to Trix's place. But we all got pretty tired, so we just headed back to Trix's and crashed there for the night."

Jack hesitated, he could tell that there was something else that Zach was hiding from him, he could tell from the perspiration that had once again begun to form on the edge of his hairline, forming little rivulets of sweat that threatened to trickle down to his chin with the slightest of movements. He thought for a moment, wondering what could be worse to someone his age than his parents finding out about a party he'd gone to without permission. There was little more frightening at that age than the wrath of one's parents, yet Jack couldn't figure out what that could have been. So, he asked.

"Is there anything else Zach? I might be able to help."

Zach shook his head, as though shaking away the very notion that Jack would be able to offer any semblance of help to his situation, "There's nothing sir, nothing at all."

Jack nodded, realizing he wasn't going to get anything else out of him at that moment, "Alright Zach, would you be able to send in Robert. I believe I'll ask him the same questions next."

Zach nodded slowly then closed his eyes as he stood, as though building himself up to something. He turned and started towards the door, pausing before he turned the knob.

“Take it easy on Robby, okay? He’s been seeing - er - he’s had a tough time with Noah’s death.”

With that he turned and left the room, leaving Jack alone momentarily with his thoughts. His mind poured over their conversation, unable to quell the feeling that something happened after they went to that party. Perhaps they went somewhere, but where? Did they piss someone off that decided to take it out on Magrath?

His thoughts were interrupted by a small boy walking through the door, nervously glancing around the room, as though afraid of every single surface. Jack regarded him with curiosity, this is more than simple grief.

Robert slowly crossed the room and moved to the seat across the table from Jack, not meeting his eyes once. Jack studied him, setting his hands palm up on the dark oak, as if in supplication. As Robert sat down, he noticed how pale he’d become; his face was beaded with sweat and his shirt was now telegraphing several dark spots where the sweat had begun to seep through.

Despite this, Jack also found he looked dreadfully tired; his shoulders slumped forward, and occasionally, after a spout of his neurotic eye twitching, he looked almost like he was about to fall asleep. He’d be looking at one particular wall and his head would slowly begin to dip as his eyes began to flutter closed, then at the last second he’d snap awake and his eyes would resume the frivolous activity of trying to see all spots in the room at the same time.

Jack spoke cautiously, “Is everything alright Robert?”

Robert flicked his frantic eyes over to Jack, and Jack noticed for the first time, the dark rings that sagged underneath his eyes, like he hadn’t slept in days. He hasn’t been sleeping.

Finally, when Robert finally spoke, his words came out quickly, “What? Oh yeah, I’m fine, yeah. Just a little tired. That’s it, yeah, tired.”

As Robert began to descend again, Jack pressed on, “have you been sleeping Robert? You look more than ‘just a little tired.’”

Roberts eyes snapped open for a second as he shook off the sleep once more, “uh - sleeping? No - no, I can’t, haven’t been able to. Nightmares. Really bad nightmares. I can barely sleep for five minutes officer.”

Jack frowned, “I’m not an officer, just call me Jack. When did the nightmares start?”

Robert shook his head once more, trying to remain awake, “Week or so before Noah died. After the - after - after…”

His head lulled forward as he finally lost the small battle he’d been waging, and he began to snore. Jack sat back, wondering what the best way to deal with this would be. Call his parents, ask them to get him a shrink? There’s obviously some psychological trauma caused by his friend’s death.”

Jack stood, about to walk over to the other side of the table to where Robert was sleeping. However, just as he stood out of his chair, Robert bolted wide awake in a screaming fit.

“AHH GET THE FUCK AWAY FROM ME. Wait - where? Ah, must’ve fallen asleep”

He slowly settled back down in his chair and Jack responded in kind, wondering what sort of dream could elicit that sort of response from a child. Jack watched him cautiously, playing with a thought as to the nature of the dream.

“Robert, did the dream have something to do with the party? Did something happen after your group left?”

Robert’s eyes went wide, and he began shaking his head vigorously. This time, his eyes didn’t waver. He met Jack’s eyes and held them, a fierce and intense fear burning behind them.

Jack sighed, “Please Robert. Zach told me about the party, but I need to know the rest, I can’t help without the rest Robert. Please tell me. Please.”

Robert’s eyes bulged slightly, and he finally looked away from Jack to the corner of the room. Confused Jack looked over his shoulder to the empty corner.

“Robert?”

"No. no, no, no. I can't, no. I can't tell you. No. If I do, you'll go there. He'll find you. NO! You shouldn't, don't go. If you do, you'll end up like the rest. We're all headed there, you know. He comes in my dreams, shows me the world as it was and as it will be. He is fear. In time we'll be nothing, but he'll remain." He blinked the tears out of his eyes, "There was a fire, years ago. It destroyed most, but not all, it remains with a face like plastic and skin like liquid ash. He remains, he lives beneath, it remains!"

Suddenly fearful for Robert's health, Jack stood from his chair and began to rush around the table. But as he neared the end by the door, Robert fell from his chair and began convulsing on the ground as he screamed. Instead Jack altered his course and flung open the room's door; calling out to the secretary.

"Call for an ambulance, we need to get him to a hospital!" he swiveled his head to a very confused Dom, "Come here, we'll need to do basic first aid."

He pivoted and rushed back into the room, beginning to move chairs out of the way so as to prevent the seizing Robert from injuring himself on the furniture. He heard Dom come in shortly after and begin to wheel the other chairs out of the way.

"We'll need to move the damn table over. I don't think we can lift it, so we have to push it."

Jack looked up to Dom who was already on the other end of the table. They nodded to each other and pushed the table, grunting at the effort of moving the large slab of oak.

After some muscular negotiations, the table began to budge and the two let go in exhaustion as Robert still lay on the ground, now convulsing without any obstruction.

"What's the go Dom?"

Dom's eyes were wide, "Well, we shouldn't really touch him while he's seizing, as that could cause further injury. The best thing we can do is stand by and wait for it to stop. Then we can proceed."

Jack wiped the back of his hand against his head, brushing away the sweat that had formed on his forehead, "Shit. Dom, this may be worse than we think."

Dom simply nodded, though he didn't take his eyes off the still convulsing Robert. Jack turned towards the door and halted immediately upon seeing Zach and Larkin peering in, their faces showing only masks of abject horror instead of any amount of concern. Their hands were clenched into tight fists at their sides, with white knuckles threatening to burst through their skin.

Later, Jack would look back and marvel at the amount of clarity he'd had at that moment and the level of detail he'd seen as they waited for paramedics to arrive. He saw the secretary's concerned face as she held the phone up to her ear while listening to the operator on the other side. He saw the clock's second hand ticked past 8:23:59 and 8:24:00, he saw the way the clouds moved in from the horizon, casting a dark shadow under the grounds below. He saw the concerned expression crossing Dom's face and knew he was thinking about Trix, he saw the blue and red lights approaching down the road long before the sounds ever reached his ears. He noticed the grey curls of fabric in the carpet, how they looped underneath Robert's body as he struggled to regain control over his muscles and eventually fell still, his eyes closed. Jack wondered how long it would be until they finally opened again.

As the paramedics moved in, they asked everyone to leave the conference room and stand in the waiting room. Agreeing, Jack slipped his recorder off the table and back into his pocket, then slipped out of the room. He crossed the floor to the front desk and asked the secretary to call Robert's parents as they worked on stabilizing Robert. Larkin and Zach held their heads low as they looked down at their hands; in the passing moments they'd retaken their seats along the wall and had since gone silent, their faces growing somber as the paramedics worked on their friend in the other room.

Jack smiled sadly as he walked over to Dom, "What's the go, man?"

Dom met his eyes and Jack saw that they were filled with worry, "Well, I suppose he'll go on to the hospital, I'll write a report about the events that took place, and we'll carry on with the case. I don't see any other course of action here, do you? As it stands, we're both still on the clock. Did you make any headway with the boys or did you want to talk to Larkin still?"

Jack saw Larkin raise his head slightly at the mention of his name, so Jack signaled for Dom to walk with him over to the small staff room. Understanding, Dom followed him into the small room, and plopped down into one of the small white folding chairs that was set around the fold out table against the wall. Jack sighed as he lowered himself into the one adjacent to him.

Thinking about Trix himself, Jack began. “So, Dom, try to remain professional here, I know she’s practically your daughter at this point.”

Hearing this, Dom straightened in his seat; suddenly on high alert. Jack met his now intense stare and continued, “Look, so basically the five of them went to a party a few weeks ago.” Dom’s face reddened visibly, “Now, according to Zach, they had a little bit to drink and they had a relatively good time. Though, he also said they got tired and went straight home. This is where I don’t believe him. I think they went somewhere and saw something that scared the absolute crap out of them. It would have to have been something bad enough for Zach to refuse to talk about it and Robert to lose sleep over it. Did you see the looks on their faces when Robert started seizing?”

Dom nodded slowly, “Looked like they’d seen a ghost.”

Jack nodded and continued, “Exactly, and before Robert’s episode, he began spurting out things about a fire and something that lives in a basement. I think they saw something they couldn’t comprehend, and it perhaps snapped poor Robert’s mind.”

Dom frowned, “So you mean like an actual ghost?”

Jack hesitated, “Maybe, maybe not, all that matters is what they believed they saw, and where they went. Perhaps it was a hiding ground for a serial killer or something of the sort and he’s hunkered down in Magrath. Perhaps he’s the one that killed Noah.”

Dom nodded, “So all we need is a location?”

Jack nodded, “Yeah, and I think we could get it out of Larkin, but not if Zach’s there. I’m thinking of sending him off with the paramedics, so Robert at least has someone familiar with him in the ambulance.”

Dom smiled, “Smart, alright, let’s do it.”

Jack walked out into the waiting room as the paramedics were coming back into the office with a stretcher, Zach and Larkin watched with wide eyes as they passed. Jack followed them into the room, and they looked up as he entered.

One of the paramedics began to tell him to leave but Jack cut him off, “Look, I know you want to do your work, but I also have to do mine. Listen, I’m a PI employed by the Magrath police department, so I was wondering if I would be able to send one of the students with you. Just to keep company with Robert until his parent’s show up.”

The one he hadn’t interrupted spoke up, “Sure, that’s fine, I assume his parents will meet us at the hospital?”

Jack nodded, knowing they’d need to wait for them so they would be able to get their billing information. He walked back out into the room and met eyes with Zach, his eyes were lined with red.

“Hey Zach, do you want to go with them? They’re bringing Robert to the hospital and I think you’d be able to keep him calm if he wakes up on the way to the hospital.”

Zach nodded sullenly and stood, “I’ll need to just grab some things from my locker if that’s okay?”

Jack smiled, “Sure, just be back here quick, alright?”

Zach smiled weakly and quickly walked from the room, leaving Jack, Larkin, Dom and the secretary alone in the office. Jack looked to Larkin, who’d gone back to looking down at his hands, and walked over to him.

He sat down next to him, “Hey Larkin, how are you doing?”

Larkin looked up, revealing red eyes and a tear streaked face, mucus hung partially out of his nose, “I just wish I could even hope he would be alright.”

Jack frowned, “What do you mean?”

Larkin’s eyes dropped, “Well, I already know he won’t make it. Noah didn’t, and he was the best of us.”

Jack looked to Dom, but he just shrugged in his confusion.

“Say Larkin, I know you probably don’t want to talk about it now, but Zach mentioned the party and Robert mentioned that you guys went somewhere afterwards. All I need is the location, please. We're trying to put a stop to whatever is going on."

Larkin's eyes went wide, "I doubt you can, but at least you're trying. Sure, we - uh - went to that old abandoned building. The one that kind of sits over the town. We'd been wondering if there was anything left, so we explored it."

"Which building Larkin."

"The old one with all the rumors of being haunted, y'know? The old Lewis manor."

~ 3 ~

Jack's thoughts lingered on Larkin's words long after they left the school, his mind playing over the thoughts that were his childhood home. As he and Dom pulled out of Fairmont Secondary's parking lot, he couldn't help but gaze off towards the husk of a structure that stood over Magrath like an angry god. He shuddered and wondered - not for the first time - why it hadn't been destroyed since he'd burnt it down.

He blinked hard and narrowed his focus on the road as he drove, to where? He glanced over at Dom, but noticed that like himself, Dom was deep in thought.

Wanting to break the air of silence that had befallen them Jack spoke, "So, what's on your mind Dom?"

Dom looked over at him, taken aback by the normalcy of such a complex question. It was something he'd thrown out to Shannon numerous times over the years, yet, its impact had never been so apparent to him. It spoke not of menial matters, but matters that people often kept to themselves; ranging from the perverse to the benign.

He looked over to the Jack, who'd resumed looking out the windshield as he drove, "Honestly, man, I'm thinking about Trix. I'm kind of hurt that she didn't tell me she went to her first party. It's not even a big deal for her to do so, hell I'm glad she did! Remember the ones we went to when we were younger? I just... I wish she told me man. Hell, I sound like a clingy boyfriend and less like an uncle right now, don't I?"

Jack wasn't sure how to respond and again he found himself marveling at the way he'd built Dom up in his mind as an infallible deity in his mind of sorts. But Dom had emotions, valid emotions, so Jack needed to be there for his friend.

"She probably didn't tell you because you're a cop, I'm sure it has nothing to do with you and more to do with your profession. Legally, you would have been obligated to stop the party from continuing knowing there were minors drinking, correct?"

Dom nodded and his face started clearing, "But she could have told me after, couldn't she?"

Jack shook his head, "I don't think so, whatever those kids found at my old home was enough to scare them into secrecy. Even after one of them died."

Jack shuddered, Larkin said it was haunted… no. That couldn't be right. A vivid image of the little girl sprung up in his mind. Though this time it caused his stomach to knot and twist as fear set in the pit of his stomach. Fearing he was about to vomit; he pulled the car over to the edge of the road and put it in park.

As Jack hyperventilated, Dom stared at him with concern, "What the hell? What's wrong Jack?"

It took a while for him to calm himself enough to speak, the thoughts of having to face the very thing he tried to conceal in flames tore pieces of him away with every passing second. The fear that overcame him was so pure and so intense, his entire body began to break out in a cold sweat, as though that would provide a suitable defense from his own mind. Eventually though, he was able to slow down his breathing and get himself back under control.

Finally, he met Dom's gaze, "Given what Larkin told me, I don't think it can wait. I have to tell you the story of my past, I need to get this out in the open, holding it inside of me is killing me."

Dom nodded slowly, "alright, we can go back to the precinct-"

Jack cut him off, "no, not the precinct. Let's go grab a coffee or something and talk it over there."

Dom eyed him warily, but Jack didn't notice, his mind was too busy running through the mere prospect of spilling his closest guarded story, the one that had caused him so much pain and suffering over the years. The one that made him leave Magrath nearly ten years ago. The one that sometimes made him wake up mid scream with tears running down his face; forcing him to reach for the bottle to drown out the pain all over again.

--

Jack pulled over outside of a small cafe on Magrath's market road. As he stepped out of his car, he noticed the faint gold lettering of a familiar storefront down the road. He repressed the wave of guilt that washed over him and continued into the shop. Now wasn't the time to go down there - he saw Dom walking towards the shop as well - no, now was the time to dig up old wounds and tear them open.

They stepped into the cafe and walked up to the cashier, each of them ordering a large black coffee; standing in silence as the barista went about preparing their drinks.

With their coffees in hand, they found a seat by the window, Jack stared down at the cup as the steam billowed upwards from it. Jack closed his eyes and thought for a second before opening them back up and looking into Dom's eyes.

It was time to relive the past he'd fought so hard to forget.

Chapter 6: Memories

~ 1 ~

Jack's mind wandered back to the month of October in the year 2005. He recalled the way the snow came early that year, falling delicately from the clouds like wings from angels. He remembered the way the snow had already been plowed into banks that stood like guardrails on the sides of the road, the tall mountains that stood resolutely on resident's lawns formed in the evenings as they shoveled their walkways. And though it was close to hallows eve, the citizens of Magrath opted to string lights of color from their homes; turning Magrath into a winter wonderland months before St. Nicholas was due to make an appearance.

Standing outside, he admired the way the snow fell under the streetlamps, cascading gently through the night sky like fireflies, illuminating the air around him. The world was calm and the streets quiet, no cars, trucks, or residents wandered down the road at that hour. That was something for which he was glad.

As he stood there under the streetlamp, he could feel the faintest of smiles creeping its way up his face, and for a moment, if only one, he forgot the dismal home life he'd walked away from that night. But it wouldn't be long before the memories would come rushing back; grim reminders of the life he lived always did.

He sighed and turned towards Emma's house, trundling up the familiar walkway to the comforting home that was cloaked in the falling snow. Yellow light spilled out from the front facing windows, pouring gold through the night, filling his mind with thoughts of times from his youth. Better times from before life had gone so awry. With that, his smile faded, and he climbed the stairs to Emma's front door.

He knocked three times and just as he was going in for the fourth, the door swung open and he was greeted by her smiling freckled face and a wave of warmth as the inside heat braved its escape into the cold world outside.

She smiled warmly, "hey mister, you missing? You must be cold, wanna come inside?"

She winked and Jack's heart fluttered. He crossed the threshold into her house. He wrapped her tightly in a hug that she reciprocated in kind, entangling herself with him. He breathed in and held her close, not daring to let go for fear she'd drift away.

After several minutes, Emma broke off the hug, concern lining her eyes. She grabbed his hands in hers and looked into his eyes, as though divining the truth from within them. He struggled to keep himself from crying; he felt helpless to his situation and didn't want to burden her with something she couldn't fix.

Her voice came out shaky as the words flowed from her, "Babe? What's wrong? Did it happen again?"

He smiled weakly in a vain attempt to make everything appear alright, but the tears began to trickle gently down his face; dripping from his chin onto the indifferent ground below. The cold pouring in from outside cooled the wet spots on his face, causing his cheeks to sting even more. Silence encroached on them as they stood in the doorway, wrapped in each other's arms, filling the intangible space growing between them. Jack detached from Emma and moved his hand slowly to the top of his shoulder, wincing as his hand ran over the spot that until recently had been stinging. Not the superficial sting of a slap or a punch. No, this was the sting of the mind and of the soul as well. The type of injury that could only be placed on by someone in a position of authority, someone who he had grown to respect and love over the years. Some who until recently had been a loving and caring man. His very own father.

Jack's control over his facial muscles slipped momentarily and he found himself unable to hold back the barrage of tears that began to work their way forth; bringing on a torrent of sobs. His shoulders sagged and cast his eyes downwards as the sobs racked his chest.

Emma swung her arms around him once more, "Shush. It's okay now Jack, I've got you now. You're safe. You're always safe in my arms."

After some time, Jack pulled back and looked at her, noting the tears running lines down her face, glistening in the faint light that leaked out from the room behind her. Her makeup began to run in streaks down her face, creating charcoal lines down towards her chin. He thought about the normalcy of this seemingly endless ritual, it was one they'd done numerous times over the past several months. And though it brought them closer, it also made him dependent on her. For in her arms he felt safe. In her arms he felt as though his father couldn't reach him. And in the nights spent wrapped in her arms, the walls couldn't speak to him in the silence of night, they couldn't whisper of the atrocities committed by his father. They couldn't remind him of the things his father had done and the things he would do. In her arms, Jack felt as though he was in a world that was free of his father.

He stared into Emma's eyes, his voice coming out shaky, "I can't keep this up Em. He pushes all his shortcomings and insecurities onto me. Fuck, maybe I deserve it, maybe I should 'turn the other cheek,' take the beatings with a smile or even thank him for them. But the screaming Em. My god, the screaming. I can't handle the damn screams anymore. I don't know exactly what he's doing, but I know he must be doing some awful things, things that I have the power to stop. Tomorrow I'm going to walk down to the precinct and talk to Hamlon, I'll tell him everything my father has done. He'll be able to do something."

Emma nodded weakly at Jack, though she didn't say anything. She knew he wasn't looking for any verbal reaffirmation of his future actions, he just wanted her to listen. She had become something of an emotional lightning rod for him, he'd soundboard off her and allow the emotions to pour from him to her - the pain, the guilt, the shame - all of it was shared with her.

--

They entered the house and Emma seized Jack's hand in hers. He looked at her curiously, about to speak, but Emma raised a single finger to his lips, effectively silencing him. Though her parents had long since gone to bed, she lead Jack silently to her bedroom, so as not to disturb the quiet air of the small house.

He followed her up the stairs, watching intently as her hips swayed with each step, his mind slowly beginning to narrow on a singular objective. When they finally reached her room, she turned to look at him and he pulled her in, unable to quell the growing desire.

She loosed a surprised squeak as he unexpectedly pressed his lips against hers; but her lips quickly softened and she began to return his kiss, her eyes fluttering closed. His hands slid over her shirt, tracing the curves of her sides and back with his palms while she placed one hand on his chest and clawed his back with the other.

She bit his lip and he moaned appreciatively before picking her up and walking her over to the bed. He laid her down, and kissed his way from her lips, to her jaw, down her neck and slowly down the front of her shirt. He raised the hem and slowly kissed his way back up, kissing and licking her skin as he gently removed her shirt. When the shirt was finally brought over her head and cast to the side he pulled back slightly and looked into her eyes, heart thudding vigorously in his chest as he gazed into the pools of liquid chocolate.

He found himself entranced, not only by her body, but the radiating love that flowed between them. The coalescing companionship they'd formed in the darkest part of his life. In the darkness of his father's shadow, he'd found love, he'd found a light that couldn't be quelled, couldn't be vanquished so long as she was there. He'd found the very thing that he needed to face each day and fight for survival. In the darkness of life, he'd found his own personal sun. He found Emma.

--

They spent the next few hours making love, entangling their bodies and souls into one. Their bond solidified further than it had ever before that night, the lust that fueled their actions was spurred by their mutual admiration and love for one another. Although it wasn't their first time sharing the same bed or having sex in general, it was one of the most passionate, raw and emotional experiences either of them had ever had up until that moment.

Their desire allowed them to blossom, to become one, and embrace the primal urges that had been dormant within them; growing deep inside. It was with each other that they attained something more; something pure, something beautiful, and something meaningful.

As Jack lay there, wrapped in Emma's tender embrace, his mind lingered over the events of the day and he vowed; not only to himself, but also to Emma that he would do anything for her. The vow, although innocent in nature, spurred a great deal of pain for them over the coming weeks. Unbeknownst to them, the dark wave that had been washing over the town of Magrath was finally coming to a crest and it wouldn't be long before it all came crashing down; changing their world forever.

~ 2 ~

Jack awoke to the warm yellow glow of the morning sun streaming through the bedside window; undisturbed by the thin white curtain that hung loosely over it. He rolled over and wiped the sleep from his eyes, trying to remember the events of the previous night as the dreams slowly flitted from his memory as consciousness forced its way back in. Jack's eyes fell on Emma lying next to him and smiled as he remembered the events of the evening.

Jack scooted closer to her, marveling how even with her hair splayed out over the pillow and a small trail of drool spilling from the corner of her mouth; she was still the most beautiful girl he'd ever seen. Smiling, he wrapped his arms around her and pulled her in tightly. She slowly stirred back into consciousness and looked at him through narrow eyes. After rubbing the sleep from the corners, she smiled delicately, exposing just the faintest bit of her white teeth beyond her upper lip. Jack leaned in and kissed her gently, breathing in her scent as he got close. He realized that even though it was laced with sweat from last night's activities, it still breathed heaven into his lungs.

He broke off the kiss, smiling. Emma's brown eyes widened, "What is it mister?"

Jack met her curious gaze with one of unfathomable affection, one that resonated with the feelings bubbling around inside of his chest, "Em, let's run away from here, get out of this town and start over. Just you and me, let's go. Let's be free. Em, you're all I'll ever need."

She smiled tiredly and tried to say something else, though it came out as indiscernible babble, which to Jack, sounded awfully suggestive. She tried once more, and again; Jack could just barely hear it. It appeared as though that was enough for her as she placed her head down on the pillow and promptly fell back asleep. Jack smiled and rolled onto his back, staring up at the ceiling. He remained awake, however, for he was resigned to the statement he'd made the night before on Emma's doorstep. Today, I'll tell the police about my father, the people he keeps in the house against their will and the secrets contained within our large, intimidating manor.

He had no issue leaving Emma's house, he sneaked out multiple times over the several months they had been dating and had since reduced the strenuous activity of scaling out her bedroom window to a science. He would open the window and position himself with both feet on the sill, then he would rocket himself towards a branch that jutted out from the tree just next to the house and catch himself with both hands. As he would only be dangling a mere couple feet off the ground, he would then gently drop from the branch and land gracefully on the ground below.

There was rarely any issue with getting out of the yard. Luckily, Emma's room was on the back of the house, and past the fence was a small alley by which Jack could use to get back onto the main road without passing any of the house's other windows. Though on this day, there was a thin layer of snow covering the backyard, it proved little significance. There was a small path that Emma's father had undoubtedly shoveled that morning leading from the door to the back gate. Jack thought about the best course of action for the scenario and then jumped for the outstretched branch. He nimbly passed his hands to the other side of the branch, using momentum to lessen the weight on his grip, then swung his legs out to land on the path before him. He smiled and walked out of the yard with little issue.

There would be issues however, with returning home. His father never worked, not in the past few years anyway. Though they lived in the largest house in the town; the manor that overlooked all of Magrath, there was little need for his family to work. The Lewis family had helped to build the town; thus, they owned a significant portion of the properties within the city limits. The shopkeepers would pay a small rent each month and they would allow them to conduct their business. His mother worked a little florist shop in the market as a 'hobby', though Jack had always suspected it was to get away from the drunken stupor his father was always in.

At one point, years ago, his father had been a rather active community figure. He would help run the library, run charity events and even facilitate meetings with the leaders of the other towns. In some capacity, he was the Mayor, though that was never officially declared. However, slowly, he began drinking more, and that's when the abuse started. He'd slowly devolved from the loving center of the community to an abusive father who'd take any chance he could to kidnap some hitchhiking passer-by and lock them somewhere in the house. At times, when the screaming became too much, Jack had set out to find them, though he never got closer than his parent's bedroom before his father would cut him off. He'd reek of alcohol and even though he'd smile at Jack, Jack could see the malice hidden behind it, the urge to cause harm to anyone and everyone he could. This would always cause Jack to turn and walk the other way, trembling with fear.

Jack recalled this as he slowly approached the house. Though, to call it a house would be paramount to calling a great Dane a poodle. No, the house was a mansion. It boasted two full levels, each sporting numerous windows from which to see the surrounding land. The entrance was covered by a large overhang held aloft by four thick wooden pillars and from above that overhang, one could see the breathtaking view of the city sprawled out before them. The house loomed over the town like an idol, imposing its presence and the social status of its occupants to an otherwise indifferent audience.

Jack took hesitant steps up the stone brick path, head hanging low as he thought of his father's abuse from the day prior, a tear began to trickle slowly down his face. He turned his head skyward - as though to use gravity to hold the tears in - and noticed a lone black cloud floating in the sky above.

It was a colder morning than usual, and Jack found himself shivering. Though he was unsure if it was a result of the chill that clung to the air, or the trepidation that was working its way through his bloodstream. He reached the threshold to the house, a thought flickering by momentarily as he weighed the grandeur of the home, what an absurd waste of money.

With that, Jack turned the knob and pushed open the door, stepping into the empty foyer of his absurdly large home. He was unsurprised to find the house silent, it wasn't atypical of the time of day, though, he was certain his father had already drunk himself into a stupor. On a typical day, he'd finish a two-six of rye by himself, starting early in the morning and finishing late at night when he finally passed out on whatever unlucky piece of furniture he could find.

His mother would undoubtedly be at the flower shop. Those days she opened it at six in the morning and closed at ten at night, always managing to be home when Jack's father was blacked out. She was home less and less; which meant less intervening in his father's "punishments" and less worrying over the bruises and cuts he'd receive.

Jack shook his head and trundled down the familiar hallway, past the preposterous amount of room, trudging his feet along the rich cotton of the carpet. He kept his head low as he continued on his path towards his bedroom, not wanting to draw any attention from his father who - if he was unlucky - would be in his study. Though as Jack began to pass the open French doors a sigh halted him.

His father stood in front of the ornate fireplace. The fire danced off the glass tumbler in his hand, illuminating the glistening ice that twirled around in an amber liquid. He brought the glass to his mouth and swallowed the contents in a couple gulps, sighing once when he finally brought the glass away. He was wearing a plush black velvet bathrobe and the front swung open as he turned, revealing the jeans and black top he was wearing underneath.

Jack didn't dare move as his father laid his eyes on him, "now what am I going to do with you Jackie? My little disappointment of a son. Now, this morning I was walking by your room and decided I would poke my head in to see if you were actually in. Imagine my surprise when I find your bed empty. Where were you last night Jack? Don't you dare lie to your dear old daddy?"

Jack shuddered. He never liked being inspected so finely by his father, it unnerved him. Any confidence he'd gained by spending the night with Emma had vanished under the skewering glare of his father; replaced by a fear of knowing exactly where this conversation would eventually end. He realized he'd have to pick his words carefully, although there would be no way to prevent the oncoming blows, he could at least, he wagered, soften them, if even just a little.

Jack's tongue felt too heavy, though he managed with a shaky voice, "I was at Emma's, sir."

A flash of rage crossed his father's face and he scoffed distastefully. "That harlot? Jackie, we've been through this how many times now? We are of a superior blood to those peasants that mill about the town like ants. We cannot afford to taint our bloodline by mixing with the common rabble! Surely by now I have beaten at least that much into, you insufferable child!" He paused, as though thinking of a punishment, "Now, seeing as our family has overseen this town for generations, we must keep our blood clean, for we are cut of a different, better cloth. I will not tell you again; stop associating with the peasant girl, or do I need to remind you of what happened to that last girl you use to bring around here?"

Jack paled as his mind swarmed with memories, memories of falling to his knees in front of his father. The memories surged in his head, even as his father withdrew his belt and stalked over to him, crossing the space in seconds. They rendered him defenseless as his father struck him across the face with the belt, causing tears to well up in his eyes and obscure his vision. Even as his father struck him across the jaw and sent him sprawling onto the floor, they caused him to freeze up. As his father climbed on top of him and began hammering blows into his head, the memories kept him subdued, prevented him from moving, well into the time when the darkness began to encroach on his vision, and he was rendered unconscious.

~ 3 ~

Jack struggled out of unconsciousness several hours later. Flailing, he noticed two things. The first was that he had somehow ended up in his own bed, the second was that there was an ungodly pain in his head. He opened his eyes to the darkness of his room and frowned, surely it should still be bright outside. A casual glance to his left revealed that the curtains had been drawn over the window; what little light came through shone only around the border of the curtains, giving it a faint aura of a secret entrance, or exit.

Jack's eyes scanned the rest of the room, struggling to make out any shapes in the dim light that barely penetrated the overwhelming darkness of the space. On his nightstand there was a simple note, handwritten in his father's elegant scrawl.

You deserved it Jackie

Tears rolled down Jack's bruised cheeks as he read his father's message. Over the years he'd been beaten multiple times by his father, though he reckoned this was one of the worst. As he read the note once more, he sighed a long breath of resignation, it's time to report that bastard.

--

It took Jack longer than anticipated to leave his bed. The pounding in his head only got worse as he worked himself into a sitting position. With the pressure building in his head, he bided his time, staying seated until he was finally able to breathe evenly, and the pressure was tolerable. He held his breath as he rose to his unsteady feet, though he felt nauseous as the world tilted around him. Losing his balance, he fell back onto his bed in a painful heap, knocking his elbow on his nightstand as he fell. He cried out in pain, due to both the now screaming pressure in his head and the pulsating agony that radiated from his elbow down his forearm.

Clenching his teeth, he tried again, this time standing for a slightly shorter amount of time before the world turned black and he fell back onto his bed. Frustration growing, he tried a third time, and this time he was able to reach out and steady himself against the wall as the darkness washed over him and then faded.

He nodded in appreciation for the slight victory, then worked his way down the hall toward the bathroom. He pushed open the thin wooden door and stepped inside, headed for the small medicine cabinet they kept above the sink. He pushed it open and smiled as he reached in and took out the small bottle of Aspirin contained within. He slowly took three out and popped them in his mouth, grimacing as he chewed the bitter pills into a fine paste. He found they worked quicker that way and had been chewing them since the beatings began.

He shut his eyes against the wave of pain that passed through his head as he chewed and only opened them when the pain eventually began to fade. He smiled at himself in the mirror, taking note of the flecks of blood that dotted his teeth and gums, realizing his father had done more damage than he'd anticipated.

He blinked hard and turned for the door, walking through the quiet hallways of his large, empty home. He stopped, only once, to grab his jacket on the way to the entryway. Without knowing what awaited him at the precinct, he stepped out into the cold, ready to reveal his father's crimes against humanity and use his own face as proof if he had to.

--

Within the hour, Jack was standing outside of the brick building that was Magrath police department's sole precinct. His mind had been running over the various conversations he could have with the detective and thus, his feet carried him through the familiar streets on autopilot, working his legs while he worked the scenarios.

He walked through the front doors of the precinct, shaking nervously as he considered what he would say to the officer manning the front desk. He looked up and eyed Jack, a young man, only slightly older than Jack, maybe by five or so years by the name of Hanson. Jack regarded him and approached the desk.

"Hi - uh - would I be able to speak to someone, perhaps a detective?"

Hanson raised an eyebrow, "for what purpose?"

Jack's eyes flickered from him to the hallway that he knew would lead to the bullpen, "uh - I know a few things about the people who went missing in Magrath over the past couple years. I know who took them."

Hanson's eyes widened, "if you're serious then I definitely thing that Detective Hamlon will want to speak to you. I'll page him right now."

Jack watched as officer Hanson plucked the telephone off the desk and quickly typed in a three-digit number; undoubtedly Hamlon's extension. He caught Jack staring as he waited and Jack bashfully looked away, instead moving his eyes over the posters that lined the walls. He saw one with a cartoon officer pointing towards whoever happened to stand right in front of it, ONLY YOU CAN STOP CRIME. Jack nodded appreciatively, thinking it was a sign that he was doing the right thing, that things would work out for him and everything would be okay once his father was taken care of.

"Hello? Detective Hamlon? Yes, this is Officer Hanson from the front desk."

Jack looked over to see Hanson now speaking on the phone to who could only be presumed as officer Hamlon, "I have someone here who thinks he knows something about the missing people. Yeah. Yeah. His name? One second."

Hanson looked over to Jack, well aware that Jack had been listening in, "Jack Lewis sir"

Hanson continued, "He says his name is Jack Lewis. Yeah. Most likely. Okay. Yeah I'll send him in."

He placed the phone back on the receiver and once again looked up to Jack, “he’ll see you. Follow me”

Jack followed Officer Hanson down the precinct’s hallway, past the filing room and bull pen, and into one of the small interrogation rooms. He shot Hanson a quizzical glance, but Hanson just shrugged and muttered something about offices before turning and walking back to the door.

He turned before leaving and met Jack’s gaze, “look, kid. I don’t know exactly what you’re expecting Hamlon to do… but don’t get your hopes up.”

Jack’s eyes widened in confusion, “what do you mean?”

Hanson just shook his head sadly, “you’ll see.”

With that, Jack was alone in the room, seated at the metal table, staring at his reflection in the two-way mirror. Though the door had been left open, Jack suddenly felt like a prisoner in that room. The claustrophobic walls and bright fluorescent bulb overhead gave it the air of a cage and within moments, Jack found himself shifting anxiously in his seat.

He heard heavy footsteps slowly approaching and turned apprehensively towards the door, eager to see what Detective Hamlon looked like and nervous as to his reaction to the information Jack had to tell him. He furrowed his brow as a large, pot-bellied man rounded the corner, waddling slowly; this was not what he expected Hamlon to look like.

He was wearing a baggily fitted yellow button up shirt that was tucked into tight blue slacks held up by suspenders, his thin grey hair was swept back over his liver spotted scalp and was held in place by what looked to be a mixture of sweat and oil. He smiled a gummy smiled at Jack as he entered the room that caused Jack to squirm in his skin.

Instead of taking the seat opposite of Jack, Hamlon walked to the edge of the table and placed his left buttocks on it, angling himself towards Jack in a way that caused his rolls of fat to twist and bubble. He eyed Jack studiously, as though trying to read Jack’s mind.

Jack returned a flimsy smile, “Hi, sir, I’m Jack Lewis.”

Hamlon belted a hearty laugh, "Oh yes son, I know who you are. Does your daddy know you're here?"

Jack's eyes widened; he supposed he should have known that the police would already know his father's name as they surely would have been looking into him, though their name was a common enough one that Hamlon shouldn't have known about Jack.

"Uh no sir, that's actually why I came to talk to you."

Hamlon nodded, "I see. Yes, Officer Hanson - good boy that one - mentioned you knew something of the people who have gone missing over the past couple years."

Jack nodded, feeling a little apprehensive about divulging things, yet he soldiered on, "Yes sir, that's right. I know where they are and who took them."

Hamlon's face turned to one of thought, and for a moment Jack considered he was thinking of the potential perpetrators, "I suppose you're going to tell me that it was your dad that did it?"

Jack nodded excitedly, "Yes! I hear the screaming at night and he's always home, so it only makes sense."

Hamlon nodded again, "I suppose that makes sense, so what? You want me to get a team together, go storm your house, save the people and convict your father on multiple counts of kidnapping, intent to cause harm and potential other crimes against humanity?"

Jack nodded again, though, he detected a vague amount of condescension from Hamlon, "yes sir. They need to be saved. They -"

Hamlon cut him off, holding up one thick greasy finger. A disconcerting smile rippled across his face, causing his several chins to jiggle. He moved his other hand to wipe off the drool that had begun to dribble from the corner of his mouth.

Condescension leaked into his words, "Jackie boy, you really ought to keep your nose out of your daddy's business. And to make up such lies! I could write you up for defamation of character if you go around spouting such nonsense. He does so much for the community, it would be a shame if the public began to think he was some sort of a monster."

Jack's mouth hung open, disbelief coursing through his body, "Look at my face! Where do you think these bruises came from? He did this to me this morning!"

Hamlon smiled wider, "more lies Jack? Is he a child abuser or a kidnapper? Which is it son? I think you need to get your stories straight."

Jack began to grow furious, "What do you mean! I have proof that the asshole beats me, and you sit there smiling like a pompous sack of shit!"

Hamlon's brow furrowed, "You need to mind your manners boy. Your father is a good man and I will not tolerate your beratement of him."

Jack was dumbfounded. The man who'd at one point sworn an oath to protect and serve; to put the needs of the public before his own was defending his father? Jack felt like he'd been struck, not like the physical blows of his father, but the blows one sustains when the innocent veil of childhood gets peeled back and you see the world for the way it is. Jack saw the corruptness of the Magrath police department, a force that for the longest time he'd deemed an immovable object of justice. Never in his life had he even considered that his father would have them under his thumb. Jack realized then why no one had ever turned up at Jack's house looking for his father.

"He's paying you all off, isn't he?"

Hamlon's smile grew wider, "Your father makes sizable donations to the force. He ensures that we all live a life of comfort so long as he's allowed to conduct his business in private. It's a don't ask, don't tell sort of relationship. If his deeds end up being nefarious, we can always look the other way."

Jack stood up and backed away from Hamlon, "you're all dirty cops!"

Hamlon's smile vanished entirely as his face took on an angry shade of red, "you don't know shit about the world kid. You think everything's all sunshine and rainbows? Well it may be for you. You'll get life handed to you on a silver platter and so much money you'll wipe your ass with it. You see, us normal people live with something called class struggle, in other words, we have more debt than money and we eventually find ourselves swimming in it and eventually drowning in it. Everything has a goddamn price in this world, you take your beatings for a financially stable future, we look the other way from time to time so we can afford things like food and electricity. So, you sit your ignorant ass down and listen you ignorant shit."

Put off by his sudden outburst, Jack slowly pulled the metal chair back towards him and sat down in it without saying a word, wondering how Hamlon had ended up at this point.

Hamlon continued, "kid, I wish there was something I could do. I really do. It doesn't make me feel any better knowing the kind of stuff your dad gets up to. I see your bruised and beaten face and I want to run up to that fancy house of yours and bash his face in just as badly. But I can't. He owns this town. There isn't a single piece of land in Magrath that doesn't have the Lewis name stamped on its deed at one time or another. Your father knows that and he fucking revels in the fact that he can strut around town untouchable. His word is law here. There's nothing we can do. Even if we tried to do something, anything, he'd have us killed. He has people all over this town on payroll, keeping tabs on 'persons of interest'. You're at the top of that list kid."

Hamlon sighed, moving from the edge of the table to the second metal chair, then slumped into it. For a moment, Jack didn't see him as the corrupt, grotesque man he'd seen before. He saw him as someone who at one point or another had signed up to make a difference in the world; set out to make it a better place but came up short. The system ate him up and shit him out and he was defeated, beaten long ago. There was nothing he could do for Jack, despite his desire, and he understood that now. This understanding led to a realization in Jack: that he was the only person that would be able to stop his father. He was the only person that could end the town's suffering at his father's hands.

Having received all the answers he didn't know he needed, and being nowhere closer to seeing his father behind bars, Jack stood, turned for the doorway, and slid on his jacket. Detective Hamlon followed suit, rising from his chair and resting his thumbs under his suspenders. He extended his thick, slab-like hand towards Jack, who took it and shook it sadly. Jack turned and walked from the room, back out into the hallway that ran down the side of the precinct. As he began walking, he noticed that Hamlon was escorting him out.

When he finally left the building and stepped into the cool October air, happy to be free of the oppressive walls of the precinct, he turned back to Hamlon, "thank you. I know you would have done something if you could have."

At first, Hamlon said nothing and simply stared into the horizon, watching the clouds roll across. "You may be right about that, but listen, Jack. There's a storm rolling in on Magrath. Please, just be ready for when it hits."

Jack nodded as he watched Hamlon turn and walk back into the precinct. He knew there was a storm coming in more ways than one. He wasn't sure how he would stop his father, but he was sure he would find a way.

Jack began walking, though he focused little on the action itself. His mind was enraptured by the coalescing greys and blacks that clashed vehemently amidst the sky, flashing streaks of light against the black backdrop of the encroaching storm. Marking a path of inclement weather over the town he'd called home for so many of his formative years. He smiled dryly as he made his way down the path, seemingly floating above his body as he observed the chaos erupting in his world around him. He needed to see Emma, needed to wrap her in his arms and allow her to subdue the emotions bubbling rampantly in his mind; she would be the one to break him free of the clutches of the clouds in his mind. The clouds that wrapped around all reason and thoughts, leaving one sole objective, I need to get the hell out of Magrath.

As his mind struggled to free itself of that thought, the lingering realization of Emma's voice thundered through his head with stunning clarity and Jack knew then what she'd said on that morning so long ago. Before the phone call that brought him back, before he'd ever stepped foot back in the dreary town of Magrath, "Jack, let's just run away."

Jack nodded; he could leave his father behind; leave this whole shitshow in his rear-view. Run. He could speak truth to the wind as he put rubber on the road, and he realized. He could leave the whole town behind; so long as he had Emma by his side.

~ 4 ~

Jack's subconscious guided him down the lonely Magrath streets towards Emma's house, taking him over cracked and well-maintained sidewalks alike, carrying him towards his sole destination. His mind was clouded, still focused on escaping the confines of the city limits, though more narrowly focused on retrieving Emma first.

He stepped over the mutilated carcass of dead crow that had met its unfortunate end at the hands - or paws - of one of the neighborhood's dogs. He smiled sadly at the corpse as he passed, as though it understood the gravity of his situation and the weight of the choices he had yet to make. This would not be an easy task for him, for asking someone who'd only just come to be legally recognized as an adult to pack up and move was not an easy task in the slightest. He had no idea of the level of responsibilities that he would face or the struggles he would have while trying to find work or a place to stay; though he figured with Emma, it would be easy enough. Straightforward enough.

As if on instinct, he moved his eyes to Emma's front door as he turned the corner onto her street and frowned. It appeared to be open. Rushing now, fearing something had gone horribly wrong, he closed the distance between himself and the door, wincing slightly as the blood began to rush in his concussed head.

As he peered through the screen door, he noticed two things. The first was that the inner metal core door appeared to have been pushed through the latching mechanism of the lock, and the second was that there was a small red speck on the white tile of the entryway.

Jack flung open the flimsy screen door and stepped inside, bending down to inspect the fleck of red he had seen from the outside. He rubbed a finger through it and felt his heart drop as it smeared a semi-congealed crimson paste across the tile. Blood.

Heart pounding, he called out into the empty house, "Em?"

When no response was issued, he called out a little louder, "Emma?"

When no one answered the second time, he dismissed any notions of intrusion or mannerisms and flung himself up the stairs towards her room; barely noticing the throbbing in his head as he reached the upper level. There he noticed several more of the red dots marking the carpet and his panic turned into hysteria.

On the verge of tears, he tried once more, “Emma!? Come out babe, this isn’t funny.”

The house remained silent, indifferent to his pleas for his absent girlfriend. He surged towards her room and froze when he threw open the bedroom door.

Spattered along the wall with a layer of viscous crimson blood, was a single word. “Harlot” Surrounding it was a smattering of more blood and the tatters of one of Emma’s favorite shirts.

Shaking, he read the word repeatedly; his mind registering the one person who could have done this. His father. With his panic turning to rage, he backed out of the room and vacated the house, leaving behind the wall, the ripped shirt, and the ill spotted bloodstains as he went to find his girlfriend.

--

Years later, Jack still wouldn’t be able to recall the events between the time when he left Emma’s and the time he spent running back to the manor. The blind emotions eclipsed all rational thought as he closed that distance, focused solely on getting home.

He threw open the doors to the absurdly large house, with lungs stinging and legs burning from his sprint over, though those feelings didn’t bother him. No, what he was focused on; what was driving him was the rage that spurred him onwards and an undying desire to save Emma from the monstrous clutches of his father.

He ran down the hallways, searching rooms and turning over furniture in search of a secret hatch to another room, a hidden entrance to the area his father had kept all the prior captives. He looked for signs that could give away where he’d brought her, yet found nothing, no traces of blood, no dirt, no proverbial breadcrumbs of any sort.

Eventually he found himself in his parent’s bedroom, flipping the mattress over in search of a secret entrance to a hidden room when his eyes flitted over to the walk-in closet. There, nestled in the depths of the white carpet was a single scarlet droplet, no larger than the head of a pin. From the way it glistened in the overhead light, Jack could tell that it was fresh.

He slowly approached the closet, to hide his presence from his father. He crossed foot over foot as he closed the short distance, homing in on the small droplet of Emma's blood that stained the carpet. His heart rate picked up the closer he got, as though building to a critical point. He closed his eyes and breathed deeply to calm himself, yet the effort proved fruitless.

When Jack finally entered the closet, he saw no path in which his father could have taken Emma, yet, he'd always been suspicious of his parent's bedroom and thought that there may be a hidden entry way somewhere in the room. Afterall, whenever he'd sought out his father's previous captives, his father would always stop him as he neared this very room. If there is one, it must be here.

Jack pushed aside his mother's dresses, looking for anything on the wall that could mark out a secret compartment or anything of the sort. Next, he moved to his father's suits, brushing his hand along the back wall as he pushed them off to the side. He paused as his fingertips brushed a small protrusion in the hardwood behind the suits. Curious, he moved his hand back to where he felt it, and sure enough, there was a small bump. He frowned and jutted his thumb into it, hearing a soft click before numerous mechanical whirrs filled the air around him. The wall panel began to slide smoothly over the floor and Jack took a step back, allowing it to pass. As the door shuddered to a halt he gazed down the dark staircase it had been concealing; leading down into a basement he never knew existed.

Jack stepped onto the first step leading down, wincing as the board creaked under his foot. He tried slowing his approach to conceal the groan of the old wood, yet as he went down step after step each board groaned loudly. At last, he saw the end of the staircase, though the thought of what end truly awaited him at the bottom caused his heart rate to increase once more.

The stairs opened to a large, empty room with walls of concrete. Suspended above by hanging sockets were small lightbulbs. They covered the small area in a faint incandescent glow. Using what little light they produced, Jack worked his way around the room, passing his eyes over the grey walls and cracked foundations. Anxious to find any trace of Emma, Jack began inspecting the small rooms, going from entryway to entryway.

Jack's ears picked up the faintest sound of whimpering coming from one of the rooms on the perpendicular wall and immediately began heading towards them, stepping over debris that seemed to have been pushed into the corner he was crossing. He frowned, but continued towards the sound of the noise; now barely able to hear the faint sound of his father's voice saying "harlot," and "peasant" or any string of the vilest words he could think of to describe the "lesser" class.

Fury growing in Jack's heart, he looked around frantically for a weapon of some sort and knelt to grab one of the thin pieces of lumber he'd stepped over to reach the doorway. He frowned as he held the long cylindrical object in his hand. The piece of wood felt too light, too smooth, it didn't feel like wood. Unable to make out the details in the dull yellow light, he raised the lumber towards the nearest bulb, nearly screaming as everything clicked into place.

The wood was too white, and not wood at all. Jack threw the bone back in the pile and shuddered all over, trying to push the gross feeling he was experiencing down lower in his mind. He nodded slowly to himself, realizing he would not have a weapon to fight his father with. His mind clicked several facts into place, and he realized the one way he could get close enough to his father without hurting Emma.

He stepped into the room, jaw set, and face twisted in anger, "Father, I thought you proclaimed she was a harlot, a peasant, common filth. You dare bring her into our home? What was it you told me this morning father?"

Emma's eyes widened as she saw him, though they had twisted in confusion as he started talking and by the time he'd finished, she was terrified. His father on the other hand only smiled. It was a stretched out, maniacal smile that didn't meet his eyes that were looking at the several bruises he'd left on Jack's face earlier that day.

Jack studied his father, noticing his bloodstained hands as one wrapped through Emma's hair and the other held a wicked blade close to her throat. His eyes were glazed over with alcoholic stupor that had washed over him. His father noticed Jack staring and only smiled wider. Jack swallowed and walked closer, until he could smell the alcohol that flowed off his father's breaths.

The penetrating smell of whiskey rolled off his slurred words, "Ahh Jackie, how nice of you to come around, my boy. It's good to see you finally embracing your heritage and taking it seriously. Do you want this one? I figure you could hogtie her and keep her in the basement as your own personal… slave. If you catch my meaning. I mean, after all, she is nothing but swine." He traced the tip of the blade down Emma's cheek, "She is a pretty one, though… in any matter, swine was made for the reaping of man. Was it not boy?"

Jack fought down the rage boiling inside of him and reached out for the knife, "I should end her here to remove the temptation of breeding with a commoner."

His father nodded delightedly, "but of course my child."

Jack reached out and plucked the knife from his father's outstretched hand, feeling the comfortable weight of it as he turned his eyes back to Emma. The tears cascaded from her eyes, dripping from her chin and hitting the ground with a quiet plip. Plip. Plip.

Jack pressed the knife's blade to her throat and choked back the tears welling up in his own eyes. He closed his eyes and exhaled, when he opened them again, his teeth were clenched.

He whirled and attempted to stab his father, who stepped back in anticipation of the attack. He tried again, but this time his father reached out and caught his wrist, stopping the motion outright.

He laughed darkly, "Do you think I'm an idiot? Did you honestly believe that I wouldn't have known that you've been plowing this fucking pig for the past few months? There was no way you would even try to kill her Jack; you don't have the balls. Get a grip kid, you're nothing but a wasted failure."

He reached out and snatched the knife from Jack's hands, then turned and began stalking towards Emma, who lay sobbing on the ground in fear and pain. She noticed him approaching and began to wiggle away from him, pushing off the ground with her bound feet and hands. He laughed maniacally and pursued her while Jack stood there dumbly, frozen by his father's words and the futility of trying to stop him. It was only when Emma's gag slipped out that Jack was spurred into action.

"Jack! Help!"

Jack turned and charged his father, tackling him moments before he reached Emma. They flew onto the ground and the blade skittered away, far out of reach.

Jack hit the ground hard, though his father managed to catch himself in a roll and rose quickly back to his feet, leaving Jack able to do nothing but watch as he contemplated his next move.

Instead of chasing the blade, Jack's father stood up and began slipping his belt off, catching Jack off guard. He stood there, unsure of the best way to proceed as his father pulled the belt into a loop, holding the buckle and tail end in one hand. He snapped it several times, taunting Jack as he inched backwards slowly.

Jack slowly rose to his feet as his father spat venom into his words, "Come on Jackie, you know this belt well. You want it don't you?"

Jack felt the rage course through his veins and strengthen his muscles, as he began to charge at his father. His father laughed as he readied himself to strike Jack down with the buckle of his belt. Though as he began the short arc that would undoubtedly connect the buckled with Jack's temple, Jack reached out and grabbed his wrist, halting the motion almost entirely. The buckle whipped around given its new pivot point and smashed Jack's father under the jaw, causing him to cry out in pain.

Using his father's momentary disorientation, he gripped the belt with both his hands and ripped it free of his father's vice-like grip.

He brought it down twice on the back of his father's head, then pushed him onto his knees. While his father wobbled, Jack walked around him and looped the belt around his neck, quickly slipping the tail through the buckle. His father's eyes shot open and he began to resist as Jack fought to tighten the belt around his neck. Jack pulled tighter and tighter, until he realized he was lifting his father off the ground. His father's legs kicked out as they struggled to find purchase on the ground, though they kept slipping.

Jack pulled tighter and tighter, hearing his father's gurgled attempts to free himself from the restricting tightness of the belt. Jack persisted and continued to pull, even as his father began to go slack and stopped restraining as much. Even as his meager claws at his neck were rendered to pitiful swipes; and even after he finally went still. Several minutes passed before Jack let go of the belt and looked down at his father's face. It was hideously bloated and purple, his eyes bulged out of the sockets. Jack had killed his father, and freed Magrath from the wrath of his father.

In the years following, Jack would often see that final image of his father whenever he'd close his eyes. The grim reminder of the patricide committed in the basement of his own home. Did he regret it? Of course not, though the image would still haunt him.

Jack knelt and loosened the belt around his father's now clammy neck, then removed it entirely. He threw the belt to the side as he walked over towards where Emma lay sobbing on the floor and knelt next to her.

"Shush my love, it's alright now… I … I killed him."

Her eyes widened at his admission, though she said nothing as he worked about untying her bonds.

A thin gash ran up the length of her thigh, and Jack had no doubt that it was where all the blood he had seen had come from. It didn't appear to be deep, however, and Jack was relieved to see that the wound had already started to clot. He helped her onto her feet and together they walked outside into the evening light and Jack noticed that the dark clouds over Magrath had been replaced with softer ones.

He helped Emma into his father's Mercedes and walked around the car, breathing deeply. He looked down to his hand as he reached for the handle.

It was shaking.

~ 5 ~

The following hours blurred by as Jack's mind went into autopilot. In the years following, he wouldn't be able to recall the short drive from the manor to the gas station, nor would he remember using his father's credit card to buy two large jerrycans. He wouldn't be entirely sure of where he was headed or what he was doing, but he would remember small things in the years to come.

He'd be able to recall the bright red of the jerry cans, and the metal nozzle poking into the opening of each of them. He'd recall the sloshing sound as the sharp scented liquid filled the spaces around him, reminding him of childhood days seated in the back of his parents' car waiting to go on another adventure.

He wouldn't cry though. For tears would come later, much later; when the memories had time to settle and the fog that clouded his mind that evening finally went away. He'd cry in the quiet moments, when he'd miss his family and the life he had when he was a child, before the abuse and pain. Though he wouldn't cry that night.

He didn't cry when they pulled back up to the Lewis manor. Each toting a large red jerry can full of gasoline. He didn't cry as the familiar scent filled his nose as the fluid splashed over the carpet, staining persian rugs and silk tapestries. He refused to cry.

He walked back through the house, leaving a trail of gasoline behind him as he met back with Emma at the door. She was standing, though keeping weight off her injured leg. She smiled wearily at him.

"Are you sure you want to do this?"

Jack heard his own voice flow out his mouth, "Yes, it's the only way. This house… too many evil things have happened here. It's best to just burn the whole thing down; forget about it. It needs to be destroyed."

Emma nodded as a small ball of flame curled up from between her fingers, she looked back to Jack and smiled once more as she dropped the bundle of matches onto the gasoline path. They watched the trail ignite, like a snake made of fire exploring its new habitat.

Jack tipped his head sadly to the loss of his childhood home and turned, assisting Emma once more into the passenger seat of the Mercedes. He met her eyes and smiled, knowing that there was nothing left but the two of them and the road. He slid the transmission into first and slowly pulled out from the manor. He passed several fire trucks on their way over to the highway, though they paid him no mind. They drove off down the highway, leaving behind Magrath and it's brilliant orange sky.

The snow fell over Magrath that night, though initially the residents all thought it was the ash from the fire that had finally cooled enough to fall back to earth. Though they were partially right, the snow did fall. It tried unsuccessfully to snuff out the raging inferno that engulfed the manor. Though, in hours passing, when the fires dwindled to mere stains one the grand walls of what was once a proud manor; the snow would begin to collect on the boards that had cooled enough to no longer melt them.

As Jack and Emma pulled into the first of many motels, the Lewis manor was reduced to nothing but charred logs and…

--

"...ash."

Dom's eyes remained focused on Jack's face; transfixed on the space just between his eyes, as though trying to dig his way into the depths of Jack's thoughts. Jack lulled his head forward, exhausted after recounting the story that had plagued him for all these years. To Jack, it felt good to tell Dom, it felt good to let it out and address it rather than leave it buried to collect dust and alcohol vapor.

Jack looked up as Dom stood, his jaw set and his eyes a million miles away. He panned his eyes around the room in thought, as though trying to find the right words to say what was on his mind.

Jack didn't take his eyes from him as Dom patted his pockets, as though in search of something, "What's wrong Dom? You lose something?"

Dom looked over, as though Jack had frightened him and loosed a nervous chuckle, "Not quite. I'm unsure why, but for whatever reason I thought I had cigarettes on me."

Jack laughed, "The good and noble Dominic Thompson, smoking? Yeah right."

Dom looked over at him with a surprisingly grim face, "Honestly Jack, if I've ever needed one in my life; it's now. Could I have one."

Jack's mouth opened slightly, even as he dipped his hand into his jacket pocket to retrieve the box of smokes, "sure thing, so long as you don't mind me joining you."

Dom chuckled good-naturedly, “I wouldn’t have it any other way.”

Jack smiled and stood, slipping into his jacket before withdrawing two smokes from the box and passing one to Dom, “don’t say I never gave you anything.”

Dom shook his head playfully as he took the smoke, “wouldn’t dream of it.”

They walked back out of the small coffee shop onto the quiet street. Jack lit their cigarettes and they stood in silence; Dom looking for pedestrians, Jack looking at the clouds, marveling at the blue sky hidden just beyond the white clouds.

He looked over to the Lewis Manor and took another heavy drag of his cigarette. As the smoke flowed slowly from his mouth, he looked past the manor into the far reaches of the sky; he could almost swear he saw black clouds.

Chapter 7: Lewis Manor

~ 1 ~

Jack and Dom drove in relative silence to the Lewis Manor. While Jack's mind was rife with trepidation over returning to his childhood home, Dom's was full of guilt and worry. Worry for his friend who'd faced such adversity in his childhood that he was only able to escape upon killing his own father. More importantly though, he was worried about just how much had been left out of Magrath police records.

As far as he was concerned, there was never a formal investigation into the fire, the disappearance of Jack or his father. As far as the town was concerned, the house burned down and they fled, leaving Jack's mother behind.

He passed his eyes over to Jack, whose white knuckled hands rested on the steering wheel as he focused on driving. Dom wanted to reach out and talk to him, but he knew now wasn't the time. Jack had just relived the most tragic night of his life, and Dom knew that he would need to sort the ideas floating around in his mind on his own.

Dom suspected that Jack hadn't ever taken the time to sort his feelings on the matter, in fact, he was certain. It was evident in the way Jack shut down slightly at the mention of the house or his father. It was evident in the drinking he displayed on his first night in Magrath and the faint smell of whiskey on his breath that very morning.

He looked back out his own window and lost himself further in his mind as he tried to place himself in Jack's shoes. But he couldn't. Growing up Dom had a great family life; his father managed the local bank, and his mother was a shift supervisor at the grocery store, they were always home on time and always had supper together at five o'clock sharp. They'd talk about their day and what goals they had set for the week. He couldn't imagine not having that growing up.

He supposed there was always a stigma surrounding Jack when they were growing up as well. Everyone thought he had it easy, being the son of the richest family within a hundred miles. Yet no one, not even his closest friend truly knew what was going on behind the closed doors of his friend's house. Before telling Dom, the only person that had known was Emma, and with her gone, Dom couldn't imagine the amount of stress weighing down on him.

He sighed and settled down further into his seat, "So Jack."

Jack cocked an eyebrow but didn't turn his head from the windshield, "hmm?"

A coy smile splayed over Dom's lips, "how come if your firm is so successful do you drive a Sunfire."

Jack's brow furrowed, "reliable car."

Dom laughed, "The sputtering when you start it suggests otherwise."

Jack turned to look at Dom and scowled, "now you have an issue with my car? What'd she ever do to you?"

Dom raised his hands, "nothing man, just asking, if you could afford a lot nicer of a car, why wouldn't you?"

Jack nodded in thought, "well, to be honest, I bought this car shortly after Emma and I left. We drove for a while in my Dad's merc, from motel to motel as we put Magrath far behind us. When we finally stopped, we decided to trade it in, see if we could get some cash to put ourselves up in something better than a motel, maybe slow down, take our feet off the pedal. I'd snatched my dad's wallet earlier on when we went to get the gasoline to burn down the place, and I was grateful that I still had it on me. I looked enough like him at the time, hell, I probably look a lot more like him now.

"Anyway, I had his driver's license and I could forge his signature easily enough. We drove into a small dealership, not quite a "used car lot" but one of those more diverse dealerships. Like uh, what's that one... I see ads for it all the time."

Dom helped him out, "go-auto?"

Jack nodded, "yeah that's the one. So, we brought in the Mercedes, which I hadn't realized was worth over eighty grand, and traded it for this Sunfire, brand new, and twenty thousand in cash. We were aware that we were on the losing side of that trade, but we were just happy to be rid of the car."

A smile spread across his face, "we put the first thirty-K on in the first year. We still city hopped for a bit, but eventually we settled down. So, to answer your question, yes, I could buy practically any car I wanted, but there's no car like this one."

Dom nodded, "I guess that's that then."

Jack grunted in agreement as he continued to trundle the car the remaining several blocks to the manor. Dom went back to staring out the window, thinking about when Jack left. He supposed that the car represented his freedom from a tyrannical father more than it was just a car. He thought about it for a moment longer and eventually nodded; he supposed that was something you couldn't quite put a price tag on.

~ 2 ~

They drove up the cracked asphalt drive leading to the Lewis manor; the passing years of neglect yielded a collection of dirt, ash and plants to cover most of the road. Jack kept his eyes on the road as they travelled maneuvering around holes where water had collected and bumps from where tree roots had threatened to poke through the surface of the asphalt. He slowed drastically as they neared the top of the road and the hill where the manor resided.

The ruins spanned before them, though the bulk of the structure remained. The exterior was blackened; the white paint flecked off in bubbled sheets, the roof caved in in several parts and the house itself looked rather flimsy; as though one strong push was all that was needed to send it toppling over.

It filled Jack with a deep sadness to see the house in its sorry state, for although he was the one who'd committed it to such a fate, he mourned the lost legacy of his family. His grandparents and theirs before them had lived in the house; though they died long before he was ever born.

He slipped from the car and wiped a stray tear that had begun to form in the corner of his eye. He'd grown weary of being so emotionally volatile over the past couple days, but as the smell of decaying wood graced his nostrils, he was filled with a rage alongside his sorrow. Rage at the actions of his father and the night he left; that purple bloated face staring blankly at him with its bulging eyes. The tears that began to slip down his face were a reminder of the emotions that coursed through him that night. The wet sort of emotion that bubble forth from your throat; you know it would be hard to speak, even though you could scream.

He walked stiffly over to the mailbox that sat several feet before the twin fences that surrounded the property and curled along the path. He reached out hesitantly, as though afraid the box would fall apart under his touch. Though, as his hand brushed atop the metal it didn't crumble, didn't wither or even fall. It stood resolutely, still vigilant despite the dilapidated ruins that stood behind it.

Dom sauntered down the path towards the house, stopping as he passed the fence. Jack watched him curiously as he shifted his eyes over the front of the structure. After spending a time studying the bulk of the house, Dom resumed walking towards it. He stopped when he got to the door and reached out towards the knob, moving slowly as if afraid it would still be warm from the fire that blazed years ago.

Jack stared as Dom tried the handle and the door swung open; surprised that the basic motion of opening the door would still work. When Dom knelt to look at the blackened floor. Jack looked once more to the mailbox, running his fingers over the bolted-on letters spelling his family name before turning and heading over to Dom; a profound sadness working its way through his chest.

He spoke up as he approached, to not scare Dom, "Did you find anything?"

Dom shook his head, though he didn't look up or rise to his feet. Jack hunkered down to see what Dom was looking at. As he looked down, following Dom's line of sight, he noticed wet spots, spattering the otherwise dry ash just in front of his feet. Dom was crying.

Jack placed a hand gently on his shoulder, "what's wrong man?"

Dom finally looked up at him with hazel eyes that were rimmed with sadness, "it's just that… I held it against you. All these years I held you leaving town against you. I've taken it personally, but to hear that all that time you were struggling with that, I couldn't imagine it. Jack, I hated you, hated you for leaving. Not only for leaving me behind, but Shannon too. You didn't even say goodbye, no letters, no postcards, nothing. Now I realize there was probably so much pain even wrapped in thinking about this piece of shit town."

He paused to take a deep, shaky breath, "Listen, when you came back, I was mad. I didn't show it because that's not who I am, but boy was I mad. You stroll into town like some bigshot and take over the case like it was nothing. You started making progress on a case where there were only dead ends. You followed up with people, did things we didn't even consider, and you made it look so easy. It was humiliating."

Jack said nothing, instead he allowed Dom to vent the feelings he's been burying for years. *Welcome to memory-fucking lane Jack, you piece of shit.* He felt bad, awful in fact, though, he mulled about just what that feeling was in hindsight. Guilt. He felt guilty for all the people he left behind; all the ones that weren't even an afterthought. He'd put himself and Emma first without even considering reaching out to anyone. He felt like an asshole and rightfully so, he'd left his best friend behind to deal with the aftermath of his departure, without so much as a warning or explanation. He'd left Dom in the dark for a long time, and let a hate grow that he could have prevented. Sure, his world had flipped on its axiom, he'd killed his own father, but he fled like a child. He knew it was time to behave like an adult and face the consequences of his actions.

Dom continued, his voice growing shakier, "I'm a piece of shit, Jack. That's the best way to put it, but so are you. We were friends, hell, best friends and you abandoned me. You could have told me anything, let me into the world you protected to closely from the public eye, yet you didn't. You ran away. You left everyone behind. You left me behind. You never told me anything, no contact over the past ten years, then you finally show up out of the blue 'I guess if the money's good enough then I'll show up.' Fuck you Jack. What about your mother? You mentioned her once or twice in your story, but did you ever stop to think how that night impacted her? She returns from work to a dead husband, a burnt down house and a missing son."

Dom paused, catching his breath, "Fuck Jack, I'm sorry. I'm sorry, I shouldn't have, I didn't –"

Jack stopped him, "no, Dom you're right. I never stopped to consider any fallout of my actions; I was just concerned about getting Emma out of town safely. I was focused on things that only related to me; I was focused on myself. Hell, even now I am. This entire case I've been blinded by my past. It's been flaring up in places and I'm just dying to see a connection because maybe it'll let me bury another hatchet. But Dom, I'm truly sorry for leaving you behind and never reaching out to you afterwards. And yeah, I may be an asshole and I'm sorry for humiliating you, but right now I may just be the best shot this sorry excuse for a town has at solving these murders."

He stood up and reached down to Dom, "so what do you say? Friends?"

Dom looked up with the faintest remnants of tears in his eyes, "till the end."

A question lingered in Jack's mind, something Dom had said, something that would need to be addressed, "Dom… is my – is my mother still around?"

Dom looked at him, eyes wide, "yeah Jack, never left the flower shop. She's been tending to it all these years, though I'm sure she just gives them out now. Afterall, she inherited all your dad's money as well as the insurance on the house. She's set for life, that one – but alas, although she doesn't need to be, she's there every day. Sunup to sundown."

Jack nodded and looked up to the sky, the clouds were moving slowly overhead, casting shadows along the overgrown grass that surrounded the place he once called home. When the demons he'd come to know were finally put to rest, he'd set about repairing that burned down bridge and he'd go see her. It wouldn't be easy, but he'd begin to pave the road that would lead to making amends.

Dom wiped his tears from his eyes next to him and spoke so soft Jack could barely hear. Jack smiled but said nothing, instead he continued looking to the clouds above, thinking about the impending inclement weather they would bring. With it, came a warning. One that had been bouncing around in his head all of that day and the day prior.

"The road you are travelling will lead to nothing but misery"

~ 3 ~

Jack and Dom began searching the dilapidated structure, searching for anything that could be of importance to the case. Jack found that the extra set of scrutinous eyes didn't expedite the process as Jack liked to take the time to meticulously comb over every single piece of charcoal and rock that appeared to be out of place. He moved from room to room, stepping over collapsed walls and toppled over furniture, marveling at times over the way some of them had been preserved despite the roaring blaze they ignited that night. Looking at the state of the house, he reckoned that the fire department had put the blaze out in quick fashion; considering the walls were still standing in most places, though he would never risk going onto the second floor.

A chill went through his body as he stepped into his old bedroom. Though the room's walls remained standing, there was a clear trail of dark black residue from where he'd splashed the gasoline on the night he left, surrounding it were scorch marks that trailed along the floor and up the walls in several places. A fine layer of ash had settled atop the furniture; turning the top of the once white vanity a light shade of grey. Jack stepped into the room slowly, looking around in awe as he witnessed himself in third person milling around the house, playing with toys on the floor and lying in bed as his mother and father read his stories when he was just a boy.

He walked over to the bed; the last piece of furniture he'd spend any length of time on top of and saw the fine dark spots on his pillow from where his face had bled on that last day. Instead of happy memories he was then confronted with images of himself laying on that very bed, crying into his pillow after the first time his father struck him. He recalled the feeling of betrayal and embarrassment as his lack of control.

He knelt and placed his hand on the pillow. *I guess this is what the little girl meant about finally facing my demons. Even if it destroys me, I'll face it all.*

He stood and began looking through the room for any sign of the children, hoping beyond everything that he wouldn't have to descend to the basement, he wished he could find out what happened to the kids on the night they visited this house. His house.

When the room provided no clues, he took one last look around the familiar room, over the blood speckled pillow and the small dresser holding the Star Wars collectibles he'd received as a child. He smiled as a lone tear weaved its way down his cheek and stuck in the corner of his upturned mouth.

He spoke out into the ashen room, "I want you to know, I turned out alright. I'm a bit messed up in the head. But I turned out okay."

His smile faded as he turned back towards the hallway and his body filled with anxiety. He took a deep breath and stepped out into the hallway, nearly bumping into Dom, who'd been walking past the room at the time.

Dom turned, surprised, "Oh, it's just you. Fuck, I never knew just how big your damn house was Jack. I mean, I know I came here as a kid, but we'd typically only go to your room. I never grasped just how many rooms there were. It's crazy." He paused, "anyway, how's the hunt going? Find anything?"

Jack pondered, "No, I haven't. How about you?"

Dom shook his head, "me either, I'd ask to check the upper level, but with the amount of structural beams that fell during the fire, I'd wager that we'd sooner die up there than find anything."

Jack nodded, "yeah, I thought the same thing. Oh, by the way, have you noticed a lack of graffiti here? I mean, I've been to a lot of abandoned buildings over the years, but they've always been covered in tags. But there's nothing more than a 'Mark was here' scribble that I noticed near the entrance."

Dom hesitated, though a solemn look passed his brow, "well, you know… when you left, there were rumors about the place. This place was a kind of symbol to the town, though to see it go up in flames, that scared a lot of them, you know? Rumors started about six months after you left, and they grew from there."

Jack thought back to what Larkin had said earlier, "Larkin said it was haunted, or at least that there were rumors it was haunted. What did he mean?"

Dom nodded knowingly, "I think that it all started because of the nature of the house. As you know, it was always here, it stood above the town as a sort of landmark. When it burned, the remains looked like a sort of mangled corpse standing above the town like a demon. The kids who were in the primary school at the time started talking about it, as did the parents."

Jack chewed his lip in thought, "How come they never tore it down Dom? I mean, the house can be seen from nearly every part of the town, yet it's still here; all burnt and gross. Why not get rid of it?"

Dom shrugged, "your mother. She refuted the decision to take it down. She's the current owner of the house, though I don't think she's even been up here since the fire. It's my thought that her never even going near it despite wanting to leave it standing added to the rumors that the house was haunted."

Jack's eyes widened, "my mother? I figured she would have been the one that wanted to take it down."

Dom smiled, though the smile didn't quite meet his eyes, "everyone assumes it was because of you and your dad disappearing. They figured it was her only way to be close to you two. Everyone thought you died as well. Though, people did eventually find out some of the stuff your father had done, they never held that against you or your mother. Especially after all she did in the following years"

Jack frowned, "what do you mean?"

Dom's smile finally reached the corners of his eyes, "Well, she took down the police department, rid it of corruption. She single-handedly brought about the federal investigation that took down the old chief, Hamlon and half the force. Jack it was amazing! It really helped with my rising through the ranks, I just wish Hanson was out of the picture. He doesn't exactly know how to be a detective. He only got the job because of seniority. It's not hard to rise when everyone above you gets incarcerated."

Jack looked down the hallway, wondering what awaited him in his parent's bedroom, but he looked back to Dom, anxious to delay going in there as long as he could, "So when did the rumors start then?"

A look of realization crossed Dom's face, "oh yeah, I guess we kind of got side-tracked there. They started after the police department was torn apart. The word got out about your father abducting those women, and well, the stories went from being about a gas leak or lightning strike starting the fire, to being either you or your mom. When that theory got tired, they switched to the paranormal or supernatural. Some suggested demons, other ghosts, hell, Trix told me someone said it was satanic ritual gone wrong."

Jack chuckled, "So Trix is your informant then?"

Dom nodded, "yeah, as I said, I visit a few times a week, she likes to talk about what's going on in her classes. Magrath is a quiet town, so the only thing they really talk about are parties, which teachers they like, and the big burnt down house that sits over the town. They all kind of live in fear of it."

Jack chewed his lip thoughtfully, "so which story did they settle on?"

Dom laughed, "I don't think they've really made up their minds yet. Though if I had to put any money on it, I'd say that it's beginning to solidify in their minds that your father was a devil worshiping sadist that used his victims as a sacrifice."

Jack's expression fell, "he just might have been Dom, hell. He just might have been."

Silence befell the two men as they stood in the blackened hallway of the Lewis manor. Jack's eyes wandered the space between them, desperate not to meet Dom's eyes, he couldn't bear to see the sorrow held in them on his behalf. So, he turned and wandered back into his room, gesturing for Dom to follow him.

He pointed to the bed, past the fine layer of ash that settled on top of it, "Dom, the bloody spots that line the pillow are from the day my father died. His purple bloody face haunts my nightmares and always flashes behind my eyelids when I close my eyes. There's a place in this house I'm absolutely afraid of entering, and I think you understand why."

Dom looked up from the pillow, back to his friend, "why are you telling me this, Jack?"

Jack cast his eyes over the dresser and the small figurines on it, "because I have my suspicions of where the kids went in this house. It's kind of like a rite of passage, and I'm sure they would have found their way there. But I want to be sure, so I need to ask you a favor."

Dom nodded slowly, "Sure Jack, what is it?"

"Could you call Trix, I want to know if they went into the basement."

Dom said nothing, but nodded slowly, as he reached down slid his phone from the holster on his uniform's utility belt. He unlocked his phone and punched in the number then brought the phone up to his ear. After several seconds, he frowned and lowered his phone, checking to make sure he'd dialed the right number. He repeated the process again, his face becoming more and more concerned.

Dom looked over to Jack, though his voice came out shaky, "something's wrong Jack, she's not answering her phone, she always answers when I call."

Anxious to leave his childhood home, Jack quickly responded, "alright then, let's go check on her. This place isn't going anywhere, and we can risk the fifteen minutes it would take to check on her."

Dom looked up, grateful, "Thank you Jack, it's probably nothing, but with all that's going on, well, I'd like to be sure." Though, he looked a lot more afraid than someone who thought it was probably nothing.

Chapter 8: Children

~ 1 ~

Jack drove hurriedly down the path from the Lewis manor into Magrath city limits. Though the drive was short, Jack knew the emotions flooding Dom's head; they were ones he had experienced several times himself. It was the feeling of helplessness; of knowing you're too late, yet not having the validation to back it up. It caused a bubble to form in Jack's throat.

Anxiety clung to the air like fog as they flew along the edge of Magrath. White knuckles bulged through the backs of Jack's hands, threatening to split the skin at a moment's notice. His mind lingered on Emma, remembered the feeling of betrayal he'd experienced when he'd come home to an empty house, though he knew now it wasn't of her own volition that she'd left. Now understanding that she was somehow tied into this case, he only felt profound loss, something he was hoping Dom wouldn't have to experience as well.

He looked over to Dom briefly; having seen him shuffling in his seat out of the corner of his eye. He worried for him, for what he would do should they find Trix's house abandoned and her belongings missing. He turned his attention back to the road as they neared the turn onto her street. He sighed, knowing the two outcomes that this visit could have, and not liking the odds that it was the less favorable one.

As they pulled up outside of her house, Jack looked over to Dom and placed a hand on his shoulder, "let's go inside, hopefully she'd just sleeping."

Dom nodded and opened the passenger door, letting the anxious air from the inside of the car spill out as cold air rushed in. Jack slid out from behind the steering wheel and turned towards the house. Breathing deep in an attempt to quell the anxiety building in his chest.

Jack watched as Dom half-ran half-walked to the house, as though he couldn't decide on whether to be terrified or to act normally. He got to the front door and pounded on the door. When he got no response, he stuck his hand into his pants pocket and produced a small keyring with several keys on it. He looked over the arrangement of keys and picked out a thin silver one, then slid it into the locked door. He turned the knob and walked inside.

Jack sighed and followed, he hoped beyond all hope that Dom wouldn't find the house empty.

--

The air inside the house was stale, although it hadn't been disturbed in quite a few hours. Jack frowned, realizing that the air itself wasn't stale, but the smell and the feeling of it were familiar. As he wandered around the living room, listening to Dom in the kitchen repeating Trix's name, the realization came over him.

Jack's voice came out shaky, yet loud, "Dom!"

Dom rushed into the living room, eyes wild, "What is it Jack?"

Jack looked at him, not knowing how to put what he was going to say next, "We - uh - we should check her room Dom."

Dom's eyes widened further at the implications of Jack's words, having seen the results of one of the disappearances firsthand, "You don't mean…" he trailed off.

Jack nodded sadly, "I think it could have happened here too."

Dom abruptly turned and started deeper into the house, Jack followed, worrying not only for his friend but also for his friend's niece. Dom stopped outside of one of the doors and slowly opened it.

He loosed a cry as he looked inside, "Whu-where'd she go? Where the hell is her stuff? What the fuck is happening!?"

Jack closed the distance and peered into the room to see for himself. His heart sank as he saw the empty room. Inside there was no bed, no dressed, no personal effects of any kind. Everything was gone, the only thing remaining in the room was the dark red walls.

He hesitantly turned to Dom, who simply stood there with his mouth agape, "Dom, something happened the night they went to that house, something that's happening to all of them. We need answers. Now. Let's go to Larkin's house."

Dom slowly turned his head, visibly shaken by the state of Trix's room, "Okay. But we'll put everything aside if we can figure out where she went. Okay Jack?"

Jack smiled sadly, "Okay Dom."

~ 2 ~

While Jack and Dom were rushing to Trix's house, Robert Fielding was dying.

He lay in his bed in Magrath hospital's intensive care unit. His parents hadn't left his side once since they'd received the calls from the school secretary earlier that day. They'd both left their respective jobs in a hurry and came to be by his side.

They recalled Doctor Thompson's puzzled look as she relayed the news, "Typically we see this sort of reaction in older patients, when the heart is weak. Based on his lab results, his heart sustained a lot of damage from a high amount of adrenaline. It doesn't make sense, at his age, weight and physical state, this shouldn't have happened. He's slipped into a coma and we have no explanation as to why. I'm sorry there's nothing we can do right now other than hope he pulls through this."

Their tears did little, so they attempted to remain strong for Robert, talking to him and holding his hand as he lay there on the bed. It had only been a few hours since they all arrived at the hospital and his status was getting visibly worse. His skin had begun to pale, and his heart rate would spike at random intervals. In an effort to calm his wife down, Robert's father - Harold - decided he'd bring her to get coffee, figuring it would do them some good to get out of room B1-07.

They were gone maybe five minutes. But five minutes was enough. Neither them nor any of the staff saw him enter the room, nor did they hear the sickening crunches and tearing noises that filled the air for nearly three minutes straight as he conducted his work.

When Robert's parents returned, both dropped their coffee in horror as they saw the broken body of their only son laying on a bed of his own blood.

Doctor Thompson and several nurses rushed in at the sound of the fielding's screams as they filled the air of the intensive care unit, though there was nothing they could do given the state of his corpse.

On October 5, 2015 Robert Erskine Fielding was pronounced dead.

~ 3 ~

Dom received the call as they were walking back towards Jack's car, "Hello?"

Jack watched with growing concern as Dom went paler than he thought possible, "Okay, yeah, we'll be right there."

Dom hit the "end call" button on his screen and Jack watched as he lowered the phone back to his belt, evidently fighting the building hysteria inside of him. He shuddered, as though he wanted to lay down on the cold hard earth and curl up into a ball, though eventually he got himself back under control as he slid his professional face on and pushed down the emotions boiling inside of him. He wiped away a tear that formed under his eyes as he looked back to Jack.

Jack steeled himself before asking, "What was that call about?"

Dom shook his head as though trying to break free of his own thoughts, "That was my sister in law. Trix's mom. Robert's been murdered."

Jack's eyes widened, "but he's in the hospital!"

Dom loosed a shaky breath, "I know, but from the sounds of it, it matches the killers MO. Pretty gruesome. We'll have to head there."

Jack bit his lip as he slid his hand into his pocket, "Yeah, then we can try to find Trix. You'll have to tell her mom that she's missing you know."

Dom nodded as Jack handed him a cigarette, "yeah I know. It's going to be another long night for us it looks like."

Jack raised his lighter to his own cigarette and sparked up the end, taking a heavy drag as he passed the lighter to Dom who did the same. He checked his watch and was surprised to see that it was just after one o'clock.

He grabbed the lighter back from Dom and walked the rest of the way to his car, stopping to look back at Dom only once, just to make sure he was following.

--

The arrived at the hospital twenty minutes later. Normally, the drive would have normally taken them half an hour, though by speeding, Jack was able to reduce that time drastically. As they walked through the automatic doors, the scent of hand sanitizer, gloves and nylon flowed through the air and into their nostrils.

To the doctors that milled about the halls, it would have smelled like a solid day's work, the smell of medicine, or even the smell of making a difference. However, to Jack and Dom it smelled only of stomach aches and pains, long waiting hours and last visits to loved ones.

They walked down the linoleum hallway towards B1-07. As they walked Dom absentmindedly explain the significance of the letter and numbers, "'B' is the letter they use to denote the ICU, '1' signifies the floor and '07' is the actual room number within the ward. I'm not sure why they couldn't just call it 'ICU-07' as this hospital only has two levels, and only a handful of wards."

Jack shrugged and looked into the other rooms that they passed. In one, he saw a man covered head to toe in bandages, presumably the victim of a rather serious burn, in the next he saw a woman that -other than the large apparatus shoved down her throat- looked relatively normal, he presumed she was in a coma and lastly they came upon a room with a mangled corpse lying on the bed.

The body wasn't even recognizable as it was broken beyond any humanoid resemblance. Robert's limbs jutted out in precarious angles, each one hanging off broken bones, like a marionette in the hands of a child. What used to be his elbows were now pointed inward towards where his sternum should have been, with additional bends in the arms so that his hands were touching the crook of each respective arm. In the center of his torso was a giant hole and pushed through his internal organs, as if threading a needle were his legs; bent behind his back and broken so that his feet rested where his lungs should have been.

Jack's horrified eyes moved up slowly to where the boy's face should have been, but instead, what he saw caused bile to rise in his throat. As he struggled to choke it back down, he took in the bloated mass of flesh that used to be Robert's face. It looked to be around the size of a bowling ball, though his face was stretched over it as though it was removed and stretched in some attempt to cover the entirety of the head. His eye sockets were in line with the hair line and the lower lip was pulled over his jaw.

Jack took a hesitant step forward to get a closer look. He peered over the edge of the bed, into the fissure that used to be Robert's chest. Inside, his ribs jutted out from the flesh, broken to puncture the remaining organs within. He turned back to Dom, who'd grown paler than even before. A second later Dom turned and gripped the edge of the garbage can positioned next to the door; throwing up as soon as he was able to. As his body racked repeatedly and he made retching noises, Jack got even closer to Robert's corpse, nausea bubbling in the depths of his throat. The sounds Dom was making weren't helping.

As Jack peered into the mangled corpse of what was once a perfectly healthy boy, he saw a small folded sheet of paper perched precariously on the edge of where his spine was snapped off. Jack shuddered before reaching in and pulling it out, wincing as the coagulated blood clung to the edges of the note. The queasy feeling rose in his gut as the blood stretched and snapped. He looked at the outside of the note studiously before beginning to open it slowly. The note was small, but the message was clear, written in a scratch like scrawl.

You'll never find them Jackie.

Jack froze; his chest tightening as his heart began to thud hard against the surrounding tissue. Fear gripped him, pushing adrenaline through his veins. He turned slowly to Dom who'd only just raised his head from the rim of the garbage bin. Dom's eyes didn't meet Jack's at first as he struggled to regain his composure. He wiped the remaining bile from the corners of his mouth, then checked the front of his uniform to ensure he hadn't gotten any on himself. As his eyes met Jack's he froze and shot a look towards the note sitting in Jack's hand.

His voice came out hoarse, shaky, and tired, "what is that?"

Jack's voice betrayed him, cracking as he responded, "It's - uh - I found it in… I found it in… Robert. Whoever did this wanted to mess with us."

He handed the note to Dom who took one note and turned pale, before being flushed with the red of anger. He turned and nearly walked into a doctor.

Startled, the red began to recede, "Diana, how are you?"

The doctor - Diana - looked at him, "Dom, I should have figured it would have been you that would show up first. It's pretty bad isn't it?"

Dom nodded before Jack coughed, his eyes widened, "Sorry, Diana, this is Jack Lewis, Jack, this is Diana Thompson, my brother's wife."

Both Diana's and Jack's eyes widened at hearing each other's name, though Jack was able to speak first, "You must be Trix's mom."

She faltered, "How do you know my daughter?"

Jack looked to Dom, who remained silent, Jack shook his head, "Diana, Dr. Thompson, Trix is missing, we were just there before we came here."

Confusion, anger, and fear flashed behind her eyes, "That - no - what? What do you mean?"

Jack spoke slowly, so as to pierce the veil of grief that had just cascaded over her, "I'm afraid I can't tell you anything in detail right now, it's part of an ongoing investigation, as is the nature of Robert's death. I'm sorry I can't tell you more, but I promise you, we will find her."

Her eyes moved past Dom into the room, where Robert's mutilated corpse lay on the bed, still glistening with the blood that coated the rest of the sheets. Jack could see the gears turning in her mind as she attempted to put together the scarce details he'd provided her.

Finally, she clasped her hands over her mouth, "are you saying she'll end up like Robert? My baby will be tormented like him?"

Jack shook his head, "We don't know that yet, and I'm afraid I can't tell you what we do know." He looked over to the tall pale man standing next to him, his hazel eyes staring miles into the distance, "Dom, we should head out, we need to begin the search for her."

Dom slowly moved his eyes over to him, as though the implications of looking for Trix meant they weren't trying to save her but trying to find a corpse. He nodded slowly then blinked hard. When he opened his eyes, they were focused and intense.

As he moved past Diana, he plucked his phone off his belt. He punched in a number and held the phone up to his ear as it connected, all the while he kept moving; his mind focused on the task in front of him.

Though he'd been visibly shaken moments before, his voice came out calm and even, "Hanson, yes, this is Thompson. Look, Jack and I have a lead we need to follow as soon as possible, would you be able to come to the hospital and take care of things here?" He paused as Hanson answered on the other end of the line, "You're already on your way?" pause, "yeah, room B1-07. Uh - hopefully you haven't eaten recently." another pause, "Thank you. I'll be in touch."

He turned his eyes to Jack, "One more call, sorry."

As they reached the hospital's lobby he punched in another number. Jack watched in awe at his friend's level of professionalism in the face of such an overwhelming scenario. As Dom pulled the phone up to his ear and waited for the call to connect, Jack looked around, taking in the room with uncertainty. The few people that he saw, walked on, ignorant of the situation taking place in the town they call home. Though, Jack supposed that was the purpose of police work; to protect civilians from things they are better off not knowing about.

His thoughts were interrupted by Dom's voice, "Hey Shan. We're just at the hospital." Pause, "No, nothing happened to either of us… though, there was another murder." Pause, "yeah, just stay inside tonight, alright, it'll be safer there. Listen, Trix is missing." Pause, "Yeah, we're going to figure out what happened right now, and bring her back by any means. I promise." Pause, "Thank you love. Okay, I have to go babe, love you. Bye."

Jack avoided making eye contact as Dom clicked off the phone call, "you ready to go find Trix now Dom?"

Dom nodded before saying something that made everything else fade into the periphery, "Emma too."

Chapter 9: Fear

~ 1 ~

They broke several traffic laws on the way to the manor, speeding along the streets of Magrath with their minds focused on the sole task of saving Trix. Jack weaved through any traffic they encountered; the thought of any legal ramifications they may face for reckless driving waved by the presence of the officer seated next to him. As they flew over the dulled asphalt, Jack's mind wandered to Emma. What Dom had said instilled a level of hope he hadn't expected; even though he knew she was most likely dead, the premise of finding her alive and well proved too bright for his cynicism to dull.

They pulled up to the manor in a fraction of the time it had taken them to reach the hospital and before Jack could bring the Sunfire to a complete stop, Dom had already thrown open the door and was halfway out of the car. He looked back to Jack only briefly before sprinting up the cracked cement path leading up to the entrance of the house.

Jack's heart thudded in his chest as he slid out from behind the steering wheel and followed suit. He was afraid to enter his father's room and descend into the only area of the house they hadn't checked. He not only feared what they may find down there, but he also feared seeing the setting that had haunted so many of his nightmare over the past decade. He feared for facing the demons he'd tried so hard to bury in alcohol and nicotine. As he followed Dom through the threshold of the house his trepidation only grew. He felt adrenaline begin to course through his veins as his fight or flight instincts kicked in.

Jack entered the all-to-familiar hallway and saw Dom frantically looking into each of the rooms that lined the hallway, from his father's study to his old bedroom. Jack closed the distance between them quickly and placed a hand on Dom's shoulder, stilling his panicked friend.

Though it felt cowardly to him, Jack felt he had to say it, "Dom, I'm sorry, but I think I know where we have to go… I'm saying this now though; I can't go in there. I can't go back into that basement. I'm afraid of what will happen if we do."

Dom said nothing but turned and started towards the end of the hall, towards the blackened door that stood slightly ajar. Jack's heart pounded in his chest as he followed, unsure of what was going through Dom's head. As Dom reached the end of the hall and swung open what remained of the door leading to his parent's bedroom, Jack felt short of breath. Though, with little else to do, he carried on following, knowing full well that there were lives on the line. If it's going to end here, so be it.

His skin broke out in goosebumps as he entered his parents' bedroom. The room was visibly worse than the rest of the house, the walls were charred beyond recognition; the carpet had been reduced to little more than ash and the roof above had burnt away, revealing the blackened sky above. The bed he'd tossed aside on the night he saved Emma from his father was flipped over where he'd left it, though it was now reduced to disjointed springs and metal wires. Jack cast his eyes around the room, soaking it all in. Lastly, he turned his eyes over to the closet, and the indent just past it; covered haphazardly in large pieces of debris from the roof above Jack frowned as he looked closer at it.

A chill shot up his spine, and his mouth hung open as he realized what the state of the debris implied. He barely noticed Dom taking note of his reaction to the closet, though he did notice the way he followed his eyes and moved closer to it.

As Dom bent down to heave the first piece of debris off the entryway, Jack stopped him, "Dom, look. The kids definitely went down there."

Dom frowned, "how do you know?"

Jack looked at the way the debris was laid, "notice how there's almost no ash on any of the pieces of debris?"

"Yeah, what about it?"

Jack continued, "well, that alone is enough to suggest those pieces were moved, but also look at the sheer amount of debris. That didn't all come from the roof right above the staircase. That was moved there from the room. They must have covered it after they went down there. Whatever they saw frightened them so much they tried to cover it up before leaving."

Dom paled, "I have to go down there then, Jack."

Jack shook his head frantically, "I can't Dom, last time I went down ther-"

Dom didn't let Jack finish, "Jack, I'm not asking you to, hell, I'm not even sure if there's anything of use down there. But if what you're saying is true, then there may be something that could shine a light on this case." His voice grew strained, "nothing about this case makes any sense Jack. How is any of this happening? A kid was murdered in his hospital room in the few minutes his parents stepped out. How does that happen? How does someone do that without being caught?"

Jack stood in silence as Dom fell to his knees and started crying as the confusion and exhaustion overcame him. He sobbed as his emotions finally broke through the professional demeanor he'd constructed as they left Trix's house. His poker face was gone, and now everyone would see he had a losing hand.

Jack looked up to the sky through the hole above him. It was almost beautiful as the black clouds moved overhead; casting shadows over the land as they blotted out any sunlight that tried to penetrate them. Jack thought back over the past couple days, thinking about the first victim he'd laid eyes on; Elizabeth Wildbrooke.

He wondered if she'd ever come to the manor, if she'd somehow gotten into the basement as well. Looking at everything he'd collected on this case; he was becoming more and more convinced that the entire case hinged on this house and was somehow tied into his past. He knew he'd get to the bottom of it eventually, even if it killed him. He'd do it for Dom and all the people he left behind. He'd face his demons.

Jack sighed and walked over to Dom, sitting down next to him on the charred ground. He placed a hand on Dom's upper back, but remained silent as Dom's cries were carried up and out of the manor he'd grown up in. He felt weak, scared and vulnerable as they sat there, but he wouldn't move. He'd stay vigilant, after all, the whole town may fall victim if he was unable to put this case to rest.

~ 2 ~

To Jack, they sat there for what felt like hours, though it may have been mere minutes. The hidden sun had descended past the horizon, causing what little light had penetrated the clouds to vanish, plunging Magrath into a pitch-black night. Though darkness had washed over the land, Dom and Jack remained at the manor, wallowing in the futility of the case they'd set out to solve.

It had been some time since Dom's cries had stopped, and he had been sitting in silence for a time. Jack watched as Dom seemingly gained his second wind and rose onto his unsteady feet. He slowly began to stalk up to the caved in portion of the floor, eager to get into the basement below. He began throwing the pieces of charred wood and other debris from the opening off to the side. After some time, he finally revealed the concrete staircase that lead into the depths below.

Jack met his eyes as he looked back and flashed a weak smiled, revealing white teeth beneath his charcoal covered face. His eyes betrayed the emotion that Jack saw beneath; he was scared and rightfully so. Jack watched as he took the first step down the stairs and continued watching, until his head disappeared into the murky depths below the Lewis manor.

When his footsteps faded into the obscurity of the stairwell, Jack laid back on the charred ground and stared up into the dark clouds above. As the moonlight slipped through several places, he frowned; the clouds looked darker than they had before.

--

Jack awoke to the sound of screaming.

It penetrated the sleep he'd been unaware he'd entered, causing him to wake with a start. At first, he thought it was nothing more than a waking dream, until the sound came again, emanating from the closet where he'd found the staircase down all those years ago. He quickly sat up as his mind began to place in the pieces that had flitted away during his bout of unconsciousness. His heart sank as he realized what the source must have been. Dom.

Jack threw aside any reservations he had about entering the basement and quickly rose to his feet, mind set on entering the basement where he'd killed his father. He started down the stairs and pulled out his phone to light the way in front of him. The weak flashlight only illuminated two feet in front of him, though it helped with gauging how many stairs were left on his descent.

The trepidation tightened in his chest as he neared the bottom of the stairs and was only pushed further when his phone's flashlight turned off as "LOW BATTERY" flashed across the display. He was contemplating the cowardly option of turning back when he heard a groan followed by a sickening tearing sound coming from further within. Knowing he couldn't leave Dom behind; he pushed onward.

Being unable to see anything in the encroaching darkness, he felt his way along the wall; straining to hear the faintest of noises. He heard a faint dripping noise as he neared one of the many doors that ran the length of the concrete wall. As he neared, his foot bounced off something; sending it skittering a few feet away. He had just begun walking slower - lifting his feet higher than normal so as to avoid kicking the object again - when his foot came down on top of something cylindrical. Curious, he bent down to pick it up and was elated to find that the object he'd stepped on was Dom's police flashlight.

He pushed the button at the end of the shaft and winced as the small flashlight shot forth a blindingly bright light that cut through the darkness. Once his eyes adjusted, he panned the flashlight over the concrete floor; searching for any sign of where Dom had ended up. He froze as it hovered over several fresh specks of crimson blood.

Fear crept through him as he followed the dots of blood to a dark mass in the corner of the room. His need to know got the better of him as he finally moved the flashlight over the mass and his breath caught in his chest.

Half of Dom's body lay in front of him, his left eye unseeing as it stared blankly at the space behind Jack. Jack felt a sob work its way up his throat as he saw the other half just a couple feet past it, connected only by the intestines that spanned the floor between the two halves. Tears started to rise in his eyes as he looked over the corpse, not sure of what could have one such a thing to Dom.

He looked around the room frantically panning the flashlight over the surfaces of the walls and ceiling, anxious to find any indicator of who could have done this to Dom. His heart thudded hard as he saw something standing in the opposite corner of the room.

It was an anthropomorphic figure, and it cocked its grey and fleshy head to the side as it looked at him; its small black eyes glittered in the flashlight. A ghastly grin stretched across its slimy grey face, revealing a set of gnarly, wet and jagged teeth that protruded haphazardly from its black gums.

Jack turned and bolted back towards the door, taking his eyes off the creature and leaving Dom's body lying there on the floor. His mind went blank, leaving only one thought in the forefront of his consciousness: survive.

He flew up the stairs as a maniacal, twisted and dark laugh followed him up the stairs; filling the air around him. He took the stairs two at a time, flying up and up towards ground level, not so much as even stopping to look back.

As he reached the top, he collapsed, breathless from his sudden rush of adrenaline and the overwhelming urge to flee. He looked around, searching for any sign of the monster that had torn his friend in half. He struggled to his feet as he caught his breath, knowing he wouldn't be able to stay there, but also not wanting to leave Dom behind.

He looked back down the staircase into the depths of the manor. He didn't know what that thing was, but as he stood there, he became all too aware that it was most definitely the creature that had killed those children and kidnapped Trix. His entire being was begging for him to run, but he wanted to go back for Dom, needed to.

As he took the first shaky step down the stairs, a deep, ancient voice emanated from the depths, stopping him in his tracks.

"Come on Jackie, you know this belt, you want it don't you?"

~ 3 ~

Fear. It overcomes, incapacitates, and hinders all normal thought processes. In some cases, people even develop the fear of fear itself. Fear can be taught just as easily as anything else. Insects, for example are played with by most children. Though, as they grow up, external forces such as their parents, peers, and entertainment foster the fear's growth, regardless of their actual feelings towards the insects. They become afraid of being afraid of the insects.

Jack Lewis had always felt his fear towards the basement was something akin to that sort of fear. Though, as the deep melancholic voice emanated from the depths, a sort of pure, primal fear overcame his body, triggering his fight or flight response.

As he turned and ran from the staircase that would have taken him to the depths of the Lewis manor, he became aware of a realization he'd been denying for years. Subconsciously, he must have been afraid of the basement because there was something worth being afraid of down there.

This realization helped little as his legs carried him down the path past his car towards the town, leaving the manor - and Dom - behind.

With fear overtaking his body he didn't care where he was heading. His legs pumped as he ran through the street causing his muscles to cry out in protest and his lungs to scream from exertion. His instincts took over and pushed his body to keep going, lest he meet the same fate that had befallen Dom. He pushed the thoughts of the thing he saw deep down, not allowing himself to rationally mull over the idea that such a creature could exist in this world.

As he pushed himself, the clouds above began to unleash a torrent of rain onto the town of Magrath. The droplets hit Jack's face, though he noticed, little, just as he failed to notice the streams of tears flowing from his eyes and down his cheeks.

As the rain and darkness closed in on him, his body became increasingly exhausted and he found himself collapsing on a familiar sidewalk. The cool feeling of the concrete against his cheek made him smile as the exhaustion grabbed hold of his body and he began to slip into the comfort of unconsciousness. Before the darkness enveloped him entirely, the world exploded in a bright light as thunder sounded from somewhere overhead as the black clouds unleashed their fury on Magrath.

Finally, Jack was whisked away from the waking world.

~ 4 ~

Dreams washed over the blackness that had befallen his consciousness and without alcohol to suppress them, Jack was hit full force with the weight of them. Though, even in his unconscious state, Jack was aware that these were more than dreams. They were based on the events transpiring in Magrath, and although he was aware he was lying face first on a sidewalk somewhere in the town, he felt keenly aware of everything that was happening in this dreamscape.

In his dream, he was standing at the end of the long linoleum hallway of the Magrath hospital. He stared down to all the open doorways, getting the irresistible urge to go into each of the rooms regardless of what he'd find on the inside of them.

He began walking slowly down the hallway, towards the first room, his heart thudding in anticipation of what he would see past the open door. He hesitantly looked inside and saw a woman in her mid-thirties laying on the bed with her eyes closed and her fingers interlaced on top of her chest. Her dyed brown hair spilled over her shoulders and onto her chest elegantly, unlike the blood-spattered halo he'd seen two nights prior.

He walked up to the side of the bed; guilt rising like bile in his throat. She lay perfectly still; displaying not even the rise and fall of her chest as she breathed.

Curious, Jack slowly extended his hand towards her neck to check her pulse. His fingers pressed into her pale neck as he searched for any sign of life. Yet, her cold flesh provided no indication of the beating of her heart.

Confusion crossed his face momentarily, though he figured it was a simple mistake on his part. He began to withdraw his fingers so he could try again, when he noticed her skin clung to his fingertips like tape. His confusion turned to panic as he continued to withdraw from her. The panic turned to horror as her skin began to peel off the muscles in her neck; still clinging to his fingers.

He jolted back his hand and yelled out as her skin tore off her neck entirely, dangling off the tips of his fingers in sheets. Using his other hand, he tore the skin free of his fingertips, grimacing as the flesh splattered onto the ground below.

Now thoroughly horrified, Jack looked back up to Elizabeth. Blood slowly trickled from her neck, though it wasn't as though it was being assisted by her heart. No, it looked as though it were simply emptying out of her, as if she were being bled dry. The blood pooled on the ground below her.

He watched as two long, slender and grey arms reached out from the darkness at the edge of the bed and began slamming repeatedly on her body, caving in her face and breaking her arms. Slowly they began to fold her body like a pretzel, tucking her arms and legs under her back in a sort of mutilated gymnasts arch.

Jack backed away in shock; shaking his head as he witnessed her body breaking and snapping in unnatural ways. The two grey hands retreating into the darkness over the side of the bed having completed their work on Elizabeth's body.

She lay there twitching atop the now blood-soaked hospital bed. For one fleeting moment, Jack's thoughts turned towards the impossibility of the situation; she'd died next to the apartment building in Magrath. In the exact same manner. With fear gripping his chest he quickly stumbled out of the room, all to grateful as the light turned off inside and the door closed.

He shook his head of the image of her writhing, twitching corpse as he turned back to the long hallway of the hospital. With no alternative measures to take, he proceeded onward, towards the second room.

The fluorescent light flickered over the occupant of the second room. Jack knew instantly it was the second victim of whatever that thing had been in the basement of his old home. *Don't refer to them as victims, they have names you idiot.* Veronica. Her body lay across the bed; bruised and beaten; displaying signs of the incredible violence inflicted on her. A red ring of irritation encircled her neck, as though a more intense amount of pressure had been inflicted there.

Jack stepped forward; his curious nature taking over and quelling the fearsome scene he'd witnessed in the prior room. She wore nothing but a sports bra and baggy shorts, allowing Jack to see the severe pressure wounds that lined her ribs, abdomen and arms.

Not wanting to repeat what happened in the last room, he refrained from touching the angry looking red on her neck and instead observed it. A pang of sympathy overcame him as he realized what it was. She'd tried to kill herself at some point, in some attempt to escape from whatever torment the creature had bestowed upon her. A pang of sympathy swarmed through him as he realized her escape had been hindered by that thing.

A tear trickled slowly down his cheek and he shook his head sadly as he recalled the way Robert had acted that same morning; the utter fear that drove him into a coma. He blinked hard, trying to will away the tears; knowing that whatever this dream - or vision - was, he would experience a lot more sorrow before it was over.

He opened his eyes as a hand weakly gripped his wrist. He looked down to the bruised fingers as they clung to his wrist with all the strength they could muster. He looked back up to Veronica's face, surprised to see she was conscious in any measure.

Her tearful eyes stared into his for a moment, before her hoarse voice filled the space between them, "Jack, there's something you must do. Something only, you can!"

He winced as her face turned into one of pure fear and she began to scream. Her eyes rolled back as a single grey hand appeared from just beyond the head of the bed, holding a length of rope tied in a loop. It placed the loop over her head before grabbing hold of the end and pulling her off the bed, into the black oblivion beyond.

Jack closed his eyes as her hand was torn from his wrist, *it's not real. It can't be real, she's already dead, this is just a dream.*

When he finally mustered up the courage to open his eyes, he found himself face to face with the door; soon realizing he was back in the hallway once more. He tried the knob, but the door wouldn't budge. Just as with Robert, he realized he'd been too late; the room, and Veronica, were lost to the darkness. He turned his head back to the hallway and steeled himself. There was more to be seen, more to be heard. He took the first step hesitantly and found that the others followed with relative ease.

The lights were off in the third room, save for the yellow glow emanating from a bedside lamp positioned on a nightstand in the corner. Not very hospital-like. Jack walked in and looked at the figure sitting on the edge of the bed facing away from him. Jack placed a hand on the shoulder of Noah Brackman and made no attempt to walk around to see his face as he remembered what the casefile had said. Remembering that he'd died by suffocating on his own face.

Jack smiled sorrowfully, "I'm sorry Noah, you were another one I was too late to save."

A lone tear worked its way down his cheek as he remembered Noah's father sitting in his dirty house, in his stained clothes. A broken man with no hope after the loss of his family.

To his horror, Noah turned to face him; eyeballs sliding out of the cavities; unhindered by eyelids. He struggled to speak, his teeth clacked, and his tongue moved, yet without lips to help form the words, they were nearly unintelligible.

The grey hands reached up once more from the edge of the bed and began to pull Noah into the darkness just beyond. As Jack watched helplessly, he finally heard what Noah was trying so hard to say.

"It has to be you, Jack. You must remember."

Jack shook his head in confusion as Noah was lost to the darkness. He didn't know what the words meant, or what he was supposed to remember. Sorrow washed through him, and although Noah had been lost before Jack had even come back to Magrath, he saw Noah as another person whose death was on his hands.

Jack reached up and wiped his tears away with the back of his sleeve, closing his eyes as he did so. When he lowered his arm, he realized he was back in the hallway, once again facing a closed door. This time he knew not to bother with the knob, though as he turned down to the remaining rooms, he was hit with a pang of panic. She'll be down there, somewhere, won't she?

He turned back to look at the way he came, but instead of seeing the doorways he passed, he saw only a vast expanse of darkness. He supposed there was no turning back, only moving forward. With that knowledge he began walking again, towards the fourth room.

He stopped just outside of the room, noticing how unlike the previous rooms, this one was numbered. "B1-07" was displayed next to the door in typical hospital fashion, the one where in the real-world Robert had been killed. Jack sighed, and stuck his hand into his pocket absentmindedly, seeking out the comfort of the cigarettes he'd always kept within. Frowning, he withdrew his hand; realizing he'd have to face this endeavor without assistance from his old friend nicotine. Hesitantly, Jack peered around the corner into the room, not knowing what to expect given the last condition he'd seen Robert in.

Robert, like Noah sat on the edge of his bed. Though unlike Noah, he slumped slightly forward, whether that was of his own volition or the lack of muscle and organs in his giant chest cavity Jack was unsure. As Jack continued to investigate the room, he realized he could see right through Robert's chest, he could see the boy's spine keeping the upper and lower parts of his torso from collapsing in on each other. Just the sight made him queasy.

He hesitantly stepped into the room, unsure of what awaited him in this one and wondering what sort of cryptic information he'd glean from this conversation. He saw an old, yellowing visitor's chair off to the side and instantly knew he was meant to sit in it. He walked over and settled himself on the cracking pleather and waited to see what would happen next.

The broken boy turned to him then, pivoting the top half of his body all the way around while leaving the bottom in place; giving his midriff the appearance of a macabre double helix. Robert's face was stuck mid scream, and Jack's blood began to run cold as his eyes rolled forward revealing his irises.

A breathless sound began to flow from his mouth and slowly his jaw clicked back into its sockets, only then, was it made clear that he was trying to speak.

His voice came out as though he had been winded, which, given his state, should have been impossible, "I just wish it had come sooner. I'd been seeing it for days, you know. Lurking in the periphery of my vision. I tried to tell my parents, but they assumed I was on drugs. The others wouldn't speak to me about it, about what we found down there. At your house. Nothing I did could have freed me from its sights. But you already know that Jack, don't you? Afterall, it's haunting you now, isn't it?"

Jack swallowed heard but didn't reply. He couldn't reply.

Robert's corpse continued, "He's coming now, claiming whatever is left of me. There's not much time for me to say what I must. It's tied to you Jack, though not only because of the fire you started or the father you killed. Look further back, you must. It's in your blood Jack, only you-"

His words were cut off as the two long arms reached out from the darkness and seized his spine before dragging him off the bed with a sickening crack that penetrated Jack's ears and shook him from his stupor. At the last moment, Robert's eyes locked on his, and he smiled, accepting his fate. What could that mean? Further back?

Jack remained in the visitor's chair longer than he'd intended, his mind swarmed with a swathe of thoughts he hadn't the first clue on how to deal with. He thought of his failure, the line of people falling in his father's wake like dominos, and the ones who fell the decade later in some sort of delayed aftershock. He shook his head once more, not knowing what any of it could mean.

He clenched his fist, knowing full well who the culprit was but not knowing how on earth he could deal with it. Criminals were easy to a degree; you build up enough conclusive evidence to build a solid case and pass it on to the cops who move the case further. Collect your paycheck and move on. But he couldn't do that now. This thing couldn't be arrested, it had ripped his best friend in half like he was nothing, the police couldn't do anything about it.

Sure, from what Jack could tell, they were no longer corrupt, but they weren't the most competent bunch he'd ever worked with. All these years later and the town was still picking up the pieces of the life he'd left behind. He slammed his fist into his thigh, trying to remember, trying to figure out what Robert had meant; not knowing how to do anything with the information. Something was there, lingering on the tip of his tongue, but he couldn't quite grasp it; couldn't coherently think up the right string of words to explain exactly where the idea may lead.

He rubbed his hands over his face as he closed his eyes in some vain attempt to think clearer. If only I could remember. He clenched and unclenched his jaw as he mulled over everything he'd heard, learned and uncovered over the past forty-eight hours. Frustration grew like a fire in his gut as he kept coming up empty, not knowing what sort of future awaited him in Magrath. Finally, he opened his eyes.

He was back in the hallway, though this time the chair had come with him. He stood and walked forward, finally accepting his fate to check all the rooms that lined the dreamscape's hallway. He glanced back, noticing that the darkness had now swallowed the chair as well. His courage swelled as he walked to the next door and crumbled as he looked inside.

Dom lay on the bed, his two halves seeming stapled together, allowing him to lay there as a complete person as opposed to two parts of the same person. Jack held back a sorrowful scream that rose inside of him, though the emotional barricade he'd been building fell apart as his legs unhinged beneath him and he crumpled to the ground, sobbing uncontrollably.

His cries came out in slurred profanities to the God he stopped believing in long ago. He screamed out that whatever God truly existed, they'd grown indifferent and uncaring long ago, maybe they just no longer believed in humanity as a whole and had grown cynical over the millennia.

Jack's tears flowed down his face and dripped onto the floor, he shifted onto his hands and knees as he struggled to regain his composure. His cries finally subsided as he felt a gentle hand on his shoulder. He looked up to see Dom standing over him; a sad smile splayed over his face.

A tear rolled off his cheek, "Jack, don't be sad. It was always meant to end this way for me, I see that now. It's not your fault and it never will be. All of this, none of it is on you. And Jack, you need to know that I know."

Jack stared at him blankly, so Dom continued, "You and Shannon. I know Jack, and it's nothing I can hold against you. I know why you guys split up."

Tears began to well up in Jack's eyes, and Dom moved his hand to Jack's face, "Jack, she's forgiven you, I've forgiven you. It wasn't your fault to begin with. It's time you forgive yourself, Okay? Take care of her for me, you two will need each other."

He patted jack on the shoulder and Jack watched as he walked back to the bed and sat down on it, smiling sadly as he waved goodbye, saying one last thing before the hands reached out and tore him in half before pulling him into the darkness like all the others.

Jack stood and turned, knowing that he had to go through the rest of the rooms regardless of the pain. Suddenly fully aware that Emma wouldn't be the only one awaiting him in further rooms. He closed his eyes for a few seconds. When he opened them, he was relieved to be out of that room and back in the now familiar linoleum corridor.

With tears still rolling from his eyes, he stalked onward to the next room; unsure of what could possibly be awaiting him inside. As he reached the door, he saw several people milling about, all of varying age, height and sex. They looked absent-mindedly at the walls and floor as they walked, bumping into one another.

Jack felt no desire to enter the room, but only to search the faces for the one he feared to find. Just as he was beginning to feel some semblance of relief, he saw her. Emma. Her brown hair was the same as he remembered it, but the clouded expression on her face was not. He turned quickly towards the hallway, not wanting to linger on the idea that he could have saved her from this fate. He proceeded to the next room.

This one was like the last, though it was filled with more people that the room before. I had no idea there were this many missing people. He turned and kept moving, anxiety overcoming him as he reached the final room.

The bed was empty, though Jack knew the bed wasn't the focus of this room. No, in the corner of the room was a baby blue crib. Jack's body moved of its own volition and he soon found himself running his hands along the painted wood and turning the carousel that hung above it. He smiled as the familiar jingle played.

He finally looked down into the crib; towards the child that never was. Jack reached down into the crib as tears began to fall from his eyes again.

The baby grabbed onto his finger and held tight, babbling as it brought Jack's finger closer to its mouth. Jack smiled sadly and thought of the life he could have had as the baby gummed his finger.

A woman's voice came from behind him, "oh Jack, look at what we made."

Arms wrapped around him from behind and he could smell the faintest tint of lavender rolling off her. He smiled sadly once more but frowned a he was jerked back away from the crib, as though he was being dragged.

He turned, expecting to see her, but instead he was met with the hauntingly grey face of the creature from the basement. He screamed as it drew its hand back and plunged it into his chest, returning him to the darkness.

Chapter 10: Bedfellows

~ 1 ~

Jack awoke with a start, arms flailing as he returned to the realm of reality. Tears continued to flow down his cheeks as sound failed to reach his ears and a foggy haze filled his vision. His chest hurt, and in a fit of fear he began patting his chest repeatedly where the creature had punched through, loosing a sigh of relief when he felt the damp material of his sweat soaked shirt clinging to his chest.

As his vision finally began to clear he saw Shannon standing over him; a mask of concern etched into her features. Guilt flooded into Jack's mind as the events of the evening came back in full force, briefly pushing aside the memories of the dreamscape.

At first, he struggled to speak, due both to the burning in his chest and the emotions swelling in his throat. He realized the pain he'd felt upon waking hadn't been from the creature's punch, but from the exertion he'd subjected himself to on his run back to Dom and Shannon's house. Her concern only grew as she witnessed the state he was in.

After several attempts, through tears and his raspy voice, he managed to get out, "I'm so sorry Shannon… we went to my old house. There - there was something in the basement. D-Dom. Dom's dead."

Shannon's eyes widened, and her mouth hung open. For several moments, it appeared as though she didn't know what he'd said or simply couldn't comprehend. Though as she stared into Jack's broken expression, her brain finally caught up with her eyes and what started as a shocked expression slowly devolved into her sobbing uncontrollably. Jack hung his head as the tears began to spill once more from his eyes, sliding down his cheek before dripping onto the sheets of the familiar guest bed.

Shakily, he managed, "Shannon, I'll tell you everything. All we've learned over the past couple days and everything I've seen."

Yet, as he lay there with his best friend's wife sobbing just mere feet away from him; the guilt began to wash over him all over again. He looked into her pain filled eyes and felt the wall he'd built up in that false room where he'd shared his final words with Dom break apart and crumble all over again.

His sobs filled the air alongside Shannon's and the words he meant to utter in reassurance devolved into incoherent nonsense. Shannon looked up at him and smiled sadly before walking over and wrapping him in a gentle hug.

They embraced for some time, taking a miniscule amount of comfort in the fact that they weren't alone with their emotions. As their sobs began to peter out, Jack divulged the vents of the past few days to Shannon; taking care not to mention the more gruesome details. He started with the mysterious phone call he'd received the night he left for Magrath, and slowly worked through the events of the past couple days, explaining the sheer oddity of the situation.

When he reached the part about the creature they'd found in the basement of the old house, he feared that she'd call him crazy; but instead she only clenched her jaw in focus as he described what he saw in that basement.

Jack was offered little relief as he let out all the pent-up secrets and told her of the tale of the night he left Magrath ten years ago. He warily danced around the topic of his father, afraid of what other old wounds that may tear open for Shannon. Though, before he could delve into that territory, he figured it may be time for the old friend he spoke to every night before bed. Alcohol.

--

They sat at the kitchen table drinking Jim Beam straight from the bottle. Though their eyes still glistened with tears, the crying had slowed some time ago; primarily due to the numbing of the liquor. Jack supposed alcohol helped with anything; so far as forgetting went. Though he knew that as soon as the buzz of inebriation wore off, they may be faced with the stark reality of their situation. With the bottle of Beam in his hand, however, he simply didn't care what the future held.

Jack met Shannon's eyes, feeling his own breaths grow deeper as the alcohol took hold, "do you remember when we were younger? The sort of stupid shit we'd get up to, y'know, the three of us?"

Shannon smiled sadly, "yeah of course, like that one game you'd always get us to play! What did you call it? Ding-dong something..."

Jack smiled widely, "Ding-dong danger! I loved that one. Dom said he hated it, even though he'd always hop on the bandwagon as soon as I'd bring it up."

Shannon smiled, "I forget; why did you insist on calling it ding-dong danger?"

Jack gave a mockingly serious expression, "Mr. Lance would always answer his door with his shotgun in hand. We'd ring the doorbell repeatedly to make him fire a warning shot into the air. The danger came from the thought that he'd just end up shooting us with it."

Shannon's eyes widened, "Oh my god, I remember now. God, we were dumb kids."

Jack nodded, "yeah, but what else were we supposed to do? There's never been much going on in this town as it is. You could almost die of boredom here."

At the mention of death, Shannon's face clouded over with grief and Jack sat there wishing he could suck the words he uttered out so carelessly back in. An uncomfortable silence befell them, causing Jack to once more pick up the bottle and take a long, deep swing from it; allowing the warmth to rise his cheeks and cover his entire face.

Shannon watched him, then held her hand out for the bottle, which he happily passed over to her. She took a long swig from it and set it back down between them, her eyes growing clouded with a mixture of both thought and the early stages of drunkenness.

She reached across the table and put her hand on Jack's, then surprised him by launching into a story of her own, "it's kind of funny, you know. When Dom and I first started dating, both our parents were against it. Though my parents didn't know the whole story about our breakup, they knew it had harmed our friendship quite substantially and they didn't want to see that happen again. Dom's didn't want him dating his best friend's ex out of respect for you. After some time, we eventually destroyed those protests. Well, Dom did. He proposed, and suddenly, they became aware that we were more than just a one-off fling. We didn't have a large wedding, just a small Magrath-fashion one. Afterwards, people stopped by and told us how happy they were that our love had blossomed."

Though she smiled sadly throughout recalling the events to Jack, he noticed a slight grimace as she said the last part. He didn't press, however, and simply allowed her to continue without interruption.

Shannon sighed, "it wasn't all sunshine and rainbows though Jack. Hell, by the time you got back Dom and I weren't doing the best. He was working long hours and taking double shifts at the precinct. For the past month, I'd only see him maybe once a week. It was beginning to wear our marriage out, I started going to bed before he'd even get home. Jack, I was avoiding him. It's just that - and I feel like a bitch just for saying this - even though he was always a sweetheart, I never really felt special, you know? He was nice to everyone and I was just someone along for the ride on the Dom train."

She made a small noise like she was disgusted with herself but continued, "I'm sorry. I know he just died, and maybe it's this alcohol talking but I kind of feel the faintest bit relieved. Is that awful? I feel like that's just an awful thing for me to say. It's just that… Dom was married to this town and his job more than he was ever married to me."

Jack nodded, though his mind was clouded in the familiar high of the alcohol. It whisked him away to a place where he couldn't quite contribute to a meaningful conversation of any magnitude. Instead he stared into Shannon's emerald green eyes and marveled at the way the faint stream of moonlight that poured in through the open kitchen window caused them to glimmer. He saw a tear well up in the corner of her eye and without thinking, he reached up and slowly brushed it away for her using his thumb; slowly tracing along her lower lid so the tears would be pushed out without causing more to follow.

He brought his hand back without moving his eyes off her and watched as she tucked a loose strand of her fiery hair behind her ear, the bright red contrasted vividly against her pale skin.

He licked his lips, making a mental note that the attraction was still there, and though he knew he needed to tell her something -

something that had been hidden deep within himself - the alcohol blurred his mind. It obscured his thoughts and released any inhibitions he had. So, although he was subconsciously aware of how wrong it was, and although he knew they were both in mourning; he reached across the table and placed his hands on hers, and lustfully dragged his eyes over her.

Jack looked back up to Shannon's face and noticed her chewing on her lower lip as she studied his face. Without thinking, he leaned slowly leaned across the table and placed his hand on the nape of her neck with his thumb just on the crest of her jaw. Her eyes widened as he closed the space between them and kissed her.

It wasn't a magical kiss. It was a wet, sloppy kiss born out of desperation and drunken stupidity; the kind of kiss that they both knew they'd come to regret when the alcohol no longer clouded their better judgement, but for that moment they didn't care. Nothing mattered to them except for that very moment, and as Jack kissed his old lover, he felt that he could have spent his life with her had circumstances been different; that together, they could have faced the world as one and made something more of it.

Jack ran his hands through her soft, lavender scented hair and could feel the tears running down his cheek melding with the tears running down hers. He breathed in and a soft sob escaped Shannon's lips as she tried to as well. Her hands worked on his shirt buttons and for a second he saw with utter clarity that this was wrong and shouldn't be something they do. Not now, mere hours after her husband had died.

Jack pulled away, feeling his mind overheating as it tried to penetrate the fog of his drunken state. Though, as he opened his mouth to protest, Shannon pulled him back in, silencing him, quelling any desire he had to stop it from happening.

Jack submitted to his lust and ran his hands up her side as he removed her shirt; losing himself to his desire.

~ 2 ~

Hours later; under the covers next to his deceased friend's wife, the sobriety began to take hold. It started in a sort of waking dream as the alcohol slowly faded and the drunken visage crumbled away before his eyes. As the darkness of the real world came back to him in full force, Jack's mind delved once more into his past, to the days when his father began the metamorphosis from loving father to abusive authoritarian figure. To the days when the social status of his girlfriend began to matter to him.

He thought back to the child that never was; laying in the crib at the hospital in his earlier dream. The way it'd babbled as he stood there looking at it, reaching for his finger and clenching it tight.

He couldn't recall why he was running late, though looking back, he figured it had something to do with grabbing snacks from Ferguson's for the evening he was planning on spending with Shannon. He'd told her to be at his place for five, and yet, as he walked back under the warmth of the sun, he realized he was no less than twenty minutes late.

He'd just walked through the threshold of his house when Shannon ran out from the hall, tears pouring down her cheeks and blood dripping from beneath her dress; leaving a trail of crimson in her wake.

Jack's eyes widened, "Shannon, what happened? Is everything alright, are you okay?"

She pushed past him as he reached out for her, "Don't fucking touch me! You're all crazy, all insane. Fuck off."

She stormed out of the house and into the sun, leaving Jack dumbfounded as he stood in the doorway with the white plastic bag in his hand. He'd place his first step down in front of him to follow her when he heard footsteps coming from the hallway she ran out of.

He turned then, and saw his father standing just above the trail of crimson with a blood-soaked towel in his hands. His white dress shirt sleeves were rolled up, revealing his muscled forearms and his lips were pulled back in a menacing smile.

His eyes flicked over to Jack, "Hey Jackie, follow me, I have something to show you."

Thinking back, Jack knew he should have run after Shannon. He should have stopped her and had her explain what happened. But in hindsight, everything becomes infinitely clearer and at the time, he had no idea what awaited him down the hall and in his father's study.

A hollow feeling spread in his chest as he followed his father - and the trail of blood - back to his father's study. As they walked into the room, he saw the trail join a puddle of crimson on the floor, where the congealing blood mixed with the dark carpet below.

His father walked over to his desk and lifted something off it, though Jack couldn't see exactly what, he could only distinguish that it - like the floor - was covered in blood.

His father outstretched his hands and dropped it to the floor in front of him, "Jackie, this is what happens when you try to breed with swine."

Jack looked down to what his father had dropped and suddenly felt like throwing up. It wasn't an object. No, the fleshy mass on floor was that of his unborn child. It's unformed face seemed to stare up at Jack, as though questioning why he didn't save it, didn't protect it.

Jack fell to his knees and picked up the child that never was, cradling it as he wept. He clutched it to his chest as the sobs overcame hi; accompanying a faint thought that resounded through his head. *We never even told him she was pregnant.*

Jack's father laughed apathetically as he wandered out of the room. Leaving Jack alone with his unborn child.

--

Jack awoke in a cold sweat sometime later, hyperventilating as he realized he'd slipped into another dream. Dom's words echoed through his head, "Jack, she's forgiven you, I've forgiven you. It wasn't your fault to begin with. It's time you forgive yourself, Okay?"

He nodded quietly to himself as his heart slowly settled and tears began to spill out once more. He turned and looked at Shannon - who began to stir from his labored breathing - and clung to her, desperate for the touch of another. Though he'd been filled with guilt after sleeping with his friend's wife, in that moment, the pain of losing the child he'd never had a chance to meet outweighed everything else.

Shannon placed a tired hand on his shoulder as he wept. He cried well into the time when the sun re-emerged in the east and cast its magnificent orange haze over Magrath; indifferent towards the adulterous act it had illuminated with its rays. The town slowly began to awaken, unknowing of the horrific events of last night or the horrors that happened years prior in the Lewis manor, and unknowing of the monster that resided in the ruins of the building that once stood proud over it.

Jack shrugged himself out of bed and shambled into the shower, hoping to wash away the guilt that rode through him, resigning himself to apologize to Shannon. Not only for the prior night, but also for what his father did to her all those years ago. He mentally prepared himself for the day as well; he knew he needed to save Trix, it was the least he could do for Dom. Though it was an act of friendship or a plea for forgiveness, Jack wasn't sure.

What he was sure of, however, was that he was a shitty human being, but he was going to face his demons.

~ 3 ~

Shannon sat at the kitchen table, eyeing the now empty bottle of Jim Beam that sat precariously before her. It refracted the sunlight and cast a rainbow along the table's wooden surface. The sunlight hit Shannon's hair shining brilliance through it that gave her a goddess-like visage that cause Jack's breath to catch in his chest. As he stood there marveling at her gorgeousness, he swallowed the guilt of their actions from the prior night. Though, the guilt was not founded in regret, for he did not regret making love to her. No, the guilt was founded in the timing of it. He knew they should have waited.

He walked over to her, and took in a breath to say what he wanted to, though she beat him to it, "Jack, about last night... I - since you came back - well. I couldn't help but think about us. What we could have been. You've changed. Matured even. I've changed too. Your dad - he - he changed a lot for us and for a time I blamed you. But I don't know. I know that wasn't your fault. I'm not going to hide the fact that I have feelings for you. What we did last night was more than just the alcohol. For me at least. But - the timing, it just wasn't right. We shouldn't have done that; not that soon. I fear, well, I fear I've ruined things between us. Please tell me that's not true."

Jack smiled and placed his hand on her shoulder, "You're overthinking things Shannon. We were drunk, and those feelings we suppressed got the better of us, they made us act out what we wanted to without holding back. Without our better judgement. The timing wasn't right, that's true, but it doesn't change how I feel about you."

She smiled sadly before tears began to fall from her eyes, "I'm glad. Do you - do you think Dom would hate us for this?"

Jack thought for a moment and shook his head, "I can't say for sure, but I don't think he would. He always strived for other people to be happy, I don't think he had it in him to hate anyone. Especially you."

Suddenly Jack's mind was filled with the thought of Dom telling him that he hated him for leaving Magrath and he felt a pain flare up in his chest. Thankfully, he managed to hide his expression from Shannon who'd resumed staring into the empty Jim Beam bottle.

Jack put his hand on her shoulder, "Look, Shannon, I can't stay here right now, that thing that - that thing that killed Dom, it's still out there. I need to kill it, if it even can be killed. But before I go, I want to say something."

She looked up to him and he gulped so as to not choke on the words that came out next, "I'm sorry Shannon. For what happened when we broke up. I know you don't hold it against me, but I do. I should have run after you, better yet, I should have been there to prevent my father from doing that to you in the first place. To prevent him from taking our child away from us."

Just like that, the emotional wall Shannon had been hiding behind crumbled and she began sobbing uncontrollably. Jack watched her for a moment as he constructed his own emotional walls, there'd be time for crying later. For now, he had a job to do, one that tears would not help with. He walked over to Shannon and wrapped her in a tight hug that she reciprocated. He knew how difficult the path forward would be for her as it was one he had travelled and had seen travelled many times over the years. It was one he would travel alongside her, if her heart so desired.

He left her there in the sunbathed kitchen. Her cries filled the space of the tiled room as she sobbed into her hands. She had whisked him off, understanding that he had a job to do. He kissed her on the forehead before leaving and stepped out into the cold and bitter morning air. As memories of the prior night with her filled him with warmth, he reflected on the oddity of his newfound situation and felt a twinge of guilt work its way through his body.

As he walked onto the sidewalk, he realized he'd need to retrieve his car from the manor. He looked back towards the house once more and saw Shannon sitting at the table still, with her face in her hands as she sobbed.

There was no amount of preparation for what he was about to face, though he knew he would do whatever it would take to avenge his friend's death and the deaths of the others. Though he knew he was a shitty friend, he would try to make amends by saving Dom's niece. Even if it killed him.

If he didn't, well, he wouldn't quite know what to do with himself.

Part 3
What's Left Behind

October 6, 2015

Chapter 11: Larkin

~ 1 ~

After retrieving his car from outside of the manor, Jack trundled it down the residential street leading towards Larkin's house. He checked each of the house numbers as he proceeded, checking against the where Noah Brackman's father had written his address two days prior. He pulled up along the curb in front of an old looking bungalow with grey siding and crumbling masonry.

Jack turned off the car and stepped out from behind the wheel, sighing into the early morning air as he steeled himself for the upcoming conversation. He looked up to the sky above and smiled as the sun radiated the faintest amount of heat over Magrath. He double checked the address once more before stepping up onto the curb and heading up the cracked cobblestone path that bisected the dew strewn lawn in front of Larkin's house.

The droplets of dew glimmered in the sunlight, reminding him of Shannon sitting at her table crying. He paused for a moment, wondering how she was faring. He stopped and shook his head clear of the thought, for now was not the time to dwell on her. No, right now he had to ask Larkin some questions about what really went down on the night he and his friends visited his old home.

The school had given the student's a day of mourning over Robert's death; which Jack was grateful for, as it meant he didn't need to go back into the anxiety riddled building where he witnessed Robert's mental breakdown. Chiding himself for being so selfish, he shuffled up to the metal screen door that stood as a barrier protecting the home of Larkin Grace.

Jack reached a nervous had forward and pressed in the pearl-like plastic doorbell, hoping Larkin would be home alone and he wouldn't need to explain to the boy's parents why he wanted to speak to their son so early in the morning. Much to his relief, it was Larkin who opened the metal core door just on the other side of the screen. His eyes widened as he saw Jack, though Jack was able to see that his eyes were red and weary looking. Perhaps from losing his friend, perhaps from something else.

Jack cleared his throat, "Hey Larkin, do you remember me?"

Larkin nodded, "Detective Lewis, right?"

Jack chuckled, "Not quite. I'm a PI, not a detective. Just call me Jack."

Larkin furrowed his brow, but nodded slowly, "okay. Yeah, what's up?"

Jack thought for a second, "perhaps I should come in, there's something I need to ask you."

Larkin thought, then nodded once more, "sure; my parents are at work, so it shouldn't be an issue. Come on in."

He yawned as he unlocked the screen door and opened it for Jack to come through. Jack nodded as he passed and took in his surroundings.

From the large worn leather couch and matching loveseat, Jack could tell that the room just off the entryway was either used frequently, or they didn't care much for their furniture. He shrugged to himself, reckoning that it was most likely a mixture of the two. Like Dom's brother's house, hardwood spanned the floor, though, unlike that house, this hard wood was worn and in several places had deep, angry looking gouges.

Jack slid his feet from his shoes and followed Larkin over to the couch where he plopped down and looked at his distorted reflection in the tube television that sat adjacent to him. He smiled, it had been a long time since he'd seen one so old, and he could imagine Larkin and his friends sitting on these couches during easier times; before two of their members had passed away. Jack's smile fell at the thought. Larkin had lost so much in the past month.

Jack smiled warily to Larkin, who was moving a cast iron kettle onto the table, "what type of tea are you drinking?"

Larkin looked up and smiled soberly, "It's a breakfast blend that my mom likes, figured I'd give it a shot, would you like some?"

Jack nodded and Larkin turned and walked into the other room, presumably to get another mug. While his footsteps petered off, Jack thought about how he would go about asking Larkin the questions he wanted to without repeat the same sort of episode that Robert had displayed.

First, he thought of the answers he needed to help with the case, 'why was Noah killed a week after they went to the house versus Robert just over two weeks later,' 'what really happened the night they went to that house,' and 'how do the other two murders tie into this?' He thought for a moment longer, rationalizing that although Larkin wouldn't know the actual answers to those questions, he may be able to give insight by retelling his story. So, Jack figured that would be the best course of action.

Moments later, Larkin returned with a clean mug in his hand. As he handed Jack the mug, Jack noticed that his motions were sluggish, as though he hadn't been sleeping, just like how Robert was the other day, though less extreme.

Jack took the mug and poured dome of the tea into it, "Thank you Larkin, I really needed this."

Larkin nodded, "no problem detective."

Jack winced at the word but said nothing, "how have you been?"

Larkin glanced up from his own mug and met Jack's eyes, "fine - actually, no. I'm not doing so hot. I didn't sleep last night. Actually, it's more like I couldn't sleep last night."

Jack put as much concern into his voice as he could, "Why haven't you been sleeping Larkin? Is everything alright?"

His expression stiffened, and he gave a cursory glance off to the corner of the room, "Just didn't, I don't know, it could have been the weather. I didn't even find out about Robbie's death until this morning."

Jack wasn't buying it, "so, it wouldn't have anything to do with what you saw at the manor?"

Larkin's eyes shot wide open, and for a quick second he looked extremely panicked, he tried to hide it, though his voice betrayed him, "Wh-what do you mean? Saw? W-we didn't see anything at the manor. We just -"

Jack cut him off, "look kid, I don't have the time or the patience to dick around right now. You know your friend Trix? Well, she's missing. Now, I'm hoping she doesn't end up like the other five that were killed by that thing. Everything is going to shit in this town and for some reason I'm crazy enough to think I can stop it. Now help me out and tell me what the hell happened at the manor."

Larkin's eyes widened once more, though this time he nodded in resignation, "yeah, okay. I guess you've seen it too. Uh, what did Zach tell you about after the party?"

Jack smiled grimly, happy he would finally hear what happened, "He said that you all were tired, so you went to bed. Though, we both know that was a lie."

Larkin nodded, "Yeah. Well, we went to that house, thought it would be fun to dick around up there and see what all the fuss was about, y'know? We just wanted to see if there was any merit to the rumors we'd been hearing. We were all fairly toasted at that point and were all maybe a little bit too courageous for our own good.

"We walked up that hill and went straight into the house like we owned the damn place. Now, we thought it would be really burnt on the inside, but to our surprise, it had only been blackened in some places, as though the fire was focused on several spots as opposed to the whole thing. I mean, the roof was pretty charred and in some places, you could see through into the sky, but all things considered, it was too bad. Like, I was six when it was set on fire and I remember it being a lot brighter than that. I guess the fire department was better than we thought or something. You know, I wanted to be a fire fighter once, but my mom thinks I should focus on my grades and go off to college or something. I don't know. I think I'd make a good firefighter."

Jack nodded, realizing this tangential thing may keep happening with Larkin, "you were saying about that night?"

"Oh yeah, well, as we walked around the house, we all sort of started feeling uneasy, as though we were all in danger. Look, it's hard to describe, but it's like the feeling you have when you're being watched, then you look up and see someone staring at you. Yeah, it was like that, but when I looked around, there was nothing I could see, and the feeling was more like someone wanted to cause us harm as opposed to just stare at us. Does that make sense?"

Jack nodded, "yeah it does. So, what happened next?"

"We began searching rooms, we didn't climb up the hill in order to run as soon as we got into the house. We began moving from room to room separately. I found this one room that looked like one of those fancy offices you seen in movies with the fireplace and the high back chair. You know what I mean?"

Jack just nodded as he saw his father's study in his mind's eye.

"Well, I was looking around in there for a while. There were a bunch of books from a few authors I knew and a few I didn't, but when I got to the desk, I realized that a lot of the drawers were locked. That's when it hit me that something was off. The house had been abandoned for over a decade, and yet no one had been through to loot it? That really struck me as odd at the time.

"Anyway, I begin trying the handles, trying to see if any of them open up and if there's anything inside of them. But none of them budge, until I finally break one open. Inside there was just this single leather book with a lock on it. I put it in my jacket's pocket thinking 'who the hell locks a book?' I figured that maybe it had something interesting in it. Then I heard some grunts coming from another room, so I decided to check it out.

"So, I go back into the hallway and try to listen to where the grunts are coming from. I mean, it wasn't hard to find it out; one end of the hallway leads back towards the entrance and the other had another room, so I walked towards that, figuring it was a better chance.

"Anyway, I was right and when I entered, I saw Noah, Robert and Zach all working to move these fallen planks off this indent in the floor. Now, I'm not sure what compelled them to move those planks, but they just kind of looked at me and said 'what are you doing watching you two? Get your asses over here and help us move these planks!' So that's what we did.

"It took us maybe fifteen to twenty minutes, but we cleared all of the debris away from this indent and realized there was a staircase underneath it. Trix, Zach and I weren't too keen on going down it, but Noah and Robert, who were also the most drunk insisted. With little option but to follow them, we did. It was dark, but we all used our phones to light the way. It was really something I tell you; that staircase seemed to go on forever. But eventually we got to the bottom and saw that there was a big concrete room. Kind of like a bunker. I've watched a few YouTube videos about doomsday bunkers, and it was kind of like that. I mean, I don't think the family that lived there would have done much with a bunker, but they had the money for one. If I had that sort of money, I think I'd buy a boat or something, you know? Just travel the ocean for a year or something, that would be fun. Sometimes I wonder -"

Jack cut him off, "Larkin, you're getting side-tracked again."

Larkin blinked hard and shook his head, as though trying to shake off the tiredness that was grabbing hold of him, "sorry about that. It's - uh, where was I?"

Jack chuckled lightly, "you just got into the basement…"

His eyes widened, "oh yes! Well, we had walked down the stairs in the dark, so our phones were already out, and our flashlights were on, but the darkness of that room seemed to be thicker, our light just didn't go as far. It's hard to describe, but the closest I would say that the best comparison would be if you tried to shine a flashlight through your shirt. You can still tell there's a light in there, but it just doesn't go as far.

"Anyway, we were walking around that basement, trying to find - well, trying to find anything that we could bring back to show we'd been down there. We probably spent around fifteen minutes looking down there, though it felt closer to an hour. Noah found this old doorway that was blocked by some more debris - honestly, now that I think about it, I don't know how that debris got there, the roof was concrete, same as the ground…"

He tilted his head as he furrowed his brow in thought, "anyway, we wanted something to show to our friends - and we were kind of, well, drunk - so we began removing the debris. As we moved the last piece from the front of the door, it was like an explosion went off. Zach and I were closest, so we were sent flying the farthest. We were thrown into the wall and I blacked out. I heard after that Trix was thrown into the middle of the room, but Noah and Robert remained close to the door.

"I woke up to the sound of Robert screaming. It was the worst thing I've ever heard in my life, detective. It was the kind of sound people make when they die. Now, I didn't see anything at first - it was really dark down there. But they were right by the door, so by the time I closed the distance between us, I could see it too. You said you've seen it, right?"

Jack nodded, "yeah I did. It tore my best friend in half like it was nothing."

Larkin gulped, "yeah, well, as soon as I saw it, I turned and ran, I didn't care who else made it out, I was afraid of it getting me. I ran until I got to the top of that damned staircase and then I waited. It wasn't long before the others made it up and Larkin, Zach, Robbie, Trix and I began throwing the debris we'd removed back on top of the hole. We hoped it wouldn't make it out, we were so wrong."

Jack watched Larkin as he took a moment to collect his thoughts; obviously trying hard not to break down at the memories of losing his friends progressively over the past several weeks. He held his hand up to his mouth and closed his eyes. For a second Jack thought he was going to scream, though, as he pulled his hand away from his mouth, Jack quickly realized that he had been yawning. The kids tired and can hardly process emotions properly.

Jack swallowed, "was there any behaviour Noah displayed before he was killed?"

Larkin nodded slowly, "yeah. After we left, we just thought things would go to normal. Hell, the next morning we laughed it off as though it were some sort of shared hallucination. It wasn't until Noah stopped sleeping himself that we realized something was horribly wrong.

"At first, he simply refused to talk about it. He just said he couldn't sleep, much the same as Robert had been close to the end there. Although, as the week moved on, he started getting more and more paranoid, looking over his shoulder and cowering whenever he was startled. I don't think he told the others what he was seeing, but he told me."

Jack's eyes widened, "what did he see?"

Larkin chewed on his upper lip as he thought, "okay, this is going to sound a bit crazy, but, he said that thing was following him. He said he'd see it outside his window or at the end of the block. Sometimes he would even see it at school, even though no one else could. He saw more of it, so I thought maybe he was just, you know, losing it? But then he died… and well," Larkin chuckled harshly, "I couldn't do anything to stop it."

Jack's expression softened, "there was nothing you could do Larkin, you know that, right? That thing, whatever it is, it's strong."

He shook his head and furrowed his brow as he thought of the situation he was in; unable to believe he was talking to a sixteen-year-old about the best way to kill a monster. *Ghosts are one thing, this, this is fucking insane.*

He was snapped out of his thoughts when Larking began speaking again, this time with tears trickling down his cheeks, "After what happened to Noah, we all knew what was going to happen once Robbie started seeing it. I'd tried telling the others after Noah died, but Trix didn't want to hear it and the others didn't want to believe it. That is, until Robbie began to come to school with bags under his eyes and started dosing in class whenever he could. Trix isolated herself in her house and Zach took it upon himself to try and save us all.

"But he couldn't save Robbie, none of us could. He's not holding up so well, especially now that I've -"

Jack frowned as Larkin cut off his words, "now that you're what? Are you seeing it now?"

Larkin said nothing, but the terrified look in his eyes told Jack everything he needed to know. Jack gave him a somber look and reached over to put his hand on Larkin's shoulder, "look, kid. I'm going to stop that thing. If it's the same as with the others, you still have a few days until it actually comes for you, right? If I have anything to say about that, it'll be dead before then. Trust me."

Larkin smiled sadly, but shook his head, "I don't think you can. I don't think anyone can. I mean, did you see its hands? It was almost like each fingernail was its own blade and you said it tore your friend in half - What could you do against something like that?"

Jack looked down to his hands; imagining his father's blood staining the surfaces, "whatever it takes kid. Whatever it takes."

They sat in silence for some time, each of them lost in their own heads. Jack mulled over the courses of action he'd need to take in order to bring this thing down but kept coming up empty. He didn't think a gun would work and he doubted he could get close enough to use a knife. Though as a thought rose forth from the depths of his subconscious, he frowned.

He turned to Larkin abruptly, startling the boy out of his own tired stupor, “the night, when you guys found it. Why do you think it didn’t come after you?”

Larking furrowed his brow and thought for a second before replying, “when I saw it, it was slowly walking from the room, kind of like it was still partially asleep - I only say that because I get like that sometimes, you know? My mom says I get it from my father because he always gets up to grab sandwiches in the night, but never remembers it. Almost like he’s just on the edge of waking up. I think it’s just something guys do -”

“Larkin,” Jack interjected.

Larkin blushed, “sorry, that just kind of happens.”

Jack waved his hand, “no worries kid, I get it.”

Larkin smiled tiredly, “is there anything else I can tell you, detective?”

Jack chuckled, “I’m not a detective kid, I’m a PI, but please just call me Jack.”

Larkin frowned as though some puzzle pieces were falling into place, “Jack… Lewis? Are you Jack Lewis?”

Jack’s forehead wrinkled in confusion, “yes, but I already told you-”

Larkin’s face contorted into one of realization, “holy shit - pardon my French. But you used to live at that house, didn’t you?”

Jack nodded solemnly, “yeah, I grew up there. It was my family’s”

Suddenly Larkin got up and walked briskly out of the room. Jack frowned but didn’t call out after him as he heard Larkin’s footsteps draw down the hall then proceed back toward him. He rounded the corner with a small, pocket sized notebook bound in leather clutched tightly in his hands.

He held it out to Jack and explained as Jack took it and turned it over, "that's the one I found in the desk. I haven't tried to open it, figured it was locked for a reason, but I think you should have it. I mean, the house belonged to your family."

Jack studied the small padlock attached to the small ring of metal pressed through the book, "I don't know what to say kid. I mean, what a coincidence that you would give this to me. Thank you."

Larkin frowned, "my mom says there's no such thing as a coincidence. Things happen as they need to. She always says, 'it ain't no coincidence the sun makes the flowers bloom or makes the snow fall in our little city, why is anything else different?'" he shrugged and met Jack's eyes, "my father always brushes her off about that saying, calls them wives tales. But I'm not so sure. Ever since I got that book I've been dreaming about flowers and I gotta tell you, they feel important."

Jack tilted his head as though it would dislodge the nagging feeling that had been growing in the periphery of his mind. As the tiles of thought moved around in his mind and slid into place, he realized what he needed to do and where he needed to go next.

He stood up and reached out towards Larkin, "thank you kid, so very much. I know where I have to go next."

Larkin frowned but reached out and shook his hand. His grip was unsteady though Jack held firm as he pumped his hand once, then turned and walked towards the door, bidding Larkin farewell on his way out.

As he stepped into the cold air once more he glanced down at the leather book clutched gently in his hands and the small name pressed into the bottom right corner.

Jack S. Lewis

With his body trembling - though not from fear - he slid behind the wheel of the Sunfire and turned over the engine. Resigning to follow the signs to wherever they will lead him and allow the case to splay itself in front of him, as it always did. This sign of flowers would take him to where he needed to be, despite how anxious he was for this reunion. It was time to see his mother.

Chapter 12: Family Ties

~ 1 ~

Jack drove down the well-maintained road that marked Magrath's shopping area. Storefronts lined either side of the street and near the end stood the cafe where he and Dom had shared coffee just the day before. He smiled sadly to himself as the memory moved through his mind. He didn't allow it time to linger, however; knowing that indulging in his memories would not help in this situation. He needed to figure out if Larkin's dreams of flowers meant anything.

He drove past his mother's flower shop for the sixth time, thinking to himself that it was ridiculous. Not the fact that he was so anxious to face her, but the fact that some teenager's dreams about flowers could have any bearing on the direction this case was taking. Though, as he rounded the corner for the seventh time, he resigned himself to his fate and trundled the car to a stop just outside of his mother's shop.

Before moving from the vehicle, he looked down to the battered and locked journal that now lay on his passenger seat. He reached over to his glove compartment and pulled out a new pack of Marlboros from within, knowing full well that he would need something to take the edge off. Perhaps several.

Shakily, he put the cigarette in his mouth and lit it, cracking the window slightly to allow the smoke room to flow freely from the cab of the vehicle. The mélange of emotions bubbled within him, mixing and colliding recklessly as he puffed absentmindedly on the filter. As he sat there, he thought of what he was feeling as though attempting to understand himself.

Fear was the most prominent emotion at the second, for inside of the journal, he may find another spite filled message from his father detailing the ways in which they were "better than the rest." He feared it would be something his father had written pre-emptively to traumatize him further and stir up old memories he tried to keep buried. He feared it would give insight into the mind of the man who'd beaten him almost nightly and caused him to cry himself to sleep on several occasions, wondering why he wasn't good enough anymore.

Hope burned fiercely inside of Jack as well, for in the recesses of his heart, he hoped that there was still some semblance of the man he had grown to love as a child written between the covers. He hoped that there was even the most miniscule reminder of the man who'd build forts with him in the summer and igloos in the winter instead of the man who'd turned his room into a prison and his body into a punching bag. He hoped that contained within the pages were the memories of a man who existed long before Jack had wrapped the belt around his neck and pulled until his face turned purple and his eyes threatened to burst.

Jack stared at the book as though it was cursed, contemplating burning it or even throwing it out of the car as he drove out of Magrath. He thought about leaving everything behind once more. Though, as he contemplated fleeing, his mind returned to Shannon and he knew he couldn't leave her behind. Not now, not after he'd caused so much pain to come into her life, and not when she needed him the most.

He picked up the cursed object and looked at his name impressed upon the leather and thought of the times when the three of them were a family, full of happiness and love instead of hatred and resentment. With a tinge of wonderment, Jack found himself hoping beyond anything he'd ever experienced that the pages contained words that would stir up those happy memories and not the hellscape he'd come to bury deep inside over the years.

He ran his fingers over his name and thought to himself, realizing that although he'd come to hate the man; although he'd come to despise the man with everything that he was; there was some part of him that held on. There was some part of him that still loved him unconditionally, that yearned for not only his praise, but his affection. Despite having seen the man carry his unborn child, he still wanted to feel the lost sensation of his father's muscular arms wrapped around him in a hug. It made him feel queasy.

As these thoughts enveloped him, he thumbed the lock, wondering how he would get it open if he wasn't able to find the key. Though, he supposed that could come later, first, he needed to speak to his mother.

He cast his eyes over to the storefront as he placed the book back on his passenger seat. The golden lettering looked well-polished despite its age; reflecting not only the quality of the material, but the dedication his mother had to its upkeep over the years.

He stepped from the car and paused as he stood between the open door and the body of it, wondering if there were some chance, he was mistaken. He backed up and closed the door with a decisive *thunk* as the weather stripping softened the blow of the metal colliding with the frame. Sighing, he stepped onto the sidewalk and began walking towards the door just below the gold lettering. Stopping to look back towards his car once more as though wishing Dom were there to encourage him to take the final steps.

He snickered, that wouldn't be like Dom. No, Dom would be right there beside him, figuratively holding his hand along the way, making sure he went through with his word. *He'd say something witty, something to make me laugh and take the edge off. He'd make fun of me in a way I'd have no choice but to agree with.*

He looked down to his shoes as he resumed the walk to the glass door, stopping once more as a raindrop splattered against his shoe. He frowned and looked upwards to the clear sky above him, wondering where the droplet had come from. With no cloud in sight, he shrugged and walked up to the glass, only noticing that it wasn't rain when he saw his reflecting in the transparent surface. No, it wasn't rain at all. He was crying. *I miss you already man.*

He wiped the tears off his cheek as he grabbed the handle of the glass door in front of him, hesitating slightly before pulling it open.

--

The bell above the door jingled pleasantly as he entered the flower shop and his nose was instantly graced with the smell of lilacs and roses. He smiled as the scent stirred up the memory of playing there as a child.

He wandered no more than two steps when a familiar voice drifted from the back, "I'll be right there, just tending the bromeliads!"

Jack stopped at the sound of the voice. His mind was filled with memories of Sunday morning cinnamon buns and picnics in the park. His stomach performed somersaults and flips as he recalled the very same voice singing calming melodies and reading him stories as he lay in bed. The voice carried with it not only the memories of better times, but the time before his innocence shattered and his life was flipped upside down. Jack smiled at the sound of his mother's voice.

Jack looked past the rows of flowers that spanned the space between him and the door to the back room, smiling as a woman emerged from around the corner, stopping immediately. Her eyes shot wide open and her hand flew up to her mouth as she stifled a surprised cry. Slowly, they began to walk toward each other, their eyes never leaving the other's face. As Jack neared, her hand drifted up to his face; hesitantly as though he may disappear if she touched him. She pulled back at the last second, her eyes full of bewilderment. Smiling Jack reached out and grabbed her hand, bringing it rest on his stubbled chin.

"Jack?"

"Hey mom."

All hesitancy was gone as he replied to her simple question. Though he supposed to her, it wasn't a simple question at all and as he found himself wrapped in a tight hug and she happily cried into his chest. He wrapped his arms around her, and held on tight, not wanting to let go, for he had not realized how much he needed that hug.

After some time, they pulled apart, and Martha Lewis wiped her tears away while Jack committed her new look to memory. Her once vibrant brown hair was now streaked grey in areas, reflecting the stresses she'd undergone over the years. Her eyes, though still sharp enough to root him to the spot, had softened around the edges by both wrinkles and tired bags that formed underneath.

He watched as she studied him, reckoning she was gauging whether he'd grown into a man or he was still the boy he'd been the last time she'd seen him. He found himself hoping it was the former, for after all the hardships he'd endured, he felt significantly older than twenty-eight years old. Jack's smile wavered, and he knew her studious eyes caught the slightest inflection in his facial features.

She reached up and cradled his face in her hand, "my son. You've come home, I was wondering how long it would be before you came here."

Knowing she could spot a lie, he decided the truth would be the best option, "Honestly mom, I'm not so glad to be back. Magrath's changed, and I'm not sure if it's for the better."

She nodded slowly as she clenched her jaw, "It's changed alright, that's one way to put it." She paused, "Jack, I'm truly glad to see you. I've dreamt of this day for years, though, I know you wouldn't have come back unless it was absolutely necessary." She sighed, "I'll put on some tea. We need to talk."

--

Jack followed her through the door he'd seen her come in through, curious as to where they were heading. In the back rooms of the store, there were even more plants and flowers. Though he couldn't name many of them, he recognized the orchids and tulips, the aroma was almost overbearing, though it still graced his nose in a way he hadn't experienced since childhood.

Martha stopped just in front of a wooden door and smiled, "did you by chance notice that the store next to this one was closed?"

Jack frowned and thought back. He recalled seeing that the windows were blacked out, though he had figured that the store was just under renovations and had moved along, "yeah, but I just thought they were undergoing renovations, why?"

His mother smiled and pushed open the door behind her; revealing a large, furnished area within that had been remodeled to look like a loft, "Well, after your father died, I had no desire to rebuild the house, after all… bad things happened there. I'm sure you're aware that your dad owned a lot of the properties in Magrath, yes?"

Jack nodded, "yeah, but not exactly. He did something similar to the royal family and put all the properties in the family name so that none of them could be seized due to legal matters. Same with all the money, right?"

Martha's eyes widened, "you did your research, Jack, I'm impressed. But yes, when your father died, everything came under my possession rather easily. I evicted the previous tenants of this location and gave them a fair bit of money to get set up somewhere else. They were happy and I set about making this into my new home. It's not much, but it's enough for me."

Jack looked over the entirety of the room, soaking in the way she'd laid out the space she'd come to call home. The street side wall was covered by thick black curtains, that Jack had mistaken for coverings on the way to his mother's shop. Miniscule amounts of sunlight flitted through the small spaces between the curtains; casting beams of light across the room onto the plants that lined the wall between the living space and the flower boutique.

The plants were unlike anything Jack had ever seen; the lush greens were contrasted heavily by magnificent hues of reds, pinks and purples; all seeming to glow in the faint light. It was clear to Jack that his mother had never lost her green thumb or her passion for botany; for the plants held an air of health, each leaf's color was vibrant without the nutrient deprived yellowing or wilting displayed in many homes. He smiled as he reflected on the times he'd come to this shop as a child and learn the various potting techniques and watering methods his mother employed. Though he couldn't replicate any of those methods now, he found himself smiling at the memory of spending those afternoons with her.

He turned to survey the rest of the room, and noticed the opposite wall was lined with bookshelves. Some of the books looked new, and others looked old and cracked, as though looking at the pages would be enough to cause them to wither and disintegrate. As he moved his eyes over the numerous spines, he realized that there were far too many for him to count; there were hundreds, if not thousands of books contained on those shelves. He had always been aware of his mother's fondness of literature, though he never quite grasped just how much she read.

Martha chuckled, snapping him out of his thoughts, "I know, there's a lot of books, it took me a long time and a lot of talking to get them all here." She paused, "I - uh - I haven't left this place in a while. I don't typically go outside unless absolutely necessary. People coming through keep me up to date with on goings in the town, Mr. Ferguson delivers the groceries and the books were brought to me by Fiona Haggard."

Jack dubiously raised his eyebrow, "the librarian brought you all these books?"

"Yeah, but she's more than that. Come, sit down. I'll put on some tea, you tell me everything that's happened since you got to Magrath and I'll try my best to explain what all of this is."

Jack nodded, though he was perplexed. He walked over to the small dining table and pulled out the chair; sitting down while his mother placed a steel tea kettle on the oven then turned the dial to high. He watched as she mechanically set about cutting some herbs she had scattered atop the counter, then realized she was making the tea from scratch. He smiled and began to tell her all about the past few days.

"Well, a few days ago I got this strange call…"

~ 2 ~

Jack and Martha sat at the table, mugs in hand. Tears rolled freely down Jack's face as he came to the part about Dom's death and his mother reached across the table to grab his hand, reminding him of Shannon's similar action the prior night. He couldn't tell his mother about that, just the thought of it caused his cheeks to go red.

As his retelling of the events since his return to Magrath caught up to the present, his mother got up and retrieved several notebooks off the bookshelf. Jack frowned, but said nothing, instead he took a long sip from the bitter tea his mother had prepared for him.

She set the books down in front of him and cleared her throat, "that *thing* you encountered, well, it was encountered years before by one of your ancestors and one of the Haggard's ancestors. Around four hundred years ago to be more accurate. They encountered it during their search for new lands to inhabit. See, they were part of a larger group of more than one hundred families, yet they were chosen to lead the expedition. Your ancestor, a man named Nathaniel Lewis and the Haggard's ancestor, a man named Anlon Haggard were those two family's heads.

"Nathaniel was a physically strong man; the son of a carpenter. Whereas Anlon was the son of a cartographer and was very strong mentally. He'd committed himself to learning the language of the lands from a young age, a skill that proved useful in their travels. Anlon's mother tongue was Irish; thus, he recorded the journals of the exploration west in the Irish language. These are the translated versions of those journals. Now, I could tell you the story myself, but it may be easier to hear it from someone who actually witnessed it and recorded it first-hand."

Martha picked up the first one and began turning pages, "now, I don't think you're going to care about the earlier parts of the expedition or the actual founding of Magrath itself," she flipped to a page and stopped, "but here is roughly where their encounter starts. Bear in mind; it's not quite complete Jack, there will be many unanswered questions."

Jack frowned, but reached forward and grabbed the notebook from his mother's hand, "so where do I read until?"

She smiled weakly, "you'll know, trust me. Start at entry one-oh-seven and read through to one-fourteen."

Without knowing how to respond, Jack looked down to the notebook and began reading.

Entry 107 *April 22, 1642*

The lands still span before us and I am unsure of when we'll find suitable land in which to settle. Nathaniel seems to think that the further west we go, the more likely we'll be to find a river or lake on which to base the settlement. This land is uncharted, if only my father was here to read the land. Alas, the clouds are forming amidst the horizon and I don't believe that Nathaniel has seen them as of yet. I will advise to set up camp, based on the blackness of them, we're in for inclement weather.

Entry 108 *April 22, 1642*

The storm is raging all around us, I am sheltered in this caravan and it is only through this lamp's light that I am able to see anything at all. The others lay in wait for the storm to blow over, they assume it is the work of their God. I wonder how they'd gaze upon me should they know I don't believe in such things.

Entry 109 *April 22, 1642*

The air was pierced by a horrendous sound. Upon its inception, we believed it to be nothing more than the wind. Yet, it continued to grow in volume, eventually reaching its tumultuous crescendo that was nearly deafening. I would say it was akin to the squeal of a horse stuck in the mud. It evoked feelings of utter horror within each of us. Children screamed for their mothers who cried out for their husbands. The very sound evoked such fear in all of us that it would be unjust to call it anything other than fear itself.

I have begun to consult the bestiary granted to me by my father. Although I have scoured every inch of every page, there is no explanation for what could have produced such a sound. No manner of animal possesses the vocal cords, nor the lungs required to emit such a terrible sound. I will speak to Nathaniel; I believe that our only way of reasoning for this is to find the Indians that roam these plains. Perhaps, if communication is possible, they will shed light on this situation. Though, that will have to wait for the storm to pass and the screeching to cease.

Entry 110 *April 23, 1642*

The worst of the storm passed in the night, leaving us with little more than half our original number. Several families were found slaughtered in their tent this morning. Their innards were displayed on the outsides of their tents and wagons, what remained of them was mutilated. Their skulls were fractured, and their arms were bent in odd angles. I only hope they found peace in death. The rain continues to pour over our encampment. We'll be excavating the land for a grave in due time. Once mourning has passed, I will speak with Nathaniel and try to convince him of my plan.

Entry 111 *April 23, 1642*

Nathaniel has agreed to the plan, we set out soon. We'll be taking the fastest of the horses to take as little time as possible. The longer we leave the rest unattended, the worse off they will be. They are in mourning and need the firm hand we offer at this time. Unfortunately, our priorities lie elsewhere. In time, we will find answers to this predicament. Nathaniel has just flagged me over; I sure hope we find the answers we need.

Entry 112 *April 24, 1642*

We've been riding for over a day now. We made a small camp last night, and spent the night telling each other tales of our homelands that have been passed down through generations. I've grown to consider Nathaniel a brother in this short period of time, I only hope he sees me the same.

This morning the rains finally stopped, and the clouds began to clear. In the absence of rain to hold it down, smoke rose into the sky southbound of here. We will begin to head towards it once the horses have eaten. My only hope is that we condemn whatever beast produced that sound, and we are able to establish a new settlement soon.

Entry 113 April 24, 1642

I'm seated in one of the teepees of this tribe currently. We arrived shortly after midday and as we breached the perimeter, we were confronted by several of the Indian tribesmen wielding spears and daggers of varying lengths. Not for the first time, I am glad that I spent learning the various languages of the land in addition to the customs and traditions of the various tribes that remain untouched by my people.

As two sentries approached us, I reached into the saddle bag and grabbed the tobacco I'd been keeping for such a meeting. Nathaniel, however, began to reach for the flintlock he kept on his belt, however I was able to stop him in time.

As the men approached, I attempted to speak to them in several languages, though the one they responded to the best was the Massachusett language. It's a language spoken by several tribes both in and around New England; although they didn't speak it, they did seem to understand it.

They soon realized that we weren't a threat that they couldn't deal with and brought us further into their small village. It was there that I was able to witness the death ceremony.

A large fire blazed in the center of the village and standing around it was a circle of warriors clad in full ceremonial gear. They danced as the others beat their drums to the rhythm of the earth's heartbeat. They screamed their songs to their gods as they celebrated the lives of those they lost. I found myself unable to do anything but slide off my steed's back and get as close as I could. Though the sentries eyed me warily, I was able to get close enough to obtain a full view of the ceremony as it took place. In due time I found myself weeping alongside the villagers gathered around the inferno for the ceremony was one of the most raw and passionate spectacles I'd ever bore witness to.

When the music came to its staggering decrescendo, an older man with a headdress of feathers approached me and helped me to my feet. Again, I attempted to speak in the Massachusett language; he smiled and replied, telling me to follow him. I left Nathaniel as I followed the man who I would soon find to be the village chief into the very teepee I reside in currently. I offered him the tobacco and we smoked it together as a sign of peace between our two parties.

After exchanging pleasantries, he revealed that he knew the reason we had come; for the very same creature had killed several of their men that same night. Though, when I asked if he knew of how to stop it or if he had the knowledge required to stop the beast, he asked a strange question instead.

He asked me, "how does the sun know to rise, or the bird know to fly south? There are things in this world that we cannot comprehend, for that is the knowledge of the Earth Mother and her servants. I can grant you the knowledge you seek, though not only because I possess it, but because you are unlike the others of your kind. They squash those who hinder their goals underfoot, you, well you desire knowledge not for your own gain, but for the sake of knowing, for the sake of the betterment of the people and the preservation of tradition. That much was evident by your joining in at our ceremony. So, I will tell you what I know about our ancient foe. I will tell you how to deal with it."

It took me a moment to fully translate the chief's words in my own head, though the query on his wording was in the forefront of my cognition. He used the word "deal" and not "stop" nor "kill" to describe the knowledge he held. Not knowing what to say, I simply nodded, accepting whatever held he would offer.

To paraphrase; the chief explained that in order to "deal" with the creature, they would need to seal it. When I asked him why we wouldn't be able to kill it, he explained that there were other conditions that would need to be met. Ones that we could not perform as the creature would need to be significantly weakened and bonded to a mortal form in order for that to work.

I asked him why he didn't seal, or why the tribe hadn't taken care of the matter. He simply shook his head and told me that they had entered a pact long ago. The same type that Nathaniel and I would have to enter in order to seal it. We would have to form a verbal contract and pass down instructions through the generations for it to work.

Curious, I asked what would happen should either of the pacts be broken and he paled. He said the creature would "inhabit" the one who broke the pact and force them to live a fate worse than death. Upon their demise they would be forced to see things through the creature's eyes for all eternity.

Normally, I would have written this off as superstitious nonsense, however, I'd witnessed the scream and I'd seen what it did to my traveling companions. There was no refuting that, no matter how farfetched the premise seemed. Thus, I agreed to enter whatever oral pact the Chief suggested.

We're just waiting for Nathaniel to join us, then the ceremony will get underway.

Entry 114 *April 26, 1642*

It is done. The beast which I've taken to calling the Liath is sealed. Although the beast is sealed, it will be on Nathaniel and I to ensure it is never woken up and that our descendants know how to take care of it when it reawakens. We must ensure to pass down the tradition orally and never commit the process to paper as that will break the pact formed between us and the earth as I understand it.

Nathaniel has decided to construct his house above its resting place to act as a sort of safeguard against any escape. I'm not a religious man by any means, but God help us if it gets out.

Jack set down the transcribed journal and looked up to his mother, "is that it? There's nothing else?"

She looked at him in bafflement, "what do you mean?"

He clenched his jaw, "they sealed it, but it doesn't say how. The chief mentioned it could be killed if it was weakened but he never said how that would work either. Surely there must be *some* instruction as to how we could deal with it."

Martha shook her head sadly, "That information could only be passed on by your father to you, or Fiona's husband, Douglas Haggard, but he died shortly after you left."

Jack slammed his clenched fist on the table, "So what you're telling me is we have nothing but some journal that sounds like a fucking fairy tale? This is bullshit! I can't do anything with this."

Martha flinched at his sudden outburst and looked down to her wrinkled hands, "I'm sorry Jack… but that's all I really have on it. Fiona told me a few things that Douglas had shared in his sleep but it's nothing more than incoherent babble about plants."

Jack's face flushed as the guilt rose in his gut, "I'm sorry mom, it's just, I was hoping I'd have something to use against it. Anything at all. But with this, well, there's nothing that can be done."

Jack ran his fingers through his hair; feeling the smallest amount of sweat that started to form near the roots. He sighed, thinking over the story he'd just read. The tale from another time, surely passed down alongside the oral tradition by means of explaining the situation. *What do I do now? Dom's dead, Trix is gone, three children have died, people have been going missing and what's more is I'm nowhere closer to figuring out how to kill this damned 'Liath'.*

Martha stood and grabbed the notebooks off the table, then turned and walked back over to the bookshelf without saying a word, leaving Jack to sort out his own thoughts in the process. If his mother was unable to provide the answers, then perhaps Fiona would, after all, if the Haggards kept an account of anything, then surely she would have some insight into the on goings of the town.

Jack's eyes widened as the thought presented itself, "hey mom, just a question."

Martha placed the notebooks on the shelf and turned, wiping tears from her eyes, that Jack didn't notice, "yes dear?"

"Is Fiona around? I'd love to be able to ask her some questions."

His mother looked down and shuffled her feet, "I'm afraid I don't know. She hasn't been around here for the past week or so. I can give you her address if you want to check in on her though."

Jack nodded, thinking of the worst-case scenario already, "that would be great mom, is it close to here?"

Martha gave him a smile that didn't reach her eyes, "yeah, it's just a couple blocks south and then one or two west."

She turned back to the shelf and tore a sheet of paper out of one of the notebooks and walked back to the table, "here, I'll write it down for you."

She scribbled the address onto the paper and handed it over to Jack. He raised an eyebrow as he read it, "isn't this right beside the library?"

Martha chuckled lightly, "yeah it is, I guess the Haggards liked to be close to their life's work."

Jack smiled and stuffed the paper into his pocket, then walked over to his mom and wrapped her up in a hug, "thank you mom. I promise I'll spend the time catching up once all of this is dealt with, okay?"

Tears began to drip down her face as she pulled back to look at him one more time, "sure Jack, just promise you'll come back alive, okay? Otherwise, I don't know what I'll do."

Jack nodded, "of course, I'll do my best."

With that, he turned and started for the wooden door they entered through, taking long, deliberate strides. When he reached the door however, he turned back to his mother, one thought lingering in the back of his mind.

"Hey mom, did you ever find dad's body?"

Her eyes widened as memories flooded her vision, "Yes Jack and I had him buried in the cemetery in the family mausoleum."

Jack swallowed, "Then… you know that I -"

She cut him off, "Yes Jack, and like that time, once this is all over, I'll ensure that nothing happens to you. I still have some sway over the police department. After all, chief Harlow is only there because I removed all his competition. He still owes me for that one."

Jack nodded and tried his best to ignore the illegality of the situation, "thanks mom. I - uh - have to go now."

He turned awkwardly to the door and walked through it, eventually finding his way to the front door of the flower shop. He stopped only once on the way out, hearing the faintest sound of sobs coming through the corridor that lead to his mother's house.

~ 3 ~

Jack sat in his car outside of the Magrath public library, his mind mulling over the idea that his mother had to pull his father's body from the wreckage of the house, or at least had to identify his body after the firefighters did. *I wonder what they did with all the bones down there.*

He frowned, wondering how they could have missed the room with the Liath in it. It didn't make sense; perhaps they didn't feel the need to remove the debris because there was no possible way for anyone to be down there. Perhaps the debris wasn't there when they went down. After all, there was no way the debris that Larkin and his group of friends could have come to be piled up just outside of the door in any sort of organic fashion.

Someone would have moved it down there, though he couldn't begin to fathom who or why. The Liath, although 'tired' - as Larkin had put it, was strong enough to rip a grown man in half, surely it could push open a door and move the debris on the other side of it. *Right?*

Jack shook his head and reached for the door handle of his Sunfire, figuring he'd done enough contemplating in his car for one morning, and that sooner or later, he would have to see what awaited him in the Haggard's home.

He pushed open his door and stepped out into the familiar cool October air that he was beginning to expect. He reached into his pocket and pulled out a cigarette, rationalizing to himself that he had enough time to finish one in the brief amount of time it would take him to walk past the library and over to the house where the Haggard family had lived.

Placing the comfortable filter in his mouth, he set the end ablaze and began puffing steadily on the end of it, reveling in the familiar feeling of the smoke filling his lungs. He began walking past the old stone building that stood at the center of Magrath. Like the Lewis Manor, this building had stood strong since Magrath's foundation in the 1600's, and though it had undergone a few renovations over the years, it was more or less the same building that had been built by the people who had survived the Liath and subjected it to a nearly four hundred year slumber.

Slowly, he passed the building and moved on to the house next to it, releasing cloud after cloud of smoke up into the air behind him; a mixture of steam and the burning remnants of his addiction.

The Haggard's home was very unlike the Lewis manor. Where the Lewis manor was grand and intimidating, the Haggard's house was small and homely. It seemed inviting, like the sort of place you'd want to spend time with the people that mattered to you and have a yearly potluck. It felt *safe*.

Jack smiled as he started up the path that led to the white front door. Unlike the other houses in the area, the Haggard's house didn't have a metal screen door at the front, it only had the metal core door with a small glass peephole. As he finally reached it, Jack noticed that like Trix's home had been the prior afternoon, it was slightly open.

A feeling of dread overcame him as he pushed open the door and peered into the emptiness inside of the house. It looked like the Liath had beaten him to Fiona. Once again, he'd been too late. Though he'd had his own suspicions, he had hoped he was wrong. He hoped he'd simply approach, knock on the door and be greeted by the smiling woman the town had come to know as 'the librarian.'

He stepped into the empty house and cast his eyes across the barren floors and desolate walls that surmised the entirety of the entryway and connecting room. To someone who didn't know what was going on, it would simply appear that Fiona had moved on, packed her things and left to greener pastures. However, Jack had seen this before and had read about it in case files concerning missing the people who had gone missing over the past few weeks. He sighed and ran his fingers through his hair as he slipped his feet out of his shoes. He would allow himself a quick look around, hoping that something may have been left behind to help him with this case.

He stepped cautiously onto the hardwood and began looking around the various surfaces, seeing by chance, there was a note or anything of that sort that had been left behind for him to find. He moved from the living room to the bedrooms, noting how unlike the other missing cases where only one room was emptied, this house had been completely stripped of all belongings. *Almost like it was personal.*

The master bedroom was carpeted, and impressions had been left where the furniture had once been. *What does it even do with the furniture or other items it takes?*

He walked over to where the nightstand would have been; perplexed by the Scratches etched into the wall just above aslight fray in the edge of the carpet. He grabbed one of the loose threads and began to pull, realizing with excitement that the carpet was lifting. He smiled as he pulled back the section of carpet and revealed a small trap door style crease in the hardwood below.

He reached down and lifted the small piece of wood, gasping as his eyes fell upon a small, folded white sheet of paper bound in a red ribbon tucked inside. The ribbon was secured using melted wax as opposed to being tied, impressed in the wax was a seal he'd seen many times as a child. It was the seal of the Lewis family. Though it had already been torn and the note read, it was clear as day that whatever was contained on this sheet had been written by his father.

His heart began to beat faster and harder as confusion washed over him, *what does it contain? Did he hide it because he knew the Liath would take everything else?* He frowned and slowly tore off the ribbon, following the same path that Douglas would have torn when the note was first read.

With shaking hands, he began to slowly unfold the sheet, careful not to rip any of the edges. As the final fold came undone, a small metallic object fell from the page and landed on the soft carpet. Jack looked down as his confusion only grew more; for what lay on the ground before him was a small key, one that would fit into a lock he'd seen meer moments before. On the passenger seat of his Sunfire. Jack slowly reached down and picked up the key, studying it, convincing himself that there was no way that it had literally just fallen right in front of him. *There's no such thing as coincidence.*

He slid the key into his pocket and turned his eyes over to the sheet of paper held in his other hand, curious as to what the letter said; hoping it would explain why the key to that book was inside. He immediately recognized his father's handwriting on the page and began reading.

Douglas,

The Liath has begun to stir, though not as was initially thought. I'm afraid that when the day draws near and it finally rises, we will be unable to put it back under the seal. Afterall, we both know that it only fell victim to our forefathers because it had no idea that such a thing could happen to it.

For the benefit of the community and the longevity of my family I'm afraid I must break our sacred oath and shatter the pact that was made on that day. I will prematurely release it from its slumber. I believe it to be the only way. Please. Forgive me.

Samuel Lewis

P.S. enclosed is a key, please give it to my son Jack when he comes of age. I fear I'll be long dead before then. Thank you.

Jack staggered back, unsure of the meaning of what he had just read. He couldn't understand why his father would willing release that creature and what he meant by 'doing it for the benefit of the community.'

Jack slowly refolded the paper as his mind raced over the details of the letter, the tone his father had used and what he'd written in the book that he left for Jack. From the sound of the letter, he had written this before he turned abusive, yet he couldn't understand exactly why. He shook his head as he walked from the Haggard's house and back onto the street.

He dipped his hands into his pockets, his right hand closed around his cigarettes and the other closed around the small metal key. He chewed his lip as he considered which one he should pursue first. She shook his head at the prospect of choosing smokes over the last thing his father had written to him and began to jog as he tightened his hand around the key.

He slipped his right hand out of his pocket as he neared the Sunfire and opened the door as he withdrew the small key with his left. *Let's see what this book contains, shall we?*

He climbed into his car and closed the door behind him.

~ 4 ~

Sitting once more in his Sunfire just outside of the Magrath public library; Jack Lewis held the leather book on his lap. He'd been staring at the cover for no less than five minutes, once again debating internally as to the nature of its contents. Sure, he saw the letter from his father inside of the Haggard's house; though he couldn't be one hundred percent certain if his father had written that merely as a ploy to drive him to read this book and stir up old memories. Dom's words rang through his head as though he were sitting there next to him, '*It's just a book Jack, it's not going to bite you.'*

He took a deep breath and slid the key into the lock; his heart rate spiking as it clicked open. He pulled open the cover to reveal the first page. Instantly, the fear of his father's malicious intent faded as he lay his eyes on the five simple words written in his father's handwriting and the two short sentences written below.

For Jack Lewis, Love Dad

I wish I could give you the world, though instead I bestow upon you the end to a curse and a responsibility passed down through generations. I hope you can forgive me Jack; it was never meant to be like this.

Jack closed the cover as tears began to well up in his eyes. The words brought forth the memories of his father chasing him down the halls of their manor as they played tag. They brought memories of family picnics and the times his father would bring him into town to talk to some of the other children. They moved his mind to the games of tag and picnics in their yard; memories of watching the stars shoot across the sky while wrapped in a large blanket. The three of them. In happier times.

Jack realized the book was not the last words of his father, but the man he once knew. Long before the beatings and abuse, before the tear-filled nights and the times when Jack longed for angels to swoop down and carry him from the earth. Tears began to stream down his face as he read the last words written by the father who tucked him into bed each night with stories and love.

As he reopened the book, he pushed aside the thoughts of the father he killed and replaced them with the one who filled his heart with love and his mind with wonder. With his mind on the father he longed for, he turned the page and began reading.

Jack,

I'm certain that by the time you read this, I will be well passed dead. You most likely know about the creature that dwells in the basement of our house. The thing our ancestors called the 'Liath.' It's an immensely powerful being that has been wandering the earth since long before mankind even dreamed of conquest.

I don't know what the world is like out there anymore, though I assume I was unsuccessful in stopping it. Though, perhaps I was successful, and this is nothing more than the meaningless ramblings of a madman now. If this is true, then perhaps I also told you about it, maybe as a bedtime story; one of the brave soldier that succeeded in winning the war that was waging in his own head. Though I know is most likely not the case.

Most likely, if you find yourself reading this then I failed. The auxiliary plan will need to be set in motion. I need you to know that by writing down the following, I will be breaking an ancient pact between the Haggard and Lewis families and an ancient tribe of indigenous people that used to call the plains to the east their home.

While our family has maintained the containment of the Liath since it was sealed roughly three hundred and fifty years ago, the Haggards have been responsible for tracking down any additional information that could be used to end the beast once and for all. You must ask the Haggards to share the journals with you, they will set the stage for what I'm about to tell you.

See, what I need you to understand is that this isn't the first time it's begun to stir. It first reawakened after a century of lying dormant, longer than Nathaniel and Anlon thought it would be. There's a ritual that was given to us by the tribe and passed down the family for generations. It is a ritual of blood and a ritual of sacrifice. Though not the type of sacrifice you may think.

The sacrifice is a lifetime spent within the borders of the town, forced to live out your days with the creature just beneath the place where you sleep, never too far away. Our ancestors took over the task with grace, Magrath was all they ever wanted, it was their life's work. Why would they ever want to leave?

They had the ritual, the means to keep it contained, so what more could they desire? Unfortunately, you may have noticed that I never had the liberty of leaving the town, for even if I took but one step beyond the border, the Liath would slowly reawaken and the pact would be broken. But that was just one piece of the larger puzzle.

Certain herbs were needed from the lands, ones that your mother keeps in the shop at my request, for if events transpire in the manor, I suspect they will; I would end up destroying them. But I'm getting ahead of myself.

When two men began their journey to seal the Liath, they were given a small pouch, a knife and were tasked with drinking a fluid that the elder had mentioned would protect them; though he never explained how, only that it was brewed from the plants that the land provided.

Listen. Jack, I'm about to do something that was ingrained in my mind as taboo by my father and his father before him. It's something that once written will break our ancient pact. I need you to understand this.

So, before I tell you anymore, I want you to know that I love you. Always have and always will. At the time I'm writing this, you are nothing more than a young man entering his early adult years. I can't describe how proud I am of you. You always tell me so much about your friends and that Shannon girl you fancy, though you've never brought them around. I assume it's because of the house, and though I understand, I want you to take the risks you deem necessary. I want you to reach out and take what you want from the world, but I also want you to help people, explore the world, see places, find a girl you like and settle down. Most of all, I want you to have a life full of love and joy where the Liath and our family history can't reach you.

I hope you can forgive me for taking this choice from you, taking it from everyone. I just want to give you a life that's more than Magrath.

Jack frowned as the page dampened in a small spot, only to be quickly joined by another wet mark, and then another. Setting the book aside, Jack looked up to his car's roof; checking for any sign of a leak or damage that would give water access to the cab. It was only when he raised his hand up to his tear-soaked cheek that he realized he was crying.

As the tears bubbled forth, he realized that they were not tears of sadness, nor joy. These were tears of resignation, tears that come only when resignation hits and one s perspective changes. Jack realized that his father had not been a horrible man like he'd thought, but one with an insurmountable obstacle to face, one that no matter how he'd challenged it, it would not only cause pin to himself, but also his family. Jack wiped the tears from his cheeks using his sleeve and looked at himself in the mirror, noticing that he looked tired. He'd been tired. Tired of harboring a grudge for years against someone who wasn't even alive anymore. Against someone who for all intents and purposes wasn't the man he'd known in the end.

With a weak smile to himself in the mirror he picked back the book containing his true father's last message and resumed reading.

Jack, I want to stress that what I'm about to tell you is something that has never been recorded on paper, nor wall inscription, or anything for that matter. This may seem strange to you, hell, it seemed strange to me at first as well. However, I will do my best to explain as my father had years ago.

To summarize, words have power. They contain the very essence of the meaning placed into them. By themselves they are benign, they are meaningless. However, when you spin them into something, you impart part of yourself into them. It's not to say that you lose a part of yourself when you commit something to paper, however, you loosen the story's impact on your actions. Does that make sense? No, I suppose not.

Let me explain it this way; the pact that was formed had the caveat that it must be shared orally, it could not be written down. It had something to do with the way that both Nathaniel and Anlon prepared themselves when the ritual was first performed and the numerous times it has been performed over the centuries. In order to use the objects given to them by the village chief, they needed to accomplish three distinct tasks.

The first was a purification of the mind. They were subjected to meditate in one of the tribe's teepees under the guidance of the chief. This part had proved hard initially for Nathaniel, for unlike Anlon, he did not understand the words spoken by the chief. He couldn't quite home in on the meaning of the chief's words, nor the areas of the body he was supposed to focus on. However, after several hours of sitting with the smell of burning sage, his mind began to focus, it began to home in and understand the underlying meaning of the chief's words and eventually he found his mind 'purified'

The second task was a purification of the soul. Much like the first, they had to meditate, however, for this task, they were required to meditate on two large rocks protruding from the surface of a spring. The high salt content dried their bodies and drew out any 'evil spirits' from within. While they did this, they each held a bundle of white sage in their hands and after a whole night of sitting on those rocks, they had to light the sage on fire to drive away any of the spirits that remained.

The third, and hardest for them to grasp was the absolvement of wrongdoings. While they had known of confession, their minds immediately went to wrongdoings, breaking the ten commandments and having impure thoughts. However, the chief informed them that it was something very different. For this task, they had to account for the actions of their people, the disruptions they had made to the greater cycle. For this, they needed to account for their people's wrongdoings, they needed to atone for the acts against the earth. For this task, they spent hours confessing the wrongdoings such as mining, conquest, expansion and all manners of crimes committed against the world they called home. As they spoke of the European society, the chief became distraught, not knowing that such destruction was occurring all over the land.

When the chief told them they were ready, they stood and were each presented a second satchel filled with dirt. They were told it was earth that had been blessed by a medicine woman who'd performed a secondary ritual on it. The dirt was supposed to contain traces of the 'spirit of the earth.'

Trust me Jack, I know how crazy this all sounds. But having a monster asleep in your basement really opens your eyes to a whole slew of possibilities. In the time I've known about it, I've gone to see it twice. It lays on a slab of earth, unmoving. Creepy looking bastard.

Finally, we reach the end of what has been passed down through the generations. When they finished their meditation rituals, they followed the chief back to the village where they enjoyed venison, foraged greenery and a bitter tea that was passed to them by a girl with hair as black as a raven.

They slept under the stars that night, surrounded by bushels of sage. In the morning they awoke feeling more rested than they had in their entire lives; it was as if their bodies were thrumming in tune with the nature that surrounded them.

The chief approached them and spoke softly to Anlon, who translated for Nathaniel. As they looked over the supplies that had been gifted to them, Nathaniel took note of a peculiar knife and its white, uneven texture. He turned to Anlon and got him to ask the chief about it.

The chief explained that it was the bone of the very same medicine woman who had blessed the earth that they had been given the night prior. She'd sacrificed her own arm to create it and had blessed it in the process. He claimed it could strike evil out of the world, though it wouldn't be able to kill the Liath. No, although it would be able to cut its flesh, it wouldn't be able to kill it outright. It would be used as a means to get the other items into its system and place it in a death-like stasis.

In order to do so, they would need to force the creature to ingest the sacred earth then stab it through the chest with the blade where its heart would be. From there they would need to pack the wound full of the dirt and the herbs they were given. Once again, he insisted they would not be able to kill it. Not if they wanted to live. No, to attempt to kill it would mean they would have to allow it to bond to their soul and give it control over their body, allow it to live among humans and soak up as much fear as it wanted. It would be able to move around freely among us, using its vessel to commit atrocious acts against mankind.

Sometime later after riding into the town that was now called Magrath, they were able to halt the creature and slip it into a stasis.

Though whether a matter of pride or necessity, they refused to pass on any information about the battle they fought with it.

My son. My research and years of dedication has brought me to this. I will allow the creature to overcome me. I will sacrifice myself to let you be the one to kill it. I know this is putting a heavy burden on your shoulders, but it is the only way to stop it. Jack, I pass the torch onto you. Even now, I can feel the faintest tinge of its voice, whispering with an ancient power. I may only have enough time to send the letter to Douglas and lock this book away, then I fear I will have no strength left.

Before I slip into the abyss of darkness that awaits me, I must impart some fatherly wisdom that I never got the chance to share with you.

Do not shut out those you love, for they define who we are and the people we become. Family is important, but more important is the bonds we form, the friends we make and the people we meet along the way, for those come from choice and blood cannot define who we are. Shave with the grain first, then against it; this applies to so much more than just shaving. Find the flow before you disrupt it, it's easier to sway people to you if you know the way they operate first.

Remember, your dad will always love you. Your dad will always care for you. I will be with you Jack, in this book and in spirit. Though I fear I will lose my body to the Liath, I will not lose my soul. Remember me as I was, and not what I become.

I hope everything in this book helps,

I love you,

Dad.

Jack turned the final page over as the emptiness of reading his father's last words settled over him. He hoped there was more to the book, and judging by the remaining thickness of the pages, there should have been. However, as he tried to turn over the back page behind his father's closing thoughts, he noticed something was off about it and the remaining pages. They were far too rigid, too secure and the page he was attempting to turn appeared to be glued to the rest of them. Slowly, he peeled back a layer of the pages; revealing a thin white blade that looked more like a bayonet than an actual knife.

I guess now I have my weapon.

Jack placed the book on the seat next to him as he ran the tip of his finger over the white blade. From the human bones he'd seen over the years, he'd assumed they bee to porous to form any sort of weapon from. Yet, the blade he held appeared to have been from the outside of the bone, where the highest build-up of calcium was. Even then, given the amount of time that had passed, it should have degraded a fair bit. Yet, as he held the blade up to his fingertips, he could feel a slight vibration. *A thrumming.* It was as though the blade itself had been imbued with an otherworldly power.

He ran his fingers over the small handle, noting the faint symbols that had been carved into it. He chuckled to himself as he realized that should he try to explain this to anyone else, they would view him as insane.

The faint smile escaped off his lips as he reached over and placed the knife within his glovebox, atop the numerous cigarette boxes within. He closed it and slid the car into first, knowing full well that it was time to face the creature his family had guarded for centuries. He would bring about vengeance. Not only for Dom, but for Emma, his father and all the others it had claimed over the years.

It was time to return to the Lewis Manor.

Chapter 13: Darkness

~ 1 ~

Jack drove back up the path towards the Lewis manor; mind racing over the events that transpired the last time he'd been there. A pang of guilt shot through his chest as he remembered running after seeing the remnants of Dom's corpse and his unseeing eyes. He recalled the shrill terror that coursed through him, causing him to turn and flee in fear. Like a coward that wasn't worthy of Dom's friendship. He shook his head, remembering Dom's words in his dream. Finally, he pulled up in the same spot he'd parked the previous evening and set his eyes on the ruins of his old house.

The previous night's rain washed away any build-up of dirt that had been on the front of the building; revealing the dark and angry burn marks that had been obscured underneath. Jack reached over and popped open the glove box. His hand gripped comfortably on the handle of the white knife that he'd placed inside earlier. He thought for a second then moved aside the various boxes of cigarettes inside and reached deeper inside, wrapping his fingers around the flashlight he'd placed at the bottom some time ago.

A primal fear washed over him as he stepped out of the Sunfire and stood there staring at the husk of what had once been his home; the place he had been raised and the place where he'd killed his father. Though it had come to mean many things over the years to him, he knew that it would also be the place where he would finally take care of his family's legacy and kill the Liath.

He turned his head to the sky and looked at the dark clouds that began to move in from the horizon; casting the ground below in shadow as they closed in once more on Magrath. Jack watched them for a moment, noticing the silence that had seemingly settled over the world. No crickets chirped nor birds sang, the still air clung around him, undisturbed by any breeze. Jack began walking down the cracked yet familiar path towards the front door of the Lewis manor.

As he passed through the front door, he tightened his grip on the small knife, suddenly all too aware that the only noise he could hear was that of the wood creaking beneath his feet. It was as though the manor was holding its breath; causing a sense of dread to rise along his neck. With an unsteady smile to reassure himself, he began down the all too familiar hallway. He passed his room and his father's study without a moment's hesitation, not even a passing glance was sent into either of the rooms. No, he had little time for such trivialities. He was here for one thing and one thing only; to stop the Liath at all costs and find Trix. He tightened his hand on the bone dagger as he stepped into his parents' bedroom and started towards the closet and the staircase that would bring him to the depths below.

Jack looked down the stairs and into the inky blackness that they would bring him too. Swallowing down the nervousness that was ever growing in his throat he reached into his pocket and brought out the flashlight. Armed with both the knife and flashlight; he took his first hesitant step, all the while thoughts of turning back ran rampant through his head. With a deep exhale, he continued down the staircase; each step becoming noticeably easier as he surrendered himself to his objective.

His stomach began to churn halfway to the bottom, threatening to bring up what little food he'd consumed recently and spill them over the horrid steps. *Come on Jack, you've come this far, there's no turning back now.*

With his thoughts spurring him forward he continued down, shaking as he resigned himself to the fate that awaited him in the depths below. Visions of the grey hands reaching from the depths and tearing him apart flooded his vision, causing a panic to well up inside of him. Though, when he reached the bottom of the steps without incident, he sighed and raised his light to look around the room.

First, he shined it to where he'd seen Dom's body the night prior. Much to his surprise; Dom's body was no longer there and in its stead were two large pools of partly-dried-partly-coagulated blood with trails of the mixture leading off into the far recesses of the darkness.

Larkin's words returned to him, '*it was like the light just didn't go as far. The darkness swallowed it.*' Jack realized his words were spot on; for in the depths of the concrete basement the light from his flashlight only covered the spaces within a few feet of himself. He swallowed and continued to pan the light over the spaces, expecting to see the familiar grey figure of the Liath in front of him at any moment.

He paused as his foot brushed something. Instinctually, he shined the flashlight on it and his breath caught in his chest. He knelt and picked up the familiar leather of his father's belt and held it as memories of that night flooded through his mind. His fear turned to a pained rage as he recalled his father's message. As a lone tear went down his cheek, he reasoned with himself. *It wasn't him you killed; it was the Liath acting through his body.*

His emotions got the better of him as he called out into the darkness, "Where the fuck are you beast! Come out and face me!"

The faint sound of scuffling came from further within the room and Jack trained his light in its direction. His hand clenched tighter on the handle of the knife, causing his knuckles to bulge through the skin. He took several more hesitant steps in the direction of the now constant scuffling noise and halted as his light illuminated its source.

Standing in front of him wasn't the Liath, but a girl. For a moment Jack couldn't place her face. It was as though the skin had been pulled tight over her skull and any fat had been removed from her body.

She spoke, "J-Jack?"

Suddenly Jack recognized her. He lunged forward as she fell and caught her before she could crash into the ground. Knowing full well he couldn't face the Liath with her in such a state, he jammed the knife through the belt loop at the back of his jeans and placed the flashlight in his mouth as he carefully maneuvered her frail form into his arms. A wave of guilt washed through him as he realized how light she had become despite the short amount of time she'd been missing.

Jack heaved her up the long flight of stairs and back into his parent's bedroom, where the small amount of remaining sunlight illuminated her pale face. He stifled a gasp as he set her feet down to remove the flashlight from his mouth. Her emaciated face looked much worse in the natural light as it caused the hollows of her cheeks to darken drastically. As he slid the flashlight back into his pocket he sent his thoughts out to Dom, telling him he'd fulfilled the promise he made and saved the person that had caused him to charge so recklessly into the basement the night before.

He brushed her dark brown hair from her face and smiled weakly at her as she opened her hazel eyes for a moment before falling unconscious again. As Trix Thompson fell back into the world of darkness, Jack heaved her back up into his arms and set about bringing her to his car.

As he walked down the path towards his car, his muscles twitched and tightened, anxious for a fight they'd been promised but denied. Jack realized that he'd been ready to die in that basement, realized that perhaps it was some vague hope that he'd finally be able to end it all; rid the world of either the monster or himself, though ideally both. He shook his head at the epiphany. It was an act of pride. An act of pride brought on by a promise to a dead friend, himself and a father he'd killed all those years ago.

As his father's purple face flooded his vision, Jack absentmindedly kicked a pile of soot that had collected in the hallway, causing a cloud of ash to raise into the air. He coughed and gripped Trix tighter, afraid to drop her in his fit. When he coughs subsided and the ash began to settle again, he carried on, leading Trix through the front door and out into the chilly October air. He hurried over to his car, not wanting to let Trix get hypothermia in the cold air as her thin body wouldn't be able to regulate heat as well as it once had.

He opened the back door of his Sunfire and placed Trix inside. He then removed his coat and placed it over her to help keep her warm. After buckling her in, he removed the knife from the read belt loop of his pants and walked around to the front of the car.

Before climbing inside he looked back over to the Lewis Manor, *I'll be back for you later. Beast.*

He closed the door behind him as he slid behind the wheel. He popped the knife and flashlight into the glovebox and turned over the engine. Jack cranked the eat and fans up to their max before sliding the car into first and starting down the road back into Magrath.

He knew he couldn't bring her straight to the hospital, though he also knew that was for selfish reasons. No, he would bring her to Shannon so she could look after her as Jack went back up to the manor to resume his hunt. He nodded to himself as he continued through the residential seats towards the house he'd come to stay for the past few days.

~ 2 ~

As Jack pulled up outside of Shannon's house he was greeted by a familiar sight. Though he'd seen her in the days prior, he was not expecting to see her small frame and pink muddy dress anytime soon. Yet there she stood, planted firmly in the doorway of the house as her eyes fixed themselves onto Jack's now shocked face.

He cautiously slid out from behind the wheel of the Sunfire, leaving Trix in the backseat as he began to walk towards the house. Though, as Jack neared, she slowly brought her hand up to stop him, as though warning him of whatever might await him inside the familiar walls.

He shot her an incredulous look, "I thought you weren't going to be able to come back anytime soon? What happened to '*This may be the last time I'm able to appear before you*'? What's the matter?"

She ignored his questions and instead gave him another one of the cryptic messages he'd grown to expect, "You've carried down the path. Has it brought you pain? You wouldn't have had to relive the woes of your past had you heeded my warning in the alley, Jack. People are dead. Surely, they would have perished had you left, though their lives may have lasted slightly longer. You've made all the right steps yet you've both caused and received so much pain over just the past sixty hours alone. Have you stopped to wonder why, Jack? Perhaps you wish it on yourself, your self-destructive tendencies and volatile behavior alone is enough to support that theory. Or perhaps it's your pride, regardless of how many you hurt upon the way, be it yourself or others, you desire the self-gratification of being the one to solve the case. Alas, heed my warning this one last time. Turn back, leave, drive away from Magrath and never look back. Go so far and leave for so long that Magrath is nothing but a footnote of the past. If you enter this house, there's no turning back."

Jack scowled and set his jaw, "There's no turning back, not once I agreed to come back here. Not when I first stepped into this town. I've been running from the past all my life, I'm not about to continue that. There's no more running. Not when I can save so many others from meeting the same fate as Dom. Not when there's others that need my help in this moment. I need to stop fretting over myself, my past and what happened on that night. I need to get over myself and do this for the other people this effects."

She looked at him curiously as he continued, "Listen, I appreciate all you've done for me over the years with these cryptic messages and hints as to where the cases I'm on will lead. But I don't need you anymore, so please, find whatever afterlife awaits us and move on. You're free from this *bond* we happen to share. You're free."

He took a step back as her expression changed and the dried dirt and blood began to lift from her clothes and skin; leaving a smiling little girl in a bright pink dress standing there before him. As she began to dissipate into a warm glowing mist, Jack realized it may have been the first true smile he'd ever seen on her face. The mist swirled around in the dim evening light and as she drifted into the great beyond, Jack walked up to the door and wrapped his fingers around the brass knob; steeling himself for whatever lay inside.

--

Jack stepped into the small entryway of the house and was instantly greeted by a faint coppery smell that almost reminded him of raw steak. He frowned as he was unable to place it, though as he stood there, confused, his brain began to process the incoming stimuli. Slowly, the incoming information translated, and his mind was able to comprehend the cacophony of information that was swirling around inside his nose.

He slipped his feet from his shoes as he pondered the smell a moment longer. Finally severed from his own thoughts when he heard a splash echo from the floor above. Suddenly, he was all too aware of what the smell was. Blood.

Jack flung himself down the hallway and up the carpeted mountain to the upper level, each step seemingly taking forever. He found himself unable to move fast enough, unable to drive his legs hard enough to close the seemingly endless expanse between the top of the staircase and the door that would take him to the source of the smell and Shannon.

He threw himself into the room, fully expecting to see her mangled corpse laid out in front of him as the Liath claimed another victim. Though instead he let out a horrified gasp as he saw Shannon laying intact in the bathtub. The rosy water lapped against her naked body as her head lulled forward. Her left wrist was submerged in the water and thick tendrils of blood flowed from the long cut running across her forearm as the water eased its transport. Her right wrist dangled off the side, loosing a steady stream of droplets of the crimson substance onto the floor in a steady *plip plip plip.*

Jack ran to her side, noticing fully just how red the water was, "Oh no, Shannon, no no no."

He reached into the tub and pulled her out, not bothering to check if she was still breathing or even had a pulse. He hugged her close to her body. She was cold, though as he carried her from the tub into the master bedroom, he heard the faintest sound of her raspy breaths escaping from her lips.

He carefully laid her on the bed before running back into the bathroom to find something to staunch the bleeding. He threw open the medicine cabinet and scoured the three shelves within, seeing nothing other than a bottle of Pepto and several prescription bottles within. *Thank god she didn't take those.*

Not seeing a first aid kit inside he began cursing to himself, "shit!"

He gripped the edge of the counter as he racked his brain for another idea of where to look. On a whim, he checked under the very sink he was standing over and began pulling out the various bottles of cleaning supplies within. As he reached past the last bottle his hand struck something metallic. He craned his neck to allow himself a better view and exhaled as he saw a white metal box with a single red cross on the front of it. Quickly, he pulled it out and shot back into a standing position before running back into the room, nearly dropping the box twice in the process.

He ran up to the bed and nearly cried out when he saw that Shannon's blood had flowed from her wrists into the sheets. He watched her chest rise with each shallow breath as he fumbled the latch of the first aid kit and finally got it open. Inside were two tensor bandages, several individual packages of gauze, a small bottle of peroxide, several butterfly stitches, and a box of assorted bandages. He reached and pulled out the butterfly stitches and all the packages of gauze.

He hastily tore open the gauze and began wiping blood and water off each of her wrists. Using the butterfly stitches, he pinched the cuts together before laying pads of gauze on top. Next, he pulled out the tensor bandages and wrapped them tightly around her wrists, ensuring to maintain pressure throughout to help stop the bleeding. Once he was done, he looked at his work. *Not the best, but it'll do until I can get her to the hospital.*

He ran back into the bathroom and brought a towel out to dry off the remainder of the bloody water from her body. Once she was fully dry, he ran to the dresser and pulled out a pair of Dom's sweats. He slid them onto her and heaved her up into his arms, knowing full well he needed to bring both her and Trix to the hospital.

Jack carried Shannon down the stairs and placed her in the passenger seat, growing ever more concerned that she hadn't woken up yet.

~ 3 ~

With Shannon tightly secured in the passenger seat and Trix still fastened haphazardly in the back, Jack reversed out of the driveway and sped down the road towards the Magrath Hospital.

He sped through several red lights, jostling the car as he narrowly avoided collisions and pedestrians alike. He didn't care about breaking the law, however, he had two women in his car that were in dire need of medical attention.

They rolled up to the hospital in less than ten minutes; making considerable time despite having to drive over half of the town. Jack slid out from behind the steering wheel and ran through the double doors into the empty triage, where a rather bored nurse sat with her cell phone in hand as she tried desperately to pass the time.

Frantically, Jack rushed up to the front desk and caught the nurse's attention. She attempted to hide her enthusiasm as she met his bewildered eyes.

"Please, I need help."

She nodded quickly and plucked the phone off the desk in front of her before uttering a muffled code that failed to reach Jack's ears. Within moments, several other nurses flooded into the foyer, looking between Jack and the nurse working the desk expectantly.

Jack turned and beckoned them to follow, rushing back to the car and the two unconscious women that lay inside. He went to Shannon while instructing two of the nurses to Trix, thought they would have only needed one due to the state of her body. They quickly maneuvered them onto stretchers that had been brought over by the other nurses.

The nurses wheeled them into the ER while Jack went through the tedious process of checking them in.

--

Jack had been filling out forms for the better part of half an hour - tirelessly attempting to figure out the best way to word Trix's condition - when he finally stood up and brought the now completed entry forms over to the nurse at the desk. Since things had settled down, she'd regressed to looking bored once again but smiled as Jack approached and reached out for the papers. *I just hope I get to see them soon.*

She looked over Shannon's form and nodded, then looked at Trix's "Symptoms… sudden emaciation?" Her eyes flicked back down the sheet, "Mr. Lewis, I'm just curious as to how they both ended up with you. I mean, attempted suicide *and* this emaciation thing. That just doesn't add up."

Jack sighed, "It's a long story and one I'd rather not tell, not that you'd believe it anyway."

The nurse frowned as she resumed scanning her eyes over the page, "wait, you're not one of *the* Lewis' are you?"

Jack thought for a second, "Yes, but I haven't thought of myself like that in quite some time."

She placed the papers back down, "Mr. Lewis -"

"Just Jack is fine." He interjected.

"Well, Jack… what is your relationship to either of the two women you brought in. It still strikes me as odd and I should probably let the police know..."

Jack sighed, "As I said it's a long story. Trix is Shannon's niece, I'm kind of a family friend. I grew up with Shannon. But there's no need to call the police, I'm actually employed by them. I'm helping with an ongoing investigation. I found Trix… well where exactly doesn't matter, but I thought I should ask for Shannon's help. When I got to her place however, I found her like *that*. I did my best to stabilize her before bringing them both over."

She smiled, "I wasn't really going to let the police know. I know Dominic; he comes by quite often. He's a sweet guy, he shows up once or twice a week to visit his mother; she's just been admitted for a hip surgery. He mentioned you were in town the other day - he stopped by to have lunch with her. Where is he by the way?"

Jack strained to keep the pain from making its way up his face, "I'm not at liberty to say unfortunately." He thought for a second, "now can I please go in, I would really like to see Shannon and Trix."

The nurse shook her head sadly, "Right now I can't unfortunately, but I'll let you know as soon as they're ready for you."

Jack smiled weakly as his shoulders slumped, "Thanks."

He turned and walked back to one of the waiting room chairs; where he plopped down and turned his mind back to the case once more. *Once I know they're good, I'll go back and end this. Once and for all.*

--

Hours passed as Jack sat waiting in that chair with nothing but his own thoughts to prevent him from boredom. The growing concern did not aide in the passage of time and Jack found himself rising up to his feet and pacing several times over the passing moments; though for the most part he sat with his elbows resting on his knees with his head held low in thought.

He thought of the people he lost and the true reason he was pushing so hard to kill the Liath. Uncertainty coursed through him as the little girl's words weighed on him, causing him to question if he was truly working the case for his own gratification or for the people it would save. Was it due to the burning desire for revenge for the people it had taken from him, or was it for the reasons he'd given her earlier? He truly didn't know, and though in the grand scheme of the case it had mattered little; he wondered what it said about his character.

He shook his head as one of the nurses from earlier entered the room through the two large swinging doors and approached the nurse at the desk. Jack raised his head and watched in anticipation as the man bent down and whispered something into her ear. She nodded and watched as the man walked back the way he came.

Jack looked away as she turned her head to him, "Mr. Lewis - er - I mean, Jack. They're ready to see you now, if you follow me I can bring you to them."

Jack was on his feet before the last sentence had even left her mouth. He watched as she calmly slid her phone into her pocket and stood, before coming out from behind the desk.

He followed her through the doors into the emergency war, anxious to see Shannon and Trix, but his anger re-emerged. Anger that was directed not only at himself for not being able to protect them, but also to the thing that had caused all of this. Anger that bubbled up at the world for just existing. As he walked through the double doors, he cursed the God he didn't believe in, for if there was such a being, they were nothing more than a kid with a magnifying glass and all the people were nothing but ants.

--

He followed the nurse through the open space towards a curtained area on the far side of the ward, passing a doctor on the way. He was hopeful; thinking that they perhaps they'd awoken in the time he'd spent waiting. However, as the nurse pulled back the curtain his heart plummeted.

Lying unconscious in two beds spaced a meager six feet apart were Trix and Shannon. Jack looked to the left bed where Shannon lay with her eyes closed and her face expressionless. Her dressings had been removed and redone in a more professional manner causing Jack to suspect that they'd stitched back together herself inflicted lacerations. Connected to the back of her right hand was an IV connected to a quart of blood. Jack's stomach turned at the sight as he recalled walking in on the grisly sight in the bathroom just hours prior. Suddenly ashamed of having left her that morning, he turned to look at Trix in the other bed.

Trix lay wrapped in a heavy blanket and had a long feeding tube going through her nose and down her throat. Though some color had returned to her, her face was contorted into a fearful expression. Jack could only wonder what it was she was seeing.

A gruff voice from behind him cut off his train of thought, "they're both damn lucky you brought them in when you did."

Jack turned to see the doctor he'd passed in the hallway earlier and realized he must have been the one who'd been overseeing one if not both of them. He had a strong jaw and a resolute look on his face that hit Jack with a vague wave of recognition, though he couldn't place where he'd seen him before.

He looked down to his notes, "Sudden emaciation as you put it. Hell, if she wasn't friends with my son, I'd have pegged her as someone struggling with an eating disorder."

Jack suddenly recognized the man in front of him, "you're Zach's dad, aren't you?"

The man frowned momentarily, then his eyes widened, "you must be the man that questioned the boys at their school yesterday. But to answer your question, yes, Zach is my son. The name's Harry, though you can just call me Hank."

Jack nodded, thinking he most likely wouldn't use the man's name at all, "how's he doing, y'know, after what happened yesterday?"

Hank's expression grew dark, "not as well as I'd hoped to be honest. Though, he's just lost two of his closest friends, I don't know what I expected."

Jack nodded understandingly as he looked back over to Shannon and Trix, "What about them, doc? Are they going to be okay?"

Hank smiled then, “Yes, your work on Shannon’s wrists damn well saved her life. Good thinking with the tensor bandages to maintain pressure, if you hadn’t, I’m sure she would have bled out before you even got here. As for Trix, she’ll recover, though, we have no idea how that could have happened. Her entire digestive system was empty, as though she hadn’t eaten in weeks, any idea how that happened?”

Jack shook his head, “No, I just found her while working the case, did you let her mother know she’s here?”

Hank nodded, “I couldn’t find her, so I got one of the nurses to page her down here. I’m glad you found her Jack. Hell, after yesterday this place really needed a win.”

Jack smiled weakly but said nothing as the man looked down to the sheets once more before excusing himself. *Lucky? No, I’m the one who caused all of this.*

Jack walked over to Shannon and took her hand in his, wincing as the bandages brushed the edge of his pinkie finger. He had no idea just how close to the edge she was when he left that morning, but then, as he held her hand in his he felt nothing but guilt. And Anger. He hated himself for leaving her but hated himself more for dragging Dom into a situation where he was killed so easily. As he ran his thumb over the back of Shannon’s hand, his heart rate picked up once more and he found himself fuming with rage. He looked up to the clock that stood indifferently on the wall between the two beds and decided he needed to go back to the manor and end this once and for all.

Jack knew that the creature’s hand was dealt, and it had nothing that would be able to hold him back from ending it. He bent down and kissed Shannon on the forehead before turning and walking from the room. It was time to finally lay this case to rest. Either with his death, or the Liath’s.

~ 4 ~

Once again Jack found himself parked outside of the place he’d once called home. As he sat in the Sunfire staring at the old shell that was once his house, he thought of all that had transpired within its walls over the past couple days. It had come to be a murder house of sorts, containing within the concrete bunker the remnants of the numerous victims the Liath had claimed throughout the years. It had also come to serve as a tribute to the life he'd once claimed; one full of abuse and pain, one where he'd lost his child and his first love. Once more resigning himself to the idea that it could be his final resting place, Jack reached over to the glovebox and pulled out the knife as well as the flashlight from within.

"Let's get this over with."

With that, he removed himself from the Sunfire and followed the same path up to the ruins of his old house that he had taken earlier that day. He flicked on his flashlight as he entered the old house and once again found himself acutely aware of how quiet everything seemed to be. The wood beneath his feet creaked its familiar creak, yet as he walked through the pile of ash he'd absently kicked earlier, he heard not one other sound. His hands grew slick around both the knife's handle and the flashlight as his fear began to grow with each step.

The fear reached its summit as he stood over the familiar stairway that descended into the depths of the Lewis manor. The very same steps he'd gone down only three times before. Memories flooded his vision. Memories of following his instincts as he tracked down Emma only to find her in the concrete bunker below. The feel of the leather belt as he held it tightly in his hands. The look on his father's face as it bit into his neck, restricting the airflow. The way his tongue hung out from between his purple lips, as though prodding the air for a viable source of oxygen. Jack recalled the bulging eyes and purple face as he finally let go of the belt and let his father fall onto the ground before him.

He shook his head and took the first step down the stairs, "Come on Jack, you know there's no turning back now."

"You're absolutely right. No turning back."

The voice penetrated his mind and Jack lashed out at the dark with the flashlight, hoping to illuminate the foul creature. His heart clambered to a tumultuous staccato; thudding and palpitating with each and every ounce of the fear that worked its way through his body. Yet, the Liath still didn't reach out from the inky blackness and grab him. Its thin sharp talons didn't strike out and tear the flesh from his bones nor did they emerge and pummel him.

With no indication as to the creature's whereabouts, Jack turned his attention back to the stairs in front of him; fully aware that he had no option other than to continue down and face the very creature that he'd set out to destroy.

Jack descended the remaining steps quickly, anxious to get revenge on the monster that had snuffed out Dom's life, had ruined his childhood and had taken his father from him. Slowly, the rage began to boil inside of him as he reached the bottom of the stairs.

He stepped into the large concrete room, noting how the walls appeared to be more imposing and intimidating than the last time he was there. He shined his flashlight onto the now fully dried pool of blood then over to the lone belt that lay across the concrete floor. The same belt he'd used to end his father's life all those years ago.

The rage suddenly forced itself out, "Come on out you piece of shit! Are you still hiding like a little bitch?"

A deep breath came from further in the room as its deep and melancholic voice filled the space, **"Oh Jack, you really are a tiresome and weak human, aren't you? Your taunts won't work on me, I am a *god.* I stand above you insects, I'm above the very fabric of existence. I've roamed these lands for millennia, taking what I want, *claiming* who I want. Your kind always thinks that it belongs to you. No Jack. It belongs to *us.* We've been here longer, you call us 'creatures' or 'monsters' and you try to shame us for living in the darkness and feasting on the weak. Your very fear feeds my soul,"** It paused, as if thinking, **"and now your father's"**

Jack grunted, "Where the hell are you?"

It continued, ignoring his question, **"Your father's here. He's been trapped inside of me for years; watching as I used his body to torment you and beat you down. He watched as I shattered your weak heart and broke your spirit. His soul nearly fractured when I killed the child you implanted in that girl. Such paltry things, you humans, latching onto others because you're far too weak to stand alone. Tell me, how'd that work out for your friend? You know, he's in here too. Squirming to get out and be free of my grasp. So is that girlfriend of yours *Emma.* How they must ache to know you fucked his wife without a second thought, mere hours after I killed him."**

Jack's anger built, "You don't think I fucking know that! I've come to terms with my sins beast. Now enough talking, face me, die!"

It stepped out of the shadows and into the ever-dimming light of Jack's flashlight. Jack felt his mouth fall open as he was finally able to see the Liath in its entirety.

It stood nearly a foot taller than him, with nothing covering its grey, slimy flesh. It's body, though anthropomorphic in nature, was devoid of all human features. There were no genitalia to speak of, for it had no need for breeding. Its long, stick-like legs comprised nearly two thirds of its height, and its nipple-less torso was devoid of any muscular features. Jack felt his mind twisting with confusion as he studied it, not finding himself able to feel anything other than fear while he took in its unnerving proportions.

Under the grey skin were thousands of rippling, black veins that moved under the skin freely like thousands of thick worms. It reached a long, slender hand up to its face and picked a lump of flesh from between its sharp, yellow teeth. Its small black eyes narrowed on him as it flicked the piece of flesh onto the ground in front of him.

The Liath smiled sickly at him, stretching its non-existent lips over its teeth. It cocked its head as though trying to better angle the ears it didn't have. It locked its obsidian eyes on him and extended the same finger it had used to pick its teeth towards him.

Then, in its deep and fear inducing voice, it spoke. **"I've watched you suffer. Watched you flail blindly through a life unfit for you. I watched you drink yourself to sleep night after night, dreamless sleep after dreamless sleep. I've seen you smoke like a chimney in some feeble attempt to cure yourself of the anxiety that presents itself in every waking moment of your life. You feebly fight for a life that you don't want to live, for friends you couldn't care less about. So come at me Jackie, let me taste in that magnificent fear."**

Jack's hand trembled, causing the light to bob along the features of the Liath. He tried to move, attempted to lunge forth; to swing the blade that he'd been gripping so tightly into the belly of the beast. Yet, his body refused to respond; doing little more than trembling as he looked into the arrogant eyes of his adversary. His mind began to swim with thoughts of doubt and fear, rooting him to his very core as it plunged him into the purgatory of absolute terror. He realized that yes, he'd found the beast, had come to face it in its own territory but what came next? How could he hope to face something that stood as the embodiment of absolute terror?

The Liath cocked its head to the other side, **"Where is your talk of ending me, Jack? Didn't you say you were going to kill me? Turns out that you are all talk, but deep down you're a coward. You could never face me as a boy, let alone as a man. You do nothing but stand there and shake, it's a wonder you haven't pissed yourself. Your fear, your sweat, your adrenaline, it's delicious; so, come now Jack, let me consume your soul."**

The Liath lunged, closing the space between them in an instant. Its long, taloned hand came down and Jack finally found himself able to move again. His muscles constricted as he threw himself backwards a couple feet; narrowly avoiding the creature's razor-sharp claws. The Liath roared as it lunged again and this time Jack threw himself to the ground as its claw passed overhead, dropping the flashlight in the process.

He fell into a roll, noting with great relief that the flashlight had landed in such a way that it illuminated the space they occupied. Jack looked to the ground as he came out of the roll, noting the deep gouges left in the concrete by the Liath's first swing. He shifted his eyes to his right hand and tightened his grip around the knife. *If I get sloppy then I'm dead. There's no coming back from a hit like that.*

Fury crossed the Liath's face as it starred at the white blade in Jack's hand, **"WHERE THE FUCK DID YOU GET THAT?"**

It closed the space between them in an instant and swiped downward with impossible speed. Jack turned at the last possible moment and felt the incredible surge of displaced air as the Liath's hand severed the space just in front of him.

Jack wasted no time at all as he turned and plunged the knife hilt-deep into the Liath's abdomen. Relief coursed through him as blood spurted from the wound, covering his hand in the thick, black ichor. Jack repeatedly stabbed the Liath in the abdomen, causing more and more of the black ichor to spurt out of the multiple stab sites. Jack's heart rate quickened, and he found himself smiling as he gained the upper hand.

And then the Liath screamed.

Horrific images flooded Jack's vision as the sound pierced his ears. Tears welled up in his eyes as scenes of unbridled grotesquery spread out across his mind. Jack cried out and fell to his knees before the screaming, bloody form of the Liath.

Images of war and famine stretched out before his eyes, he saw the slaughter of millions of indigenous people as settlers swept over the land, killing them indiscriminately in the name of both God and the Queen. He witnessed women, children and elders harmed for the sake of conquest. He saw the concentration camps of the Second World War, experienced the fear as his brothers and sisters were killed around him, hoarded into gas chambers and buried in mass graves. He saw himself joining millions as they slowly became more and more emaciated; living off scraps and 'mystery meat' as they scrounged for sustenance. He saw sadistic murders torturing their victims as they cried out in pain, he saw rapists exert their will onto their undeserving prey.

Jack fell on the ground in a heap and brought his knees up to his chest in a vain attempt to calm himself. Though, as era after era of cruelty and pain flashed before his eyes his heart lurched and he found himself unable to calm down. His heart thudded incessantly against his sternum, threatening to explode under the sheer amount of stress and terror it was being subjected to.

He struggled as he brought the knife up to his chest, suddenly filled with an unfathomable desire to end this feeling that had overcome him. With fingers clenched around the hilt, he brought the lade up to his neck and began to press.

The moment the blade broke the skin however, Jack found that the effects of the scream began to melt away and the fear that had rendered him all but immobile began to withdraw. The blade fell from his trembling grip and clattered dully onto the hard ground. He lay there, sucking in deep, unsteady breaths as he whimpered; feeling the cold concrete as it pressed into his side. The sounds of something hard on the ground snapped him back to reality and he looked around in a desperate panic to see where the Liath was.

Just behind him, the Liath rose onto its unsteady feet; its face was twisted in a mixture of pain and rage. Knowing he had little time to get to his own feet, Jack rolled onto his front and rose onto his hands and knees; once again picking up the blade as he rose onto his own feet. Just as he finished the motion, the Liath roared and charged him once more; swiping clumsily with its large, taloned hand.

Jack stepped back as the creature's hand came down on him. He swiped upwards; raking the blade along the Liath's palm. It roared again and clamped its hand down on the blade; squeezing tightly despite the pain the blade inflicted upon it. Jack tried to pull back, but the creature's grip held. Fearing it would use the opportunity to attack with its other hand, Jack realized he had no option but to let go and step back.

Though, as he moved away from the Liath, its eyes narrowed on the small, white object now clutched tightly in its hand. Its lips spread into a sneering smile as it clenched tighter on the blade. The sneer turned to strain as it continued to apply pressure and soon, Jack saw the faintest traces of white emerging from between the creature's fingers. Instinctively, he shielded his eyes as the blade cracked and then exploded; casting the entirety of the room in a brilliant white light.

Jack was thrown back in the explosion and slid across the length of the floor; back towards the very staircase he'd entered the room from. He groaned as he tried to blink out the light spots that had taken over his vision and began groping around on the ground for a weapon - for anything he could use to finish the Liath. His hand brushed something vaguely familiar and he gripped onto it tightly, frowning at the way it fit in his hand.

He rose onto his feet once more as he continued to blink away the last of the light spots and his eyes readjusted to the darkness surrounding him. Surprisingly, the light of the flashlight now penetrated the darkness as it normally would have; as though whatever had been released during the explosion had thinned out the ever-imposing darkness of the basement. He looked down to his hand to see what his weapon was, and his heart fell.

Coiled in his hand like a cobra waiting to strike; was his father's belt.

Jack's heart thudded as he stretched the familiar leather cord between his hands as he walked over to where the Liath had been. A feeling of intense purpose and understanding rose in him as he looked over to the smoldering mess that was once the Liath. Its arm had been nearly obliterated in the explosion; the hand it had used to break the blade was nothing more than a mangled mess of sinew and black blood. The remaining stump held on only by the tiniest amount of tissue. As Jack rounded the Liath, it attempted to let out another scream. Though instead of another fear inducing other-worldly noise, all that came out was a sad whimper.

Jack firmly placed a foot on its remaining hand, then reached down and tucked the belt under the Liath's chin. He wrapped the length around its neck once and pulled the ends up towards his chest. Jack pulled hard, cutting off the Liath's air supply. As it began to struggle, Jack only pulled harder; remaining steadfast despite the creature's incessant bucking and kicking.

After several minutes of fighting the creature - constricting the belt tighter and tighter the Liath finally stopped moving - the final twitches of death having ran their course. Though Jack continued to pull, not willing to give any ground lest it still be alive. Time passed slowly as Jack stared down at the creature; unable to believe he'd bested it. He'd been standing there for what felt like an eternity when he felt a soft, warm hand place itself on top of his.

Jack looked up - surprised - into the eyes of his father, "it's okay Jack, you've done it. We're free. You can let go now."

Jack stumbled back in shock and dropped the belt as disbelief coursed through his body, "N-no. There's no way you're here. Dad. I killed you. There's no way."

Tears began to spill from his eyes as his father responded, "You did, and I thank you for it. I wish I had more time with you Jack. More time to watch you grow and mold you into a great young man." He chuckled lightly, "looks like you didn't need me for that, though. I'm proud of you, son. You've grown to be so strong, so courageous. I just wish I was able to see more of it."

Jack wiped his eyes and smiled through his tear-soaked cheeks, "I'm not strong, look at me, I can hardly hold myself together right now."

His dad reached out and put his hand on Jack's shoulder, "True strength doesn't come from restraining your emotions. No, it comes from embracing them and being able to move forward. You excel at that Jack; you are truly strong."

He frowned, but continued, “I wish I had more time Jack - that we had more time. But I’m afraid I can’t stay. This place isn’t where any of us are meant to be,” he gestured to the others standing behind him, “Thank you for freeing us Jack. I love you.”

Jack watched as his father took a step back into the crowd of others that he was unable to save. Back into the group of those he’d loved and lost, next to Noah Brackman, Robert Fielding, and all the others whose lives had been claimed by the Liath over the past decade. A tear rolled down his cheek as his father stepped next to a smiling Dom and Emma; who looked not like they harbored any hate for him, but like they were thanking him for ending their suffering. As Jack met their eyes he felt nothing but the immense love they felt for him. He watched in awe as they were encompassed in a faint blue glow before their bodies slowly dissipated into a fine mist that drifted through the air surrounding him like leaves in an autumn breeze.

Jack’s smile slowly faded as the three people he longed to hold one last time dissipated into the air surrounding him; leaving him alone in the basement once more. He bent down and retrieved the flashlight from the ground before turning back towards the stairs and walking up them for the last time.

Part 4
Aftermath

Chapter 14: Relay

~ 1 ~

Jack walked back through the linoleum lined hallways of Magrath hospital; feeling hollow despite his victory over the Liath. As he walked through the corridor, he found himself taking his time; unsure of what he would say to Shannon and Trix other than simply relaying to them that he'd killed it. Though, as he rounded the threshold to the room where the two women lay, he found himself smiling.

Trix was now sitting up in bed; her hands resting in the hands of both her parents who sat on either side of her. Her eyes widened as she saw him and gave him a weak smile. Though she hadn't miraculously put on the forty pounds she'd lost to the Liath in the past hour, she did appear to be significantly better in the awareness department. She smiled weakly.

Diana and Liam Thompson looked over to Jack; their eyebrows raising as they took in his sorry state. He walked over to the foot of Trix's bed and smiled.

She frowned, "Wait, where's Uncle Dom?"

The expression was instantly reflected on her parents' faces as well and Jack struggled to figure out the words to tell them that Dom was dead. Despite his constant guilt at his friend's death, it hadn't crossed his mind in the slightest that he would need to pass on the information to anyone other than Shannon.

He choked on his words, finding himself unable to form them properly, "He - uh - that *thing* got him Trix."

Stunned silence fell over Trix as she attempted to process what Jack had just told her. Diana and Liam looked at Jack in confusion as he walked over to the other visitor's chair and dragged it next to Shannon's bed.

He sat down and took her hand in his, "Shannon, I did it. They're free."

He looked down at his lap as the tears began to flow once more from his eyes and he realized just how tired he was. He sobbed silently, ignoring the Thompson's confused stares as he held Shannon's hand. It was only when he felt a gentle hand on his cheek that he looked up.

Even though she was in a hospital gown with hair sticking up at odd angles and smudges where her makeup had been, Jack was still taken aback by her beauty. She smiled sadly at him and mouthed the words "thank you" before putting her head back down and falling back asleep.

Jack smiled and wiped the tears from his eyes before finally turning and meeting the Thompson's eyes, "I guess I owe the three of you an explanation. I hope you have time; this may take a while."

Diana and Liam looked at each other then back at Jack and nodded; prompting him to fill them in on all the vital details of what transpired over the past few days.

--

Tears streamed down Liam's face and Diana's was a picture of horror. Though Jack had expected some resistance to his recount of past events; the black blood that stained his clothes along with Trix's confession of what happened on the night of the party aided in the Thompson's coming to terms with the truth.

When Liam's crying finally ceased, he spoke, "so what do we do for the funeral? There's no body, so do we just bury an empty casket?"

Jack thought for a moment, "unfortunately we'll have to. As far as convincing the police of what happened, we can leave that to my mother; she still has pretty strong ties with the chief."

Liam nodded slowly before turning to his wife, "will you help me make the arrangements? I don't know if I'm strong enough to do it all by myself."

Diana nodded and took his hand in here, "of course my love. Though, we should plan it for a week or so from now, that should give Trixie enough time to get a fair bit better."

Liam smiled gratefully, "thank you." He turned back to Jack, "Thank you for avenging my brother. I know you meant a lot to him and he wasn't the type of man to judge you for…" His eyes flicked over to Shannon.

Jack blushed, "Thank you Liam. Listen, I have to step out for a bit to check on something. Will you be okay here for a bit?"

Liam nodded, "yeah, sure thing."

~ 2 ~

Jack pulled up outside of the familiar storefront with the large gold lettering above it. The journey had been uneventful, and he'd found his mind wandering to the one part of the case that still hadn't added up for him. Though it was early morning, the door to the flower shop swung open when he pulled on the handle; she'd been expecting him.

He walked between the rows of plants to the door at the back of the store and headed down the small hallway that connected the two spaces. He stopped outside of the wooden door and exhaled, then raised his hand to knock.

The door swung open the moment his knuckles first rapped against the surface and his mother flung herself at him; momentarily startling him. He chuckled as he returned the hug.

When the embrace was broken off, he looked into her eyes and relayed the only message that mattered in the moment, "I've freed him, mom. Dad's free."

She smiled as tears welled up in her eyes, "thank you Jack. I'm sorry it fell on your shoulders to do all that. And - I - I'm sorry I never helped you when you were young. It was wrong of me."

Jack smiled sadly, "I never blamed you mom, I don't know what I would have done in the same situation. I'm just glad I was able to make things right."

She nodded, "I'm glad you answered that call Jack."

Jack frowned as his mind snapped back to his thoughts in the car, "Mom? Were you responsible for that? Did you bring me back here?"

Martha chewed her lip thoughtfully, "I may have had a hand in it. I figured you wouldn't come back if I called, so I had to disguise it as a job offering."

Jack thought over the past few days as pieces began to slide into place, "So then you're the reason that none of the cops got heavily involved in the case and basically let me have free reign."

She nodded, "Yeah. I guess you could say that. The Lewis name still carries a lot of weight in Magrath though, you could have had free reign all by yourself."

Jack thought for a second, "So what will you do with the manor now that there's no reason to keep people away?"

Martha smiled, "Well, the inheritance from your father has only been growing as renters continue to pay, and the fund has grown significantly over the last decade… maybe I'll rebuild."

Her eyes glazed over as her mind drifted to thoughts of rebuilding the house and Jack smiled. *She's been keeping herself isolated for ten years, now she can finally live her life again.*

Without another word, he wrapped her in his arms and hugged her tightly. She gripped onto him and laughed into his chest. Jack's smile grew; it was nice to have his mother back in his life.

Jack spoke again once they broke off the hug, "So, will you still be able to convince the chief of what happened here?"

She nodded, "Yeah of course Jack. Oh, and there's one more thing I wanted to tell you."

Jack raised his eyebrow, "Sure, what is it?"

She smiled at him, "Well, when your father died, everything went to me. The properties and the money are all mine now; and I want to give you half."

Jack's eyes widened, "No, mom, you don't have to."

She shook her head, "'I know, but I want to. We can work out the details later, but I just wanted to let you know. You can buy a house and get settled somewhere - maybe carry on the Lewis bloodline."

Jack chuckled, “of course, we see each other after ten years and you’re already on me to give you grandchildren. Thank you mom. I should be getting back to the hospital now… Shannon needs me.”

His mother raised an eyebrow but didn’t push it, “okay Jack, give her my best. I’ll see you soon, right?”

Jack felt a pang of guilt for the years he spent away from her, “of course mom. Love you.”

Chapter 15: Farewell

~ 1 ~

The golden-brown oak shined with a mirror-like polish; suspended above the earth as the priest said his closing remarks. Jack looked to the people gathered around for the ceremony. He saw faces he recognized and some that he didn't. The priest's words didn't meet Jack's ears as he once again turned his attention to the empty casket that sat over the gaping hole in the frozen earth.

"... the Father and of the Son and of the Holy Spirit. Amen."

He looked over to the priest, who slowly closed the old, well used book from which he'd read the prayer. Jack doubted very much that the priest even needed the book at this point in his career; he would have said that very same prayer hundreds of times over the years, maybe thousands.

Jack looked up to the sky; half expecting to see black clouds moving in; marking another day where he'd have to face the force of nature that lay dead in the basement of his old home. Though, no such phenomena were present. Instead the pale blue sky was dotted with numerous specks of wispy white clouds. Though the cold bit into his face and made his breath inherently visible; the state of the sky filled him with warmth. He smiled sadly and looked back towards the burial procession.

A sickly-looking woman hobbled over to the casket - supported by Liam and Diana - and Jack realized that it was Dom's mother. She walked up to the casket and placed her hand on top as tears rolled down her sallow cheeks.

"No mother should have to bury their son. I love you Dommi, don't wait up for me, I'll be there soon."

Jack swallowed as the urge to cry welled up in his throat. Next up was Shannon, who - much to Jack's chagrin - insisted that they stand together during the burial. It wasn't that he was embarrassed of being with her, no, it was more that he found it inappropriate to bring their relationship forward so soon after Dom's passing.

She walked up to the casket and placed her own hand on top of it before whispering her own words to the empty box. Although everyone there knew there was no body in the coffin, Jack found it still offered the same level of acknowledgement to the situation. It was as though they subconsciously decided that the coffin itself was Dom.

Shannon walked back, and Jack could see the tears that streaked down her face through the thin black veil she wore. Magrath was an old town and still followed the same funeral traditions they had for centuries. Jack blushed as she slipped her fingers through his and clung to his arm in front of all the attendees.

Once everyone said their farewells Jack walked up to the casket and placed his hand gently on top of it, "Hey - uh - Dom. I'm sorry for bringing you along on the case and I'm sorry for not being there for you over the past decade. I hope that wherever you are - wherever we end up when we die - that you're happy. I'll take care of Shannon and treat her how you would have; I'm going to miss you man."

He walked back over to Shannon and she reclaimed her place clinging to his arm. A sad silence fell over the crowd as the coffin was slowly lowered into the ground and the first handfuls of dirt were thrown on top. Tears flowed freely down everyone's face, but Jack held his in; staying strong for Shannon and for himself. He knew if he broke down that emotional barrier again and let the tears flow, they wouldn't stop for a long time.

~ 2 ~

Jack slipped away from the crowd once the service was done. Shannon was speaking to Dom's brother and his wife, and his mom was speaking to Dom's mother. Jack excused himself and walked down the cobblestone path into the older part of the cemetery towards a place he knew he'd eventually be buried. The Lewis mausoleum.

It was his family's tradition to be buried inside; though the doors remained locked to everyone but the groundskeepers. Thus, the only time a Lewis would ever enter the old and stony crypt would be once they themselves had shuffled off this mortal coil.

He walked up to the structure and placed his hand on the large black granite door. He closed his eyes and imagined his father inside, sleeping his eternal sleep.

He sighed and spoke softly, for only him to hear, “Hey dad, it’s me Jack. I wanted to apologize for hating you. For killing you. I know you did what you did to allow me a future that was free of this town and of the burden placed on us by our forefathers.

“God… I don’t know what to say right now. I thought it would be easy to just get this off my chest and let you know that I’m sorry, but it’s not. These words feel awkward and I can’t form the sentences I want to say to you. I guess… what I’m saying is that I wish we had more time. More time like when I was young, and you’d teach me about the bugs that wandered our backyard and the science behind the clouds in the sky. I wish you could have truly met me as a man, and I guess I wish I could just hear you say you’re proud of me. Is that shallow? I think it is. I love you dad, thank you for everything.”

He lowered his hand and stayed there for a while; his head bowed with closed eyes. He only looked up when he heard the faint sound of footsteps approaching. When he saw Trix walking over to him he smiled. She looked a lot better than she had when he found her in the basement the week prior, yet, she still hadn’t regained all the weight she’d lost.

She smiled back, “Hey Jack, I saw you walk off, so I figured I’d come check up on you.”

Jack’s smile grew, “Thank you Trix, I - uh - I came over here to speak with my dad. I had something things I needed to tell him; you know?”

She nodded, “Yeah I do. It’s going to be tough without uncle Dom. At least for a while. He’d always come visit me when he was done work and we’d sit, drink tea or coffee and just talk about our day. I guess I saw him as a sort of second dad.”

Jack chuckled, “I remember him telling me about that. He sure loved you kid.”

Trix beamed, “You too. I mean, he’d always talk about you, tell me stories of when you guys were young and stuff. I think wherever he is, he’s happy that he got to see you again.”

Jack smiled and tried to speak as tears began to work their way up but found himself unable. He blinked hard in an attempt to keep them down, though as the first tear broke free, he realized it was futile. He reached up to wipe at his eyes when he felt two arms wrap around him as Trix hugged him.

He returned her hug and they stood there for several minutes, silently crying out for Dom. Eventually, when Trix pulled away, he finished wiping his eyes.

He looked at her, desperate to change the topic, "so, what's next for you?"

She chewed her lip before smiling, "Well, I've missed a lot of school this year, so my parents are pulling me out for the remainder of the school year. Next year I'll go back and finish grade eleven then I'll do grade twelve the following year."

Jack nodded, "Oh yeah? Any plans for after school?"

She looked up to the sky for a moment, "Noah told me I'd make a great vet, so I think that's what I'll do. Maybe I'll open a practice here in Magrath or maybe I'll move way. It's all pretty unclear still. What about you?"

Jack smiled, "Shannon and I are going to move just out of Magrath and sell her house here. We both figured that there's far too many bad memories for us here in town, so we've been looking into acreages just beyond the city limits. We'll come back and check in every week or so, but I think for the most part, our future lies outside of Magrath. Hell, maybe I'll hand up the old investigator's hat and focus on keeping animals or something."

Trix nodded but raised her eyebrow, "So you and auntie Shannon are shacking up?"

Jack laughed and gestured for them to begin walking back towards the group, "Yeah, I guess we are. Is that weird?"

Trix thought for a second before replying, "Kind of, but not really. I feel like Uncle Dom talked about you enough that I've known you all my life. And I guess it makes sense."

He smiled, "Well I'm glad, maybe if we get animals you can be our private vet?"

Trix beamed, "Sure thing! But it'll cost you!"

They laughed as they re-joined the others and fell back in with the other's mourning the loss of Dominic Thompson.

Epilogue

The cold air washed over their small acreage; despite this, Jack sat on the porch smoking as his son played in the snow. Though he'd kicked the habit of drinking some time ago - and was now four years sober - he could never quite rid himself entirely of the cigarettes. Granted, he'd gone down from a full pack a day to four or five.

He looked out over his land, thinking of days passed and times when he hadn't been so happy. Though it was cloaked in the late afternoon darkness that accompanied winter, he could still see the area where his son played thanks to the floodlight suspended just above their porch.

Jack reflected on how far he'd come, how much he'd gained - and lost - due to that one phone call his mother had arranged just over four years prior and smiled. He'd been living with Shannon and though some nights the nightmares would return and either one would wake up screaming, they could always take solace in knowing that the other was there to calm them; there to quell the demons. He ashed his cigarette and watched the snow fall.

They still returned to Magrath, visited his mother - who now lived in the rebuilt manor; although she'd spent a small fortune filling the basement to the top with cement. They also visited Dom's brother, wife and Trix quite frequently. Though, these days Trix was quite preoccupied with College, she'd always take at least a couple minutes to come say hi.

Trix told him that Larkin and Zach had moved into a small apartment in the city and were currently looking into starting a business together. Jack was just glad that none of them tried to end it in the time following their friend's murders.

He exhaled the smoke that he'd been keeping in his lungs before calling out for his son to come and sit with him. As his son joined him, Jack felt nothing but love for the boy and felt himself once again happy that he'd retired from his job to focus on his family. He'd always be there for them; there for him.

He pointed to the snow falling just in front of the flood light and his son's eyes widened as each one lit up like fireflies against the dark tapestry of the night sky.

Jack looks at him. He looks at the way he marvels over each and every flake as it shimmers down from the sky like teardrops from the angles, and Jack is filled with love. He's filled with love so pure that it forms a single thought, one that rings true of his little miracle's namesake.

As Jack ruffles his son's hair he turns and looks at him, and says, "I love you daddy."

Jack smiles as the snowflakes fall over their property and whispers quietly, so as not to disturb this serene night;

"I love you too Dom."

September 2019 – January 2020

Author note and Acknowledgement

In rural Alberta, Canada, there exists a small town with a population just north of 2,000. Its name is Magrath. Though the real town and the town in this novel share the same name, they are not the same town. The Magrath represented in this novel along with any of its inhabitants are fictitious in nature. Any similarities are coincidental in nature and any likeness was not intended.

This novel started as a series written to the reddit community r/NoSleep. As I was writing the series, I realized that the constraints of the subreddit really didn't allow the story to flourish. Once the series was completed I set out to rewrite it in its entirety, keeping all the scenes from the series, but adding more scenes and more in-depth dialogue between the characters. This resulted in a novel that I am insanely proud of and am overjoyed to be able to share with the world.

Before I share some vital information below, I would like to thank my beta-readers; Marni, Nailah and u/zulal88. You really helped with the editing process.

Thank you to those who shared their kind words on the series, the ones who spurred me on to continue writing. A lot of sleepless nights went into writing this and I'm so glad it got the attention that it did on reddit.

No for the vital bit of information; this novel dealt with some pretty dark themes and at times I questioned whether or not I was pushing it too far. However, this story was meant to be the way it is, Jack Lewis was always meant to have a tragic past and Dominic Thompson was always meant to be a casualty.

If you're reading this and feel like life can sometimes be too much to bear, please consider contacting one of the suicide hotlines below. They're anonymous and toll-free, even if you don't share the novel with people, at least share these numbers. One day they could save someone's life.

Argentina: +5402234930430
Australia: 131114
Austria: 142; for children and young people, 147

Belgium: 106
Bosnia & Herzegovina: 080 05 03 05
Botswana: 3911270
Brazil: 188 for the CVV National Association
Canada: 1.833.456.4566, 5147234000 (Montreal); 18662773553 (outside Montreal)
Croatia: 014833888
Denmark: +4570201201
Egypt: 7621602
Estonia: 3726558088; in Russian 3726555688
Finland: 010 195 202
France: 0145394000
Germany: 08001810771
Holland: 09000767
Hong Kong: +852 2382 0000
Hungary: 116123
India: 8888817666
Ireland: +4408457909090
Italy: 800860022
Japan: +810352869090
Mexico: 5255102550
New Zealand: 0800543354
Norway: +4781533300
Philippines: 028969191
Poland: 5270000
Portugal: 21 854 07 40/8 . 96 898 21 50
Russia: 0078202577577
Spain: 914590050
South Africa: 0514445691
Sweden: 46317112400
Switzerland: 143
United Kingdom: 08457909090
USA: 18002738255
Veterans' Crisis Line: 1 800 273 8255/ text 838255

Lastly, I'd like to thank you for getting this far and hope I've at least inspired you to seek out more of my work. If not, I hope you at least enjoyed this story.

Manufactured by Amazon.ca
Bolton, ON